SPELLC

BARBARA ASHFORD

Spells have a way of coming back to haunt you....

DAW
No. 1589

DAW
No. 1589

$7.99 U.S.
$8.99 CAN

ISBN 978-0-7564-0729-2

5 0 7 9 9

S ▷ EAN

SOMEONE WAS BREAKING INTO MY
GODDAMN THEATRE
ON MY GODDAMN OPENING NIGHT . . .

Reinhard refused to let me call the police. Instead, we all trooped down the hill from Janet's house to investigate.

Maybe it was some kind of practical joke. Catherine and Javier had been sent ahead to oversee the final preparations. And when I walked in, everybody would yell, "Surprise!" But the last thing I needed after the past few days was yet another surprise.

By the time we reached the parking lot, I was beginning to wonder if I'd imagined the whole thing. I almost hoped there *was* a burglar. If we walked in on Catherine and Javier having a quickie on one of the orphan's beds, I'd feel like an idiot.

The wrought iron lamps along the walkway flared to life. For a moment, we just stood there, gaping. Then Janet gripped my hand and Reinhard flung his arm around my waist. I looked from one to the other, suddenly scared. Whatever this was, it wasn't a practical joke. . . .

☆ ★ ☆

SPELLCROSSED

BARBARA ASHFORD

DAW BOOKS, INC.

DONALD A. WOLLHEIM, FOUNDER

375 Hudson Street, New York, NY 10014

ELIZABETH R. WOLLHEIM
SHEILA E. GILBERT
PUBLISHERS

http://www.dawbooks.com

First Printing, June 2012
1 2 3 4 5 6 7 8 9

ACKNOWLEDGMENTS

Thanks to everyone who helped in the creation of *Spell-crossed*:

My writing friends who provided feedback and critiques: Michele Korri, Michael Samerdyke, Susan Sielinski, and the NOVA critique group.

My friends and colleagues in the theatre who offered scripts, suggestions, and memories of past productions: Jeanne McCabe, Nellie O'Brien, and Steven Silverstein.

Ellie Miller who gave me the title.

My sister, Cathy Klenk, who confirmed and corrected details of Wilmington (and even traipsed out after a snowstorm to reconnoiter the Brandywine Zoo).

My editor, Sheila Gilbert, whose insights and suggestions were—as usual—invaluable.

And my husband, David Lofink—my first reader and my best friend. His encouragement has nurtured my writing career and his love has nurtured me since we starred opposite each other on the stage of the Southbury Playhouse. As always, this one's for him.

To learn more about the world
of the Crossroads Theatre,
visit www.barbara-ashford.com.

CONTENTS

OVERTURE

I AM DANCING WITH FIREFLIES.

Part of me knows that this is only a dream, that I must wake up and resume my responsibilities as director of the Crossroads Theatre. But for now, I dance in their golden light.

I am a child, chasing fireflies with her father. I am a woman, hearing Rowan Mackenzie laugh as fireflies swarm around him on Midsummer's Eve.

The light flickers uncertainly, as if my fireflies understand the mingled joy and sorrow those memories evoke.

I sense the others before I see them, the family that I found at the Crossroads. My family in blood as well as spirit. They hover at the edge of the glade, half-seen among the shadows.

Hal rushes forward and embraces me. He is dressed in a flowing gown of green. He, too, wears many faces tonight: costume designer, lingerie shop owner, and Titania, queen of the faeries. That must make Lee his Oberon, although he wears his usual T-shirt and jeans. The light grows brighter as Lee crosses the glade, as if he were bringing up the house lights in the theatre.

Javier waves his hand, and the fireflies obediently move to the far edge of the glade like members of his stage crew. Catherine waves hers, and they construct a glowing pyramid of light. The pyramid dissolves into a dance again as

Mei-Yin stalks forward; even fireflies know better than to defy their choreographer. Alex raises his hands, the conductor cueing his orchestra, and the erratic flashes of light become a single steady pulse. On. Off. On. Off.

Reinhard jots a note on his ubiquitous clipboard, checking off fireflies like cast members reporting for their seven o'clock call. Janet rolls her eyes. Hard to believe I once considered her my enemy. But I knew so little about her—about all of them—during that first summer at the Crossroads.

They begin to dance—Lee with Hal, Javier with Catherine, Reinhard with Mei-Yin. Husbands and wives, partners and lovers. Janet pulls Alex into the dance. The widow and her widowed son. Alone in life, but in this dream, they are partners. In this dream, everyone has a partner.

Everyone except me.

Sadness touches me again. And then Bernie rolls his walker forward, observing the dance with wonder, as if he finally understands the secret of the Crossroads Theatre.

"Faery magic," the fireflies whisper.

Bernie cannot hear them, but he casts his walker aside and dances with me. We all dance, caught up in the spell of the fireflies and the spell of the Crossroads.

Only the one who created the spell is missing. My faery lover who was the heart and soul of the Crossroads Theatre—and my heart and soul as well.

"Rowan will always carry you in his heart. Remember that, my dear. And know that you will always have a home at the Crossroads."

I search the shadows, but I cannot see Helen. Yet I know she is here, taking her bow with the others.

This is not the time for curtain calls; the season is just beginning.

There is work to do.

I must stop dreaming.

I must wake up.

I must forget Rowan Mackenzie.

ACT ONE

SOMETHING'S COMING

THERE IS NO UPSIDE to losing your lover—especially in Dale, which is not exactly the singles capital of Vermont. But having a faery for a lover does teach you to accept the impossible and cope with anything that life throws at you.

Since Rowan Mackenzie returned to Faerie one year, eight months, and twenty-two days ago, life had thrown me a lot of new and unusual experiences. I had helped judge the watermelon seed spitting contest at the Farmers Day Fair and frozen my ass off collecting buckets of sap during the Maple Sugar Festival. I had enjoyed fishing with Reinhard, Christmas caroling with Alex, and a romantic Valentine's Day sleigh ride. With Janet.

As manager of the ramshackle Golden Bough Hotel, I had dealt with a flooded basement, a kitchen fire, and the mysteries of ancient plumbing. As executive director of the newly nonprofit Crossroads Theatre, I had learned to write successful grant proposals and appeal letters. As the theatre's interim artistic director, I had staged three small musicals and plucked out twice that many long gray hairs.

After all that, auditioning dogs was a breeze.

As the latest contender shuffled across the stage, I heard soft chuckles from the seats behind me, quickly converted into coughs. Naturally, the entire staff had turned out this morning, eager to see Maggie Graham, Dog Director, in action.

It was my own damn fault. I'd pitched the idea of doing a show with children's roles. The perfect way to draw attention—and warm bodies—to our after-school program and bring in enough money to keep it alive after the grant ran out.

The board was thrilled, visions of ticket-buying relatives dancing in their heads. The next thing I knew, we were doing an entire season featuring young performers, and I was auditioning dogs to play Annie's adorable sidekick Sandy.

The lugubrious click of toenails ceased as Arthur finally made it to center stage. At a hand signal from his owner, his arthritic hindquarters drooped onto the floorboards. Doreen kissed his shaggy head. She looked exactly like the handlers I'd seen during my infrequent viewings of the Westminster Dog Show—portly, middle-aged, and tweedy.

She straightened and peered into the darkened house, awaiting my reaction.

"He's very obedient," I said.

"Arthur's a pro."

Which was true; his resume was more impressive than mine.

"And he's played Sandy twice before," she noted.

Judging from his age, he'd probably starred in the original Broadway production of *Annie*.

"He's very . . . calm, isn't he?"

"Oh, nothing upsets Arthur."

The entire set could fall down, and he'd just sit there. But he was sweet-tempered and scruffy if not exactly adorable. Who cared if he was a little long in the tooth?

"Play dead, Arthur."

Frankly, it wasn't much of a stretch. I watched him anxiously until the rise and fall of his rib cage assured me he was merely playing. Then I smiled brightly.

"I'm sold. Arthur's our Sandy."

"Oh, that's wonderful! Isn't that wonderful, Arthur?"

Arthur's tail thumped the floorboards once.

"I hope Fifi won't be too crushed," I said.

"Her time will come," Doreen assured me.

She coaxed Arthur to his feet and released Fifi from her "stay" position. Fifi shot across the stage and jumped up on her stubby legs to lick Arthur's face. He appeared unmoved by her display of affection, but clearly, wagging his tail was a monumental effort. He hobbled down the five steps from the stage, and slowly—very slowly—made his way toward the back of the house with Fifi literally running circles around him.

I kept my smile in place until the lobby door clicked shut behind them.

"Oh. My. GOD!" Mei-Yin exploded.

I swung around in my seat. "Not another sound until they're out of the theatre."

"Better give them five more minutes," Janet advised. "It'll take Old Yeller that long to reach the front door."

"Oh, hush. He was better than the hyperactive Border collie. Or that ugly pit bull."

Or Fifi who appeared to be the unfortunate offspring of a golden retriever bitch and a very determined toy poodle.

"You're as picky about dogs as you are about men," Hal complained. "I don't know how many hours I've wasted setting you up with eligible bachelors."

"Bachelors, yes. Eligible, not so much."

"What about Mitch?" Hal demanded.

"The cross-dresser?"

"He was straight."

"Which is more than you can say about Rafael."

"Rafael is bi!"

"With a decided preference for your team. As we discovered at the cast party of *The Fantasticks* when he went home with my date."

I shot a pointed look at Javier who sighed. "Yeah. I kind of missed the mark on Tad."

"Kind of?"

Catherine poked her husband's arm. "I told you he was gay."

"But he likes basketball. And fixing up old cars."

"So do I," Lee pointed out as he leaned over to kiss Hal's cheek.

"I rest my case," Catherine said.

"Well, what was so wrong with Don?" Alex asked, jumping into the fray.

"The real estate guy who never shut up?"

"That was Ron! Don! The English teacher."

Janet groaned. "He spent the entire date crying about his ex-wife."

"How do *you* know?" Alex demanded.

"I insist on hearing about all of Maggie's awful dates. Much more gratifying than charging her rent. For what it's worth," Janet added, "I'd have given Mitch the Cross-Dresser another shot. His fashion sense was impeccable."

Hal nodded solemnly. "And there are very few men his size who look elegant in a strapless gown."

"And that," I announced, "ends this discussion."

Shadowy figures rose and began drifting up the aisle toward the lobby: Hal to his lingerie shop, Lee to his law office, Javier to his antiques store, and Catherine back to the Mill to finish constructing the Warbucks mansion set. I felt a pang of regret; last year, everyone had sat through auditions to lend me moral support.

But I was a big girl now. And I had Mei-Yin, Reinhard, Alex, and Janet to get me through the rest of the day. If I could survive dogs, how bad could children be?

❦❦

"Shoot me NOW," Mei-Yin whispered. "Just put a GUN to my head and SHOOT me."

As yet another Annie wannabe stuck out her chin and grinned and warbled that the sun would come out to-morrow, I was sorely tempted to grant Mei-Yin's request and then turn the gun on myself.

Instead, I envisioned a sold-out house and a big, fat program filled with "break a leg" ads placed by adoring parents. And the opportunity to mount two shows that had never been staged at the Crossroads Theatre, a thought that filled me with enough excitement to weather a hundred renditions of "Tomorrow."

The blonde girl onstage gulped a breath of air and belted out that final "aaa-waaay." Alex pounded out a succession of triumphal chords on the piano. Janet and Mei-Yin heaved simultaneous sighs of relief.

Then the applause started.

"Brava, my dear," the mellifluous voice called. "Brava!"

Mei-Yin leaned close to whisper, "When did HE sneak in?"

I gave a dispirited shrug. It was harder to shrug off the déjà vu that shivered through me as I recalled Hal bursting into spontaneous applause after my ever-so-reluctant audition.

Rowan had quelled Hal's ebullience with a single glance. I had to swivel around in my seat, clear my throat, and call Long's name twice before the applause died.

I swung back to face the stage. "Very nice . . ." Quick glance at the resume. ". . . Chelsea."

"I know all the songs," Chelsea informed me. "I played Molly when our community theatre did *Annie* four years ago."

"Yes, I see that."

"If you'd like to hear something else . . ."

Mei-Yin's fingernails dug into my forearm.

"That won't be necessary. We'll be in touch next week to let you know our casting decisions."

Chelsea nodded briskly. "My home number and e-mail address are on my resume. But the best way to reach me is my iPhone. It's always on."

Instantly, I morphed from vital thirty-four year old to doddering crone. When I was eleven, I'd been thrilled to have a Princess Phone in my bedroom. Cell phones and e-mail didn't even exist back in those dark ages.

Cronehood receded as Janet began humming "Thank God, I'm Old" from *Barnum*; when she was eleven, the telephone hadn't even been invented.

"Thanks for coming in, Chelsea."

From stage left, Reinhard effortlessly picked up his cue and announced, "Please follow me to the lobby." He marched out of the house, leaving Chelsea to scamper after him.

Janet rose and stretched. "Thank God that's over."

Long's laughter shattered the peace. "Why so gloomy?" he chided. "That little charmer was born to play Annie."

For the gazillionth time, I wondered why I had listened to Janet. After she agreed to join the board, she'd urged me to invite Long to serve as president, citing the benefits of his wealth and influence. So far, the only benefit I'd discovered was a newfound ability to curb my temper.

A shaft of light signaled the reopening of the lobby door. I glanced around, hoping Long had slipped out. Instead, I found Reinhard striding down the aisle with Long hard on his heels.

I made a big deal of stuffing papers into my briefcase. Unlike Reinhard, Long failed to pick up his cue and planted himself at the end of my row. His meticulously coiffed mane of white hair gleamed dully in the light from the stage. When he smiled, I caught the fainter gleam of white teeth.

"Thanks for stopping by, Long."

"No trouble at all. I just wanted to pop in and see how auditions went."

He was always popping in: to observe the after-school program and the green room renovations, to check on the progress of a grant proposal, to offer a few "humble" suggestions and his usual leer. At first—like a good little executive director—I'd welcomed his interest, but lately, he always seemed to be underfoot.

I mustered what I hoped was a convincing smile. "Actually, there is something we should discuss."

His face rearranged itself into a pontifical expression.

"We saw close to forty kids today. I'd like to use them all this season."

"Are you NUTS?" Mei-Yin exclaimed.

"We have to double cast the principal children's roles, anyway. What's a few more orphans?"

"A lot more WORK!"

"You and Alex could still teach choreography and music to the whole group. But when I block scenes, I thought we could break the orphans into teams. Each headed by one of the Annies. And rehearse each team separately to avoid competition and build camaraderie." I shot a pleading look at Reinhard. "I know that'll make things tougher on you. And me. So if you think it's impossible . . ."

"Impossible, no. But to hold separate rehearsals . . . and work around their school schedules until Hell Week . . ."

"Okay. Bad idea."

"We will discuss it tonight at casting. Extra children mean extra costumes. We cannot make that decision without Hal's input."

"Extra costumes mean extra money," Janet noted.

"Oh, I don't think we need to worry about that," Long said with an airy wave. "The week we've added to *Annie*'s run will easily offset the cost. And with all those children in the show . . ." His eyes gleamed as he mentally calculated the additional ticket sales.

"So you're green-lighting this?" I asked him. "If the staff goes for it?"

"Absolutely, my dear. And if you'd like me to sit in on casting—"

"Oh, no," Janet said. "You just want the phone numbers of all the pretty women."

Long heaved a sigh. "Janet, Janet, Janet. Why do you always ascribe the basest motives to me?"

"Long, Long, Long. Because you're a bigger hound than any of the dogs we saw today."

Long chuckled and threw up his hands in surrender.

Ten more minutes crawled by before he finally left us in peace. By then, Reinhard had brought up the house lights and Alex had emerged from the orchestra pit to join us.

I sighed. "We're going to have to cast Chelsea as Annie, aren't we?"

"Why not?" Alex asked. "She's perfect."

"Revolting, but perfect," Janet agreed.

Against my will, I pictured Rowan trying to suppress a smile as I questioned the wisdom of casting me as the middle-aged, anthem-singing, clambake-loving Nettie in *Carousel.*

"I cast people in the roles they need, not necessarily the ones they'd be good at. I know it sounds crazy, but it's worked for a very long time."

And it *had* worked—for me and most of my cast mates. Only later did I learn that Rowan had called us all to the Crossroads, the far-flung descendants of the Mackenzie clan who had bound him to this world in the eighteenth century. He forced us to dig deep and let down our defenses. And that season at the Crossroads changed many lives, especially mine.

Even with the support of a staff with some pretty impressive Fae bloodlines, I would never be able to accomplish what Rowan had. But I still yearned to offer our actors the same opportunity for healing that I had discovered here.

Once a helping professional, always a helping professional.

A hand descended on my shoulder, startling me from my reverie. Reinhard frowned down at me—my stage manager, my mentor, my rock.

"We all agreed that this season we would adopt more . . . traditional casting methods."

"We shouldn't even have called the Mackenzies," Janet muttered.

"It's not the Crossroads without them," Alex protested. "Besides, it wasn't much of a call."

But it had been strong enough to interrupt my dinner with Hal and Lee. Lee possessed enough Fae power to block its effects. Hal and I—who had about five drops of Fae blood between us—became totally antsy. Even Lee couldn't calm us down. Finally, we grabbed two bottles of wine and drove to the theatre.

As soon as we stepped inside, the antsiness vanished, replaced by the reassuring sense of coming home that had embraced me the first time I entered the old white barn. By the time we polished off the wine, a troupe of faeries could have been calling and we wouldn't have noticed.

"Calling the Mackenzies is a tradition," Reinhard said.

"A tradition that's going to have to change," Janet replied. "We're a professional theatre now. Well. Almost. We can't keep living in the past."

The pointed look she directed at me made it clear she wasn't referring to calling the Mackenzies.

❧❧

With an hour to spare before our dinner meeting, Mei-Yin raced off to torment the staff of the Mandarin Chalet, "Vermont's only restaurant specializing in fine Chinese and Swiss cuisine." I shooed the rest off to the Bates mansion and promised to join them after I'd collected all the resumes.

I smiled as I mounted the steps to the stage. Alex had been taken aback to learn my moniker for his childhood home, a stately Victorian perched on the hill near the theatre. Janet—whose sense of humor was as twisted as her family tree—loved it. At last year's Halloween party, she had donned a gray wig and black dress and greeted us by brandishing a butcher knife. The feathers on Hal's evening gown very nearly carried him aloft.

I paused to straighten the drooping metal cage of the ghost light and made a mental note to ask Lee to add another layer of duct tape to the ancient mic stand. It

would be a lot easier to use a standing lamp with a bare
bulb to ward off specters, but Reinhard insisted we cob-
ble ours together from backstage detritus. A Crossroads
tradition as time-honored as calling the Mackenzies.

I flung open the green room door and paused again to
admire the new furnishings. Hal might shudder at the
green-and-blue plaid upholstery and the "chunky-clunky"
tables, but even he admitted they were a huge improve-
ment over the dilapidated furniture that had graced this
room during my season as an actress.

Best of all, they were free, donated by one of our theatre "Angels" when she redecorated her den. As were
the stove (which had four working burners instead of
one) and the kitchen cabinetry (which had doors that
actually opened and closed without falling off their
hinges). Even the paint had been donated, although Mr.
Hamilton at the General Store had to special order it
because Hal insisted on a shade of pale green called
"Crocodile Tears."

The production office down the hall was still a work-
in-progress. One day, I hoped it would live up to the
shiny brass nameplate on the door that Hal had given
me last Christmas—"Margaret Graham, Executive Director & Goddess."

I plopped my briefcase on the desk and began trans-
ferring resumes and info sheets from my inbox. The towering stack said as much about the desperation of the
actors as my PR brilliance, but it was still very satisfying.

Thirty professional actors had shown up at our Bennington audition, a pitifully small turnout for any other
theatre, but a cornucopia of talent for the Crossroads. With
the community theatre actors we'd auditioned yesterday,
we would have an experienced company this season. Except, of course, for the fourteen bewildered Mackenzies.

Nearly eighty performers in all. Which posed a dilemma. In its long history, the Crossroads had never
turned away an actor. A tradition that seemed destined
to change.

Rowan would hate it. But it wasn't his theatre any longer. No matter how wistful I felt about my season here, the Crossroads had to move on. And so did I.

My fingers caressed the silver chain around my throat. Rowan's chain. He had thrust it into my hand the morning he left me to return to Faerie. Since then, I had worn it every day, waking and sleeping. Maybe it was time for that tradition to change, too.

I reached for the clasp, then let my hands fall. Talk about empty gestures. If I really wanted to make a break with the past, I knew exactly what I needed to do.

The ghost light provided just enough illumination to mount the stairs to his apartment. There was no lock on the door. When Rowan lived here, no one would have dreamed of invading his privacy. Except me, of course.

The staff tactfully refrained from reminding me that I'd passed up two opportunities to move in: last spring when Caren agreed to manage the Golden Bough and again in the fall, when she began a graduate course in interior design in New York City and I hired Frannie to replace her. If they thought I was out of my mind to accept Janet's invitation to move into the Bates mansion, only Hal voiced his reservations.

Clutching the arm of one of the scantily clad mannequins that graced his lingerie shop, he'd said, "You and Janet? Living together?"

"It's better than a cheap walk-up in town."

Which was all I could afford on my meager salary. I was saving the money Rowan had left me to refurbish the Bough.

"It's like something out of *The Children's Hour*. Or *Little Women*."

"Trust me, I don't harbor repressed lesbian desires for Janet. And the day I call her Marmee, I'll move out."

Eight months later, I was still living there. Funny, how I kept filling the spaces that Helen had once occupied:

her apartment in the Bough, her bedroom in the Bates mansion. Janet and I surprised everyone—including ourselves—by adapting easily to the arrangement. Maybe because we were both lonely: she had lost her daughter, I'd lost the man I loved. At any rate, it was nice to hear her puttering around downstairs while I worked on a grant, to take out my frustrations on the weeds in Helen's garden and share my little victories over dinner.

"I just don't want to see you turning into Helen," Hal had told me. I sure as hell didn't want that, either. I loved Helen. Missed her every day since her untimely passing. But I was not going to live with Janet forever—or spend the rest of my life dreaming of the man who got away.

My thumb traced the ornate whorls and grooves of the wooden latch. Then I took a deep breath and pushed the door open.

The office was neater than I remembered; the staff must have tidied up when they packed Rowan's journals and the other items he'd set aside for me, including the painted wooden box containing $50,000—everything he had saved after more than a century at the Crossroads.

As I stepped inside, I realized I was holding my breath. An unnecessary precaution. The air smelled a bit musty, but it held no trace of honeysuckle sweetness and animal musk, that peculiar scent of Fae desire.

Golden shafts of sunlight streamed through the three skylights on the western side of the steep roof. Instead of making the room more cheerful, the dust motes only underscored the emptiness.

I walked through the office to the large living area. Everywhere, there were reminders of Rowan: the extensive collection of books and records; the baby grand piano and the antique melodeon; the table where we had shared candlelit dinners and stories from our pasts. Yet, oddly, the room felt less like Rowan's home than a photo in one of those free real estate booklets: "For rent or lease. Sunny artist's loft. Soaring ceilings. Hardwood floors. Recently renovated to remove faery magic."

Unexpected tears burned my eyes. I'd heard that old buildings retained the energy of their former occupants. Sometimes, I swore I could feel Helen's comforting presence in the Bough and smell the faint whiff of lavender from the sachets that had scented her clothes. But I could feel nothing of Rowan here. The apartment was just a dusty shrine to the past.

Someday, these rooms might house the theatre's artistic director—if we ever scraped together the funds to hire one. A stranger could be happy here, but not me.

I returned to the office and stared at the desk where he had written his farewell letters. Then I turned toward the final doorway, steeling myself to enter the bedroom.

Warmth embraced me. Something soft caressed my cheek.

I gasped and whirled around, but of course, no one was there.

I gripped the doorframe hard and waited for my heartbeat to slow, for reason to conquer imagination. A shaft of sunlight had warmed me. And the touch . . . a cobweb, perhaps, or a draft from the open door. Stupid to allow my longing to conjure phantoms.

Rowan was gone.

I pulled the front door closed behind me. I silently blessed the man who had once inhabited this apartment and this world. And then I said good-bye.

CHAPTER 2
LITTLE GIRLS

THE NEXT WEEK WAS YOUR BASIC FRENZY of activity. Alex made up music files. Reinhard sent out scripts and vocal books, schedules and parental consent forms. I scrambled to fill roles when some of the professionals refused the ones they were offered. Bitched about prima donnas. Shot off a final batch of grant proposals. And sent exuberant e-mails to the board urging them to sell, sell, sell those tickets for the opening weekend fund-raiser.

My horde of orphans arrived a week later. Mei-Yin had grumbled that casting every young hopeful encouraged the hopelessly untalented, but she had voted with the others to include every kid who had auditioned in one of our shows.

The prospect of coordinating thirty orphans ranging in age from seven to thirteen was daunting, even with the assistance of my Orphan Wranglers. Frannie had corralled one of her Chatterbox cronies and I'd roped in Janet by promising full disclosure on any and all awful dates I went on for the rest of my life.

Janet took one look at the throng onstage and muttered, "You better go on a lot of awful dates." Frannie's chum Eleanor just shrugged. "This is nothing. Try hosting a birthday party with nineteen six year olds and a drunk magician."

Fortunately, my magicians were sober. Reinhard's power rippled through me, calm and authoritative. To my surprise, Janet's held a hint of banked excitement— that "We've got a barn, let's do a show!" vibe.

When I announced that we'd play the Name Game by way of introductions, Chelsea rolled her eyes, but even she seemed amused when Reinhard joined us. In terms of icebreakers, it's hard to beat a heavyset, frowning man sitting cross-legged in a circle of little girls and declaring, "R my name is Reinhard and I like rohwurst."

I asked the girls playing the secondary orphans to choose names for their characters; nothing says "You're part of the huddled masses" more than playing some nameless part in the chorus. An endless discussion ensued with all the girls weighing in. By the time the last girl settled on the nickname "Marbles," Reinhard's gray crew cut was standing on end in full porcupine mode and I had only ten minutes left for my Red Light-Green Light version of Stage Directions 101. Although that evoked more eye rolling from Chelsea, the rest got into it, and I was pleased to see the older girls helping the little ones sort out upstage from down.

The wranglers and I escorted the girls over to the Smokehouse. Chelsea shot a dismissive glance around the rehearsal studio, but the others seemed impressed by the recently framed posters of past shows that lined the wall above the dance barre.

Alex led them through the same exercises I had performed during my season at the Crossroads. The girls hissed like snakes to practice breath control and giggled their way through the bubble blowing that was supposed to relax their lips. They giggled even more at the tongue twisters like "unique New York" and "fluffy, floppy puppy." They yodeled and chanted and followed Alex up and down the scale. By the end of the hour, even Chelsea seemed to be having fun, a tribute to Alex's charm as much as his magic.

In subsequent rehearsals, I introduced other games,

including the ever-popular Mirror Exercise, where each
girl had to mimic her partner's movements, and the Emotion Party, where they had to "catch" the feelings of each
arriving guest. That one left me totally strung out. I asked
for sad and got Greek tragedy. I asked for scared and got
A Nightmare on Elm Street. But at least they grasped the
idea of committing to the emotional moment.

When we plunged into the real work, the girls proved
themselves more prepared than most of the professionals I'd worked with during my years in summer stock.
Even the little ones knew their songs and their lines.
They threw themselves into learning their choreography
with such fervor that Mei-Yin exclaimed, "Give me kids
ANY day. When THEY fall over their feet, it's CUTE!"

Staging their scenes proved more challenging. Blocking adults is dull. Blocking restless children is about as
rewarding as herding cats. It required the concentration
of a traffic cop and the energy of a cheerleader on crack.

By the end of the second week, I wished I had three
more wranglers and a lot more time. Two weeks of "orphans only" rehearsals worked out to less than thirty
hours to teach them their staging, music, and dance numbers before the adults arrived.

I was also beginning to worry about my two Annies.
Chelsea had all the nuance of a police siren. When called
upon to dry Molly's tears in the opening scene, she
seemed impatient rather than comforting, and her rendition of "Maybe" shattered eardrums instead of capturing
hearts. It was Amanda who discovered the bittersweet
longing of the song during the rare moments I could actually hear her.

Chelsea's "damn the torpedoes, full steam ahead" approach served her better in "Hard Knock Life." Her
team of orphans turned in a spirited performance while
Amanda's were as tentative as she was.

The Cheshire Cat and the Dormouse; if I could roll
them together, I'd have an Annie who would break your
heart and make you cheer, all in the same scene.

I tried to bolster Amanda's confidence and tone down Chelsea's. Amanda nodded and looked miserable. Chelsea nodded and looked bored.

It was Alex who filled me in on what lay behind Chelsea's tough facade. Divorced parents. Mom in banking. Father living overseas somewhere and hadn't seen his kid in more than a year. No wonder she reminded me a lot of . . . well . . . me.

"Can you help her?" I asked Alex. "Everything I try meets with a shrug or a grimace."

"Same here," he replied. "We'll just have to keep trying."

Rowan would have known what to do. But it seemed my rehearsals could only provide a distraction instead of the healing I hoped she would find at the Crossroads.

SOME PEOPLE CLAIM SUMMER BEGINS Memorial Day weekend. Traditionalists hold out for the solstice. For the citizens of Dale, summer officially began with the annual migration of actors to the Golden Bough.

Last year's migration had consisted of seven Mackenzies and one semi-pro actor trickling into town for *The Fantasticks*. This year, the line of cars crawling around the village green and clogging Main Street evoked approving nods and relieved smiles from the citizenry.

"Now it feels like summer," Frannie remarked during check-in. The professionals seemed surprised to find me behind the front desk. The Mackenzies were too busy trying to figure out what *they* were doing here to wonder why their director was doubling as a hotel clerk.

When I heard the quavering strains of "When the Swallows Come Back to Capistrano" wafting through the windows, I raced through the lobby and flung open the front door. Now it felt like summer to me. Bernie Cohen—friend, volunteer, and board member—had returned.

My smile faded as Reinhard unloaded Bernie's walker from his SUV. Naturally, Bernie noticed. Seventy-plus he might be, blind he wasn't.

"These old hips stiffen up over the winter, but a couple weeks back at the Crossroads and I'll be doing a Highland reel. Just seeing the old barn again was a tonic."

A "tonic" he had first experienced during our season of summer stock and had accepted ever since without questioning how it worked.

"Boy, it's good to be back. Leah was driving me crazy. If she had her way, I'd spend my life playing canasta at the senior center. The whole time I'm packing she says, 'Don't overdo, Dad.' I say, 'How can I overdo? I'll be living with Reinhard and Mei-Yin. He's a doctor. She's a terror.' How're your teeth?"

"Once a dentist, always a dentist." But I bared my teeth for his inspection.

Bernie tsked. "Floss more. It's the secret to good health. Look at Long."

"Must I?"

"Okay, he's a putz. But such teeth. How's ticket sales?"

"We can discuss this at the barbecue," Reinhard said.

"What's the deal with that?" Bernie asked. "Some new Crossroads tradition?"

"My secret weapon. With half the cast living off-site, I wanted everyone to get to know each other before rehearsals started."

"Smart. Did you get Long to pay for it?"

"You bet."

"Very smart."

"Bernie claims to have a secret weapon, too," Reinhard said. "One that will sell ads like pancakes."

"Hotcakes," Bernie corrected. "I got a bet with Reinhard that I can sell a thousand bucks of ads for *Annie*. You want in?"

"Absolutely."

"Loser treats the winner to dinner at the Bough."

"Deal. But it'll be like taking candy from a baby. Even you can't sell that many ads."

"Just you wait, girlie."

The barbecue broke up around ten o'clock, but it was well after midnight when Janet and I crept into the Golden Bough to carry out a far older tradition.

During my season, Helen had performed her blessing every night until her heart attack confined her to the Bates mansion. When I moved into the Bough, I carried on the tradition in her memory. Once I was no longer managing the hotel, I made do with a furtive blessing when each new wave of cast members arrived. This season, I'd decided to enlist Janet's help to back up the blessing with some genuine Fae power.

As we tiptoed up the stairs, I caressed the worn leather cover of Helen's book of spells. Although I knew the words of the blessing by heart, just holding the book brought me a small measure of the comfort and reassurance that Helen had always provided.

I knew the words on the cover page as well: "The Herbal of Mairead Mackenzie. 1817." The woman whom Rowan had called a witch. The woman who had cursed him and bound him to this world. The woman whose collection of remedies, charms, and talismans had been passed down through generations of Mackenzie women before coming to me in Helen's will.

Janet rested her palm against the first door. I held the book to my breast and silently repeated the words of the blessing:

> *Deep peace of the running wave to you.*
> *Deep peace of the flowing air to you.*
> *Deep peace of the quiet earth to you.*
> *Deep peace of the shining stars to you.*

Janet and I repeated the ritual at each door, bound by our love for Helen and our blood tie to Mairead Mackenzie. Maybe that was why the blessing seemed so potent, why I felt like I was participating in an ancient rite rather than one that Helen had invented, a rite that signaled the beginning of our summer stock season.

By the time we had bestowed our final blessing, peace flowed through me as surely as it flowed through the sleeping inhabitants of the Bough. Janet seemed to feel it, too, a rare smile curving her mouth. Then she rolled her eyes and whispered, "Let's get the hell home and go to bed." And the spell was broken.

Helen's peace and Janet's sarcasm. Somehow, they summed up all the contradictions of the new Crossroads Theatre: a board of directors unknowingly leading a Fae-powered staff; a cast composed of professionals, community theatre actors, and bewildered Mackenzies; and a director who fervently hoped she could keep her head above water while balancing all those disparate elements.

CHAPTER 4

YOU'RE NEVER FULLY DRESSED
WITHOUT A SMILE

WHEN REHEARSALS BEGAN, I found myself dog-paddling furiously to keep afloat. As excited as I was to work with professional actors, I was painfully conscious of my lack of directing experience. Last season, the small casts had made staging easy, but this production of *Annie* was the musical theatre equivalent of *The Ten Commandments*. And I sure as hell was no Cecil B. DeMille.

I'd resorted to a graph paper floor plan of the stage and moved tiny paper cutouts of actors around it like an interior designer planning the layout of a room. Naturally, Hal discovered my shameful secret. Reinhard put a stop to his teasing with the stern admonishment, "Every director works differently. If this technique helps Maggie, why should she not use paper dolls?"

Which wasn't exactly the boost I needed.

In the mornings, I blocked scenes with the principals, leaving the chorus to the tender mercies of Reinhard and Mei-Yin. Then I gobbled lunch in the production office, fielded questions from the staff, and tried to ensure that the fund-raiser was on track. More scene work in the afternoon, then over to the Golden Bough to check in with Frannie. A quick dinner at the house, then back to the theatre to work the big musical numbers in the evening. By the time I trudged up the hill to the

Bates mansion, I was too wired to sleep and spent an hour sending out e-mails and prepping for the next day's rehearsal. While the hectic pace left me jazzed, I worried that I'd be as lively as Arthur by opening night.

The staff was putting in the same killer hours. Every afternoon, Alex raced over from the high school for music rehearsals. Mei-Yin juggled choreography and the Mandarin Chalet. Reinhard somehow managed to maintain his medical practice during his few hours off. On the days his antique store was closed, Javier helped Catherine with set construction. And although we had rented some of the principals' costumes, Hal had to construct the rest and enlist volunteers to alter the Depression-era drag he had scoured from area thrift stores.

Bernie flung himself into selling ads for the program, visiting shop owners in the morning and waylaying parents every afternoon as they dropped off their daughters. He alternated between the fast-talking salesmanship of Harold Hill in *The Music Man* and the sad-eyed pleading of Puss from the *Shrek* series. Throw in "little old man in a walker" and even the most tight-fisted parents caved, convinced their daughters would suffer lifelong damage if they failed to buy an ad.

"What a con artist," I told him, watching yet another mother walk to her car, paperwork in hand.

"It's called salesmanship," he retorted, morphing from sad-eyed Puss to keen-eyed retiree. "Know how much I've sold so far, Miss Smarty Pants? Five hundred and fifty bucks!"

"Are you fucking kidding me?" I glanced around and hastily lowered my voice. "In four days? How the hell did you do it?"

I scanned the papers he thrust at me. A full-page ad— lavishly adorned with stars—screamed, "Some families are dripping with diamonds. Some families are dripping with pearls. Lucky us! Lucky us! Look at what we're dripping with! A fabulous little girl!" Another proclaimed "To a little orphan with a big heart and the talent to match! We love you!!" And yet another: "Our FILL IN YOUR CHILD'S ROLE shines like the top of the Chrysler Building!" "Break a leg!" and "We're so proud!" messages adorned other—significantly smaller—ads.

"It's brilliant, Bernie."

Tacky, but definitely brilliant.

"It was Sarah's idea. That granddaughter of mine is gonna be a millionaire someday."

"If this keeps up . . ." I glanced around, frantically seeking wood to knock on, and settled for his sheaf of papers; they'd been trees once, after all.

"From your lips to God's ears." Bernie executed a jig—quite a feat for a little old man with a walker. "Better up the credit limit on your MasterCard, girlie. I'm gonna order the most expensive dinner at the Bough!"

"I can't think of anyone I'd rather dine with."

Bernie cocked his head in the characteristic gesture that always brought to mind a bright-eyed—if balding—sparrow.

"You sure about that?"

I found myself remembering a gourmet meal, a bottle of wine older than I was, and Rowan sitting across the table, angular features soft in the flickering candlelight. And as usual, everything I was thinking and feeling must have shown on my face because Bernie sighed and patted my hand.

"Time to exchange 'Some Enchanted Evening' for 'I'm Gonna Wash that Man Right Out-a My Hair,' " he scolded gently.

I managed a smile. "From your lips to God's ears."

My crazy schedule left me little time to moon over Rowan Mackenzie or wash my hair. I was lucky to squeeze in a weekly call to my mother and to my Crossroads roommate Nancy. I kept those conversations upbeat, but sometimes found myself venting to Frannie.

She possessed Helen's boundless optimism and handled every crisis with a firm hand and a cheerful smile. My eyes and ears at the Golden Bough, she alerted me to the rift developing among the cast.

"They're clumping," she confided. "Mackenzies huddled in one corner of the lounge. Professionals in another."

So much for the "getting to know you" barbecue. And my strategy of giving each Mackenzie a pro for a roommate to encourage mingling.

"What about the locals?" I asked.

"Mostly, they head home after rehearsal. The ones who stop by hang out with the pros." Frannie clucked. "Not like the old days, is it, hon?"

No. Our cast had been a family. An occasionally fractious, somewhat dysfunctional family, but a family nonetheless. Of course, we were all in the same boat: separated from our families, desperately trying to cope with the murderous schedule, and—except for me—woefully inexperienced.

"Let's see if movie night helps."

Hal shattered that hope when he stormed into the production office and declared, "Only half the cast showed up! And most of them just came for the pizza. There's something wrong when theatre people can't bond over Judy Garland films."

"I can't require them to attend, Hal. Most of the locals are holding down day jobs. Monday's the one night they can spend with their families."

Working around their schedules made rehearsals incredibly frustrating. Every evening, we had to get the strays up to speed. They felt clumsy, the pros got impatient, and the Mackenzies shot anxious looks at both groups and clumped together even more fiercely. Mei-Yin and I began reserving the first hour of the evening rehearsal to work through the big numbers with the locals and the Mackenzies, so they could perform confidently—and competently—when the pros arrived.

Naturally, that came back to bite me in the ass.

"The professionals are griping," Frannie reported. "They say you don't give them as much attention as the others."

"They don't need as much attention!"

"I'm just saying."

For the next few days, I gave the pros "extra attention." End result . . .

"They say you don't trust them," Frannie told me. "That you're treating them like amateurs."

"I'd like to treat them to a swift kick in the ass."

Instead, I set my sights on Debra, the most experienced actor in the company. If I could win her over, the rest would fall in line.

I knew it wouldn't be easy. Debra was big, brassy, and ballsy—and completely set in her ways. She'd played the wicked orphanage director Miss Hannigan before and saw no reason to do anything differently this time.

I considered it a good sign that she arrived right on time for our first one-on-one in the Smokehouse. Then she blew a hank of brown hair off her forehead, plopped onto a chair, and folded her arms across her chest. As her gaze drifted around the room, I wondered if she was studying the posters on the wall behind me, each emblazoned with the words "Directed by Rowan Mackenzie" in letters as dark and forbidding as Debra's eyes.

I forced a smile and praised her work in rehearsals. She nodded absently and glanced at her watch. So I cut to the chase and earnestly suggested that she consider Hannigan's backstory and find moments to let her genuine desperation shine through—without, of course, losing the humor.

Debra frowned. Then she burst out laughing. "Oh, God. You really had me going. For a minute, I thought you were serious." Her smile abruptly vanished. "You're not serious, are you?"

"I'm not asking for *Long Day's Journey Into Night*. Just pick a few moments—"

"It's *Annie*! A musical based on a comic strip! You work the laughs, try not to walk into the furniture, and accept the fact that the kids or the dog will always upstage you." She heaved a long-suffering sigh. "Let me guess—first season directing?"

"No! My second."

"You'll learn."

After favoring me with a pitying smile, she waltzed out of the Smokehouse.

Way to win her over, Graham. Now she thinks you're an artsy-fartsy novice.

I glowered at the posters, but I had only myself to blame. I'd been so desperate to leave my mark on the show that I'd tried to play Rowan Mackenzie.

Stupid.

Had I delved into Ado Annie when I'd played the role? No. I'd learned the lines, worked the comic bits, and enjoyed a vacation in the country. Which was what Debra wanted to do.

Stupid, stupid, stupid.

And even more stupid to waste time fine-tuning a perfectly acceptable performance when I had much bigger headaches.

Like Paul, the earnest Mackenzie playing cheesy, breezy Bert Healy. He was about as breezy as one of Hal's mannequins and sounded more like a soloist in the Mormon Tabernacle Choir than a radio show host. If you're never fully dressed without a smile, Paul was half-naked.

Then there was Bill, the community theatre actor playing Warbucks' butler. You could drive a bus through his pauses. A simple "Everything is in order" required a glance heavenward, a considering frown, and a thoughtful nod before he delivered the line. His entrances and exits added a minute to every scene he was in.

"Could he walk any slower?" I fumed to Reinhard after the Scene 5 work-through. "I swear to God, Lurch was livelier."

"Lurch?"

"*The Addams Family*."

"Ah, yes," Reinhard replied. And followed up with Lurch's deep, shuddering groan.

"I can't wait until he brings Arthur in at the end of the show. Talk about the slow leading the slow."

"You are the director. You cannot allow him to control the pace. Or the scene."

"I've given him the same notes after every fucking rehearsal!"

Reinhard winced a bit at my profanity. "You still want to be a helping professional. With some, you must be a dictatorial director."

"Couldn't you just clout him with your clipboard?"

"No. Although it is tempting. Do not worry. You will find a way to get through to him." Reinhard sighed. "Now, if only we can do something with poor Otis."

The entire staff had taken to calling him "poor Otis." A sweet-natured bear of man with a brown moon face and a gleaming bald pate, I'd known from the moment he stepped onstage at auditions that he had to play Oliver Warbucks. But while he had all the warmth of the Daddy Warbucks who emerges late in Act One, he couldn't capture the self-important, multitasking tycoon we meet at the outset. Maybe because he was cowed by Chelsea and Kimberlee, the actress playing Warbucks' long-suffering but faithful secretary. The more he rehearsed with them, the more flustered he became. Lines and lyrics went out the window. By the time he finished butchering the lyrics to "N.Y.C.," we were both streaming flop sweat.

I tried role-play, my old reliable "list thing," and just talking with him, but the only thing that seemed to help was working with Amanda. Since that boosted her confidence as well as his, I gave them more rehearsals together, even if it meant reducing his time with Chelsea.

I resisted the urge to ask Alex to give him a magical nudge. Even Rowan had used his magic sparingly during rehearsals and then, mostly to reassure us.

When I tried out the reassuring voice I'd used on HelpLink calls, Otis asked if I was coming down with a cold. So I packed it away in mothballs and resumed my performance as The Calm Director Who Had Everything Under Control, even though I felt more like Chicken Little.

The sky didn't fall during our Act One run-through. Just a lot of props. As the orphans bewailed their "Hard Knock Life," wash buckets and mops flew around the stage as if bespelled by the sorcerer's apprentice. A wheel fell off at the top of Scene 2, literally upsetting the apple cart. In "I Think I'm Gonna Like It Here," the efficiency of Warbucks' army of servants was belied by the clang of dropped platters, an inner tube zigzagging across the stage, a cascade of gift boxes, and an avalanche of linens. Alex got bonus points for fielding the tennis ball that bounced into the pit with his left hand, while his right soldiered on with the tune.

Two hours later, Chelsea warbled the reprise of "Maybe" and mercifully ended things. Then we had to go through it all again on Sunday with Amanda's team.

I quelled my fear that the show would run longer than *The Ten Commandments* and *Ben-Hur* combined and focused on the positives. As the brainless Lily, Nora proved you could chew gum and sing at the same time. Steven made a deliciously oily Rooster, winning laughs with just an artful flip of his fedora. Debra's "Little Girls" was a comic masterpiece of defiance and disgust, her scenes with Lily and Rooster, a triumph of sleaziness.

I knew I'd had little to do with their success; I pretty much stayed out of their way and let them strut their stuff.

Unfortunately, Long didn't do the same with me. After our second Act One run-through, he trailed me to the production office, shaking his head.

"That Otis fellow. He's not very good, is he?"

"It's a demanding role."

"Pity you didn't cast a professional." When I bristled like an angry cat, he hastily added, "I'm sure you had your reasons. But he's dragging down the whole show."

"He'll get it."

Long turned on his megawatt smile. "Of course he will. But you understand my concern. There's a lot riding on this show."

My reputation. And the theatre's. The board was counting on a crowd pleaser. Now, I had to deliver.

CHAPTER 5

ALWAYS LOOK ON THE BRIGHT
SIDE OF LIFE

ACT TWO WAS MERCIFULLY SHORTER and the run-through mercifully smoother. I fretted that I should have trimmed the Cabinet scene more ruthlessly as well as the dreadful finale: "A New Deal for Christmas." Was it me or was there something creepy about the President of the United States pretending to whip his reindeer orphans?

After three weeks of giving Bill notes about pace and chiding Kimberlee for her impatience with Otis, I took Reinhard's advice and told Bill he was failing to capture Drake's brisk efficiency and warned Kimberlee to knock off the snide remarks. Mr. Method Actor looked stricken. Ms. Bitch looked stunned. But Bill walked marginally faster and Kimberlee kept her mouth shut—at least in front of me.

I saved my hugs for my girls who were working their little tails off—and for my Mackenzies. Paul was evolving from choirboy to radio singer. The others were holding their own in various chorus roles. Even Chelsea thawed once I abandoned my attempts to play helping professional and settled for theatre professional instead. If her emotional moments failed to resonate like Amanda's, they were less relentlessly upbeat.

Working with Otis had nudged Amanda from a waifish Dickensian orphan to an almost-plucky comic strip one. An admittedly silly session of scream therapy had helped, too. At first, Amanda regarded me like I had lost my mind, but after a couple of minutes—and a lot of prodding—her timid squeak became a full-fledged shout. Amanda—who barely spoke above a whisper onstage and off. She looked nearly as astonished as I felt. Minutes later, we were both screeching with such abandon that Reinhard stormed into the Smokehouse, fearful that someone was being murdered.

Otis remained my biggest hurdle. During our final one-on-one before Hell Week, I led him to the picnic area for one last try at helping him discover his inner Donald Trump. He sat down opposite me, clearly dreading another scintillating discussion about his performance. When I asked why he'd come to the Crossroads, his expression shifted to surprise.

"Tell the truth, I don't know. Just felt the urge to take a trip and somehow ended up here. Why did you cast me?"

"Because I knew you had the heart to play Daddy Warbucks."

"Takes more than heart," he said, his face gloomy.

"Come on, you're a natural for this role. You started out poor like he did. And you made a good life for—"

"I'm nothing like him! All high and mighty. Buying up fancy art and big houses and looking down his nose at all the folks he'd grown up with."

Nothing in the script indicated Warbucks looked down his nose at people. He was pretty much oblivious to everyone at the beginning of the show. Did Otis still feel the sting of growing up poor even though he was the self-proclaimed "Plumbing King of Canarsie?" He'd been married for nearly thirty years and clearly adored his wife. But he rarely spoke of his daughter, the law student, and his son, the accountant. Were they ashamed of their father's humble beginnings? Or worse, did they make Otis feel ashamed?

Reluctant to pry, I just said, "But Warbucks changes. He realizes that—"

" 'Something Was Missing.' I know." Otis' voice was quiet again, his shoulders slumped. "It doesn't always happen in real life the way it does in the theatre, Maggie."

"It can."

He regarded me for a long moment. "Happened to you like that, did it?"

I nodded.

"Here?"

I nodded again, embarrassed to feel my throat tighten.

Otis reached across the table to cover my hands with his. Big, strong hands, but as gentle as the man himself.

"Don't you worry about me. I'll do a good job for you."

"I knew that the day you auditioned. I just . . . I wanted you to find something here that would help *you*. The way it helped me."

"Found you, didn't I? And little Amanda. And some of the folks in the chorus."

"And Kimberlee. And Bill."

Otis waved them away. "Gotta pick and choose, child. Like fishing. Keep the good ones and throw the crappy little ones back."

That astonished a laugh from me. And for the first time in days, Otis laughed, too.

As we rose to return to the theatre, I casually asked, "Are your kids coming up to see the show?"

Otis studied me. "You're one smart lady, Maggie Graham."

"If I was all that smart, I would have been less obvious."

"The kids have their own lives. But Viola's coming up. And a good thing, too. Haven't been apart from her this long since we were married."

"I can't wait to meet her."

As soon as his car pulled out of the parking lot, I made a beeline for the production office. I dug Otis' contact information out of the file cabinet and dialed his home number. Viola picked up on the third ring.

It took less than a minute to discover we were both on the same wavelength. Ten minutes later, there was a knock on the door. I reluctantly ended the call, but I was so buoyed by our conversation that I greeted Bill with a smile.

"What's up?"

He glanced around the office, shuffled his feet, and cleared his throat. Realizing that the preliminaries could take another ten minutes, I tried to curb my impatience.

After enduring his solicitous concern about burdening me, his stirring endorsement of my directing, an even longer declaration of his work ethic, and an avowal of enthusiasm for his roles in the next two shows, he finally said the magic words: "I've been offered the role of Henry Higgins in our community theatre production of *My Fair Lady*."

Shoot me now.

"You know what an incredible opportunity that is. A role any actor would kill for."

Just put a gun to my head and . . .

"Well, long story short . . ."

SHOOT ME!

"How could I turn it down?"

As this was clearly a rhetorical question, I just stared at him.

"Naturally, I wouldn't dream of leaving you in the lurch for *Annie*. But I've only got a small part in *The Secret Garden*. You won't have any trouble filling that. I hate to miss out on *Into the Woods*, but . . ." He heaved a sigh. "What could I do?"

Tell them you were already committed for the summer? That you had signed a contract to that effect and had to honor it?

I rummaged through my collection of smiles and

found a very sweet one. "That's great, Bill. Congratulations! Just be sure to notify Reinhard. He'll need to dock your salary for backing out of *The Secret Garden* rehearsals with less than a week's notice."

Still smiling sweetly, I ushered him out of the office, closed the door, and waited until the sound of his footsteps receded before pounding my fist on the wall. Then I yanked open the file cabinet drawer and pulled out my stack of resumes.

Thus beginneth Hell Week.

TECH REHEARSAL WAS AS TEDIOUS as I'd expected. Yes, it was exciting to see the neon lights on Times Square, but there were only so many times I could watch those lights come up before I wanted to slit my wrists.

Hal's set design relied largely on a series of backdrops that evoked the comic strip origin of *Annie*: the orphanage sketched in shades of black and gray; sepia brownstones and shanties for the street scenes and Hooverville; a brightly colored Times Square. The only fixed set was the upstage Warbucks mansion, a stylized Art Deco confection with a central staircase and two landings.

With so little moving scenery, I figured we were on Easy Street.

Naturally, I figured wrong.

Warbucks' servants tripped up and down the stairs. Chorus members jostling for position sent shudders rippling through the painted streets of New York. The orphans' metal bunk beds clanked and screeched as if Marley's Ghost plodded across the stage, dragging the chains he forged in life. The crash of furniture and thudding footsteps of the unseen crew members would have worked like gangbusters in the final scene of *The Diary of Anne Frank*, but made it sound like the Warbucks mansion was under construction.

By contrast, our first dress rehearsal was a breeze. If Javier's crew didn't display ninja-like stealth, neither did they sound like storm troopers. The pit band only drowned out the performers half the time. The near-sighted actress playing the housekeeper only tripped on the staircase twice. Only one platter and two gift boxes dropped during "I Think I'm Gonna Like It Here." And Bill's entrances and exits were nearly as smooth as those of the well-oiled bunk beds.

As the company launched into "A New Deal for Christmas," I glanced at my scrawled notes and won-dered why I had bothered. I'd reached the "Que Será, Será" stage of directing when I had to trust my actors to carry the show. Well, maybe a few reminders about pace, especially in that endless fucking Cabinet scene.

Let it go, Graham.

It was a good production. As good as I could make it, anyway. Otis was still fumbling his lyrics in "N.Y.C.," but he'd found his inner tycoon. Kimberlee might still be a bitch offstage, but when Otis dropped the ball, she picked it up and kept their scenes moving. The audience would be too busy admiring Chelsea's pipes to notice her lack of nuance.

Stupid to look for shades of gray in cartoon characters. Or yearn for the healing magic that Rowan Mackenzie could have brought all the actors instead of the handful I'd been able to reach. We were in the business of theatre, not healing. And *Annie* would do good business.

Long seemed to think so; I could hear him clapping in time to the music.

In a minute, Bill would lead Arthur onstage. Ap-plause. Quick rehearsal of the curtain calls. A rousing speech by yours truly. Then up the hill to the Bates man-sion for a very long bath and a very large tumbler of single malt whisky.

The cue for Bill's entrance came and went. The cast forged ahead, but some shot surreptitious glances stage left.

Just when I was starting to worry, Arthur tottered on with Bill. I gritted my teeth as I watched them. Glaciers moved more swiftly. The cast appeared mesmerized, every pair of eyes monitoring the duo's infinitesimal progress toward center stage.

Arthur stopped. Bill tugged his leash. Arthur obediently trudged forward and stopped again. Bill gave another tug. Arthur stood there.

At which point, Chelsea apparently relinquished any hope that Arthur would reach her before the end of the number and skipped toward him. The chorus' triumphant "this year" was still hanging in the air when Arthur collapsed.

Alex's hands froze, still upraised from cueing the cut-off to the cast and pit band. A high keening shattered the stillness. Doreen burst out of the stage left wings. Reinhard strode on from stage right, shouting, "Stay in your places!"

But by then, I was already running down the aisle.

❧❧

As I pounded up the steps to the stage, two of the younger orphans burst into tears. I paused long enough to squeeze a shoulder and pat a cheek before hurrying over to Doreen.

She had flung herself to the floor next to Arthur and pulled his head onto her lap. My desperate hope that he was merely worn out vanished when I saw that his rheumy brown eyes had begun to glaze over.

And still, stupid Bill kept tugging at his leash. As I shot him a furious look, Javier and Reinhard's daughter Bea pushed through the crowd. In their black stage crew garb, they looked like mourners at a funeral.

Javier's fingers closed around Bill's wrist. Bill regarded him with bewilderment. Then the leash slithered onto the floor.

As I stared helplessly around the stage, a hand came down on my shoulder. The steadying throb of Reinhard's power pulsed through me. My galloping heartbeat slowed. My anguish receded a little—just enough for me to collect myself.

Janet and Alex drifted among the huddled orphans, pausing as I had to pat a trembling shoulder, to stroke a drooping head. Lee must have raced down from the lighting booth, because he and Mei-Yin were offering the same fleeting gestures of comfort to the adults, their magic easing grief and fear and uncertainty.

Bea sat beside Doreen, one hand resting lightly on her arm. It was the first time I'd ever seen her use the power she had inherited from Reinhard, but it was clearly working. Although Doreen's face was streaked with tears, she seemed more stunned now than heartbroken.

A strange lassitude settled over me, like the calm that had descended during the staff's "brainwashing" after Caren nearly stumbled on Rowan's Fae kin. With a start, I realized that tomorrow was Midsummer's Eve. This year, disaster had struck a day early.

Reinhard released my shoulder, and my languor dissipated. I shot him a grateful glance and asked him and Mei-Yin to take the cast to the green room.

As they began herding everyone into the wings, Hal moaned, "Poor Arthur."

Doreen's head came up. "It was just his time. And this is how he would have wanted to go. Not lying in his doggie bed, but performing in a show he loved. Arthur was a professional."

All of us onstage nodded solemnly.

"I should have known he didn't have the strength for another show. But he was so excited at auditions."

Excited? He could barely shuffle across the stage.

Guilt swamped me at that traitorous thought. When I recalled how Arthur had obediently played dead, I winced.

"I'm so sorry, Doreen. If there's anything we can do . . ."

"I'll be all right. But this will be so hard on the girls. They loved Arthur."

Well, the little ones did. They treated him like a combination furry futon and living doll, alternately sprawling atop him and tying bows around his tail. Arthur tolerated it with only an occasional twitch. But Chelsea eyed him with ill-disguised impatience and some of the older girls took their cue from her. I might have done a better job at hiding my emotions, but I'd certainly shared their frustration.

"Don't worry about the girls," Janet said. "We'll make sure they're okay."

I was the only one likely to become hysterical. How was I going to find another Sandy and get him up to speed before opening night?

The thought provoked a fresh wave of guilt. Poor Arthur wasn't even cold and I was worrying about his replacement. But I was the director. I had to worry.

Right now, though, I had more immediate concerns, including a grief-stricken owner, a nervous cast, and a lot of unhappy children.

"We could hold a memorial service," I suggested. "So we can all say good-bye."

A tremulous smile lit Doreen's face. "Oh, that's so sweet."

"Tomorrow," Hal declared. "Before the second dress rehearsal."

I exchanged a quick look with Long. "I'm not sure there will be a second dress rehearsal."

Doreen gasped. "You're not thinking of postponing the opening?"

"We may not have a choice," Long said.

"Oh, but you can't! Arthur would want the show to go on."

Fumbling for a solution, I said, "I could rewrite Scene 2. And cut Sandy's—"

"Nonsense! Fifi will play the role."

Unwillingly, I pictured the unholy product of mixed

breeding that was Fifi. The stumpy legs. The too-broad chest. The pom-pom tail and curly fur. Granted the fur was sandy-colored, but the audience would be too busy gawking at her bizarre physique to notice Annie.

"You didn't think I'd let Arthur take on the role without an understudy?"

No. Only the director would do that.

"I worked with her at home. She knows the blocking and the cues. And she watched Arthur from the wings."

Until Javier banished her for piddling all over the floor in excitement.

"All she needs is one rehearsal with Chelsea and Amanda and she'll be ready."

"Maybe we should talk about that tomorrow."

"After the memorial service," Hal said firmly.

Janet cleared her throat. "I'm not sure it would help the girls to see Arthur being . . . laid to rest. That is, if you're going to . . ."

"Of course!" Doreen regarded Janet with astonishment. "I don't believe in cremation. All those jars on the mantel. It's ghoulish. Besides, Arthur would want to rest with the others."

Another unwilling picture, this one of Stephen King's *Pet Sematary*.

Now who's being ghoulish?

"We could have a little gathering in the picnic area," I ventured.

"But this is a formal occasion," Hal protested.

Before I could suggest an alternative, Doreen said, "We'll hold the service at my house."

Praying we could fit a funeral into our overcrowded schedule, I nodded.

❧❦

I left Janet and Long to break the bad news to the parents who were beginning to filter into the theatre while I hurried to the green room to speak to the cast. As soon as I opened the door, the murmur of conversation ceased. I couldn't help noting that the pros clustered together on the far side of the room, while the Mackenzies huddled near the kitchenette with the orphans. The community theatre actors were in the middle, squeezed onto the sofa and chairs and crowded around the central table.

Even in grief, my cast remained divided.

As I searched for inspirational words to recognize Arthur's loss, address their concerns, and pull this cast together, Kimberlee demanded, "Are we postponing the opening?"

Thrown off stride, I fumbled to get back on script. "While Arthur's death is a terrible loss, we will still open as planned. Fifi will be taking over the role of Sandy."

"Are you kidding?" Bill exclaimed.

"Well, who else is there?" Debra demanded.

Heartened by her support, I flashed a grateful smile. Then she added, "Even if she is a weird little mutt and pees at the drop of a hat."

I silenced the titters with a stern look. "I know it's been a long night, but there's one more thing before I let you go. We're holding a memorial service for Arthur at Doreen's house. Tomorrow at eleven o'clock."

Most of the children brightened. Otis nodded. Bill said, "But we're not expected to go or anything, right?"

I'd merely planned to encourage a good turnout, but Bill's look of disbelief pissed me off.

"Arthur was a member of this cast. I realize that the commuters may have scheduling conflicts, but I hope you'll make every effort to attend. I expect all cast members living at the Bough to be there to support Doreen and show your respect for Arthur. Reinhard will e-mail directions tomorrow morning. Frannie will have copies at the Bough. Those who'd like to carpool, please meet at the theatre at 10:30. Are there any more questions?"

Silence greeted my speech. And no wonder. The moment had called for warm and supportive and I'd given them cold and bitchy. Hoping to mend things, I groped for the inspirational words that had eluded me earlier.

"Arthur's death has been a shock. But we have a terrific show and if we pull together, we'll have a wonderful opening night. One that will make us—and Arthur—proud."

Chelsea heaved a dramatic sigh. Kimberlee muttered something to Bill. Debra stifled a yawn.

So much for inspiration. Before Arthur's death, I had a divided cast. Now, I had a divided, resentful cast.

Maggie Graham. Hapless Professional.

CHAPTER 7
TOMORROW

I SPENT THE NEXT MORNING checking in with Doreen, touching base with the staff on funeral arrangements, helping Janet organize the luncheon we'd decided to hold at the Bates mansion, and fielding a gazillion phone calls from parents and board members. After my third conversation with Long, I dialed my mother's number.

"Are you serious?" she exclaimed after I told her about Arthur. "He just dropped dead? Onstage? In front of the entire cast?"

"I'm very serious."

There was a long silence. Then: "It could be worse. It could have happened opening night."

"That's the silver lining?"

"You said yourself he was a thousand years old!"

"I know, but—"

"How are you handling it?"

When I told her about the funeral and my dreadful "be there or else" ultimatum, she sighed.

"I know. I screwed up."

"You were upset. And that...whatever his name is...Lurch. He's an idiot."

"Please tell me I'm going to live through this."

"Of course you will. You're a survivor."

"Yeah. And tomorrow night, I'll find out if I'm going to be voted off the tribe."

"Don't be silly. Who could they find to replace you? Especially for that pittance they call a salary. When this season is over, Maggie, you put your foot down. Hard. Preferably on Long's neck. Chris will represent you at the trial."

"When are you going to stop shacking up with that nice man and accept his offer to make you a respectable married woman?"

"When you stop referring to an adult relationship as 'shacking up.' Now go to your funeral. And call me afterward and let me know how it went."

Janet and I waited at the theatre until 10:45. When no one showed up, we got into my car and drove in silence to Doreen's house.

It turned out to be a rambling country cottage that looked like it had last been painted during the Nixon administration. But there were about a dozen cars out front. At least, some of the cast had shown up.

Janet and I hurried to the backyard where the service would be held. As we rounded the corner of the house, I stopped short.

Dozens of people milled about on the lawn. Sixty . . . seventy . . . too many to count. Children and adults, board and staff, cast members and strangers.

I gratefully accepted the tissue Janet brandished and followed her through the maze of dog poop that littered the patchy grass. A chorus of howls, yips, and barks accompanied us, along with the occasional clang of metal as a dog hurled itself against the wire mesh of its run.

"Maybe they don't like strangers," I said, nervously assessing the sturdiness of the mesh.

"Maybe she's breeding a pack of Cujos."

Reminded of the pet cemetery, I scanned the lawn. Failing to find any gravestones, I concluded her other animals must be buried somewhere in the field behind the house.

The focal point of the gathering was a rickety, octagonal gazebo that was decidedly off-kilter. A good gust of wind would knock it down. Which might not be a bad thing since Long was standing inside it.

I wormed my way through the crowd, but stopped a few feet from the Leaning Tower of Zebo. "I thought we agreed that Reinhard would lead the service."

Frowning at a hole in the roof, Long said, "I'm just going to make a few introductory remarks."

I resisted the urge to tell him to keep it short, nodded to Bernie, Frannie, and Bea who were representing the board, and made my way toward the staff.

"Shouldn't you be standing with the board?" I asked Janet.

"No. I want to be able to yawn inconspicuously if Long gets windy."

The faces of some of the professional actors were as sullen as the sky, but they were all there. So were the Mackenzies, of course, and most of the commuters, looking harried but dutiful. Plus a few parents who had obviously ferried carloads of kids. Only the men on my staff were missing.

"Where are the guys?" I whispered.

"Pallbearers," Janet whispered back.

"Pallbearers?"

"Well, SOMEONE has to carry the coffin!" As always, Mei-Yin's whisper was loud enough to make heads swivel in our direction.

Long waved his hands and called, "May I have everyone's attention?" A wave of shushing ensued until the crowd fell silent.

"For those of you whom I have not met, my name is Longford Martindale, president of the board of directors of the Crossroads Theatre. I just wanted to thank you for coming this morning. Especially the actors. I know how hard you've all been working and to sacrifice even an hour of free time shows how deeply you cared about Arthur and how much you wanted to support Doreen. I have been impressed by your performances in rehearsals, but today, I am moved by your compassion and generosity of spirit."

Several actors preened—naturally, those who'd been conspicuously short on compassion and generosity last night. I had to hand it to Long; he might be a pain in the ass, but he had struck just the right tone—something I'd completely failed to do during my address.

A loud, nasal wheeze interrupted my thoughts. I spun around to discover Mr. Hamilton in full Scottish regalia. With measured tread, the treasurer of my board and owner of Dale's General Store advanced toward the gazebo, bagpipes blaring "Loch Lomond."

Reinhard carefully descended the three rickety porch steps and extended his hand to Doreen. The rest of the staff followed, Lee and Hal supporting one side of the small coffin, Alex and Javier the other. Like Reinhard, they were wearing suits—with white carnations in their buttonholes.

The little procession marched toward us. Reinhard escorted Doreen to a folding chair. Mr. Hamilton walked slowly around the gazebo while Reinhard took his place inside. The pallbearers laid the coffin at his feet and broke into pairs on either side of the gazebo. Long produced a floral wreath from somewhere and laid it atop the coffin, then stepped back to join the other board members.

Catherine must have labored all night on the coffin. Instead of the simple pine box I'd expected, she had stained the wood a soft honey color and varnished it to a high sheen. Two sets of shiny brass handles adorned the sides. Between the handles, Hal had painted a line of dark, multi-petaled flowers. Poppies, perhaps.

No, not poppies, I realized as I peered more closely. Paw prints. And the stain that I had initially thought of as honey-colored was—of course—sandy.

I swallowed hard to dislodge the giant lump in my throat. Glancing around, I noticed cast members fumbling in pockets and purses for tissues.

I had hesitated before asking Reinhard to deliver the eulogy, knowing it would conjure memories of Helen's memorial service. But even Janet agreed that someone on the staff should speak, and since I was a basket case, Reinhard was the logical choice.

His eulogy combined gentle warmth with humor as he described Arthur's adoption from the shelter, his performances in other shows, and the companionship he had offered Doreen for so many years. At his invitation, a succession of people stepped forward to share their memories. I stopped sniffling long enough to talk about his unfailing patience and even temperament. A neighbor described how Arthur used to give piggyback rides to her kids. Tori—who played little Molly—won smiles by saying, "He never minded when I painted his toenails purple. And he didn't smell all doggy."

After the final tribute, Doreen rose and stammered something about how grateful she was. Then she lowered her head onto Reinhard's shoulder and began to cry. Long stepped forward and awkwardly patted her back. The mourners cast uncertain glances at each other, clearly wondering what was supposed to happen next.

From somewhere off to my right, a thin voice began singing "Tomorrow."

People craned their necks, trying to identify the singer. I didn't need to. I recognized Amanda's voice—quavering with emotion, but louder than I'd ever heard her sing onstage.

I promptly burst into tears.

I'd never been an *Annie* fanatic like so many little girls. But after my father left, "Tomorrow" came to epitomize everything I hated about the show: the too-easy sentiment, the happiest of happy endings, the cheeriest of cheery orphans who overcame every obstacle with a smile and a song. What I hated, of course, was the way everything worked out so neatly onstage when our lives were falling apart.

For weeks, I'd been pushing Chelsea to discover the heart behind those sappy lyrics, the shadows as well as the sunshine. Amanda had gotten it from our very first rehearsal. An old soul, that one. But only now did she capture that perfect blend of hope and longing and doubt—the same emotions Rowan had pushed me to discover when I sang "You'll Never Walk Alone."

I'd seen my younger self in Chelsea without suspecting that she might have been resisting the message of her song just as I had resisted the truths of mine. How could I have been so damn blind?

Amanda's voice cracked. Otis slipped in behind her. Resting his hands on her narrow shoulders, he began to sing. To my surprise, Debra joined in, her strong voice and Otis' mellow one lending Amanda support.

A few of my orphans chimed in. And then some of the adults. In moments, the whole crowd was singing— professionals and Mackenzies, parents and children. Even Chelsea.

I'd spent weeks trying to create the tribal bond of community that had sustained me during my season at the Crossroads. In the end, a shy waif and an ancient dog had succeeded where I had failed.

Bless you both for bringing us together.

CHAPTER 8
BLESS OUR SHOW

AT 5:30 THE FOLLOWING EVENING, I perched on the stool before Helen's dressing table while Hal put the finishing touches on my makeup.

"Stop fidgeting!" he commanded. "We're at the critical stage." Flourishing the 3-in-1 lip wand he had insisted I purchase, he bent over me again. "A little liner ... a little color ... a touch of gloss. Perfect!"

He swung me around to face the mirror. I looked like a perfectly made up zombie. Considering I'd survived Arthur's funeral, the luncheon, two rehearsals with Fifi and the Annies, plus our final dress rehearsal, it was a miracle my head wasn't spinning like Linda Blair's in *The Exorcist*.

Little wonder Midsummer had passed unnoticed. No dance of the fireflies. No mysterious lights in the woods. No unexpected visits from the Fae.

I cursed the sudden burning in my eyes and blinked rapidly.

"What? Did you get mascara in your eye?"

"I'm just PMSing."

Hal snatched a tissue from the box on the dressing table and watched anxiously as I blew my nose. "Tonight's going to be wonderful. Now get into your dress. We've only got a few minutes before call."

For the run of *Annie*, we had changed curtain time to

seven o'clock instead of our usual eight, hoping to bring in more families and ensure that our orphans got to bed at a decent hour. We'd also eschewed the traditional "opening of the season" cast party in favor of two small receptions so both teams of orphans could share the celebration. God knows, they needed one.

Hal ducked outside while I changed. He'd helped me pick out my dress, an apricot-colored halter that complimented my auburn hair. According to him, the flared skirt said flirty and fun. My catatonic expression suggested otherwise, but maybe people would listen to the dress instead.

"I'm dying, Egypt!"

I had to smile. Ever since we'd done *The Fantasticks*, Hal had used the phrase to cover a gamut of emotions from impatience to shock to despair.

"Prepare to be dazzled!" I called.

He froze in the doorway, hands clasped over his heart. "God, I have wonderful taste. Pivot. Yes! Flirty, fun, fabulous! If I were straight, I'd ravish you this instant." He seized my hand. "Come on. We just have time to show Janet before I dash."

I snatched up my purse and allowed him to drag me through the house. After calling Janet's name for five minutes, we finally discovered her on the lower patio, staring out at the woods while she smoked a cigarette.

"Damn!" Hal exclaimed. "I have no time to revel in her reaction. As we speak, Clumsy Cow Kimberlee is probably putting her foot through her hem." He took my hands, his expression solemn. "You're beautiful. The show's beautiful. And the audience is going to love it." He hugged me quickly, careful to avoid tousling my carefully tousled hair. "See you down there!"

As I descended the steps to the patio, Janet turned.

"What do you think?" I asked, striking a pose.

"Very nice." She took a long drag on her cigarette, her gaze drawn again to the woods.

"Anything wrong?"

"No." She flicked the cigarette away and ground it out. "Just enjoying some peace and quiet." Before I could question her further, she started up the steps to the house.

It *was* peaceful here. Summer flowers filled Helen's garden with color: purple iris, orange poppies, blue delphiniums, multicolored spikes of foxgloves. Early evening sunlight turned the field gold and burnished the treetops to a glossy green that looked positively unreal—like the plastic flowers in Munchkinland.

Still, Janet's manner seemed odd. I studied the woods, already bathed in gloom although sunset was two hours away.

"Are you coming?" Janet called.

Shaking off my disquiet, I hurried to join her.

❦

After checking in with the staff to ensure that there had been no last-minute catastrophes, I hustled down to the Dungeon. Voices echoed in the empty corridor—the normal, excited dressing room chatter you'd hear before any opening, thank God.

A chorus of greetings welcomed me to the women's dressing room. Orphans and principals lined three banks of tables cluttered with theatrical makeup, combs and brushes, wig stands and good luck totems. The long mirrors reflected multiple images of their painted faces, making the dressing room seem even more crowded. In order to accommodate the large cast, we'd had to turn Hal's sewing room into a makeshift dressing room for the chorus women. Not the best solution—for Hal or for them—but the best we could do.

I told them all to break a leg and murmured a few words to each of the principals. After going through the same routine in the other dressing rooms, I hurried upstairs.

6:40. Right on schedule.

I pulled the bottle of champagne from the green room

fridge and wrestled the cork free. One of the few tradi-
tions I'd inaugurated at the Crossroads. Reinhard had
disapproved, equating it with the bad luck that came
from giving an actor flowers before a performance. I assured him we weren't celebrating the success of the show,
but the hard work that had gone into it.

One by one they filtered in: Reinhard, Javier, and Lee
dressed in black; Alex in his tuxedo; the rest in summer
stock casual. Hal wore a scarlet shirt in honor of Annie's
trademark dress.

As they picked up their plastic glasses, I said, "If I
start listing all the ways you've helped me during these
last few weeks, the curtain won't go up until midnight.
And besides, I'll start crying and Janet will strangle me.
So I'll just say thank you. And I love you all." I raised my
glass. "To us! And the start of another season together."

"To us!" they chorused.

We savored the moment for about three seconds.
Then Alex took off for the Dungeon to warm up the cast
and musicians, Lee headed up to the lighting booth, and
the rest went to their seats in the house or their positions
backstage.

To the accompaniment of muffled voices singing "Tomorrow," I poured the last of the champagne into my
glass and raised it again, this time to absent friends.

Rowan. Helen. Nancy. Mom. Nancy and Mom had
called, of course. And I'd see them this weekend. Some
of my old cast mates—Lou and Bobbie, Gary and Kalma,
Caren and Brittany—had sent "break a leg" e-mails. But
I still felt a little wistful and envied the shared excitement that was coursing through the cast.

The speaker on the wall crackled, ending my moment
of self-pity. Reinhard's disembodied voice announced,
"This is your ten minute call. All cast members to the
green room, please."

I hastily cleared the empty glasses and champagne
bottle. Took the pitcher of lemonade out of the fridge
and set it on the table between the plate of orange slices

and the bowl of herb tea bags. Straightened the banner that read, "You're Gonna Shine like the Top of the Chrysler Building."

Footsteps thudded up the stairs as the cast converged on the green room. The backstage door eased open. Janet and Reinhard slipped inside. Reinhard gave me an encouraging nod. I took a deep breath and surveyed my cast.

"I want to thank you. For your hard work. For your professionalism. And for believing in me and in each other. These last few days haven't been easy, but tonight, we're going to give the audience a terrific show."

My gaze swept across every face, just as Rowan's had on opening night of *Brigadoon*. And, like Rowan, I asked everyone to take the hands of the people standing beside them and close their eyes.

My voice guided them, but it was Janet's power and Reinhard's that filled the green room. As many times as we had performed this ritual last season, I was still surprised by the exhilaration that filled me — as if I were the one who possessed faery magic.

My hands trembled as their energy flowed into me, Janet's strong and commanding, Reinhard's steady and calming. I urged the cast to let that energy move up through their arms, and as I spoke, the power rippled through mine, leaving goose bumps in its wake. I summoned it into my legs, and a rush of sensation shivered down my thighs and calves. As it circled back to fill my belly and my lungs, my heart and my throat, I felt like a medium, filled by the spirits she channeled.

The energy raced around the circle, linking us as surely as our joined hands, building in intensity and excitement until I could not contain it a moment longer.

"Let it go!"

The power burst free to the accompaniment of muffled groans and sighs and a couple of squeaks from my orphans. None of them had known the giddy excitement Rowan conjured or felt that uniquely powerful current zinging through every cell, raising them to a fever pitch before returning them safely to earth. And I would never experience it again.

But what we had was strong and satisfying. It was enough.

"You're gonna shine like the top of the Chrysler building. Break a leg, everybody!"

❦

Although I knew the show was sold out, I still shivered when I saw that packed house. I took the aisle seat that Rowan used to occupy. As usual, Janet sat beside me; I needed her calming presence on opening nights. Mei-Yin and Hal sat behind us with Catherine and Bernie.

As the lights faded to half and Reinhard's recorded voice reminded the audience to silence their phones and refrain from flash photography, Janet handed me a copy of the program. I glanced at the piece of paper inserted into it by our volunteers—a brief paragraph I'd written honoring Arthur and announcing that the role of Sandy would be played by Fifi.

The house lights went out. A spot picked up an Armani-clad Long strolling onto the stage, white mane and teeth gleaming. His voice was particularly mellifluous as he introduced himself and welcomed the audience. As he rambled on about the theatre, the show, and the fundraiser, I fidgeted impatiently. Finally, he flung out his arms and said, "And now, I give you Alex Ross and the overture to . . . *Annie*!"

"Good God," Janet whispered. "It's the Greatest Show on Earth."

Alex briefly acknowledged the applause, then raised his hands to cue the musicians—and, apparently, my stomach, which fluttered in nervous anticipation.

A solo trumpet sounded the opening notes of "Tomorrow." A trombone offered a soft counterpoint. They climbed slowly to the high note and held it for a breathless moment. Then the trumpet skittered down the scale, the trombone slid up, and with a crash of snare drums, the band launched into the jaunty melody of "Hard Knock Life."

I took a series of deep breaths to control the butterflies in my stomach, but by the time the triumphal restatement of "Tomorrow" neared its conclusion, the linguine I'd had for supper had tied itself into knots.

Alex's hands sliced the air. The final sforzando chord was greeted by polite applause. Then the red velvet curtains swished open.

MY ORPHANS BARRELED THROUGH the open-ing dialogue, but the pace settled down as the initial burst of nerves calmed. I suppressed a sigh as Chelsea blared out "Maybe." So much for getting in touch with Annie's softer side. But the audience creamed over her voice, chuckled at Debra's grumpiness, and cheered the orphans' spirited rendition of "Hard Knock Life." When Fifi made her entrance in Scene 2 and I heard that collective "Aww . . ." I knew we were going to be okay.

Suddenly, Fifi's legs wobbled, and she lurched sideways.

"It could be worse. It could have happened opening night."

Before I could do more than recall my mother's words, Fifi regained her balance and began crawling on her belly toward Chelsea.

I slumped back in my seat, drenched by a wave of flop sweat. Maybe Fifi had stepped on something or gotten a cramp in one of her stumpy legs. It didn't matter. She was fine now.

But Chelsea wasn't. Instead of speaking the lead-in lines to "Tomorrow," she just crouched there, staring at Fifi.

I'd run this scene half a dozen times with both girls. Amanda had broken down the first time Fifi appeared instead of Arthur. If Chelsea had been shaken, she'd hidden it well.

But she was clearly rattled now. She took a series of deep breaths before she finally began to speak. Her voice was so high and quavering I barely recognized it. When she broke off, unable to say the line about taking care of Sandy, my fingers closed convulsively on Janet's arm. She shook me off impatiently, her face screwed up in a frown of concentration.

Alex signaled the band to begin the intro to "Tomorrow." They repeated the vamp once. Twice. A third time.

Oh God, oh God, oh God . . .

Chelsea's head jerked up. For a moment, she stared out at the audience. Then her dazed eyes focused on Fifi. She flung her arms around the dog's neck and began to sing.

Her voice was halting and uncertain at first. When she scrambled to her feet for the bridge, Fifi yipped once as if to encourage her. Chelsea nodded firmly and sailed through the rest of the verse with confidence.

"Good old Sandy" hit every cue during the dialogue interlude, crossing to Chelsea when called, jumping up to place her small front paws on Chelsea's thighs, wagging her tail as Lieutenant Ward strolled off, and obediently trotting downstage for the repeat of the bridge.

Chelsea ruffled the curly fur on Fifi's head. Then she stuck out her chin and grinned and belted the bejesus out of the D flat.

Goose bumps rippled up my arms. The audience broke into spontaneous applause. They quieted down immediately so they could hear the rest of the song. But when Chelsea hit the final note, they began to cheer and kept on cheering long after the music ended.

❦

As soon as the lights came up for intermission, I rushed to the women's dressing room and drew Chelsea into the corridor.

"Are you okay?"

She stared at the scuffed linoleum floor and nodded. "I'm sorry I screwed up."

"You didn't. The song was wonderful. The best you've ever done it."

Her head came up. "Really?"

"Really."

"It was just . . . when Fifi stumbled . . . all I could think of was . . ."

"Me, too. But you kept going. That's the important thing."

"It was funny. All of a sudden, I felt . . ."

"What?"

"It's stupid."

"Tell me."

"It was kind of like . . . an arm around my shoulders. Not a real arm. Just something telling me that everything would be okay. I know that sounds totally lame —"

"No. That happened to me once."

Rowan's touch before "You'll Never Walk Alone," as reassuring as if he cradled me in his arms.

"Maybe it was knowing there were so many people rooting for you."

"Maybe," she said, clearly unconvinced.

"Well, whatever happened, you were a pro out there. I'm really proud of you."

Her expression grew thoughtful. "You were right. About the song. I always thought it was stupid. But when I sang it tonight, it felt . . . real."

"I had a song like that. In *Carousel*."

Chelsea grimaced. "That 'when you walk through a storm' song?"

"You got it."

When I grimaced, too, she surprised me by laughing. I tried to remember if I'd ever heard her laugh before. It made her seem less of a world-weary adolescent and more like . . . a kid.

"Watch it," I warned her. "Or thirty years from now,

you'll be back on this stage singing about clambakes and June bustin' out all over. Unless, of course, you're on Broadway. In which case, I expect you to tell everyone that working at the Crossroads changed your life."

She laughed again, and I sent her back to the dressing room to prepare for Act Two. As I turned toward the men's dressing room, I discovered Debra standing outside one of the bathrooms. I raised my eyebrows in silent inquiry.

"Not bad," she admitted. "Maybe there's something to all this touchy-feely crap you and Alex have been dishing out. For the kids, anyway."

It was as close to a compliment as I was as likely to get from Debra, and I acknowledged it with a smile.

Janet's seat remained vacant after the house lights went down for the "Entr'acte." When she finally appeared, the stage lights were coming up for The Oxydent Hour of Smiles radio show, giving me no opportunity to ask about her role in averting Chelsea's meltdown.

Both versions of "Fully Dressed" worked like a charm. Less charming was the interminable Cabinet meeting, but Otis won the restless audience back with "Something Was Missing." His slow waltz with Chelsea standing on the toes of his wingtip shoes provoked sighs. So did Chelsea's reprise of "Maybe" which had all the bittersweet longing I could desire.

When the Secret Service agents led off Rooster, Lily, and Hannigan, the audience cheered. They even clapped along to the horrible reindeer number. And when it was all over, they gave Chelsea a standing ovation. Of course, Annie *always* got a standing ovation. I was more relieved to see the cast smiling and clowning during their curtain calls.

Maybe I would never be able to heal the wounds of the Mackenzies or help people find their paths in life or create the ineffable magic that held an audience spellbound. But I had helped Chelsea and Amanda and Otis. And with the staff's talent and dedication and just a dash of magic, the new Crossroads Theatre would be a success.

After the house lights came up, I was surrounded by board members and neighbors and parents. I made the kind of gracious remarks every director offers at such moments: "I'm so glad you enjoyed it." "The credit really goes to the cast." "Yes, they were wonderful." It was more professional than screeching, "We pulled off a fucking miracle!"

After a brief detour to the Dungeon to congratulate my cast, I headed to the breezeway to make the rounds of newspaper critics and theatre "Angels" and indulge in hugs with my staff. I kept an eye on the stage door, waiting for the cast to appear, eager to see the reaction of their relatives.

Chelsea looked embarrassed but proud when her mom burst into tears. Paul and his wife broke into an impromptu duet of "Fully Dressed." Otis' face lit up when he spied Viola, then went utterly blank when he saw his children standing behind her.

As he covered his face with his hands, the trio made their way over to him. Otis' son awkwardly patted his shoulder. His daughter hugged him. Viola's gaze met mine and we shared a conspiratorial smile. I didn't know how much persuasion—or bullying—it had required, but she had gotten them up here. I just hoped that sharing their father's triumph would help them see him with new eyes.

"Was that your doing?"

I turned to find Lee watching the family reunion, too.

"Not really. Viola and I both had the same idea."

"I remember when my mom came up to see me in *West Side Story*. It was the first time she and Reinhard had spoken in . . . God . . . forty years? And when Hal's mom dragged his dad from California to see the first show he designed."

And when Mom broke down after listening to me sing "You'll Never Walk Alone."

"This is what the Crossroads is all about," Lee said. "What it has to be about. For everyone who comes here—not just the Mackenzies."

I nodded. We might be in the business of theatre, but there had to be more than just putting on good shows. The board would never understand, but the staff did. We had all been changed by our seasons at the Crossroads.

◄◄►►

The reception broke up quickly, the adult performers eager to get to some real drinking and the parents vainly hoping to bring their kids down from the combined highs of opening night and sugary cake.

The board volunteered to handle cleanup. Instead of pitching in, Long motioned the staff to the far end of the breezeway. Acknowledging us with a pontifical nod, he said, "We can be proud—very proud. An excellent start to our season."

"Thanks, Long. I'm glad you were pleased."

"Weren't you?"

I shrugged. "You know how it is with the director. She sees every little mistake."

"Well, I thought most of the actors did quite well tonight. Even that Otis fellow. But next season, we really must get some higher caliber performers."

"Then we need to start paying higher caliber salaries," Janet noted dryly.

"Rowan Mackenzie used nonprofessionals and look what he accomplished."

Well, duh. He's a faery!

"Naturally, I wouldn't dream of comparing your efforts to his, Maggie. You're still a novice."

I bit back my retort. He was right, after all. But I really didn't need to hear this tonight.

A sudden gust of cold air made me shiver. Long used that as an excuse to wrap his arm around my bare shoulders.

"I don't want you to be discouraged if the production fell a bit short."

From "an excellent start" to falling short in fifteen seconds or less.

As I eased free of Long's arm, another blast of cold air swirled around us. Long glanced skyward, frowning. Bernie was examining the skies as well, but the rest of the staff regarded Long with stony expressions.

I had felt the chilly blast of Rowan's anger often enough to recognize what was happening. The staff was pissed—and some of them were unable to rein in their power.

"Do you suppose a storm's blowing in?" Long asked, oblivious to the one that was brewing on the breezeway. "Ah, well. It's like Twain said: 'If you don't like the weather in New England, just wait a few minutes.'" He chuckled. "Don't worry about the show, Maggie. You'll reach Mr. Mackenzie's level of excellence one day. You're like a fine wine that only grows more—"

"That's enough!" Alex thundered.

"You're damn right!" Lee exclaimed.

I had expected Lee's outburst. But I had never seen Alex lose his temper.

"Do you really think we need to hear remarks like that on our opening night?" Catherine was literally shaking with anger. Like her father, still waters clearly ran deep.

"Maggie worked her ass off for this show," Javier said, his expression nearly as threatening as Lee's.

"We ALL did," Mei-Yin added.

"And for you to say such things is so ... so ..." Hal's face got redder and redder as he struggled to find the words. "It's just wrong!"

My throat tightened. How many times had they warned me to curb my temper around our not-so-beloved board president? Now they were ignoring their own advice to leap to my defense.

God, I love these people.

"The members of this staff are fully aware of how talented Rowan was," Reinhard said with icy deliberation. "But Maggie is our director now. And she deserves your support."

"But I *do* support her."

"You got a funny way of showing it," Bernie said.

Long's gaze darted from face to face before coming to rest on mine. "I didn't mean . . . you seemed dissatisfied with the show and I thought . . . why, you've worked wonders this past year. I've told you so a hundred—oh, no, please . . ."

As he fumbled in his breast pocket for a hanky, I swiped at my cheeks, furious at my unprofessional behavior. "Sorry. It's been a long week."

Janet took Long's arm. "I'll walk you to the parking lot."

Instead of picking up his cue, he thrust his hanky into my hand. "Forgive me, my dear. I wouldn't hurt your feelings for the world. Or ruin this night for you."

Which turned on the waterworks again quite effectively.

"Parking lot," Janet said. "Now."

As she pulled him down the walkway, I groaned. "I'm such an idiot."

"HE'S the idiot!" Mei-Yin hissed. "If the Archangel GABRIEL had touched down on that stage tonight, he'd complain that it wasn't Jesus CHRIST."

"Everything he said was true. I *am* a novice. The show *did* fall short."

"We don't think so," Alex said quietly.

"I just mean that Rowan—"

"Was *Brigadoon* perfect?" Reinhard demanded. "Or *The Sea-Wife*? Or *Carousel*? No! And neither was *Annie*. But we put on a show that none of us had ever attempted. We pulled good performances out of amateurs and excellent ones out of professionals. We gave children an opportunity to work in the theatre and experience the thrill of hearing an audience laugh with them and cry with them and cheer their performances. Is that not cause for celebration?"

I smiled up into his worried face and nodded.

"Good! Now. We will go up to the house and toast our accomplishments."

CHAPTER 10

ALL IN MY MIND

IT WAS A RELIEF TO LET THE BUSINESS of theatre slide and just enjoy the company of good friends. Unfortunately, the opening night high wore off in a hurry. Catherine and Javier made their exit only a half hour after their entrance. I followed them to the front door, my yawns almost as huge as Catherine's.

As I reached for the switch to turn on the porch lantern, Javier said, "Save the electricity. We don't need it." He grinned. "Faery eyesight," he added in a whisper. "Great for running around backstage during a blackout. And for late-night strolls."

Hand in hand, they started down the hill. After they disappeared into the darkness, I leaned on the railing to stare up at the sky. There was no moon, just a million stars splashed across the heavens. I closed my eyes, breathing in the pine-scented air. Then opened them again when I heard the faint sound of Catherine's laughter. The lights in the parking lot provided just enough illumination to show her running down the walkway by the barn with Javier in pursuit. Then they both vanished into the shadows. A moment later, a light flicked on in the Mill.

Married more than two years and they still acted like newlyweds. I suppressed an envious sigh and turned to go inside.

A faint flash made me glance back. At first, I thought it must be another lamp going on in the Mill. But when I walked to the end of the porch and peered into the darkness, I realized the narrow sliver of light was coming from the theatre.

It was the ghost light, shining through the open stage door.

A shadowy form darted through the light and into the theatre. Then the door closed.

Maybe Catherine or Javier had gone back for something. But if I could see the ghost light shining through the stage door, I would have noticed the front door of the Mill opening.

There was only one explanation: someone was breaking into my goddamn theatre on my goddamn opening night.

I flung open the screen door and strode into the foyer, narrowly avoiding a collision with Reinhard who was emerging from the powder room. "Someone's broken into the theatre," I told him. Then I hurried into the library. With shaking fingers, I dialed 911.

"Hillandale Police Department," a woman's voice said.

"Becky?"

"No, it's April. Becky was feeling a little under the weather so I—"

"April, it's Maggie Graham. At the Cross—"

"Oh, hi, Maggie! Heard the show was a big hit. Burt and I are bringing the kids Saturday."

Only in Dale can you call 911 for a cozy chat.

"That's great, April. But we have a problem. There's an intruder in the theatre."

"An intruder?"

"Or intruders."

"In the theatre?"

"I saw someone breaking in through the stage door." I glanced up as Reinhard walked in. "It's okay," I whispered. "I'm talking to the police now."

"The police!"

I waved my hand to shush him. "What was that, April?"

"I asked if you were in the theatre now."

"No, I'm at Janet's. I spotted the . . . uh . . . perpetrator from the porch."

"Maggie . . ." Reinhard began.

"Sure it wasn't one of the staff?"

"The staff's at Janet's, too."

April chuckled. "You theatre folk sure keep late hours."

"Maggie, give me the phone."

"Wait! No, not you, April. Look, there was something distinctly furtive about the perpetrator's manner."

"Furtive, huh."

"Nobody has keys to the theatre except the staff. And Reinhard always locks up . . . you locked up, right?"

Instead of answering, Reinhard wrested the phone from my grip. "Hello? This is Reinhard—yes . . . yes, we were very pleased with the show. April, I think Maggie might be overreacting."

"I am *not* overreacting!"

"I am sure it was only Catherine or Javier. They left a few minutes ago."

"It wasn't—"

"Yes, she *is* from New York."

"That has nothing to do with it!"

"I will go to the theatre now. But I am certain there is nothing to worry about."

"Reinhard, would you please—?"

"And I shall look forward to seeing you then, too, April. Good night."

"Are you crazy?" I demanded as he hung up the phone.

"Maggie. We do not call the police. Ever."

"This isn't some Fae thing," I whispered, conscious that Bernie was in the house. "This is a burglar!"

"I very much doubt it. Please calm down. And let me handle this my way."

Still protesting, I followed him to the living room. In a few terse sentences, he told the rest of the staff what had happened. Hal and Mei-Yin and Bernie all began talking at once. Janet and Alex exchanged glances.

"It was probably Javier," Reinhard said. "Or a youngster who wanted to poke around backstage. I will go down now and find out."

"I'm coming with you."

"No, Maggie. You are not."

"Let her go," Janet said.

Alex's head jerked toward her.

"Short of tying her up, she won't stay here." Janet shoved herself off the sofa. "Let's just find out what's going on."

❧

Bernie pleaded his hip and stayed behind. Mei-Yin pleaded four glasses of whisky and stayed with him. The rest of us marched off.

All the way down the hill, I tried to make sense of Reinhard's behavior. I knew the staff had an aversion to dealing with the authorities, but surely, in a case like this it was warranted. What disturbed me most were the looks that had passed between Reinhard and Alex and Janet—almost like they knew something was up.

Maybe it was some kind of practical joke. Catherine and Javier had been sent ahead to oversee the final preparations. And when I walked in, everybody would shout, "Surprise!" But the last thing I needed after the past few days was yet another surprise.

By the time we reached the parking lot, I was beginning to wonder if I'd imagined the whole thing. I almost hoped there *was* a burglar. If we walked in on Catherine and Javier having a quickie on one of the orphans' beds, I'd feel like an idiot.

Reinhard held up his hand. "Lee and Alex and I will go in. The rest of you wait outside."

"Why do I always have to wait with the women?" Hal complained.

Before anyone could answer, the wrought iron lamps along the walkway flared to life. For a moment, we just stood there, gaping. Then Janet gripped my hand and Reinhard flung his arm around my waist. I looked from one to the other, suddenly scared. Whatever this was, it wasn't a practical joke.

As they guided me toward the nearest picnic bench, I heard a protesting creak of hinges. My head jerked toward the stage door. Hal gasped. Alex whispered, "It's okay, honey."

No sneaky little sliver of light this time, but a big, bold rectangle that cut a shining swath across the brick walkway.

A figure stepped out of the shadows. With the light behind him, I could make out little more than his dark pants and pale shirt and the gleam of glossy, black hair.

A shiver crawled up my spine. Cold sweat broke out under my arms.

Janet's fingers closed convulsively around mine. Reinhard squeezed my waist. Alex gripped both shoulders. Calming energy flowed through me, but it wasn't enough. Not by a long shot.

Slowly, he walked toward us. The light from the lampposts confirmed what I already knew but still couldn't believe. Then he hesitated, his gaze fixed on me, a frown carving two furrows between his brows.

"Don't be afraid," Rowan Mackenzie said. "It's only me."

CHAPTER 11
THIS CAN'T BE REAL

*THE WORLD HASN'T STOPPED REVOLVING.
You haven't stopped breathing. You haven't entered*
The Twilight Zone. *Those are Janet's fingernails digging
into your hand. That's Hal whispering, "Oh, my God, oh,
my God." This must be real. He* must *be real.*

Rowan is here. He's here!

*His hair's longer. He looks so tired. And his clothes
look like he's slept in them. Has he been wearing the same
clothes all this time? Didn't the goddamn faeries give him
some goddamn clothes?*

*Focus, Maggie. Janet's saying something. He's saying
something. Apologizing for causing an uproar.*

*I'm moving. Good. But I'm going the wrong way. Why
am I—?*

Something hard. Picnic bench. Okay. Sitting works.

*Why is he just standing there? Hovering on the walk-
way like it's some kind of DMZ? The middle ground between light and shadow, between—*

Forget the fucking Twilight Zone*! Focus. Breathe.*

In. Out. Slow. Deep.

Calm . . .

*Janet. She's keeping me calm. And Reinhard and Alex.
I can't feel Rowan at all. Why can't I feel him?*

*Get a grip. Everyone's staring at you. Everyone's wait-
ing for you to say something.*

Say something!

"Hi."

"Hi?" You've thought about him every day since he left and the best you can come up with is "Hi?"

Rowan smiled, but the lines remained etched between his brows. "I know this must be a shock for all of you, but I'd like to speak with Maggie. In private."

"No," I whispered. When I saw Rowan's shock, I realized he'd misunderstood me. "They knew. They had to. They always know when you're nearby." Anger surged, a welcome relief from the numbness that had enveloped me. Dragging my gaze from Rowan, I turned to Janet.

"I . . . suspected," she said.

"Why didn't you—?"

"Because you had opening night to deal with! And I wasn't sure. Even after you told us someone was breaking into the theatre."

Rowan frowned. "I didn't break in. I used the keys I always kept at the cottage."

He kept keys at the cottage?

Who cares? Focus!

"So you were the one who helped Chelsea," I said.

His frown deepened. "Chelsea?"

"No," Janet said. "Reinhard and I did."

"Then why did you suspect—?"

"I felt . . . something . . . at Midsummer. That was when you crossed over."

Rowan nodded.

Midsummer? That was yesterday! Why didn't he come to the theatre then? Why was he sneaking around tonight?

Maybe he didn't want to see me. Maybe he just came back for a change of clothes. Maybe . . .

Don't be stupid, Maggie. Pay attention. Javier's asking Janet something.

When did Javier show up?

"It didn't feel like Rowan's power," Janet said to Javier. "Just . . . a Fae presence. And it was gone so quickly,

I couldn't be sure." She regarded Rowan thoughtfully. "You learned a few things during your sojourn in Faerie."

Maybe that was why I still detected no hint of his emotions. He'd always been able to mask his expression; now, he could disguise his power just as easily.

"Pity you couldn't have timed your entrance a little better," Janet remarked.

"This wasn't . . . I didn't intend to have this conversation tonight."

"Then you shouldn't have been sneaking around the theatre at midnight," she snapped.

"I wanted to shower! And change. Make myself . . . presentable."

Rowan smoothed his wrinkled shirt. His gaze swept over me, from my carefully tousled hair to my carefully painted toenails. It rose more slowly, but stopped short of my eyes. It took me a moment to realize he was staring at the silver chain around my throat.

As always, his sweet smile made my breath catch. His face blurred as I smiled back. Probably the goofy smile that made me look like a pole-axed heifer, but I didn't care. For the first time, he looked like my Rowan.

"Can we talk, Maggie?"

I nodded. He watched me expectantly. I realized I'd missed my cue. I was supposed to stand up. I made it halfway and sank back down on the bench.

"Maybe this should wait until tomorrow," Reinhard said.

"I'm fine," I insisted.

"You can't even stand up!" Lee said. "If you want to talk, talk here."

Rowan stiffened. "I played out my farewells in front of an audience. I have no intention of playing out my homecoming in front of one, too."

"And you shouldn't have to!" Hal exclaimed. "Neither should Maggie. They just need ten minutes of private time."

"They need a lot more than ten minutes," Janet muttered.

"Maybe so," Alex said, his voice sharp. "But Hal's right. Let's all go back to the house."

"I will wait in the Smokehouse," Reinhard said. "And escort Maggie back after she and Rowan have finished talking."

Hal tugged Lee's arm. When Lee hesitated, I summoned a reassuring smile. His frown deepened. Clearly, I didn't have a good grip on my inventory of smiles—or much of anything else except Janet's cold hand.

"I'm okay. Really."

As okay as anyone could be who had just faced an opening night, a mixed review from her boss, and the return of her long-lost faery lover.

Javier nodded to Rowan and walked back to the Mill, glancing over his shoulder several times as if to assure himself that Rowan hadn't vanished into thin air. Alex paused to shake Rowan's hand, but his expression was troubled. Janet just marched off into the darkness.

Hal tugged Lee's arm again. As they started up the walkway, he suddenly whirled around. "I didn't even say welcome back! Welcome back!"

Rowan smiled. "Thank you, Hal."

"It's so romantic! Like the end of *My Fair Lady*. Or *Gigi*. Or *The Ghost and Mrs. Muir* except Maggie didn't have to die first. Oh, I wish Helen—" Hal's hand flew to his mouth.

"It's all right," Rowan said, his smile gone. "I know about Helen."

"I'm sorry," Hal whispered. "I didn't mean . . . oh, I've ruined everything!"

Lee pulled him into his arms and murmured something. Then, one arm around Hal's waist, he guided him toward the parking lot.

"When did it happen?" Rowan asked.

"A week after you left," Reinhard replied. "How did you know?"

"I couldn't feel her. When I crossed." Rowan's gaze returned to me. "Instead, I felt you. I had prepared myself for the possibility that Helen might be ... gone, but I never imagined ... I thought someone on staff would know where to find you. But clearly, you found a home here. Just as I did."

"Is that why you have come back?" Reinhard asked. When Rowan hesitated, he shook his head impatiently. "Forgive me. You asked for privacy."

"No, stay a moment. You deserve an answer. I simply resented Lee's attempt to bully me into a public confession."

"Lee is—"

"An alpha male defending his pack from the intruder."

"You're not an intruder!" I exclaimed.

"No?" Rowan's smile was bleak.

"No," Reinhard said firmly. "But it is only natural that we should have questions. And concerns. When you left—"

"I thought I was going home. But when I got to Faerie, I realized this was my home."

Those impossibly green eyes looked deep into mine.

"*You* are my home."

I drew in a shaking breath and let it out. I knew I should speak, should tell him I had come to the same realization. Only mine had occurred before he'd even left this world."

Reinhard squeezed my shoulder and walked away. Rowan waited for the Smokehouse door to close. His expression was as calm as a teacher about to lecture his pupil. Only the trembling of the antler tine buttons on his shirtfront attested to his quickened breathing.

"Leaving you was the hardest thing I've ever done. I thought it was the right choice—the only choice—for both of us. I didn't want you to lead the sort of shadow existence I must to safeguard my secret. I was afraid of watching you grow old and dying centuries before me.

Most of all, I was afraid that my love—my power—would always overcome any doubts you might have about choosing a life with me."

"But . . ."

"Wait. Please. I know all those arguments are just as valid today as they were the morning I left you. I tried to stay away. To lose myself in Faerie and enjoy the world I barely remembered. But without you . . ." He glanced around the picnic area, as if the words he was seeking were hidden in the darkness. ". . . it was empty. Perfect and passionless and empty."

He shrugged helplessly. "I was as much of an outsider there as I had ever been in this world. Maybe I had changed too much. A better man would have stayed there. But I'm a selfish creature like all the Fae. I wanted you and this place and the chance to build a life together."

He waited for me to speak. But everything was happening too fast. The earth was spinning wildly out of orbit, the ground beneath my espadrilles shifting like quicksand. Only a few minutes ago, Rowan Mackenzie had been part of my past. Now, he wanted to build a future with me. If I'd never stopped longing for him or dreaming of him, I had accepted that he was as unreachable as the moon. Now, the moon had tumbled out of the sky.

I wanted to cry, "Yes! I want those same things!" But how could anyone hold the moon in her hands?

"I know things have changed," he said. "I saw a program in the green room." His mouth quirked in a brief smile. "Margaret Graham, Artistic Director."

"That's just temporary. I'm really the executive director. We're a nonprofit now. But we couldn't afford—"

"A nonprofit? Already?"

"It's been nearly two years, Rowan."

His eyes widened. Then he nodded slowly. "Of course. Time moves differently there."

"Funny how the Fae always know when it's Midsummer, though."

"What are you saying?"

"Nothing. I'm just . . . I don't want to be the consolation prize because Faerie wasn't all it was cracked up to be."

"Good gods, Maggie! Do you really think I would turn your life upside down just because I was having trouble adjusting to Faerie?"

"No! But it still hurts. It took me about a minute to realize how much I loved you, how much I wanted you in my life. And for you to need two years . . ."

"I didn't need two years, Maggie. Or two months or two days."

Finally, he walked forward. But instead of sitting beside me, he slumped onto the far end of the bench and rested his forearms on his knees.

"There was something I had to do. I'll tell you about that tomorrow. For now, please believe that I love you. That it took all the self-control I possess to keep from running to you as soon as I realized you were here. That I could never regard you as a consolation prize."

His face, sculpted by the lamplight, was as calm as his voice. His long tapering fingers, knotted tightly together, provided more trustworthy evidence of his emotions.

"If you don't want me . . . if there's someone else . . ."

"Would I be wearing your chain if there were? I've never taken it off since the day you gave it to me."

A tremor rippled through his linen shirt.

"You're a pretty hard act to follow."

"So are you," he replied.

Which was the part I still didn't get. He'd listed all his reasons for loving me in his farewell letter, but when you can have any woman in the world, why choose me?

"Why do you always doubt yourself?" he asked.

I wondered if he'd added mind reading to his lists of talents, but decided he was merely reading my expression. Never a tough task.

"Why are you always so sure of everything?" I countered.

"Because I'm centuries older and infinitely wiser."

"And incredibly humble."

He chuckled. "Someone once described me as an arrogant prick with a God complex."

"Someone once described me as a pit bull. And a coward. And—"

"Beautiful."

His gaze roamed over me, as intimate as a caress. Heat flushed my body and traveled rapidly faceward.

"Someone needs faery spectacles," I said a bit breathlessly.

"Someone needs—" He leaned away from me and shook his head. "If we give in to that temptation, neither of us will be able to think clearly. And we must."

I had a million questions, a million concerns—about us, about where he would fit in at the new Crossroads Theatre. But those could wait. Right now, there was only one thing I needed.

"I really want to touch you."

His breath caught.

"The picnic table won't spontaneously combust or anything?"

"No. But I might."

"Let's both go down in flames, then."

As I slid closer, he tensed, wary as a wild creature. My fingertips touched his hair. His eyes closed, and he took a deep, shuddering breath.

I traced the wild-winged brows, the sloping cheekbones, the ridge of that beautiful, beaky nose. Like a sculptor, I molded the boyishly smooth cheeks, the line of his jaw, the curve of his chin.

My fingers trembled as I fumbled with the antler tine. Then I pushed it through the buttonhole and parted the collar of his shirt to reveal the thick red weal at the base of his throat.

He shuddered again as my fingertips caressed the mark of the iron collar that the vengeful Mackenzies had forced upon him more than two hundred years ago. He would always bear the scar—and the deeper scars of memory: the agony of the iron burning his flesh, the slow but inexorable draining of his power, the long years of exile and isolation and loneliness.

So much pain burned into his flesh and his soul. And so little I could do to relieve it.

His eyes opened, soft and green as moss. And for the first time, he allowed his power to touch me. Just a whisper of his love, gone in an instant, but as tender as his expression, as warming as single malt whisky.

To my questing fingers, it seemed that the grooves around his mouth were deeper. But the soft lips were the same. And his scent, honeysuckle sweetness and animal musk.

Heat flooded my body, his desire feeding mine. He groaned and shook his head. Before he could slide away, I captured his face between my palms and pressed my lips to his.

For a moment, he remained perfectly still. Then his lips parted. His tongue rasped again mine, sandpaper-rough like a cat's, and the heat ramped up to mildly volcanic.

He slid to the far end of the picnic bench, breathing hard, and held up his hand as I began inching after him.

"Any closer and I will throw you to the ground and ravish you."

"It's the dress. Hal swore he'd do the same thing if he were straight."

Rowan's smile froze.

"What?"

He was beside me in a blur of movement, his hands gripping mine. "Do you trust me?"

"Yes, of—"

"Then don't say anything. And try to forgive me. Stay with her," he added as he strode toward the stage door. Only then did I notice Reinhard hurrying toward me.

"What is it?" he asked. "What is wrong?"

Still trying to make sense of Rowan's sudden change in mood, I just shook my head.

From inside the barn, a muffled voice called Rowan's name.

"I'm right here," Rowan replied.

"Maybe there really *was* an intruder," I whispered.

"Then it is one Rowan knows."

A head peeped around the doorframe. All I could make out was a tangle of long, white hair before it ducked out of sight again. For one unreasoning moment, I thought it was Helen. Then logic kicked in. Rowan Mackenzie might possess extraordinary powers, but resurrecting the dead wasn't one of them.

"Come out," Rowan urged. "These are friends."

Seconds ticked by while his hand hung suspended in the air. Then another reached out of the shadows to grasp it.

A figure shuffled into the light. Not Helen, but Rip Van Winkle. A skinny scarecrow of a man whose knobby knees protruded from the frayed holes in his jeans. Those had faded to so pale a blue that they looked almost as white as his long hair and beard. The right sleeve of his shirt was neatly buttoned at the wrist; the left hung in tatters from his elbow.

He darted frantic glances at us as Rowan coaxed him forward, his right arm around the man's waist, his left hand resting lightly on his bicep. In spite of the soothing murmur of Rowan's voice and the calming power that must be flowing into him, the old man held his battered guitar before him like a shield.

There was nothing about him to suggest that he was a faery; maybe they came in different varieties, like humans. But faery or human, there could only be one reason why Rowan had brought him here: if anyone needed the kind of healing to be found at the Crossroads, this poor, terrified creature did.

The lamplight revealed a face far younger than his

hair suggested. The skin of his forehead and nose was roughened by exposure to sun and wind. Judging from the freckles, he must have been a redhead in his youth.

"My name's Maggie. What's yours?"

For a long moment, he just stared at me. Then he flashed a smile and I saw the little gap between his front teeth and the ground slipped out from under my feet once more.

The dark blob on the front of the guitar. All that remained of the Gibson's teardrop-shaped pickguard.

The bright splash of yellow on the guitar strap. Barely visible as it curved over his shoulder, but I knew it was the sun. A smiling sun whose features I had traced countless times.

Those huge, frightened eyes, the same indeterminate shade of blue-green as mine.

I wanted to tell him I was sorry, that I hadn't meant to frighten him, that I was just as scared as he was. But all I could manage was a single, whispered word:

"Daddy?"

CHAPTER 12
SEEING IS BELIEVING

ROWAN GRIPPED MY ARMS HARD. The black dots swarming around the edge of my vision receded. Calm washed through me, stilling my chattering teeth and slowing my frantic heartbeat.

Then I heard Daddy whimper, and it all crashed down on me again. Not just the moon this time. The whole fucking universe.

My father was alive. The playmate of my childhood. The obsessed stranger, searching through his mountain of books for something that would explain his haunted memories. The broken man who had walked out of my life, leaving my mother to pick up the pieces.

How many years had he wandered through this world seeking a portal to the other? And dear God, what had happened to him after he found it? For he must have found it. He was the mysterious "something" that had kept Rowan in Faerie.

"They began playing with him. Petting him. Teasing him. Heightening their glamour to enthrall him."

That chance encounter with Rowan's clan had nearly destroyed him. What was left of him now, after spending years in that place?

Rowan's hands cupped my cheeks. Rowan's voice whispered my name.

"I need you to listen to me."

88

I nodded, obedient as a child.

"He's lost twenty years of his life. He has no idea how much time has passed. If you tell him you're his daughter, the reality will shatter him."

I was eight when he left. Ten when we received that final postcard. Twenty-four years without knowing whether he was alive or dead. And now I had to pretend he was a stranger?

"I know what I'm asking. But while he's so fragile, I don't think we have a choice."

Rowan's calm pulsed through me, as steady as Reinhard's arm around my waist. Reinhard who always reminded me that I was very bad at hiding my feelings.

"Maggie?"

But I didn't have to hide them. Only the fact that I was his daughter.

Only . . .

"Maggie."

Three times, Rowan had spoken my name. Three times for a charm, Mairead Mackenzie had written. Maybe the charm worked for I heard myself say, "I can do this."

Rowan pressed a quick kiss to my forehead and hurried back to Daddy.

To Jack.

The whimpering was constant now, high-pitched and terrified like a wounded animal. His fingers plucked anxiously at Rowan's sleeve. "I'm sorry. I didn't mean to make her cry. Please don't send me back there!"

A sob caught in my throat. Reinhard's hand tightened around my waist. Rowan shot me a warning glance, all the while murmuring, "No one will send you back. Maggie's all right. You just startled her."

"I'm so sorry." My voice trembled as much as my father's. I swallowed hard and tried again. "You reminded me of . . . an old friend."

"Who are they?" my father whispered.

"I told you about Maggie, remember?"

He shook his head wildly. "No. No! I don't remember!"

"Think, Jack."

As Rowan stroked his arm, he grew calm again. His eyes widened with recollection and he flashed that gap-toothed smile. "Yes! Yes, she's your girlfriend."

"That's right. And this is Reinhard. He's my friend, too."

"You have a girlfriend *and* a boyfriend?"

My laugh was too close to a sob, and I pressed my lips together.

"I am the theatre's stage manager."

Daddy's smile faded. "I don't remember you."

"I joined the staff after you performed here."

Daddy suddenly straightened. "You wouldn't think it to look at me now, but I played Billy Bigelow in *Carousel*. My 'Soliloquy?' The applause went on for three minutes. Remember, Rowan? And the standing ovation at the end? God, they loved me."

Suddenly, he was my father again, flipping through his album of reviews, pointing himself out to me in photos, boasting about his performances.

"Maggie was in *Carousel* during her season here," Rowan said.

"Julie or Carrie?" my father demanded.

"Nettie," I replied.

"Nettie! You're way too young for that role."

"That's what I said."

"Rowan and his crazy casting."

I managed a weak laugh, still stunned by his transformation. "Somehow, he pulls it off."

"Well, sure. He's a faery." He cringed and shot a frightened glance at Rowan. "I'm sorry! I didn't mean to tell. Please don't send me back there!"

And just like that, my father was gone. Numbly, I watched Rowan soothe him, watched the terror leach away yet again.

"Why don't we all go up to the apartment?" Rowan suggested.

Daddy shook his head. "I don't like it up there. I like the little house in the woods."

"Yes, but you can take a bath and—"

"No! I don't like it!"

"And finish the rest of your cake."

Daddy's face lit up. He strummed a chord on his guitar and marched into the theatre, singing, "There is nothing like a cake. Nothing in the world!"

If someone else had transposed the words of a song from *South Pacific* into an elegy on cake, I might have smiled. But my father wasn't trying to be clever; he was clinging to sanity using the only lifeline he knew.

Rowan took my hands. "He's frightened, Maggie. And confused. He'd just settled into the cottage when I moved him here." He glanced over his shoulder. "Let's go inside. He gets nervous if I leave him alone too long."

One by one, we filed up the stairs. The door to the apartment hung open, but it was dark inside. Years of experience had taught Rowan to find his way around, but I groped for the light switch and flicked it on.

Something crashed to the floor, followed by the sharper sound of shattering china.

"Turn it off!" my father shrieked. "The eyes! The eyes!"

I quickly switched off the light and slumped against the doorframe. Reinhard squeezed my shoulders and whispered, "Steady, *liebchen*."

The quick tattoo of Rowan's boots on the hardwood floor. The muffled thud as he crossed the rugs. The murmur of his voice. My father's sobs, ebbing to sniffles.

Then Rowan's footsteps again, slower now. A drawer opening. The harsh rasp of a match.

Light blossomed in the doorway of the living area. When Daddy cried out, Rowan said, "It's all right. They can't find you here. You're safe here."

Another flare of light. Then Rowan's footsteps coming toward us.

He opened his arms and I stumbled into them. Our

first embrace. Not the one we would have exchanged a mere ten minutes ago. The only desire now was to comfort and be comforted.

"Eyes?" Reinhard inquired softly.

"The skylights."

Rowan leaned back to study me. When I nodded, he took my hand and led me into the living area.

The two candles on the sideboard provided barely enough illumination to make out the shadowy outlines of the furniture. I couldn't see my father at all.

"Jack. I'm going to turn on some lights."

The soft moan made me shudder.

"I'll keep them low. And I won't turn on any in the kitchen. But you can't expect our guests to sit in the dark."

"They'll see . . ."

"No, Jack, they won't. They can't. They're in the Borderlands. And you're here—in my apartment in the theatre."

The Borderlands?

"I like the little house. They can't see me there."

"They can't see you here, either. You know why?"

A long silence. "Because they're in the Borderlands?"

"That's right. Now wouldn't you like to come out and have some cake with Maggie and Reinhard?"

"No. I'll eat my cake here."

"After I turn on the lights."

"I want it now!"

"Jack!" For the first time, Rowan's voice was sharp. It drew another whimper from my unseen father.

"For God's sake, just give him the cake," I said.

"Let me handle this, Maggie."

Unwanted memories assailed me.

"Get off my stage. Now!"

"You have no right to do this!"

"Don't tell me how to direct."

"You're not directing. You're bullying him!"

Rushing to Nick's defense had helped bring about the

confrontation that had made him walk out of *Carousel*. But it required all of my self-control—and Reinhard's firm grip on my shoulders—to keep me from rushing to my father.

Rowan turned the dimmer switch and the track lights above the bank of stereo equipment bloomed with soft golden light, enough to make out the kitchen: Daddy's guitar resting against the refrigerator; a beat-up red backpack beside it; a chair, lying on the floor; clumps of cake strewn among the shards of china. And my father, huddled under the dining table.

"Cake?" he prompted hopefully as Rowan walked toward the kitchen.

"After I clean up this mess."

"I'll do it," I volunteered, eager for some task that might distract me.

"I'm already filthy. Why don't you clear off some space on the table? Sit, Reinhard. You've had a long night."

"We all have," Reinhard replied as he sank heavily onto a chair.

Rowan had clearly raided the green room fridge. A half-empty bottle of lemonade sat on the table, along with an unopened bottle of iced tea and plastic containers filled with leftover cookies and veggie sticks. The slab of sheet cake bore a legend in red piping gel that read "ulations, Cast of An."

I moved everything to the counter and pulled plates and glasses out of the cabinets. Reinhard refused food, but accepted iced tea. I poured three glasses of lemonade; the only iced tea Daddy would ever drink was Mom's. Steeped for hours in that chipped brown pitcher. He'd always teased her that only a weightlifter could pick it up.

I set the plates down a little harder than I'd intended.

"Cake?" a plaintive voice inquired.

"In a minute," Rowan replied.

As he dumped the mess in the garbage can, I grabbed

a chocolate chip cookie and thrust it under the table. I heard a startled squeak. Then the cookie was snatched out of my fingers.

"Cookie!" my father crowed in Cookie Monster's gravelly voice.

Another flood of memories: Daddy sitting on the floor, growling, "Cookie, cookie, cookie!" while I danced around him, holding it just out of reach. His arms waving futilely, then suddenly pulling me into his lap. My delighted laughter. His unintelligible words as he shoved the cookie into his mouth. My mother protesting that he was getting crumbs everywhere.

"Me want another cookie!"

"Me want a bottle of Laphroaig," Rowan muttered, slumping onto the chair opposite Reinhard.

"Cookie, cookie, cookie!"

"Jack . . ." Rowan said, a warning note in his voice.

A pause. Then: "Cake?"

Rowan lowered his head onto his hands. Reinhard frowned. I laughed—a little hysterically judging from their concerned looks.

"You have had enough sugar," Reinhard said. "But you may have some vegetable sticks."

"Vegetables?" my father wailed.

I laughed again. I really *had* entered *The Twilight Zone*. With Rowan and Reinhard serving as stand-ins for my parents and my father reverting to the role of child—easily frightened, often entertaining, and difficult to pacify. Leaving me the thankless role of the daughter who could not be acknowledged, the helping professional who didn't know how to help.

My laughter caught in my throat. Rowan gripped my left arm. Reinhard clamped down on my right. I pressed my lips together and clenched my fists in my lap.

Something tugged at the hem of my dress. A moment later, a tentative hand patted my knee.

"It's all right," my father whispered. "You don't have to eat the vegetables if you don't want to."

I sat there, shaking silently, until their power calmed me. And all the while, my father's gentle fingers patted my knee.

The first time I had felt his touch since I was eight years old.

I seized a napkin and blew my nose. Reinhard pushed back his chair and announced, "I think it is time for us to go home."

Daddy's fingers gripped the hem of my dress. "You go. Maggie can stay."

"I'll be back tomorrow," I promised. "With breakfast."

"Breakfast!"

"Eggs and bacon and English muffins and orange juice," I said, reciting our traditional Sunday morning menu.

"Thomas'. Not the store brand."

"Of course Thomas'. The store brand never has the good—"

"Nooks and crannies."

How many times had he lectured my poor mother about that when she was just trying to save a buck by buying the cheaper brand?

"So is it okay if I go now? I *am* pretty tired." The understatement of the year. "And you must be, too."

The fingers relaxed their grip. Regretfully, I pushed back my chair.

"Are you going to come out," Rowan asked, "and say good night to Maggie and Reinhard?"

"I can say good night from here."

"Well, you have to come out eventually."

"Why?"

"You can't sleep under the table."

"They'll never think to look for me here."

Rowan crouched down. "Jack. They're not looking for you."

"Just in case."

I crouched beside Rowan and said, "We could put cushions on the floor. And bring a pillow and a quilt."

Daddy surveyed his prospective sleeping quarters with a frown. "My feet'll stick out. If they see them—"

"We'll drape a sheet over the table. Like—"

"A tent!" he exclaimed. "I used to do that with my little girl. Her name's Maggie, too. But I call her Magpie 'cause she talks a blue streak."

Unwilling to trust my voice, I simply nodded.

"We used the dining room table. It was much bigger than this," he informed Rowan loftily. "We'd crawl inside with books and toys . . . and sometimes, a plate of cookies." He flashed a beguiling smile.

"You are *not* going to wheedle more cookies out of me," Rowan replied, unbeguiled.

"Rowan and Reinhard will make up the tent. I'll show you where the bathroom is."

Daddy craned his neck to peer up at the skylights. "But what if they see me?"

"They won't if we run."

"They won't see you at all!" Rowan exclaimed. "They can't find you here!"

"Not if we run quick like a bunny!" Daddy said.

"Quick like a bunny, Magpie. That way, the gnomes'll never catch us!"

"We'll let Rowan go first so he can put a candle in the bathroom. When he gives us the signal, we'll run. Okay?"

Daddy nodded. Rowan sighed and stalked off.

Long minutes ticked by. Daddy grew increasingly restive, his questions more panicked. Finally, I hurried into the bedroom and found Rowan standing before his armoire, barely visible in the flickering candlelight.

"What is it? He's getting nervous."

Rowan slowly closed the doors to the armoire. "No toothbrushes, I'm afraid."

"I'll pick up whatever you need tomorrow."

Rowan nodded and walked over to the small chest under the eaves. When he just stood there, staring down at it, I edged around him, yanked open the top, and unearthed a neat pile of bedding and a pillow.

"Put the candle in the bathroom, okay?" I hesitated, trying to make sense of his queer expression. "Is something wrong?"

"Just very tired all of sudden."

I pressed a quick kiss to his cheek and hurried back to my father.

"Ready?" I held out my hand and smiled as he clasped it. "On the count of three. One. Two. Three!"

Hand in hand, we sprinted through the apartment. Daddy scurried into the bathroom and slammed the door behind him. I paced the bedroom until the door eased open again. We shared another ten seconds of handholding during our return sprint. Then he scrambled under the sheet.

"A pillow . . ." he sighed.

How long since he'd rested his head on one?

"Will you wait for me downstairs?" Rowan asked quietly. "It won't take me long to get him to sleep."

With a final longing glance at the tent, I followed Reinhard out of the apartment.

We slowly descended the stairs. As the uncomfortable silence lengthened, I said, "He'll be fine. After he settles in."

"He needs a doctor's care, Maggie."

"A doctor would lock him in a psych ward, pump him full of meds, and spend years trying to convince him that he'd imagined all of this. Maybe he's confused and frightened, but he's not delusional."

"I know you love him, child. And I know you believe Rowan is a miracle worker. But there are some miracles even Rowan cannot achieve."

"How do we know until we try? We have to try! Doesn't he deserve the chance to lead a normal life?"

"Locked up in that apartment with Rowan for months? For years, perhaps? This is the kind of life you want for him? For both of them?"

"He'll get better."

"But he will never be as he was. That man is gone, Maggie. Can you accept that?"

Rowan's arrival spared me from answering.

"He's asleep?" I asked.

Rowan nodded. "He's exhausted."

"So are you," Reinhard said. "When did you last eat?"

"Yesterday. I think. Jack finished the last of the food this morning. That's why I had to bring him here tonight. Helen . . . we always kept snacks in the green room refrigerator."

"Cake and cookies," Reinhard said with a disapproving frown.

"I know. But after all he's been through . . ."

"Tell me," I said.

"Let it wait, Maggie. Just until tomorrow."

"Rowan is right. Your father is alive. He is safe. As for what happens next . . ."

"I won't let you send him away!"

"Our return affects everyone on staff," Rowan said. "And everyone deserves a say in . . . what happens next."

"I will call a meeting. For eleven o'clock tomorrow morning." Reinhard frowned. "Bernie cannot be there. We cannot speak openly—"

"Bernie?" Rowan interrupted. "Bernie Cohen?"

"He has taken on Helen's jobs—publicity and program."

"Bernie Cohen . . . back at the Crossroads . . ."

"Yes. Well. I will deal with Bernie. Somehow. Can you leave Jack alone for an hour?"

"If we hold the meeting in the green room or the Smokehouse. Somewhere close where I can feel him if he needs me."

"The Smokehouse, then. I will stop by before the meeting. I would like to examine him. He seems remarkably healthy, but—"

"Would you stop arranging things?" I exclaimed. "I

need to know what happened to him. Nothing you tell me will be as bad as what I imagine. Please."

Rowan and Reinhard exchanged glances. Then Reinhard sighed and nodded. Rowan led me over to Reinhard's stage manager stool and eased me onto it.

"I don't know how long I searched for him in Faerie. Months, probably. None of the clans I visited had heard of any human who'd been adopted. And I couldn't feel Jack's energy. At first, I thought he might be too far away for me to sense. Then I realized I'd stupidly overlooked the obvious."

"The obvious?"

"The older Fae can always sense when a human has breached the borders of Faerie. But none of the elders I spoke to had detected such an intrusion. That's when I thought of the Borderlands. It's a place between the worlds. A sort of . . . buffer zone."

His grim expression made me ask, "Is it . . . awful?"

"Some of it is as beautiful as Faerie. But its magic is wilder. You can be walking through a darkened thicket at moonrise and suddenly find yourself on the brink of a sunlit precipice. Even time seems to follow no rules. That's why it seemed that only a few months had passed while I was searching for him."

He hesitated, clearly reluctant to say more. Then he took a deep breath.

"The Borderlands draw the darkest elements of Faerie. Guardians, we call them, for they keep out hapless trespassers from both worlds. But some use their power to lure the innocent and the foolish. Once inside the Borderlands, few manage to escape."

Until now, I'd been terrified about the ordeals my father must have undergone. Rowan's haunted expression made me wonder what he'd had to endure in order to find him.

"These . . . creatures," Reinhard said. "Could they have followed you back here?"

"No. I sealed the portal behind us and warded it against intruders."

"And Daddy?" I prompted. "How did he survive there for so long?"

"Jack was no hapless trespasser. He had prepared for his crossing. He brought extra clothing, a medical kit, cooking utensils, a tarp—anything and everything he could fit into that backpack."

Mom protesting that we were only going away for the weekend and couldn't possibly need everything he was stuffing into suitcases and carryalls and shopping bags. Daddy invariably responding, "Be prepared. That's the Boy Scout motto."

"Once his food ran out, he hunted and fished. Gathered fruits and nuts and berries. Much as I did during my early years in this world. He hid from the dangers as best he could. And when he discovered that the magic was wilder in some places than others, he sought out the pockets of relative safety. Most of all, he clung to his memories. He read—and reread—the few books he'd brought. Recited his old theatre monologues. Sang show tunes. In spite of everything, I think he was relieved to find the Borderlands. To know that the things that had happened to him here were real. That he wasn't crazy."

Lying in bed, listening to the muffled shouting. Cringing when I made out his words: "I am not losing my mind! I'm finally beginning to see things clearly!" Pretending to be fast asleep when Mom eased open my bedroom door to check on me.

"I couldn't leave him in the Borderlands. My clan would never accept a . . . damaged human. And if I'd taken him to Faerie, I knew I'd never convince him to leave."

No. He had sacrificed everything and everyone he loved in his search for Faerie. Once he found it, he would never give it up.

"So I have thrust both of us upon you. I hope you can forgive me."

"Forgive you?" I echoed. "You came back to me. You brought my father back. Nothing is more important than that."

Rowan's sweet smile faded when he noticed Reinhard's dubious expression.

"Nothing," I repeated firmly, "is more important than that."

ENTR'ACTE
THE JOURNAL OF ROWAN MACKENZIE

"Nothing is more important than that."

She loves me. After all this time, she still loves me. She is still my Maggie. As long as I have her, I can accept the rest. Even the loss of my theatre.

Of course, no one expected me to return. Those empty wooden hangers in my armoire brought that home far more powerfully than their incredulous looks.

At least they didn't throw out the contents of my desk. I'll have to ask Maggie to buy me a new journal. For tonight, I will make do with blank paper.

If only my mind were equally blank.

A nonprofit. Had I remained here, it could never have happened. Helen would not have allowed it. She knew I could play no role in a theatre where accountants issue paychecks to employees with Social Security numbers.

Foolish to have expected everything to remain the same, to imagine that I could simply pick up the threads of my life again. Places change. People change. Even Maggie. She is stronger now, more confident about herself and her place in the world.

What a colossal irony that she has taken my place.

How could I have ever imagined that she would be content to be my assistant? But that was the play I wrote in my head. I would direct the shows. She would work with the actors, doing her list thing, helping them with their music. We'd work together and live together and love each other. We would give Jack a home and he would grow strong in mind and body.

A pipe dream. The kind of happy ever after found in musicals.

She is still my Maggie. But I am not the same Rowan Mackenzie. Can she really love a penniless beggar with nothing but the clothes on his back? A man as ill equipped to deal with this world as her poor damaged father?

If only I had never left.

If only I had given up the search sooner.

I could have returned months ago. And faced Maggie without shame and told her without lying that I could not feel his presence in Faerie. I would still have my theatre and my life.

My first completely unselfish act and look how it turned out.

I mustn't blame Jack. It was my choice to leave, my choice to search for him. He would not have been there in the first place had I protected him all those years ago.

I failed him then. I will not do so now.

The staff will let us stay. Maggie will insist on it. And when Maggie Graham digs in her heels, she is as immovable as the Green Mountains.

And then?

I must help Jack heal.

I must help Maggie succeed.

I must find a new purpose, a new life, a new place in this world, just as I did more than two hundred years ago.

And never allow Maggie to suspect how much that prospect terrifies me.

ACT TWO

LIVING IN THE SHADOWS

CHAPTER 13
WHO ARE YOU NOW?

AS I STAGGERED FROM THE PARKING LOT with the first four bags of groceries, the stage door banged open and my father poked his head out. He surveyed the picnic area, the Smokehouse, and finally craned his neck to study the sky. Then he bounded out of the barn and sprinted toward me.

I felt like I'd stumbled into *The Twilight Zone* again. Although his clothes were still ragged, the terrified Rip Van Winkle was gone, replaced by a smiling stranger, white hair secured at the nape of his neck, white beard and mustache neatly—if inexpertly—trimmed.

My delight faded as he wrested a bag from my hand and began rummaging through it.

So he's more excited about the groceries than you. Just be grateful he isn't cowering under the table.

"Jack!" Rowan called as he hurried toward us. "We'll unpack the groceries upstairs."

"There's more in the car," I said.

"I'll get them!" Daddy replied.

I watched him race toward the parking lot, still shocked by his transformation. If Rowan could accomplish so much in a single night, I'd have my father back before the end of the season.

As I turned to thank Rowan, his gaze rose abruptly from my legs to my face. I wished I'd worn something

107

flirty, fun, and fabulous instead of throwing on shorts and a T-shirt. Then his desire flashed through me, and I decided that shorts and a T-shirt were just fine.

His lips brushed my cheek. I heard his deep intake of breath. Then he suddenly recoiled.

"Did you cut yourself?" he demanded.

I shook my head before I remembered. "I nicked myself shaving. How did you—?"

"The iron. In the blood."

"You can smell it?"

"I just wasn't prepared."

In spite of his reassuring smile, his face was even paler than usual, and he kept swallowing as if he might vomit.

"But people cut themselves all the time. And women . . ." Heat burned my cheeks. "Women . . . bleed. Every month. Not old women, but . . ."

"I understand the female reproductive cycle, Maggie."

I envisioned him retreating to the cottage every time a woman got her period. But if he'd done that during my season, he never would have gotten around to directing.

Rowan cleared his throat. "I'm usually careful to keep up my . . . shields."

Now all I could envision was some *Star Trek* character shouting, "Red alert! Shields up!" And menstruating women bouncing off them like ping-pong balls.

What is wrong with you? Focus!

Which wasn't easy on two hours of sleep and five cups of coffee.

"So you left your shields in the apartment today?"

"Not exactly."

I tugged my ear. "Sounds like . . . ? Three syllables?"

"I wanted to smell you."

Six rather surprising syllables.

"I know that sounds disgusting, but—"

"It's sweet," I replied and smiled at his astonishment. "Did I smell okay? Other than the blood?"

"You smelled wonderful." He closed his eyes, his expression dreamy. "Something ambiguously herbal in your hair. The dusty fragrance of lavender permeating your shirt. Lemongrass soap. A salty hint of sweat. A sweet whiff of baby powder . . ."

"All that? In one breath?"

He regarded me through heavy-lidded eyes. "The musk between your legs. And your scent. Sweet and spicy. Like ginger."

"My perfume," I managed.

"Yes. But it's also you. Your essence."

I took a shaky breath and let it out. So did Rowan. Then he said, "We'd better help Jack."

We found Daddy bent over the open trunk of my car. He straightened as we approached, a guilty expression on his face as well as a great many crumbs.

"I said we'd unpack upstairs," Rowan reminded him.

Daddy muttered a protest, spewing crumbs everywhere. "It's Entenmann's crumb cake. My favorite!"

"Mine, too," I said.

"But you bought English muffins, right?"

"And new clothes."

"Good thing. I'm a regular Raggedy Andy. I hope you bought clothes for Rowan, too."

Belatedly, I realized that he was still dressed in the stained and wrinkled clothing I'd seen last night.

"Mine seem to be . . . missing," Rowan said.

"Missing?"

"Along with my toiletries. Jack and I showered with Joy this morning. The dishwashing liquid, not our state of being."

"You don't have any clothes?"

"I imagine Janet or Reinhard cleaned everything out."

"And left the fucking dishwashing liquid?"

Daddy hooted. "That's what I said!"

I scowled and heaved two bags out of the trunk. "Let's get this stuff inside."

As we headed back to the theatre, I said, "I can't believe they gave away your clothes. I mean, I can. But still . . . what a shitty homecoming. Well, I have one of your shirts. I'll be able to find the manufacturer's name and—"

"You have one of my shirts?"

"Reinhard packed it for me. With your other things." Another embarrassing wave of heat suffused my cheeks as I recalled the times I had pressed it to my face and breathed in the faint scent of him that clung to it. "Anyway, I can order more. I'll run out and pick up some other stuff to tide you over."

"Naturally, I intend to pay for the clothes. And the groceries."

"Don't be silly."

"I don't have any money, but—"

"You have the money you gave to me."

"That's yours."

"Well, you're back now. That makes it *your* money."

"I don't *want* the money!"

"Please don't fight," Daddy whispered.

That silenced us. After an awkward exchange of glances, we both began apologizing, then broke off. Finally, Rowan said, "Suppose we wrangle about finances tomorrow."

"Okay. But I'm paying you back everything I spent on the hotel."

"The hotel?"

"The Bough. I spent most of your money fixing it up."

"Why would you—?"

"I own it."

"You *own* the Golden Bough?"

"Helen left it to me."

"But I thought Janet—"

"I'm hungry," Daddy complained. "And I want to try on my new—"

His head jerked toward the Smokehouse. Then he dropped his bag and shrieked, "Run!"

I was too stunned to do anything except watch him bolt down the walkway and disappear into the barn.

"It's the crow," Rowan said, easing his bags to the ground. "In the maple tree. There were shapeshifters in the Borderlands who took that form."

"Shapeshifters?"

But he was already hurrying after Daddy.

A shudder rippled through me. Were the shapeshifters the mysterious "they" that Daddy feared? Or were there other creatures—even more terrifying—in that awful place?

Unwillingly, I pictured giant crows gorging on carrion. Or maybe they looked like ordinary humans with feathers instead of hair, talons instead of fingers, and cruel, hooked beaks that they used to tear the flesh of their victims.

I tried to banish the disturbing images as I walked toward the theatre. Rowan crouched in the stage doorway. Daddy was hidden in the shadows, but I heard him exclaim, "Get Maggie! Before the Crow-Man does." After that, there was only the murmur of their voices.

I felt utterly useless. It was Rowan my father needed, Rowan whose power could calm him. All I could do was buy groceries and clothes.

I glared at the small black form, half hidden among the branches of the maple.

"Scat!"

Daddy's anguished cry made me glance over my shoulder. He was peering around the doorframe, frantically beckoning out to me.

"Don't do that! They're worse if they're angry."

"Yeah? Well, so am I!"

I ran toward the tree, waving my arms like a crazy woman and shouting, "Scat! Shoo! Get out of here, bird!" I wrenched a clod of dirt from the ground and hurled it at the little fucker with all my might. I missed the tree completely, but the crow gave an irritable caw and flew off.

Absurdly elated at my victory, I dusted off my hands and walked back to my men.

"You're very brave," Daddy said. "But you've got to be more careful. Those Crow-Men'll rip you to pieces. I'm starving! Let's eat."

And he clattered up the stairs.

Stupid to imagine that he'd been magically cured overnight. Or to see him venture outdoors and believe that he was no longer haunted by his experiences in the Borderlands.

One day at a time, Graham.

"We need to wash your clothes," I told Rowan. "And Daddy's."

Clearly taken aback, Rowan nodded. "I'll borrow something from Jack for now."

"We can use the machines in the Dungeon."

"Why don't I unpack the groceries while you start the laundry?"

It was a perfectly reasonable suggestion. But all I could hear was Hal's voice: "I just don't want to see you turning into Helen."

One day at a time, remember? He'll learn to do his own laundry. And his own grocery shopping. Just wash his damn clothes so he has something to wear for the staff meeting!

"Maggie?"

"Sounds like a plan."

❧❧

They were still unpacking the groceries when I returned from the Dungeon. I admired Daddy in his khaki shorts and "I L♥VERMONT" T-shirt, then burst out laughing when I saw Rowan. The droopy shorts were funny enough. The T-shirt was adorned with two bizarre cartoon creatures. Each had the body of a cow and the head of a moose. In between the pair were the words "It's different in Vermont."

"It's so you," I said.

"Another remark like that," Rowan warned, "and you get dry toast for breakfast."

We settled Daddy at the table with a slab of crumb cake while we finished putting away the groceries. When Rowan unearthed the fresh strawberries and vanilla ice cream, his mouth curved in that sweet smile. For a moment, we just gazed at each other. Then Daddy exclaimed, "Don't just stand there! Cook!"

Rowan cooked. I brought him up to speed on my life. I downplayed the financial problems the theatre still faced; I didn't want him to think I was incompetent. Rowan smiled and nodded and told me how proud he was. Over and over again. Like he was putting on a performance—or we were strangers trying to find some common ground.

Stop reading into everything! He's feeling his way just like you are. You'll have plenty of time to get to know him again. To get to know both of them.

He was astonished to learn that I was living with Janet and even more astonished to discover that I was enjoying it. But he studiously avoided asking about my personal life, and when I started telling him about my awful dates, he changed the subject.

I'd expected him to laugh. What had *he* expected? That I would sit at home, staring tearfully into space and clutching his journal to my bosom? Okay, I *had* done that. For a while. But he acted like I'd spent my winters sprawled on a bearskin rug with a succession of naked strangers, and my summers sunbathing beside hunky bronzed Vikings in Speedos.

Reinhard's arrival rescued us.

"What's in the box?" I asked as he set it atop the battered wooden trunk that Rowan used as a coffee table.

"Rowan's wines."

"You stored his wine?"

"It would have been ruined if I left it here. You know how cold the barn gets in the winter. And in the summer, with all the sunlight pouring in . . ." Reinhard shook his head. "I also stored some of your books, Rowan. The first editions. You'll have to apply to Maggie for your journals."

"I don't suppose you've got his clothes, too?"

"They are in my SUV."

"You're kidding!"

"You cannot be too careful with moths. The clothes are clean, of course, but after so long in storage, I would recommended laundering them." Reinhard's mouth quirked in a brief smile as he surveyed Rowan's attire. "I suppose you will have to wear that to the staff meeting."

"I'm doing a load of wash now," I said.

"Pity. I would have liked to have seen Janet's face. Now. Jack, if you will accompany me into the bedroom . . ."

"Why?" Rowan asked.

Reinhard frowned. "If you prefer that I conduct his physical examination here—"

"Why did you store my clothes?" He seemed more stunned than pleased by Reinhard's revelations. "The books, the wine, those are valuable. But my clothes . . ."

"I thought you would return."

"You never told me that!" I exclaimed.

"And if I was wrong?" Reinhard demanded. "Should I build up your hopes for nothing?" He smoothed his crew cut and added, "As it turns out, I was right. And now Janet owes me a very expensive bottle of wine."

Rowan silently walked over to the trunk and withdrew a bottle from the box. After examining it, he put it back and chose another, which he held out to Reinhard.

"Now you can enjoy two bottles of wine."

Reinhard glanced at the label and shook his head. "Too expensive."

"Not nearly expensive enough after what you've done. Please. I would be honored if you'd accept it."

Reinhard gave one of his little bows. Then he led my protesting father into the bedroom. Rowan followed, still looking a little dazed.

Between sprints to the Dungeon, I hovered anxiously outside the bedroom, listening to Daddy's complaints and Rowan's soothing murmur. I returned from my final trip in time to hear Reinhard pronounce Daddy remarkably healthy.

"I could have told you that before you started poking me," Daddy grumbled.

"Does the wrist bother you much?"

"What's wrong with his wrist?" I asked, hastily depositing my armful of clothes on the bed.

"An old fracture," Reinhard replied.

"It aches sometimes. But I did a good job setting it, didn't I? One-handed, too! The good ol' *Field Guide to Wilderness Medicine*. Never travel without it."

"And the earlier problems?" Reinhard inquired as he closed his bag.

"What problems?"

"I understood there was a history of alcohol and drug abuse."

Daddy shot an anxious look at Rowan. "Was there? Did I tell you that? I don't remember. So many missing pieces ..."

As he began to tremble, Rowan's hand descended on his shoulder.

"Perhaps we should postpone the meeting," Reinhard said.

"Why don't you and Maggie go ahead?" Rowan suggested. "Jack and I will be there soon."

When Reinhard frowned, I said, "I thought Jack should meet the staff."

"Then they should meet him as he is. Not under the influence of Rowan's power."

Rowan stiffened, but his hand slid from Daddy's shoulder. "Give me a few minutes to talk with him."

"I'm right here, you know!"

Daddy's querulous voice made me grimace. If they met this Jack Sinclair—or the one who'd run shrieking from the crow—would they really allow him to stay?

CHAPTER 14
I'VE GOT YOU TO LEAN ON

AS SOON AS I WALKED INTO THE Smokehouse, Hal hurried over and swept me into a hug.

"I didn't sleep a wink last night." He reared back to examine my face and sighed. "Clearly, you didn't, either. And no wonder, poor lamb. First Rowan, then . . . but don't worry. Everything will be fine."

"From your lips . . ." I glanced around and breathed a sigh of relief when I discovered Bernie was absent. "What did you tell Bernie?" I asked Reinhard.

He, too, was surveying the room. "Nothing. I just dropped him off in town to wheedle more ads out of the merchants. Javier, is Catherine coming?"

Before Javier could reply, Reinhard's head jerked toward the Smokehouse door. Right on cue, the rest of the staff went into their familiar bird-dog-on-point attitude. Either Rowan's control was shaky or he was deliberately warning us of his arrival.

There was a breathless pause. Then a soft knock.

It just killed me to imagine Rowan standing outside, humbly awaiting permission to enter the rehearsal studio that had once been his. But when he walked inside, he seemed as self-assured as that morning he'd welcomed our cast to the Crossroads.

Daddy's gaze darted from face to face. When I gave

his arm a reassuring squeeze, he regarded me blankly—
as if he'd never seen me before in his life.

"This is the staff of the theatre," Rowan told him.

"I don't know these people," Daddy said in a loud
whisper.

"Most of them began working here after your season,
but they've all heard about your performance as Billy
Bigelow."

Once again, those words proved to be the mental
health equivalent of "Abracadabra!" Flashing his gap-
toothed grin, Daddy strode toward Alex and thrust out
his hand. "Hi. Jack Sinclair. Great to meet you." Leaving
a startled Alex to stammer, "Ah. Yes. Alex Ross. Music
director."

Daddy worked the room like a politician at a rally—
or an actor who had been well coached by his director.
The staff exchanged glances, obviously trying to square
this confident man with the one Reinhard must have described.

Daddy's smile slipped as Janet introduced herself.
Then his troubled expression cleared. "I remember now!
You're Helen's daughter. How come she's not here?"

"I'm afraid Helen passed away," Janet said.

Daddy's mouth began to tremble. Then he slumped
onto a chair and covered his face with his hands. Rowan
reached for his shoulder, then let his hand fall.

"I'm sorry," he said to Janet. "I know how hard it must
have been for you."

Janet nodded brusquely.

"I wish I had been here."

"I doubt even you could have saved her."

Daddy leaped up from his chair, his face twisted in
horror. "Was it the Crow-Men?"

"There are no Crow-Men here," Rowan said. "Helen
just had a bad heart."

"She did not! Helen had the best heart of anyone I
ever knew!"

"Rowan meant she had a heart attack," I said, desperate to avoid another meltdown. "But her passing was very peaceful. She died in her sleep."

Daddy let out a shaky sigh. "Thank God. Not that she died! That it was peaceful. I couldn't bear the thought of those awful Crow-Men tearing poor Helen to pieces and then gobbling her up like—"

"I think it's time to go back to the apartment," Rowan said.

"Did I do something wrong? I didn't mean to. Please, don't send me—"

"It's okay," I assured him, all too aware of the shell-shocked expressions of the staff. "I need you to try on the rest of your new clothes. And make up a list of anything else you need."

"More crumb cake! And shoes. And underwear. Briefs, not boxers. Only Rowan wears boxers."

That revelation caused a mild sensation among the staff.

Rowan took Daddy's arm and marched him to the door. Daddy shook off his restraining hand and turned to face the staff. "It was a pleasure to meet you. I look forward to seeing you again very soon."

Head high, he made his exit, leaving Rowan to trail after him.

Every head immediately swiveled toward me.

"The Crow-Men ... he wasn't making that up. They're shapeshifters. In the Borderlands. The place where Rowan found him."

Hal shuddered. "I don't even want to imagine. And meeting a bunch of strangers his first day back ... and learning about Helen ... I wouldn't have managed half so well!"

"I expected him to be worse," Javier said cautiously. "After what Reinhard told us."

"What exactly *did* you tell them?" I asked.

"The truth, Maggie. As I saw it."

Before I could press him for details, Catherine eased through the half-open door. She looked drawn and pale. I hoped she hadn't caught some sort of stomach bug.

"Have they left already?" she asked.

"Rowan will be back in a minute," I said. "After we finish talking, I'll introduce you to . . . Jack."

"How are you doing?"

"It's all so . . . surreal. I keep waiting for someone to pinch me."

Mei-Yin obligingly gave my arm a brief but brutal pinch. I was still glaring at her when Rowan strode into the Smokehouse. He checked when he saw Catherine, then hurried over to her, his smile of greeting shifting to a frown.

"What is it? Are you ill?"

"No, no . . ."

He seized her hands and became very still. "Something's . . . changed."

Catherine shot a quick look at Javier. A huge grin blossomed on his face as he put his arm around her.

"We were going to make the official announcement later, but you can't keep anything a secret around this place. We're going to have a baby!"

Rowan's astonishment crackled through the Smokehouse like heat lightning. A dizzying array of emotions inundated me: wonder, affection, joy—and a longing so palpable it made me ache.

Everyone was so shocked by his reaction that it took us a moment before we remembered to congratulate Catherine and Javier. I was the only one who seemed genuinely surprised. The staff must have picked up on some change in her energy just as Rowan had. Even Hal had heard, undoubtedly from Lee. For a moment, I felt as much of an outsider as Rowan.

"We just found out last week," Catherine told me, her expression anxious. "I didn't want to give you anything more to worry about during Hell Week."

"Are you kidding? It's wonderful news! Although I don't know where you found the time or the energy."

"Where there's a will, there's a way," Javier said.

"I know it's not the best timing in the world," Catherine added. "But I won't let you down. I promise."

"Just promise you won't push yourself too hard. We can always scrounge up some volunteers to help with set construction."

"Already on it," Javier said.

"I was sure you'd guessed," Catherine told Rowan.

He gave a helpless shrug. "Your energy felt different, but I didn't . . . I've never been around a woman who was expecting a child." His gaze flicked toward Janet, and the mask descended.

Had she left Dale during her pregnancies? Or had she remained here and shunned all contact with Rowan?

His smile returned so quickly that I wondered if I was imagining things.

"You're the only baby I've ever known. And you were already a toddler when Alex and Annie brought you here." His left hand came up to cup Catherine's cheek. His right clasped Javier's shoulder. "What a blessing for you. For everyone. To have a child at the theatre again."

He had told me that there was rarely more than one birth every few decades in his clan. Little wonder the Fae considered children such a gift. But his words hadn't prepared me for the storm of emotions that had escaped him after Javier's revelation—or for the worshipful way he was gazing at Catherine.

Hal's hand was over his heart. Lee looked shocked. Clearly, neither had seen this side of Rowan Mackenzie. And just as clearly, the others had. Alex and Mei-Yin were smiling. Even Reinhard's expression had softened. Janet just studied Rowan through narrowed eyes.

"Forgive me," Rowan said. "I'm holding up the meeting. And we have a lot to discuss."

"No, we don't!" Hal declared. "You're back. So is Maggie's father. End of discussion."

"We are all happy that Rowan has returned," Reinhard said, although his frown suggested just the opposite.

"And that he rescued Jack. But we cannot allow emotion to cloud the issues."

"Why NOT?" Mei-Yin demanded.

"We've always followed our emotions when it came to running this theatre," Alex said.

"Which explains why it never made a profit," Janet muttered.

"But we do not run the theatre any longer," Reinhard pointed out. "The board of directors does."

"Everybody on the board knows Rowan," Catherine said. "And they'll get to know Jack."

"In time, perhaps. But right now, he needs a doctor's care."

"What are YOU? A PLUMBER?"

"I am a pediatrician, Mei-Yin! Not a psychiatrist."

"And Rowan's a FAERY! Are you telling me the TWO of you can't do more for him than a SHRINK?"

Reinhard dragged his fingers through his hair. "How can I know this? Even Rowan cannot promise that he can help Jack to heal."

"Who's asking for PROMISES? I'm asking you to TRY. Maybe it'll work. Maybe it won't. How the hell should I know? You think I got a crystal BALL up my ASS?"

"They're family," Lee stated firmly. "A lot may have changed at the Crossroads, but we don't turn away family."

Rowan had been observing the give-and-take calmly, but Lee's comment startled him. Whatever misgivings our resident alpha male may have had last night, Lee had obviously decided that Rowan and Daddy were members of our pack.

"So you are all agreed?" Reinhard asked.

"Did you really expect us to show Rowan Mackenzie the door?" Janet said.

"Would you like to?" Rowan asked.

Janet hesitated, then shook her head. "Lee's right. Like it or not, we are family. And we've always protected our own." As I let out my breath in a relieved sigh, she added, "And speaking of family, I trust you haven't forgotten your mother is arriving tomorrow."

"Your mother?" Rowan echoed.

In other circumstances, I might have found the trace of panic on his face amusing. But I'd lain awake half the night, thinking about what I would—could—say to her.

"I can't tell her about Daddy." Not until he bore some resemblance to the man she had once loved. "Or you," I added, shooting a pleading glance at Rowan. "She'll storm your apartment."

"Armed with a spoon," Janet mused.

There were a few fleeting smiles; everyone had heard the story of how my mother had threatened to geld Rowan if he hurt me.

Rowan, however, was frowning. "I hate to think of you keeping secrets from her again."

So did I. And not only because she always managed to sniff out the truth. We'd worked too hard to develop a good relationship to jeopardize it now. But if I was hiding Daddy, I could keep Rowan a secret, too. Just until she was safely back in Delaware.

"You're sure?" Rowan asked. When I nodded, he said, "Then I'll take Jack back to the cottage for a few days. He likes it there. And it might be better for us to be alone. While we start working on his recovery."

"How do we explain Jack to everybody else?" Hal asked. "He can't stay locked up in your apartment. Or hidden in the woods." He shuddered; Hal's idea of roughing it was when the hot water didn't come on immediately.

"Keep as close to the truth as possible," Rowan advised. "Jack's an old friend of mine. An actor who's fallen on hard times. And I invited him to stay for the summer."

"That explains how Jack fits in around here," Janet said. "What about you?"

"I've come back to be with Maggie. To work out our relationship."

"And what about your relationship to the theatre?"

"I can't think that far ahead."

"But surely, you *want* to be a part of things," Alex protested.

"Of course I do!"

After his calm acceptance of all the changes at the theatre, Rowan's vehemence startled me. Why hadn't he shared his true feelings with me?

"Maggie is the artistic director now," he said more quietly. "And I don't intend to usurp her authority. As long as I possess no official identity, I couldn't even if I wanted to. Perhaps one day, I'll direct again. I don't know. Any more than I know whether I can help Jack heal or whether Maggie and I can make this relationship work."

Green eyes pierced me.

"I can only promise that I'll try. I will not walk away again. From you or your father or this theatre. That is my pledge."

His fierce gaze swept over the staff, lingering longest on Janet and Reinhard.

"My pledge to all of you."

CHAPTER 15

TAKE IT ON THE CHIN

NOTHING SCREAMS WEEKEND FUN like losing the two men you love most in the world yet again.

I bundled Rowan and Daddy off to the cottage with enough food in Daddy's backpack to last a week, enough clothes in Rowan's old knapsack to weather anything short of a blizzard, and enough toilet paper to withstand the most virulent attack of enteric diarrhea.

Rowan paused at the edge of the trees to wave farewell, just as he had two years ago. I firmly reminded myself that I would see them Sunday evening, that it was foolish to interpret Daddy's delight at returning to the "little house" as a personal rejection. Then I cried for ten minutes, blew my nose, and hurried to the Smokehouse for my "getting to know you" rehearsal with the two sets of kids playing Colin and Mary in *The Secret Garden*.

Yet another show about orphans. Belligerent Mary who erected walls to hide the pain of losing her parents in a cholera epidemic. Bedridden Colin who was an orphan in all but name since his hunchbacked father was lost in grief over the death of his wife.

Not exactly a laugh riot.

As the kids and I discussed the characters, I wondered if I was out of my mind to stage such a dark musical. Yes, there was a happy ending—eventually. And ghosts and magic and redemption and love. Kind of like *Carousel* without the clambakes.

Maybe that's what had convinced me that the show could be another four-hanky success story. But it suddenly struck me that I'd ended up with an entire season of shows about characters in search of a family. A therapist would have a field day.

The four kids seemed undaunted by the show's darkness or the difficult gamut of emotions they would have to convey. Their determination made me ashamed of my earlier weepiness, and we broke for the day on a wave of enthusiasm.

After which I changed my clothes and mentally prepared myself for the "lying to my mother" phase of my festive weekend.

When I walked into the Golden Bough, a little shiver of excitement zinged through me. Tourists wandered through the lobby. The muted hum of voices emanated from the lounge. And—be still my heart!—a young guy was working in our new Media Center. Okay, "Media Center" was just a fancy term for a cubicle with a computer, printer, and landline phone, but someone was actually using it.

During my first year as owner, I'd been too busy working for the theatre to do more than learn the ropes and discuss redecorating with Hal and Caren. Frannie took over as manager a week before the flood. Although many neighboring towns were inundated, Dale escaped with only soggy basements. When I breathlessly asked Janet if faery wards had averted disaster, she rolled her eyes and assured me that our salvation was due to geography; short of a Biblical flood, the Dale "River" was too small and too far from town to do much damage.

We had to close the hotel for a few days to deal with the basement. Frannie was the one who suggested we close again during March and April to dive into renovations. It made perfect sense; southern Vermont drew more black flies than tourists in early spring.

After we reopened, I obsessively checked bookings, fearful that we'd go under before the Fourth of July. But the trickle of tourists had turned into a babbling brook, if not a flood, and we were pretty much booked through early October. Even the fact that a third of our rooms went to cast members failed to diminish my satisfaction.

The secret to our success looked up from the guest book and beamed as I approached the reception desk. Iolanthe—lounging in the inbox as usual—raised her head to allow me to rub her behind the ears before resuming her twenty-two-hour-a-day catnap. Even Janet had no idea how old Iolanthe was; I'd begun to suspect the cat was Fae.

"Have they checked in yet?" I asked Frannie.

"No. But traffic on the interstate can be murder on a Friday. Don't you worry, hon."

We discussed the ongoing maid shortage and accommodations for the handful of professional actors arriving Sunday to begin rehearsals for *The Secret Garden*. Every time the bell over the front door tinkled, my head jerked up, hoping to see Mom and Chris. In the middle of perusing the horrifying estimates to install a new boiler, the bell jangled again and my mother staggered through the door.

"I thought we'd never get here," she said by way of greeting. "The entire Eastern seaboard was fleeing north. I feel like something the cat dragged in."

Naturally, she looked anything but. Black hair perfectly coiffed, barely a wrinkle marring her pale blue shirtdress. Martians could level Wilmington and the woman would emerge from the rubble looking chic.

She gave me a quick hug, then stepped back, frowning. "You look nice."

"Want to try that line reading again? Without the surprise?"

"I'm used to seeing you in shorts and a T-shirt."

"I'm dressed for dinner. I'm even skipping tonight's

show so we can have a relaxing one. God knows we won't have much time to talk tomorrow."

The cornflower blue eyes narrowed. "What's wrong? You seem tense."

Great. She's here five seconds and already picking up bad vibes.

"Of course, I'm tense! I've got a fund-raiser tomorrow, and I thought my mother was road kill."

"We nearly were. This giant wolf lumbered across the road—"

"It was a German shepherd," Chris remarked as he edged through the doorway with their luggage.

"It was a wolf," my mother declared.

"It was a wolf," he agreed. "That looked remarkably like a German shepherd."

He dropped their bags and gave me a warm hug. He was a great hugger. One of the many things I liked about him. Along with his brown eyes that could look soulful one moment and devilish the next. And the way he teased my mother whose pursed lips had curved into a reluctant smile.

Her eyes widened as she finally registered the new and improved lobby. Hardwood floors gleamed. The dark oak paneling had been stripped and restained a lighter shade. Overstuffed couches and armchairs in deep forest green and green-and-white gingham graced the seating areas. In place of the ancient draperies that had shrouded the lobby in gloom, wooden shutters allowed morning sunlight to pour through the top half of the tall windows. Ferns and peace lilies nestled atop plant stands. And scattered throughout, a collection of funky lamps that Hal and I had scavenged from flea markets.

I'd deliberately refrained from sending her pictures and my uncommon restraint was rewarded by her look of pleasure. Needy child that I was, I couldn't resist asking, "You like it?"

"It's what a Vermont country inn should look like."

"It'll never be as elegant as the Four Chimneys . . ."

"It's cheerful and homey. Like Dale. And it doesn't cost an arm and a leg to stay here. You should have seen it before, Chris. Like something out of the Victorian age."

"Those old draperies probably were," Frannie called, waggling her fingers in greeting.

Mom hurried over to the reception desk. "I was so busy gawking I didn't even say hello. How are you?"

"Just great, hon."

"And your mother? Is the arthritis still troubling her?"

"Oh, you know. Good days and bad. But she's as feisty as ever."

Mom introduced Chris, then gazed around the lobby again. "You and Maggie have worked wonders."

"Wait'll you see your room." Frannie winked. "Maggie put you in the Honeymoon Suite."

"You have a Honeymoon Suite?"

"The Rose Garden Room." I struck a pose and quoted from the Web page: " 'The romantic rose-colored décor is highlighted by a wall of windows and French doors leading out to a balcony overlooking the Green Mountains and the quaint shops of Main Street.' Come on. I'll walk you up."

As we mounted the wide stairs, I said, "Your room is the only one we've fixed up. The rest of the second floor just got new bedspreads and curtains and paint slapped on the walls."

"One step at a time," Chris said.

"Yeah. That's my new mantra." I paused outside their room, my palm a little damp as I gripped the brass doorknob. Then I flung open the door. "Welcome to your private rose garden."

Mom drifted through the "suite," making more gratifying noises as she admired the canopy bed, the floral draperies and bedspread, the bouquet of pink roses on the table in the sitting area, and the claw foot tub in the bathroom that had cost me a fucking fortune.

"It's beautiful, Maggie. When you called it the Rose Garden Room, I was afraid it would be . . ."

"Too girly?"

"Too flowery. You know. Flowered curtains and bed-spreads and pillows and wallpaper." Mom shuddered. "Who can relax in a room with flowered wallpaper? It gives me a headache."

"It gives me the creeps. Like I'm staying in Sleeping Beauty's castle and the vines will eventually strangle me."

Chris stroked his beard thoughtfully. "Now there's an idea. An inn where every room is decorated in a different fairy-tale theme. The Sleeping Beauty Room. The Snow White Room."

"With a glass coffin instead of a bed," I suggested.

"The Hansel and Gretel Room with its charming wood-burning stove—ideal for incinerating unwanted guests."

Mom rolled her eyes. "The pair of you."

She used to say that when Daddy and I embarked on one of our flights of fancy. But her voice held affection now instead of the exasperation I remembered from childhood.

"Maggie? You've got that tense look again."

"I forgot to order flowers for the fund-raiser," I lied.

❧❧

Mom continued to study me during dinner, but Chris, God love him, kept refilling the wineglasses. By the time we said good night, Mom was pleasantly tipsy and too tired to study anything other than the inside of her eye-lids.

The next morning brought a final frenzy of cleaning before the fund-raiser. Amanda did a terrific job at the matinee, but I was glad Chelsea was on the docket at night; her performance was the kind of big bang donors expected for their bucks.

After the matinee, Hal accompanied me up the hill to

oversee my toilette. Naturally, he'd helped me pick out tonight's dress, too.

"What do you think?" I asked Janet as I descended the stairs.

"I told her the jade silk brings out the green in her eyes," Hal prompted, "and the Chinese style evokes an air of exotic mystery."

"The plunging neckline should bring in some last-minute donations," Janet remarked.

"You don't think I look like the lone Caucasian cast member of *Flower Drum Song*?"

Janet examined me critically. Then began singing "You are Beautiful." From *Flower* fucking *Drum Song*.

"I hate you."

"At least it doesn't have dragons on it like Mei-Yin's."

"Mei-Yin's wearing her dragon dress?" I demanded, turning on Hal.

"How was I to know? She didn't consult me!"

"Maybe later, the two of you can put chopsticks in your hair and treat us to a rousing rendition of 'Fan Tan Fannie.'"

"I'm changing."

The doorbell chimed and Janet grinned. "Too late now."

Within half an hour, nearly a hundred guests were milling around the Bates mansion, the front porch, and the patios and garden. We'd kept prices modest, but the dozen "Angels" who'd popped for the five hundred dollar tickets ensured that the evening would be a financial success.

Three minutes with Bernie's daughter Leah made me wonder yet again how he survived the off-season. He endured her fussing with a resigned sigh, but Sarah finally said, "Lighten up, Mom," and began talking about her recent graduation.

Hard to equate this self-assured young woman with the plump, awkward girl who had been my cast mate. I'd grown so accustomed to the agelessness of the older staff that it was Sarah's transformation that seemed unnatural. Maybe by the time I was eligible for Social Security, Janet might have sprouted a few gray hairs, but Rowan would look exactly the same.

You knew that going in, Graham. Deal with it!

I could only spend a few minutes with Sarah before resuming my duties. I was so busy chatting up patrons that I merely waved to Mom and Chris. When I finally caught up with them, I found her working the room just as hard, praising past productions and the dedication of the staff and board.

"They should have appointed you executive director," I noted.

"Actually, I hate these affairs. I just put on my game face and play the devoted patron of the arts."

"The devoted and fabulous patron of the arts." Hal paused in the sunroom doorway to fling open his arms, then hurried over to envelop Mom in a hug. "You look gorgeous as always. What I wouldn't give for that complexion! Please tell Maggie she doesn't look like a Caucasian cast member of *Flower Drum Song*. She's been obsessing all evening. You must be Chris. I can't believe it's taken this long to lure you up here."

"And you must be Hal," Chris said, smiling. "Alison's told me so much about you, I feel like I know you."

"I hope she's been equally kind in her description of me," Long boomed, edging into our circle. "Alison, Alison. Don't break my heart and tell me that this is your inamorato."

"Call your cardiologist," Chris advised as he held out his hand. "Chris Thompson, Inamorato. You must be Long Martindale, Impresario."

"I have the good fortune to be the president of the board of directors. But if you've won the heart of the fair Alison, then you are the fortunate one."

"We have swords in the prop room," I noted. "If you want to fight a duel on the front lawn."

"Behave," my mother said. "And you, too," she added,

eyeing Long sternly. "Honestly, I think you'd flirt with any female between seven and seventy."

"My cut-off is eighty," Long whispered. "But I might have to revise my limit. I see a very rich, very elderly widow who's in need of company."

After he excused himself, Chris remarked, "You know, he may not be as much of an ass as you suspect. It's hard to tell with theatre people. They're good at playing roles offstage, too."

"Some are." My mother favored me with a speculative glance.

I took that as my cue to beat a hasty retreat. When I spied Nancy talking with Bernie, Bea, and Frannie, I wobbled out to the patio as fast as my spiky heels would allow.

When Nancy smiled, I realized just how much the events of the last few days had been weighing on me. She had kept me sane during our season and we'd shared a lot of ups and downs since, including my struggles to steer a course for the theatre and hers to survive the budget cuts at the library. And while she knew nothing about the secret of the Crossroads, she understood more about my relationship with Rowan than anyone. I could always count on her for sensible advice and a sympathetic ear. At that moment, I longed for both and wished I could drag her off to a quiet corner and blurt out everything.

Instead, I just hugged her. When I stepped back, everyone eyed me uneasily; clearly, my hug had been a tad desperate.

"Everything okay?" Nancy asked.

"Great!" I snagged two glasses of champagne from a passing waiter and downed the first in a few deep swallows.

"You just thirsty or trying to drown your sorrows?" Bernie asked.

"Thirsty. I've been yapping with donors nonstop."

"Well, save the second for a toast," Bea said. "Here's to a successful fund-raiser."

As we clinked glasses, Frannie giggled. "I hope we do this every year. It's fun getting all dolled up."

Bea, of course, always looked gorgeous, a statuesque blonde easily mistaken for one of Wagner's Rhine-maidens. Put her in a slinky sheath dress and she could set the Rhine on fire. Nancy looked businesslike in her tailored navy suit. Frannie's flowered silk dress made her look like a stocky nymph transplanted from the Rose Garden Room. Judging from her fuchsia finger-nails and newly brown hair, she'd stopped in at Bea's Hive of Beauty.

I glanced nervously at my watch. "Should I start rousting people out? It'll take forever to get them all seated."

"I'll give Janet the high sign," Bernie said. "If anyone can get 'em moving, she can."

"Great. I'll talk to the caterers and—"

"Frannie and I are sticking around to make sure everything's packed up," Bea said.

"Sorry. I'm anal. And you guys are the best. You totally busted your asses for this."

"We're going make a fortune!" Bernie gloated. "Who knows? Maybe we'll be able to afford some new lighting equipment. Or a turntable for the stage."

"Or a weekend of inpatient mental health care." My comment elicited more uneasy glances. "Lighten up, I'm joking!"

Bea and Frannie departed to supervise the caterers. Bernie followed, cautiously navigating through the crowd leaning on the same cane he'd used during *Briga-doon*.

"Okay, they're gone," Nancy said. "So do you want to tell me what's bothering you?"

Evening sunlight glinted off her glasses, making it seem that her eyes were shooting fire. As I pleaded Arthur's death, the opening, and the fund-raiser, she shook her head impatiently. "This is me, Maggie. I know you. Is it your mom? Did she—? Oh, Lord. She's coming."

In an instant, her expression shifted to one of apparent delight. It always amazed me. I was the actress with a face that gave everything away, while Nancy—the most sincere person in the world—could convince a sunbathing meteorologist that it was going to snow.

I just prayed she could snow my mother.

"I was lecturing Maggie about working too hard," Nancy said. "Right lecture, wrong time. You should already be at the theatre," she scolded. "You've got to warm up the cast."

"Warm-ups can wait," my mother said. "What's going on, Maggie? You've been as jumpy as a cat ever since I arrived."

"Hey, it's been a tough week and—"

"It's more than that and you know it. More to the point, I know it. You're acting evasive. Just like you were that first summer here."

"Maybe this should wait until after the show," Nancy suggested.

"I thought we were through with that," my mother continued, as relentless as the pit bull Rowan had once called me. "The secrets. The lies. I can't do that again, Maggie. I *won't* do it. If something's bothering you, then for God's sake, just come out and—"

"Rowan's back."

My mother's eyes widened. Then her lips compressed into a hard line.

"Rowan?" Nancy said. "Came back?"

I nodded, all my attention focused on Mom. "Look, I'm sorry I didn't tell you right away, but I know you've always had . . . reservations about him. And I wanted us to have a good time this weekend."

"I can't believe it," Nancy said.

"Imagine how I—"

"Who does he think he is?"

Nancy's vehemence left me speechless; I thought she would be on my side.

"You haven't heard boo from him since he left and now he waltzes back into your life?"

"He needed time. To figure things out. And be sure of his feelings."

"What about *your* feelings?"

"He loves me, Nance."

Her expression softened. "I knew that two years ago. But he still left."

"It all happened too fast. We weren't ready."

"And now you are?"

"Yes."

The quiet certainty in my voice silenced her. Mom's face was blank—as if she'd borrowed Rowan's expressionless mask.

"Say something!"

"What do you want me to say? You know how I feel about that man."

"Give him a chance, Mom."

"To do what? Break your heart a second time?"

"That won't happen."

She gave a harsh, brittle laugh. "You know who you sound like? Me. Thirty years ago."

"It's nothing like—"

"Enough. I'm not going to change your mind about Rowan Mackenzie and you're certainly not going to change mine about him."

"Will you at least talk with him? Will you do that much for me?"

She opened her mouth, closed it again, then snapped, "Fine."

With that, she stalked into the house. I just stood there, already regretting the impulse that had led me to suggest that she and Rowan meet. But I couldn't let her go home without trying to convince her of his sincerity.

Aware of Nancy's concerned gaze, I managed an unconvincing laugh. "That went well."

"She'll come around."

"In another ten or fifteen years."

I'd worry about winning her over later. First, I had a show to deal with.

Then I realized I had an even more pressing need.

"Do me a favor, Nance? I've got to talk with Janet. Could you go to the theatre and tell Reinhard I'll be down in five minutes?"

"If you want me to wait for you . . ."

"No. Thanks. Just keep Reinhard from pulling out all his hair."

I didn't have to search for Janet. Seconds after Nancy disappeared into the house, she strode onto the patio and demanded, "What happened?"

"I spilled the beans. About Rowan. I had to! Mom and Nancy knew something was up and Mom was going nuts and—"

"Just once, I wish you were as good an actress offstage as you are on."

"Tell me about it."

"How's Alison?"

"Tickled pink." I dropped the sarcasm and gave Janet the highlights, adding, "I'll have to go to the cottage tomorrow morning and fetch Rowan. Unless . . . could you call him?"

"Call him?"

"You know. The way you . . . communicate with each other."

"On our magic faery phones?"

"Well, I don't know how it works!"

"Not like that."

"Then I'll go—"

"No. I will. Someone has to stay with Jack."

"Right. God. I'm sorry I made a mess of things."

"Please. This barely rates a "three" in the long list of Crossroads Theatre crises. Come on. Reinhard's hair will be standing on end."

As we hurried down the hill, I admitted, "I know this

wasn't what we planned, but I'm glad it's all out in the open with Mom."

"Except the part about her traumatized ex-husband camping out in the woods with your faery lover who rescued him from shapeshifters in the Borderlands."

"Yeah. Except that part."

CHAPTER 16
RUNNING IN PLACE

THE NEXT MORNING, ROWAN WAS WAITING for us in the picnic area. He must have ducked into the apartment for a quick shower, because his hair was still damp. As my mother scrutinized him, I realized that his eyes were their usual green instead of the muddy hazel his Fae glamour had made them appear at their first meeting.

Did he think she'd be too pissed off to notice? Or hope that the passage of time had dimmed her memory? He could always claim that he'd gotten contact lenses, but it wasn't like him to be so careless. He must have wanted her to see him as he truly was.

As they nodded to each other, I jumped in to introduce Chris, adding, "He's a lawyer. And Mom's ... um ... gentleman friend."

"I trust you're not here in a professional capacity," Rowan said, shaking Chris' hand.

"I think I'm the designated referee."

"Don't be silly," I lied. "You're practically a member of the family."

"A position I have not yet achieved," Rowan said.

"No," my mother replied. "Since Chris has been part of our lives for the last two years, while you were—"

"In absentia. Yes. Shall we sit?" Rowan gestured to a picnic table. "Or we can go up to my apartment if you prefer."

138

"No. Let's just get this over with."

"Mom . . ."

"Maggie says she loves you, Mr. Mackenzie. And that you love her. While that might reassure her, it's not good enough for me. You hurt her deeply when you left. More deeply than I think you realize."

"It was a painful decision. For both of us."

"And now you realize it was a mistake?"

"No. It was the right decision. At the time. But people change, Mrs. Graham."

"Some do. Others suffer disappointments and scurry back to familiar places—and familiar people."

Rowan stiffened. "If you're implying that I came back because I was afraid no one else would have me—"

"I'm saying that if you're not in this for the long haul, it would be kinder to walk away now, instead of putting Maggie through that pain again."

"You're asking for guarantees that neither Maggie nor I can give you. I can only tell you what I told the staff: I love Maggie. I want to build a life with her. And I will do everything in my power to make her happy."

"It takes more than love to keep a relationship going. It takes hard work and commitment. If you're going to run at the first sign of trouble—"

"I am not Jack Sinclair."

Mom's breath hissed in.

"When I make a commitment, I stick to it. And I'm sticking to Maggie. I realize I've given you little reason to trust me. And I'll do my best to change that. But please understand that neither your distrust nor your lectures will drive me away. They will only create a deeper rift between us and make your daughter miserable. So I suggest we keep a respectful distance and allow Maggie to decide if I am the right man for her."

Their eyes locked in a challenging stare. Chris and I watched them anxiously, heads swiveling back and forth like spectators at a particularly lethal tennis match.

"Fine," Mom snapped. "Is there anything else?"

"Just this."

Rowan reached into the back pocket of his jeans and held out a silver spoon.

My mother's face underwent several rapid changes of expression before settling back into a frown.

"A teaspoon?" she inquired. "After that speech, I expected a gravy ladle."

"I didn't want to appear boastful."

Instead of smiling, she merely plucked the spoon from his fingers.

"The entire staff is looking out for Maggie. And if I screw this up, they'll all be lining up for a piece of me. But I promise you'll get first crack."

"I'll hold you to that." She favored me with a radiant smile. "It was a wonderful show, Maggie. No one could have done a better job."

With that final dig at Rowan, she turned on her heel and marched toward the parking lot.

"Hang in there," Chris said as he shook Rowan's hand. "Graham women are a tough sell."

"I know. I'm in love with one, too."

❦

Mom's hug was longer than usual, but all she said was, "If you need anything, call."

I waved until the car crested the lane, then walked back to Rowan.

"I'm beginning to feel I should pin a sign on my chest: 'Did not come back to hurt Maggie.'"

"The staff never said—"

"No. But they're as worried as your mother. And with the exception of Hal and Catherine, they've allowed me to stay out of a sense of duty—and because they love you too much to turn me away."

"That's not true," I protested.

"Do *you* think I'll hurt you again? Or walk out?"

"You promised you wouldn't walk out. That's good

enough for me. As for being afraid you'll hurt me . . . it's more of a generalized terror."

"Well, now I feel better."

"Hey, it's hard enough for humans to build a lasting relationship, never mind a human and a Fae. And I've never been good at the 'one day at a time' thing. I want to fast forward to the happy ever after."

"You want the Act One finale of *Into the Woods*."

"Who wouldn't? Happy ending. Journey over. Yadda, yadda."

"The journey's never over," Rowan assured me solemnly.

"I know. It's one of the more annoying things about life. And if you give me any crap about what a wonderful adventure it is, I'm going to punch you."

"How about the discoveries we can make about ourselves along the way?"

I punched him. He grinned. I grinned back. Then I noticed his bulging knapsack sitting atop one of the picnic tables.

As I struggled to quell the blind rush of panic, Rowan said, "I think Jack and I need a few more days at the cottage. He's too easily distracted here. When he heard the pit band Thursday night, it was all I could do to keep him from running down to the stage."

"But after today's matinee, there won't be a show again until Wednesday. If you bring him back this evening—"

"It will be less distracting for me, too," he said with a smile.

For a moment, I basked in my distracting Aphrodite sensuality. Then my inner Athena yanked me down to earth.

"You don't want me around while you're brainwashing Daddy."

"I hate that word."

"So do I! But whether we call it brainwashing or helping Daddy heal, it still amounts to wiping out his memories."

"I might be able to banish some of his memories, but not years of his life. Even if my power were strong enough, I wouldn't risk it. I might damage him forever."

"Then what are you going to do?"

"After he encountered my clan, I took the memories from him, as much to protect myself as him. This time, he deserves to choose. And to understand the role he'll have to play if he's going to live with his memories. Maybe it will help him to think of it that way—preparing for yet another role. But his performance will have to be believable enough to convince everyone. Especially your mother."

"Maybe he just wants to forget the Borderlands."

"The bad experiences, perhaps. But some of it was beautiful. And all of it was magical. He spent half his life looking for that magic. Do you really think he'll give it up?"

"Why can't he be content with *this* world?"

I sounded like a petulant child. Next I'd be exclaiming, "I want my Daddy back!" But I *did* want my Daddy back, even though I knew that was impossible.

"He's a restless soul, Maggie. I can't change his nature."

"I know. I just want . . ."

Everything to be the way it was when I was a child.

"Tell me," Rowan urged.

I sighed. "I want you to blow some fairy dust on him and make everything perfect. And then we can all fly away to Never Never Land."

When Rowan's lips puckered, I thought he really *might* blow fairy dust over me. Instead, he kissed me gently on the forehead, then drew me into his arms.

Calm washed over me and with it, his reassurance that even if he couldn't make everything perfect, we would face whatever happened together.

"Better?" he asked as he stepped back.

"Better. But . . ."

"What?"

"How's Daddy supposed to find his place in the world if he's hiding out in the woods?"

"It's only for a week."

"Squatting in the leaves. Living off roots and berries."

"I'd hardly describe cold chicken and endive salad as living off roots and berries."

"You can't keep food fresh for a week out in the wilderness."

"It's two miles away! And we have plenty of packaged food to—"

"Cold, fresh milk," I crooned. "Red, ripe strawberries."

"Get thee behind me, Satan."

I offered a winsome, satanic smile. Rowan threw up his hands in surrender. Then he held up a warning finger. "You have to promise to give us a few days alone."

"Absolutely."

"No popping up after rehearsal or dropping in for dinner."

"What about 'absolutely' didn't you understand?"

"I know you."

"Oh, please. I barge into your apartment one time—"

"Maggie . . ."

"I won't pop or drop. Promise."

We shook hands as we used to do to solemnize one of our pacts. And I resigned myself to spending more time apart from the men I loved.

CHAPTER 17

IT'S A HELLUVA WAY TO RUN A LOVE AFFAIR

ON THE PLUS SIDE, MY PERIOD ARRIVED the day they went into seclusion. That would spare us a reprise of the icky blood thing for another month. And give me time to pick up a box of condoms.

Like we're really going to make love when my father's in the next room listening to me yowl like a cat in heat.

I thrust that depressing thought aside and focused on more immediate concerns.

On Sunday evening, Frannie and I hosted a reception at the Bough so that the newly arrived cast members could meet the rest of the company before rehearsals for *The Secret Garden* began. To our relief, everybody seemed to have a good time and the reception was relatively clump-free.

I remained cautiously optimistic after Monday's read-through. Gregory might look more like a linebacker than my idealized version of tormented Archibald Craven, but he had angst up the wazoo. And as Reinhard sternly reminded me, "There is no rule that says you must be gaunt to be grief-stricken."

Or to play a ghost. Hal was still grumbling about casting a zaftig Mackenzie descendant as Lily. I sternly reminded him that while Michaela might not be ethereal, her lovely soprano was. But she was shy and awkward, lacking the serenity that Lily required, and I was glad to see Otis reassuring her during the break.

In the largely thankless role of Neville Craven, Roger was a tad too queeny to convince anyone that he had ever pined for his brother's wife, but if toning him down was the biggest battle I faced during the next three weeks, I'd be a happy camper.

The supporting cast—largely locals and Mackenzies—had a pretty good grasp on their characters and a decidedly shaky one on their accents. A few managed a decent "stage British," but it was hard to keep a straight face when the rest trotted out their "Yorkshire" accents.

"I don't know why I bothered making those damn recordings," Janet fumed.

"I'm sure they helped," I said. "How did *you* master the Yorkshire accent?"

"I listened to the goddamn CD! Maybe they should try it."

I refrained from mentioning that they had. As for the sections in Hindi, I just prayed they wouldn't sound ridiculous, a tall order with lyrics like "mantra, tantra, yantra."

Otis had agreed to take on the role Bill had abandoned. He played one of the Dreamers—the ghosts who drift in and out to comment on the past and try to help those in the present. Debra was back to torment a fresh crop of children as the stern housekeeper Mrs. Medlock.

"It's my Wicked Witch summer," she commented after the read-through.

Since her third role was the Witch in *Into the Woods*, there seemed little point in denying it. "Don't take it personally."

"Are you kidding? It's a helluva lot more fun playing nasty than nice. I had a ball when I played the Stepmother in *Into the Woods* a few years ago."

"Who wouldn't enjoy sawing off bits of her daughters' feet so they would fit into the golden slipper?"

"Exactly."

"If we ever put on *Psycho: The Musical*, I'll know who to call."

"Now *that's* what you should do to bring in money during the off-season. Not *Psycho*. One of those murder mystery dinners." She jerked her thumb toward the Bates mansion. "You've already got the House on Haunted Hill."

It would be perfect for Halloween. If the board would approve it. If Janet would go for yet another event in her home. And if I could pull it together, run the after-school program, and prepare for our Christmas production.

Think about it tomorrow, Scarlett.

I concentrated on blocking the Act One scenes with the principals and left the chorus in Alex's capable hands. He got dibs on the kids as well. Although Sallie and Natasha were veterans of various school productions, Mary's songs were difficult emotionally and vocally, often requiring the actress to hold her melody line against two or three competing voices. Colin's material was easier, but neither of my ten-year-old actors were great singers. Having only an hour a day to block the children's scenes made me anxious, but the extra week in *Annie*'s run meant an extra week of rehearsals, so I tried to avoid obsessing.

My "one day at a time" mantra did little to quell my anxiety about what was happening in Rowan's apartment. The two men were as ghostly as Dreamers. Not even a footstep overhead betrayed their presence.

I was true to my promise. I didn't pop or drop. I just lurked.

I took casual strolls around the barn during my breaks, craning my neck for a glimpse of their figures through the windows. I dropped off groceries and hovered at the door, hoping to detect some sound from inside.

"You must have patience," Reinhard ordered.

"You've got to let Rowan do his thing," Lee advised.

"You're creeping me out," Hal complained. "Maggie Graham, Stalker."

Rowan's letter put a stop to my not-so-clandestine

surveillance. He must have slipped it under the front door because Janet handed it to me when I came down for breakfast Thursday morning. I tore open the envelope with trembling fingers.

"I know you're anxious," he began without preamble, "but we are both fine and the work is going well. And although I can think of no one I would rather have pressing an ear to my door, you are hereby forbidden to lurk. I love you."

Not quite as romantic as the first letter he had written me, but it left me with a warm glow that survived Neil's disappointingly stilted performance as Dickon and Roger's inability to keep his hands off Gregory during the library scene.

Then we blocked the opening. Exit warm glow. Enter queasiness.

The music was difficult enough, but the staging was a bitch. It had to take the audience from India to a train platform to the door of Misselthwaite Manor to Mary's room to the gallery where Mary searches for the source of the mysterious crying while her uncle prowls around looking for the ghost of his dead wife. And like all the scenes with the Dreamers, the action had to flow seamlessly—song fragments interwoven with dialogue, Dreamers drifting in and out, past incidents mingling with those in the present.

I'd recognized early on that I would need Mei-Yin's help to stage the Dreamers' scenes. When she cheerfully agreed, I was surprised and excited. I was equally surprised—but far less excited—when she stormed into my office last February, brandishing a rolled-up script in one meaty fist, and demanded, "Where are the DANCE numbers?"

"There's a lot of dancing," I'd protested. "The opening is a—"

"A CHOLERA epidemic! With people passing around a red HANDKERCHIEF."

"It's a metaphor."

"I KNOW it's a metaphor! I'm not STUPID! And it's NOT a DANCE."

"Well, if you think about it, all the scenes with the Dreamers are like a ritualized—"

"I mean REAL dances."

"There's the waltz in the ballroom. And 'Come Spirit, Come Charm.'"

"With actors chanting HINDI? I TOLD you we should do *Gypsy*. THAT has kids. THAT has a STRIP-TEASE. THAT I can choreograph."

"Mei-Yin. Did you . . . read the script?"

"Of COURSE I did! I read it last NIGHT!"

"I mean before we chose the show."

"It was ROWAN'S job to choose the shows! And HE chose NORMAL ones where the chorus sings a big SONG, the actors WITHOUT two left feet break into a big DANCE, and the audience breaks into big AP-PLAUSE! THIS . . ." She flung the script across the room. "I don't know WHAT this is."

Moments after she marched out of the office, Rein-hard scuttled in.

"She will be fine," he assured me in a hoarse whisper. "Trust me. She will view the show as a challenge. It will excite her artistic sensibilities."

"Any idea how long that'll take?"

"A day. Maybe two. No more than a week. In the meantime . . ."

"I'll stay out of her way."

Three days later, Mei-Yin breezed into the staff meet-ing and announced, "Sometimes, I'm so good, it's SCARY! I got it all figured out. Even the goddamn STORM sequences." She stabbed her forefinger at Hal. "I'll need a KICKASS set. And some KICKASS lighting, too!" she added, redirecting the forefinger to Lee. "So you boys better put on your THINKING caps."

Hal contented himself with an offended sniff. Lee just nodded wearily. Reinhard beamed. "Now the work can begin!"

To Mei-Yin's credit, her staging *was* good. Better than anything I could have dreamed up. Since I'd endured her rants when I was an actress and her regular pleas to shoot her since I'd become a director, I remained undaunted by the prospect of working cheek by jowl with her.

I woefully miscalculated the discomfort of having my cheek adjacent to Mei-Yin's jowl. Hence, the queasiness that shuddered through my stomach as we staged the opening.

"You're GHOSTS!" she shouted after our first walk-through. "Not CONSTRUCTION workers! WAFT more, CLOMP less!"

"WAFT!" she shrieked after the second walk-through. "Not MINCE! You're GHOSTS, not CHORUS queens!"

She stormed out of the Smokehouse with Reinhard in hot pursuit. I hastily called a break. After peering outside to make sure Mei-Yin had left the vicinity, the actors dispersed.

Through the open windows, I heard someone ask, "Is she always like that?"

I couldn't identify the hushed voice, but it obviously belonged to one of the new members of the company.

"She's just getting warmed up," Debra replied.

"You should've heard her when she was teaching me to waltz," Otis said. "'ONE-two-three. ONE-two ... LEFT foot! LEFT! How many left feet you GOT?'"

"Does she get ... nicer?" asked another unfamiliar voice.

"Not much," Debra replied cheerfully. "But you'll get used to her. Eventually."

Someone groaned. "I hope I live that long."

I trudged over to the piano where Alex was trying to keep a straight face.

"Easy for you," I grumbled. "She's not shouting in your ear."

"You just haven't seen her in action since you began directing."

Actually, I had. I'd made damn sure to sit in on her first rehearsals with the orphans. She wasn't exactly warm and fuzzy, but she *had* been encouraging. The strain of storing up so much unused bile was clearly showing now.

"Maybe it bugs you that you need her help with the staging," Alex said. "But you know what? She's having the time of her life. I can't remember when she's been this excited. And it's because you've given her more of an opportunity to shape this show than she's ever had before. Mind you, she'll never admit that. And you'll probably be deaf by opening night. But it's true."

I leaned down to kiss his forehead. "You know I'm crazy about you, right?"

"No, but if you hum a few bars . . ."

Reinhard appeared in the doorway, smoothing his troubled hair. He shot us a quick glance and nodded.

As the actors filtered in, Alex whispered, "I give her two more minutes. Then she'll sail into the Smoke-house—"

"And be sweet as pie."

Right on both counts. After the actors stumbled through the scene a third time, she regarded them with a maternal smile and purred, "Now that wasn't so hard, was it?"

Debra nudged Otis. He grinned. I made a mental note to pick up a very large bottle of antacids on my next shopping trip.

The Dreamers clomped, minced, and wafted. Mei-Yin ranted, raved, and purred. I gobbled Rolaids like breath mints and slipped a note under Rowan's door that accentuated the positive and pointed out that note-slipping didn't technically qualify as lurking. He slipped a note under Janet's door that assured me of his love and remarked that if I ever changed careers, I should consider becoming a lawyer.

"This is turning into Abelard and Heloise," Janet muttered.

"Don't be silly," I replied. Then rushed upstairs to search Wikipedia for Abelard and Heloise. I remembered their passionate correspondence. I'd forgotten the parts where he got her pregnant, her father castrated him, and they were both consigned to religious orders.

Given our enforced chastity and my mother's penchant for threatening Rowan's testicles, the similarities were depressing. I didn't even have erotic letters to fall back on. Rowan's latest note had included a brief protestation of love and a much longer list of grocery items. It's hard to whip up sexual fantasies with ingredients like lamb chops and orzo.

Since there was no immediate prospect of fulfilling any sexual fantasies, maybe that was a good thing. But I felt adrift and blue. A loverless lover, a fatherless daughter, and—in spite of Alex's pep talk—a rudderless director who needed help staging her show.

Hal was sympathetic, Janet, practical. My mother avoided any mention of Rowan during our usual Sunday morning phone chat. By contrast, Nancy called three times that week to see how things were going. On Sunday evening, I broke down and told her about my father.

She said, "Oh, my God!" about twenty times. In between, she asked how I was, how Daddy was, and then added, "How did Rowan ever find him?"

Let the lying begin.

"Daddy wrote a letter. To Rowan's father."

The imaginary one we made up two summers ago.

"It took awhile for the letter to reach Rowan."

You know how unreliable the Faerie postal service is.

"By then, Daddy had moved on and it took forever to track him down."

Since those pesky maps of the Borderlands shift as often as the landscape.

"And Rowan didn't want to tell you he was looking

for him," Nancy said. "And raise your hopes. Is he going
to be okay? Your dad?"

"He's getting better every day."

"He must have been so excited to see you."

I hesitated.

"Well, wasn't he?"

"I haven't told him that I'm his daughter. I want to
give him time to settle in."

"What did your mom say?" When I hesitated again,
Nancy's sigh gusted through the phone. "Oh, Maggie . . ."

"I'm going to tell her. When he's more like his old
self."

"Oh, Maggie . . ."

"Stop saying, 'Oh, Maggie!' "

"Look how fast she figured out something was wrong
at the fund-raiser. Never mind tracking you down two
summers ago. The woman's a bloodhound!"

"I know, I know . . ."

By the time I hung up the phone, I'd hit the trifecta of
guilt, depression, and loneliness. I slipped out of the
house and wandered down to the pond. Too far from the
theatre to qualify as lurking, but close enough to feel
connected to the men inside.

The pale rectangles of light on the barn's roof cheered
me; at least Daddy was no longer hiding from "the eyes."
I sat on one of the benches, imagining them finishing
their lamb chops and orzo, enjoying ice cream and strawberries, relaxing on the sofa.

As twilight faded into dusk, the skylights deepened to
gold. As if to complement them, tiny flashes of light
drifted through the meadow—the fireflies beginning
their mating dance. I half-expected the staff to emerge
from the trees as they always did in my dream. Instead,
the breeze freshened, carrying the scent of rain, and I
reluctantly rose.

As I reached the picnic area, I caught the faint notes
of a piano and the answering strum of a guitar. When I
recognized the melody, I sank down on a picnic bench.

I had heard "Try to Remember" dozens of times last season. Tonight, the song seemed even more poignant and bittersweet, the simple words evoking thoughts of my father's youth when he was as green and tender as the grass, and love was just beginning to blossom.

At first, Daddy merely echoed "Follow, follow, follow" in a sweet but tentative baritone. But on the final verse, he took the melody, his voice gaining power as he sang of wounded hearts that could be healed and cold Decembers warmed by memories.

In the long silence after the song ended, I wondered if he was recalling the bright promise of his youth or his lost dreams and lost family. Could Rowan heal the wounds that had gnawed at his heart and spirit for so many years? Could I?

Still aching from their song, I was shocked by the sound of Daddy's laughter. A moment later, Rowan launched into "You're Getting to Be a Habit with Me." Daddy interrupted him halfway through the first verse with "You Do Something to Me."

The singing quickly escalated into a contest. Rowan sang "You Could Drive a Person Crazy." Daddy broke in with "Let's Call the Whole Thing Off." Rowan advised Daddy to "Take It on the Chin" and Daddy demanded that he "Put On a Happy Face." They "lahdle-ahdle-ahdled" their way through "Friendship" and "doodle-oodle-oodled" their way through "A Bushel and a Peck." Then Rowan warbled "We Are Dainty Little Fairies" and the contest ended in exuberant laughter.

My father sounded so happy, so . . . normal. No longer babbling show tunes in an effort to cling to sanity, but singing and clowning for the sheer joy of it. If only I could find a way to sustain that happiness.

And then I thought of the Follies. Why not invite Rowan and Daddy to join our annual evening of staff silliness? It would ease them both into the world of the Crossroads and give them something fun to anticipate.

I was so excited that I failed to notice that Rowan had

begun playing again. When I recognized "Some Enchanted Evening," I smiled. And when Rowan imitated my mocking delivery from auditions, I knew he was singing to me.

I should have realized he would sense my presence; maybe he had even called me from the house, knowing that sharing my father's happiness would ease my anxieties more than any note. Now he was offering another gift: the song we had shared at our first meeting.

As he continued singing, the mockery vanished, replaced by the quiet surprise of hearing laughter across a crowded room, the unexpected joy of discovering that same laughter in his dreams, the wonder of realizing that something impossible was happening.

His voice resonated with the passion we had shared, the pain of our separation, and the love that had brought him back to me. Our whole relationship captured in a song I had chosen on the spur of the moment, a song I had once dismissed as overblown and sappy, a song that became a reaffirmation of his vow never to leave me.

The final note faded. One by one, the golden rectangles of light winked out. A rumble of thunder urged me back to the house, but still, I lingered.

I felt more than saw him on the balcony outside his bedroom. His power embraced me and offered yet another promise: that tomorrow, we would be together again.

Ignoring the raindrops spattering my face, I skipped along the walkway singing "A Wonderful Guy." Rowan's affection and amusement bubbled through me like champagne.

So what if it wasn't the moon-happy night of Oscar Hammerstein's lyrics? I still had a conventional star in my eye and a definite lump in my throat.

CHAPTER 18
DON'T LET IT GET YOU DOWN

ROWAN WAS WAITING OUTSIDE THE BARN the next morning, his energy zinging with the same excitement I felt. He swept me up in his arms and spun me around. We were both breathless and laughing when he set me on my feet again.

My laughter died when I saw his eyes, a dull gray-green instead of vivid emerald.

"My God, what happened?"

"I had to use more of my power than I'd anticipated. To calm him," he quickly added, "not to brainwash him. He's stronger than he was, but his moods are still . . . unpredictable."

I cupped Rowan's cheeks between my palms, as if I could somehow restore the power that had been drained from him, and was rewarded by a smile.

"Spending the day with you is the best possible medicine."

"But . . . I have rehearsals all day."

His smile vanished. "On a Monday?"

"The *Annie* cast has the day off, but I'm working scenes for *The Secret Garden*."

"Well. There's still lunch."

"Staff meeting. But we could squeeze in a quick dinner."

His smile returned, but I knew how disappointed he must be.

"Why don't I print out a copy of the schedule? That way, we'll be able to make plans for the rest of the week."

He followed me into the barn. Every time I glanced back, his smile was firmly in place. I would have preferred if he'd bitched me out.

As we neared the production office, he said, "At least your evenings will be free."

"Some of them. But I have the show most nights."

"You don't have to attend every performance."

I stopped, frowning. "You did."

"I had to be there. In case anything went wrong."

"And I don't?"

He hesitated, clearly searching for the right words.

"Look, I may not have the faery magic to avert a train wreck, but at least I can be there while my cast deals with the derailment. And laugh with them later about how Jeff turned a runaway inner tube into a moment of comic genius. And how two of the Hooverville residents pulled the newspapers out of their shirts to clean up when Fifi took a dump onstage!"

"One of your actors defecated on—?"

"The dog, Rowan! Fifi's the dog!"

"Ah."

"Sometimes humans need to work stuff out for themselves."

"If I didn't realize that, I would have told you why I cast you the first day we met."

"I know! It's just . . . I need to be there. To be part of whatever happens. The way you were part of that day with Maya and Gary."

His expression softened at the memory of that completely human moment of magic that had occurred during a disastrous rehearsal of *The Sea-Wife*.

"I'm afraid you're in love with a selfish pig," he said, "instead of a wonderful guy."

"Shut up and kiss me."

He shut up and kissed me.

When we came up for air, I murmured, "I suppose I could skip one show."

That was all the encouragement he needed. His long, lingering kiss sent a little shock wave of desire rippling through my body.

"Mmm . . . maybe two."

Golden sparks flashed in his eyes. Was it my imagination or were they greener than they had been a few moments ago? He kissed me again and I forgot about his eyes. I forgot about pretty much everything except his teasing tongue and his hands sliding up under my T-shirt and his body molded to mine.

When he suddenly released me, I clung to him, dizzy and dazed. Then I heard Daddy calling Rowan's name. I was still smoothing my shirt when he rounded the corner.

He'd shaved off his scraggly beard and mustache. Without them, his jaw and neck looked pale and oddly vulnerable. But for the first time, he looked like my father.

"Where were you?" he demanded. "I've been calling and calling."

"I told you I was going outside to meet Maggie."

"You were gone a long time." He studied us for a moment, then grinned. "Someone's been making out," he chanted in a singsong voice.

"Someone would have made out much better if you had remained in the apartment," Rowan replied.

"Look at Maggie blush! Her face is as red as a tomato!"

Since the floor showed no inclination to swallow me, I quickly asked, "How are you, Jack?"

Daddy's expression grew solemn. "Well, I won't lie to you. I went through some bad times. Drugs, alcohol, you name it. But a few years ago, I finally got my shit together. Even started acting again. I was—"

"Jack," Rowan interrupted. "Maggie knows the truth. You don't have to put on an act for her."

"But it was a good act, wasn't it?"

"Very good," I assured him, still a little stunned by his recitation. "Very ... believable."

"I added the part about getting my shit together. It sounded more natural than what Rowan wanted me to say."

"That was an especially nice touch."

"And don't I look good without the beard?"

"You look ten years younger."

"I smell good, too."

He stuck out his chin, and I obediently sniffed. The rush of emotion as I breathed in the familiar scent caught me unprepared.

"Don't you like it?" Daddy asked.

"It's my favorite," I managed.

"See, Rowan? You should have used some."

"I don't shave."

"Yeah, but still ..." Daddy winked at me and crooned, "'There's something about an Aqua Velva man.'"

"Yes, there is," I agreed. "I'm so glad you're feeling better. And that you're not worried about 'the eyes' or the Crow-Men or—"

"I don't want to talk about them!"

As I recoiled at his unexpected outburst, Rowan snapped, "Jack! You don't respond to concern with rudeness."

Daddy flinched. "I just ... I don't like thinking about them."

I nodded, silently cursing myself for spoiling his happy mood.

"Let's talk about something fun," he said. "Like our picnic. Rowan's been cooking all morning ..." He glanced uncertainly from me to Rowan. "What? Did I blow the surprise?"

No, I did.

"I'm afraid I'll have to skip the picnic. I have a meeting at lunchtime and—"

"Just cancel it," Daddy said with an airy wave of his hand.

"I can't. But we could pack up Rowan's food and take it to the picnic area for dinner."

His crestfallen expression made it clear that was a poor substitute. As I groped for a solution, inspiration struck.

"Why don't we have our picnic on the Fourth of July? The theatre's dark so everyone can go to the fireworks at the high school."

"I love fireworks!" Daddy exclaimed.

Wilmington's display had always been the highlight of the summer, both of us in such a fever of anticipation that we hardly tasted the food my poor mother prepared. I loved the brilliant colors and screamed with excitement at every big "boom." It took me so many hours to calm down afterward that Mom threatened each year would be the last. And each year, he wheedled her into attending again.

"Just think, Rowan. Your first time in town and we'll have fireworks to celebrate. It's perfect!"

His dubious expression suggested otherwise. "Are you sure you're ready for this, Jack?"

"Yes! I'm sick of being stuck in that stuffy old apartment. I want to get out and see things. And eat some real food. Not that fancy-schmancy stuff you cook."

"What is so 'fancy-schmancy' about pepper-crusted grilled tuna with basmati rice and a frisée and pear salad?"

Daddy and I exchanged glances and started laughing.

"Tell you what," I told Daddy. "After I print out the rehearsal schedule for Rowan, we'll set a date for lunch at the Chatterbox Café."

"The Chatterbox is still here? Man, I'd kill for one of their chocolate shakes. And a burger. And fries!"

Smiling at his enthusiasm, I unlocked the office door. As it swung open, I glanced at Rowan to gauge his reaction to the changes. He hadn't said a word about the green room. Could he possibly miss those awful furnishings? Maybe if I'd lived with them for decades, I'd feel nostalgic, too.

His expression was completely neutral as he took in the new desk and the landline phone. Then two small furrows appeared between his brows. I realized he was frowning at the laptop. His laptop.

"I'm sorry. I meant to tell you we were using it. Reinhard found it in your armoire. And since we needed a computer for the office—"

"Of course."

"I'll just use mine. It's no big deal to carry it back and forth from the house."

"No, keep this one. At least until the season's over. I only used it to watch movies."

"What are you talking about?" Daddy demanded.

Frantically, I tried to recall whether we'd had a personal computer when he lived in Wilmington. If so, it would have looked nothing like the laptop. Would he freak out if I showed him its features—or guess that it had required decades to invent them?

"What computer?" Daddy insisted.

I gave the laptop a tentative pat.

"That's a computer? I thought it was a hot plate!"

Relieved by his reaction, I said, "They'll probably add that feature to the next model."

"But where's the screen? And the keyboard?"

I opened the laptop, and he gasped. When the wallpaper came up with its photo of Stonehenge, he gasped again.

"I was there. I saw that. What are all the little pictures around it?"

"You click on them to open the program you want."

"Wait—the stuff at the bottom just disappeared."

"It'll come back if you move the arrow down there."

As I skimmed my fingertip over the touchpad to demonstrate, he said, "Let me try."

Still dazed by his enthusiastic acceptance of all the technological changes, I eased aside. Finally, I could do something for him besides buying clothes and food.

He guided the arrow along the icons at the bottom, crowing with delight each time a descriptor popped up.

I smiled at Rowan. "It might take a little while to print out that schedule."

Rowan tensed. At first, I thought he was upset with me. Then I realized Daddy had fallen silent.

He was staring at the screen. In the bottom right-hand corner I saw a tiny beige pop-up field with the day of the week, the month, the date—and the year.

Oh, God . . .

Rowan gripped Daddy's shoulder. Daddy shook him off impatiently and pointed a trembling forefinger at the screen. "Is that the year? Is that *this* year?"

As I nodded miserably, Rowan steered Daddy over to the wooden chair near the file cabinet and eased him onto it.

"Twenty years," Daddy whispered. "I thought five, maybe. Ten at the most." His gaze slowly focused, and he glared at Rowan. "Why didn't you tell me?"

"I thought it might be . . . unsettling."

"No shit, Sherlock!"

When Rowan's hand settled on his shoulder again, Daddy leaped up with such violence that his chair toppled over. "Stop calming me! Just for once, let me *feel*!"

He backed into the file cabinet. Then the anger left his face and he slowly slid down its smooth wooden side and sank onto the floor.

Stupid, stupid, stupid!

Reinhard and I had gone through the theatre, taking down wall calendars, dated notices, anything that might set Daddy off. The rest of the staff had been warned to keep their organizers and datebooks under wraps. But I had been so eager to prove how knowledgeable I was that I'd forgotten the fucking date popped up when you passed the arrow over the time.

Daddy's shoulders began to shake. Only when he looked up did I realize he was laughing. A hoarse croak of a laugh, but not the tears I had expected.

"Twenty years. And except for that . . ." He nodded at the laptop. ". . . everything looks the same."

"Communications technology changes very quickly," explained Rowan, who didn't even have a phone in his apartment.

"What else has changed?"

This time, Rowan deferred to me. "There are mobile phones now that fit into the palm of your hand. And flat screen TVs. And something called the Internet. It's this big global network . . . thing. You can send messages and watch movies and order stuff from stores and play interactive games and—"

"Show me."

I spent the next hour teaching him the basics and conducting a whirlwind tour of the last twenty years. Daddy hurled questions at me and I fumbled for answers, painfully aware that I knew more about Tony Award winners than the events that had shaped and shaken my world.

"A black dude?" he exclaimed. "Was elected President?"

"Mixed race, but—"

"Next you'll be telling me Arnold Schwarzenegger is Secretary of Defense."

"No. But he *was* Governor of California. And Jesse Ventura—the wrestler? He was Governor of Minnesota."

Daddy burst out laughing. Real laughter this time—the same exuberant bellow I'd heard last night.

"Jeez, when it comes to crazy, this world has the Borderlands beat by a mile."

At some point, Rowan left. I suppressed my guilt at ignoring him and vowed to make up for it at dinner.

With only minutes before rehearsal began, I said, "You know, you can find other things on the Internet. Old TV shows, old friends . . . family . . ."

My heart pounded like a rabbit's as he scrutinized the screen. Then his face lit up and he began to type.

"Over two million results!" he crowed.

He was so absorbed in his findings that he never even noticed when I walked out.

I'd hoped—no, I'd expected him to search for me or Mom. But after so many years apart from us, so many years without even knowing if we were alive, what was he most eager to find?

Ms. fucking Pac-Man.

❧❧

The best part about working with magical people is that you never have to tell them you're upset. It's also the worst part because you can't hide anything. My little ups and downs generally passed unnoticed, but any major emotional roller coaster drew them like bears to honey.

So naturally, just when I needed to ride out this roller coaster, Rowan, Reinhard, and Alex all converged on me in the stage right wings. And naturally, I took one look at my three bears and burst into tears.

They clustered around me, offering masculine comfort and soothing magic. When I explained what had happened, Alex suggested Daddy might have needed some sort of distraction after the shock of finding out how much time had passed. Reinhard observed that he was unready to deal with the guilt of deserting his family.

Rowan demanded, "So he searches for some woman instead?"

I had to laugh. Alex joined me. Even Reinhard's lips twitched as he enlightened Rowan about arcade games and the true identity of Ms. Pac-Man.

The unexpected laughter eased the pain a little. Blocking Scene 4 forced me to focus on something else. By the time our staff meeting rolled around, I was able to turn the whole incident into an amusing anecdote. I didn't fool anyone, of course. Maybe that was why they agreed to invite Daddy to perform in the Follies.

After the meeting, I pulled the box containing Rowan's keepsakes out of my bedroom closet. It was the first time I had opened it in more than a year.

I set aside his script of *By Iron, Bound*, his battered copy of the 1836 edition of the *McGuffey Reader*, and the equally battered diary in which he'd recorded his first thoughts and feelings. Then I unearthed the slim leather-bound journal he had kept during my season at the Crossroads. I flipped through the pages until I found the passage I was seeking.

"Jack Sinclair. Now there's a pathetic imitation of a man. Charming, yes. And clever. About everything except himself. But completely self-absorbed. And arrogant and superior. Always making excuses for his failures."

Those bitter words filled my mind as I trudged up to Rowan's apartment after rehearsal. Daddy's enthusiastic greeting surprised me. I was even more surprised when he asked about my day.

I glanced at Rowan, wondering if he'd coached him. But Daddy seemed genuinely interested so I started talking about the show. He loved the idea of the magical garden and nodded thoughtfully when I explained its themes of healing and transformation. But he was more interested in the characters. At one point, he exclaimed, "I'd be great for Archibald!" And immediately began reminiscing about some of the roles he had played.

Rowan was very quiet during dinner. But as he walked me to my evening rehearsal, he said, "Be patient, Maggie. And don't expect more than he can give."

I nodded wearily. "Did you tell him to ask about my day?"

Rowan hesitated. "I told him he should have thanked you for teaching him. And that he should think more about other people's feelings."

"So should I."

"What do you mean?"

"I ignored you to show Daddy how to use the Internet. Like father, like daughter."

"Hush."

"I'm sorry."

This time, he hushed me with a kiss. Then he asked, "Did you ever read my journals?"

Surprised by the sudden shift in the conversation, I said, "The one from my year. And the early ones. But once people I knew began showing up . . . it just made me uncomfortable."

"Then you never read about your father's season here?"

I shook my head.

"Maybe you should."

I'd deliberately avoided reading that journal. I'd come to terms with my past—and my father—and saw little benefit in picking at those wounds. Daddy's return had pretty much ripped off the Band-Aid. So instead of going straight to my bedroom, I climbed the stairs to the attic.

Each spring, Hal and I sorted through the costumes and set pieces we might want to use during the upcoming season. The only other time I'd ventured there was when I'd helped Reinhard carry up the five boxes containing the rest of Rowan's journals.

I opened the door and groped for the light switch. A single naked bulb blazed to life over my head. I made out the shadowy forms of sheet-draped furniture. Garment bags hung like corpses from the rows of clothes racks. It looked much spookier at night than it had during the day and I was glad I didn't have to rummage around to find Rowan's journals; the boxes were only a few feet from the door, as carefully labeled as the boxes of props nestled under the eaves.

I opened the one on top and easily found the journal from Daddy's season, its first page inscribed with the year in Rowan's neat handwriting. As I straightened, I bashed my head against a slanting roof beam and got a faceful of cobweb.

Not an auspicious beginning.

I retreated to my bedroom, clutching the journal in my left hand and massaging the top of my head with my right. I sank into Helen's rocking chair and turned on the light, wishing for some of her calming energy. Then I took a deep breath and opened the journal.

I knew Daddy had arrived only days before Midsummer to begin rehearsals for the second show. Oddly, neither Rowan nor my mother had ever mentioned that it was *Camelot*. Now, I learned that he had played one of the knights defeated by Lancelot in the joust.

I skimmed the pages, seeking other references to Daddy, and winced when I found them.

"Jack was quite good at the read-through, but clearly disdainful of his cast mates."

"Jack took me aside to suggest that he take over the role of Arthur. The man has ballocks the size of basketballs and an ego to match. Yet underneath it all, his insecurity throbs like a heartbeat. He is so eager for me to like and respect him, but fails to see that his behavior accomplishes just the opposite. Still, these are early days. And my perceptions are always suspect at Midsummer."

I turned the page and braced myself for a description of Daddy's encounter with Rowan's clan. Instead, there was only a hastily scrawled word: *"Disaster."*

Ragged edges were all that remained of the next three pages. Perhaps Rowan had decided it was too dangerous to leave a record of the incident. The next entry—dated three days after Midsummer—said only: *"It is done. And if we watch him carefully, all may yet be well."*

Every entry for the rest of the season contained some snippet about my father. Reading between the lines of Rowan's cryptic entries, I pieced together his transformation from the dazed man who had rejoined the company to the hard-working one who enjoyed the fellowship of his cast mates and put so much of himself into the character of Billy Bigelow: the fear beneath the bravado; the doubts beneath the swagger; the desire to make amends to his wife and child.

Rowan's last entry for the season read:

"Met Jack's wife. I had hoped that seeing the show—and seeing how it has changed Jack—might reconcile her to his long absence. But she eyes both of us with suspicion, unable to accept his transformation and unwilling to exonerate me for luring him away.

Perhaps she's seen Jack's chameleon act too often to trust his latest incarnation. And perhaps she is wise. Whatever else I accomplished, I did not change Jack's nature. Once he leaves, his dissatisfaction with himself and his life might resurface.

I hope I'm wrong. Mostly for the child's sake. Such a pretty little thing, with that shining cap of bright red hair. And clearly her father's daughter. She was practically falling over from exhaustion until he appeared. Then her face lit up and she cried, "Daddy!" And from the look on his face and the way he swept her into his arms and spun around and around with her . . . yes, I think I'm right to hope.

If anyone can save Jack Sinclair from himself, his daughter can."

Fat chance. It was Rowan's magic that had brought him back from the brink of madness; Rowan's coaching that had helped him create a new persona. So far, all I'd done was reintroduce him to Ms. Pac-Man and promise him an evening of fireworks.

My father was as much a stranger as ever. He was my indulgent, imaginative playmate and the haunted, unpredictable stranger locked away in the basement. The "lost boy" my mother had loved and the restless, unhappy one that Rowan had known. In the last few days, I'd added new pieces to the puzzle: the terrified Rip Van Winkle; the impatient, demanding child; the charming Aqua Velva man.

How could I help my father find his place in this world when I didn't even know who he was?

I undressed and crawled into bed. Tired as I was, sleep eluded me. I tossed restlessly, beat my pillow into submission, and tossed some more.

I was reaching for the bedside lamp when warmth enfolded me. And with it, the fleeting sensation I'd experienced in Rowan's apartment of something caressing my cheek.

I breathed in the faint scent of lavender.

"Helen?" I whispered to the darkness.

The only reply was a deep peace that banished my anxiety and eased me gently into sleep.

CHAPTER 19
WHAT WOULD WE DO WITHOUT YOU?

A DAY OF LACKLUSTER REHEARSALS—during which Daddy remained glued to the laptop—eroded that peace. So did the prospect of our Act One run-through, which ranked about as high on the "Can't Wait!" meter as a Pap smear.

The kids would be fine. They'd been strong from the beginning and had only grown in confidence. Gregory had cornered the market on inner torment, Michaela on sweetness. But the chorus was having a tough time with the vocals, and in spite of Mei-Yin's hectoring, their scenes looked more like a bunch of lost travelers wandering through Grand Central than restless spirits wafting through Misselthwaite Manor.

And then there was Roger.

"He's turning Neville into an incestuous gay stalker," I complained to Hal and Lee as we bolted pizza in the green room before the run-through.

Lee grinned. "Not what you were going for?"

"Not so much."

"That's a relief. I thought it was some radical reinterpretation of the character."

"Too bad about 'Lily's Eyes,'" Hal said, nibbling a slice of pepperoni.

"The song is the one moment that works!"

"Yes, but if Neville didn't come right out and say he'd

been in love with Lily, the incestuous gay love angle might work."

"But it would still be icky."

"True."

Lee tossed aside his pizza crust and picked up another slice. "Have you told him Neville is too repressed for public displays of affection?"

"Yes."

"That everyone in the show is too repressed to—?"

"Yes, yes, yes! The weird thing is, he seems to get it. But once he's onstage, it's like he can't help himself. And now Gregory's started."

"Started what?" Hal asked.

"Touching Roger almost as much as Roger's touching him!"

Hal's face lit up. "Maybe Gregory's coming out of the closet!"

"Great. My father went home after his season, obsessed with faeries. Now Gregory's becoming obsessed with the theatrical kind."

"We have to be supportive," Hal chided. "This is a very difficult and confusing time for him. Oh, I hope he won't get his heart broken. Roger can be such a bitch."

"He's not coming out," Lee said. "I didn't get any of the usual signals."

"Gaydar or Faedar?" I asked.

"Either. There's something else going on."

"As long as it goes on offstage."

"And you call yourself a helping professional," Hal scolded.

"Right now, I'm calling myself a director. If Roger doesn't butch up soon, I'll have to have him play Lily."

"If only," Hal muttered.

"Don't you dare start on Michaela!" I exclaimed.

"I'm not! She's a sweetheart. It's just . . ." Hal sighed.

"I thought you of all people would be more sensitive."

Hal slowly lowered his glass of diet soda. "Why? Because I'm fat, too?"

"You're not—"

"I may have gained a few pounds over the winter—"

"You're not fat!"

"Then why did you say—?"

"Because you know what it's like to get bullied for being different. And you love dressing up in pretty things like she does. Only when she looks in the mirror, she doesn't see a beautiful woman with sexy curves. She sees a fat chick." I grabbed Hal's arm. "Could you push up her costume fittings? Maybe when she puts on one of those lovely dresses . . ."

"She'll see a fat chick in a lovely dress," Lee said.

"Not if I'm her mirror!" Hal declared. "She'll see in my eyes that she's beautiful. Who wouldn't be in a lavender silk ball gown with silver lace and sequin embroidery?"

Emboldened by his dreamy expression, I threw caution to the wind. "Maybe if she wore it tonight . . ."

"Absolutely not!" Hal exclaimed. "It's the most beautiful costume I've ever made and I'm not having it ruined before opening night."

"The more beautiful she feels, the more ethereal she'll look. Please?"

Hal heaved a dramatic sigh. "It'll have to be the coral chiffon garden dress. That's already been fitted. Or the white cotton-and-lace afternoon dress. No, that'll get filthy."

Still mulling possibilities, he hurried down the stairs to the costume shop. Lee snatched the last slice of pizza and headed for the lighting booth. I played housewife and cleaned up. Fortunately, that just meant rinsing our glasses and tossing out the pizza box.

I wound my way through the maze of *Annie* set pieces in the wings and dodged the first wave of actors hurrying toward the Dungeon to don character shoes, rehearsal skirts, and the few costume pieces Hal permitted them to wear before dress rehearsal. Reinhard—ever unwilling to trust them to sign in—stood guard by the stage left steps, checking off names on the call sheet attached to his clipboard.

His head came up, and he stared past me into the stage right wings. A moment later, I heard Rowan greeting Javier. The butterflies dancing in my stomach morphed into pterodactyls performing loop-de-loops. Of course, I wanted him and Daddy to see my work; I just wished their first exposure to it was a polished performance of *Annie*.

Reinhard gave me a reassuring nod, but the tension in his body betrayed his anxiety. No one on staff had objected to Rowan attending the run-through, but I wondered if they were as nervous as I was about his reaction.

Daddy walked out of the wings and glanced around warily, but if Rowan felt any discomfort at the prospect of seeing Maggie Graham, Director, it was well hidden behind his easy smile.

"We just wanted to wish you good luck," Rowan said.

Daddy stared at him, aghast. "It's bad luck to wish her good luck."

"That only applies to actors."

"No, it doesn't!"

"Just don't let Reinhard hear you," I said. "He'll want to perform a cleansing ritual."

"Hear what?" Reinhard called from across the stage. How he could detect my whispers and fail to hear Rowan speaking in normal tones was beyond me.

Before I could answer, Bernie called, "Rowan! About time you crawled out of that apartment!"

"That's Bernie," I whispered to Daddy as Rowan trotted down the steps. "He's on the board, but he helps out with the box office and program, too. He doesn't know anything about Faerie. We just told him the story you and Rowan came up with. Come on, I'll introduce you."

"Maybe later."

"He's a great guy. You'll like him."

Reluctantly, Daddy followed me into the house. Rowan and Bernie walked down the aisle, Bernie chat-

tering like an excited squirrel and Rowan smiling at him
with affection.

"Would it have killed you to age a little? I'm not asking for much. A couple lines around the eyes. A few gray
hairs. Something to prove you were miserable without
us."

"Trust me, Bernie, I was miserable."

"Good!" He smiled at Daddy. "Bernie Cohen. You
must be Jack. How does it feel to be back at the Crossroads?"

"Well, I won't lie to you. I went through some bad
times. Drugs, alcohol, you name it. But a few years ago, I
finally got my shit together. Even started acting again. I
was in between gigs and staying at a friend's cabin in the
mountains when I wrote to Rowan's dad, asking if he
had anything for me here. And who do you think shows
up at the door? Rowan! Hadn't seen him since he was a
kid. Well, you could have blown me away with a feather."

Clearly, his monologue was in danger of blowing Bernie away, too, but he recovered quickly and said, "Well,
it's great to have you here. Maggie tells me you're becoming quite the computer expert. If you feel like pitching in with the program, I'd love the help."

Before Daddy could reply, laughter rang out in the
house.

"Do my eyes deceive me," Long called, "or is that
Rowan Mackenzie?"

"Longford Martindale," I murmured to Daddy. "President of the board."

Daddy straightened. Rowan merely looked resigned.
I'd warned him that Long might be here tonight. No
matter how many times I begged him to wait until dress
rehearsal to see the show, he invariably "popped in" for
the run-throughs. The squirming usually began during
the first scene, and by the time we were finished, he was
convinced we had a disaster on our hands.

"This *is* a pleasure!" Long exclaimed as he shook
Rowan's hand. "Although not exactly a surprise. I always

suspected there was something between you two. And Maggie's blushes prove that my instincts were correct."

After favoring me with a brief leer, Long turned to Daddy, eyebrows elevated.

"This is Jack Sinclair," I said. "An old friend of Rowan's."

"Long Martindale. Delighted."

"Jack worked here years ago," Rowan said. "He played Billy Bigelow in *Carousel*."

"Why, of course!"

Hard to tell if he remembered or was just turning on the charm, but his enthusiasm made Daddy beam.

"What have you been doing since then, Jack?"

"Well, I won't lie to you. I went through some bad times—"

"But he's turned the corner in the last few years," Rowan interrupted. "Since he was between acting jobs, I invited him to spend a few weeks at the Crossroads."

"Wonderful! And what about you, Rowan? Are you just visiting? Or dare I hope that you'll be staying?"

"I hope to stay a very long while."

Rowan's warm gaze brought another wave of heat to my cheeks.

"Excellent! We must have dinner. We have a great deal to discuss. Maggie's been filling in as artistic director because of our precarious funding situation, but all that's changing. I'd love to get you back on board and free her up to focus on her responsibilities as executive director."

As he rambled on, my face grew even hotter. Was he actually suggesting that I step aside? In the middle of the fucking season? Maybe Rowan was a hundred times the director I was, but these were *my* shows.

Before I could vent my outrage, Rowan said, "There will be plenty of time to discuss next season after this one's over."

"Naturally, naturally. But you can't blame me for being eager when I see my dream team standing before me."

"Your dream team?" I faltered.

"Why, you and Rowan, of course! Normally, I'd be leery of hiring a couple. So much potential for professional difficulties if personal ones should arise. But the rest of the staff manages just fine. I'm beginning to think this theatre is the crossroads of romance!"

Sweat prickled my forehead as I realized how close I had come to going off the deep end, alienating Long, and making a complete fool of myself.

Long glanced at his watch. "Well, it's almost time. Let's take our seats, shall we?"

As he escorted my reluctant father up the aisle, Bernie whispered, "Don't worry about your dad. He just needs to get his sea legs. And I meant it about helping with the program. Get him involved, that's the ticket!"

I hugged him so hard that Rowan had to grasp his arm to steady him.

"Catherine and I usually sit behind Maggie," Bernie told Rowan. "We're the 'Pat Her Shoulders During the Train Wrecks' Brigade. But if you need me to keep Long out of your hair . . ."

"I'll manage," Rowan replied. "Besides, I'd hate to break up the brigade."

I waited for Bernie to make his way up the aisle before whispering to Rowan, "Thanks for jumping in with Long."

"Did you really believe he wanted to replace you?"

"He thinks I'm a novice."

"Well . . . you are."

"I know! But on opening night of *Annie*, he told me the show fell short of your high standards, so excuse me if I'm a little sensitive."

"Stop bristling."

"I'm not—"

"Yes, you are. And stop comparing yourself to me."

"I'm not—"

"Yes. You are."

I sighed. "Yes. I am."

"Maggie, I have more directing experience than Hal Prince, George Abbott, and Jerome Robbins combined. You could direct for the next fifty years and you'd still be a novice compared to me."

"I know that!"

"Lower your voice. Long's watching." Rowan studied me, frowning. "Why do you do this to yourself?"

"Because I know what it's like to work with you. And I want to give my actors that same magic."

"Well, you can't. You're not a faery. So give them your passion, your determination, your . . . the staff's told you this a hundred times, haven't they?"

"Two hundred, three hundred. I've lost count. I'm just nervous about tonight. I don't want you to be disappointed."

"If it's anything like my run-throughs, the cast will blow their harmonies, drop half their lines and all of their props, and exit through a window instead of a door."

"Well, as long as you have high expectations."

He smiled. "Go do your job. I've got to keep an eye on Jack."

Please God, don't let Daddy say anything damaging in front of Long. And don't let the run-through suck.

❧❧

For about thirty seconds, the run-through was terrific. In her coral chiffon garden dress, Michaela looked as beautiful as she sounded. Then Paul came on for his solo. It took me a few seconds to figure out what was off about his performance: his nighttime role as Oxydent Hour of Smiles host Bert Healy was bleeding into his *Secret Garden* role. The result was a cheesy, breezy Indian Fakir chanting the Hindi equivalent of "you're never fully dressed without a smile."

The Dreamers clomped through the rest of the opening like Clydesdales. During "The House Upon the Hill," Debra managed to shout out her lines over their impossibly loud "Oohs," but Natasha looked like a mime trapped in a glass box.

From somewhere behind me, I heard the ominous squeak of Long's seat. The squirming had begun.

The squeaking became more prolonged after Gregory's entrance. I'd complained to Hal that the first hump he'd created was barely noticeable under the layers of shirt, vest, and frockcoat. No such worries tonight.

"He looks like a goddamn DROMEDARY!" Mei-Yin whispered.

Hal was already hurrying toward the stage. The next time Gregory appeared, he was humpless.

He was also largely unintelligible. It wasn't entirely his fault. "I Heard Someone Crying" was the first of several numbers where each actor sang a different lyrical thread. In the best of all possible worlds, their voices would weave together to create a unified whole. In our world, they created a wall of incomprehensible noise. "It's a Maze" was marginally better, but only because Ben and Natasha kept dropping out, Ben when he lost his melody line and Natasha whenever she tripped over her jump rope.

In spite of my repeated notes, Roger and Gregory were all over each other during the library scene: gripping a shoulder, squeezing a bicep, smoothing a fucking shirtfront. Long before the scene concluded, I wanted to inter them both in "A Bit of Earth."

They redeemed themselves with "Lily's Eyes." And Natasha and Ethan captured all the anger and resentment, humor and pathos I could have wanted in the Scene 7 meeting of Mary and Colin. Even the blocking in the final storm sequence worked—at first. Then the number devolved into yet another wall of noise with Natasha looking more exhausted than terrified and the chorus staggering around like zombies in the final stages of decomposition.

By the time Natasha opened the door to the secret garden and Alex pounded out the final chords on the piano, I was awash in flop sweat. The staff gamely applauded. Bernie and Catherine patted my shoulders. Mei-Yin whispered, "I need a DRINK!"

Although I felt like a condemned prisoner walking the green mile, I put a smile on my face and a bounce in my step as I trotted down the aisle. Alex hoisted himself out of the pit, smiling just as brightly. The cast slumped onstage, grim-faced and silent.

"Come on, people, it wasn't *that* bad. We'll smooth out the staging and the vocals in the big musical numbers over the next few days. Now for the good news. Natasha and Ethan—you both did terrific work tonight."

"Here, here!" Debra said.

The cast applauded. Natasha and Ethan glowed.

Maybe I couldn't create magic for my actors, but I *had* helped create this sense of community. And maybe before the end of this season, my father would be able to share it.

I praised their hard work, "oyed" over some of the mishaps, and promised Gregory that Hal would give him a good hump. Gregory looked startled, I blushed, and the cast began to chuckle. I removed my foot from my mouth and said, "Notes can wait until tomorrow. For now, go home and get a good night's rest."

Alex and I kept our smiles in place until the last actor drifted into the wings. Then we sank down on the stage, our feet dangling over the apron.

"Sorry I let you down," he said.

"You never let me down."

"The group numbers were awful."

"They're hard numbers, Alex! We knew that going in."

As Lee brought up the house lights, the rest of the staff trooped down the aisle toward us. I was dismayed to discover Long heading my way as well—and even more dismayed when I realized Daddy had vanished. Maybe he'd just wanted to escape from Long. Rowan was still sitting quietly in his seat, so nothing too awful could have happened.

I focused my wandering attention on the changes we would have to make in the schedule to accommodate the extra musical rehearsals we clearly needed.

"These local actors and their work schedules are KILLING us!" Mei-Yin complained.

"Tell me about it," Alex replied. "Next year—"

"Let's get through this one," I interrupted.

"Next year," Alex repeated, shooting a stern look at Long, "we've either got to cast people who'll commit to attending every rehearsal or hire an assistant vocal coach. Or both."

"We have never had to hire an assistant in the past," Reinhard pointed out.

"Because I always managed to wheedle some poor fool actor into helping out."

I raised my hand. "Poor fool actor. Duly wheedled."

"So wheedle someone NOW!" Mei-Yin demanded.

"The best musicians are in this show," Alex replied. "And they need to concentrate on learning their material, not teaching their cast mates."

Long regarded us with a beneficent smile. "You're overlooking your most valuable resource." When we all stared at him, he called, "Would you mind coming down here, Rowan?"

"I can't ask Rowan to be my assistant," Alex said in a soft but vehement voice.

"Nonsense. I'm sure he'll be happy to help out."

Rowan joined us, his expression carefully neutral. He listened politely to Long and glanced at me before turning to Alex.

"Tell me what you need."

"Four more hands."

"I only have two. But they're yours if you want them."

"Rowan, I can't ask you to plunk out harmonies."

"Why not? You do it. Besides, I can't just be Maggie's personal chef all summer."

Although his voice was light, his longing lanced through me. Long started and glanced around uncertainly. By then, Rowan had tamped down his power and Long's smile returned.

"Thank you, Rowan. A true team player. Now that we've got that settled, I'll—"

"Hold your horses," Bernie said. "If Rowan's going to be on staff, he needs to get paid."

Janet glanced heavenward. I suppressed a sigh. Bernie was just trying to help, after all.

In the old days, Helen had simply handed Rowan an envelope filled with cash. Asking Long to pay him under the table would raise too many questions. And if Rowan refused to accept any of the money he had left me, he would never allow me to give him part of my salary.

As Long hemmed and hawed, Rowan said, "Thank you, Bernie. But if you can volunteer your time to the theatre, so can I."

Long looked genuinely touched. Bernie shook his head. "So be it. But before the end of the year, you're sitting down with the board and hashing out a long-term contract. You and Maggie both! This year-to-year stuff is for the birds. Who can plan a life based on that? Especially a young couple starting out."

I smiled at Rowan and hoped I could disguise my jumble of emotions. He obviously needed something more fulfilling than babysitting Daddy and cooking me dinner. And the actors were blessed to have someone so talented working with them. But a small part of me wanted to prove that we could mount this production without his help.

"Maggie? Alex? Are you okay with this?"

"Are you kidding?" Alex's smile was more convincing than mine, but his voice was just a bit too hearty. "It'll be great working with you again."

CHAPTER 20

THE "YOU-DON'T-WANT-TO-PLAY-WITH-ME" BLUES

INTRODUCED ROWAN AT THE COMPANY meeting the next morning. Judging from the awed expressions of the locals, they had seen the shows he'd directed. Doubtless, word would spread to the rest of the cast in the time it took to walk to the Smokehouse.

Alex and I left the chorus with Rowan and worked some of the principals' scenes and songs. Then I took Gregory and Roger aside for a little chat.

Lee's instincts were right. Turned out Gregory—a local—was so impressed by Roger that he was simply following his lead. And far from putting the moves on Gregory, Roger was groping—literally—to make his character more sympathetic.

I pointed out that his performance in 'Lily's Eyes' accomplished that and suggested he find one or two moments to use gestures to show that Neville wanted to break out of his shell, but couldn't do it. If he indulged in five or six gestures during the subsequent rehearsal, at least he and Gregory kept their hands off each other.

At the break, Alex and I wandered outside for some fresh air. As we reached the picnic area, piano music poured through the open windows of the Smokehouse. The voices of the chorus matched the wildness of the music, but each word was distinct, the harmonies perfect.

I glanced at Alex as the storm of music subsided, but his gaze was riveted on the Smokehouse.

Slowly, the piano built the chord in the bass. One by one, voices took up the chilling "Mistress Mary, Quite Contrary" chant. And then a new vocal thread—"It's a Maze"—offered a solemn counterpoint that built into a relentless round.

More voices joined in, more threads in the musical tapestry, the gorgeous complexity of the number revealed at last: the lament of the Fakir and Ayah a quiet sostenuto; Wright's echo of Mary's skipping song playing off the "Mistress Mary" chant of Shaw and Claire; the fear that shook Alice's soaring soprano; and weaving in and out of all those vocal threads, the sadness of Mary's mother and the growing desperation of her father as he searched for his lost child.

I shivered as their voices united in the dissonant harmonies of "Mistress Mary." And shivered again as the number reached its terrifying climax.

I let out my breath and heard Alex do the same.

"We knew it would be like this," I reminded him.

Alex nodded.

For a few moments, there was only the murmur of Rowan's voice, punctuated by occasional chuckles from the chorus. Then I heard the scrape of chairs and the buzz of conversation.

The Smokehouse door swung open. Rowan emerged, surrounded by a cluster of local actors. Like a king and his courtiers. The Mackenzies trailed behind, wearing the exalted expressions I remembered from my season at the Crossroads. Most of the entourage dispersed when Rowan walked toward our picnic table, but a few lingered by the stage door, whispering and watching.

As Rowan dropped his score on the table and slid onto the bench beside me, Alex regarded him with a rueful smile. "Magic wand's still in good working order, I see."

"A little magic, a lot of hard work. And as soon as they

get back onstage, half of what they learned will fly out the window again."

"Maybe. But look how excited they are."

"The cast always left your rehearsals smiling."

"Not lately."

"It's a hard show, Alex."

"But it's perfect for the Crossroads," I said. "Magic and healing and transformation. And the music may be difficult, but it's wonderful."

Rowan shrugged. "Some of it. The songs for the Yorkshire characters."

"What about 'Lily's Eyes?' And 'Where in the World'? And—?"

"I'll grant you 'Lily's Eyes.' But by the time Archibald gets to 'Where in the World,' I'm tired of his endless sorrow and just want him to go home and take care of his son. How can anyone sympathize with a man who abandons his child?"

Rowan's passionate expression froze. Then his mouth twisted in a bitter smile. "I'm a fine one to talk."

"You never knew you had a child," I said.

With a brusque gesture, Rowan dismissed the daughter he had never known, the daughter who had lived long enough to give birth to Janet and her twin sister Isobel—Reinhard's mother.

"My opinion of the score doesn't matter," he said. "The staff clearly loves the show or you wouldn't have chosen it."

Alex's gaze slid away. I nudged his foot under the table. "This is where you're supposed to chime in."

He shifted uncomfortably on the bench. "I'm afraid I have to agree with Rowan."

"Well, why the hell didn't you say that when we were discussing it?"

"Because you were so excited. And the message *is* perfect for the Crossroads." He shrugged helplessly. "That's what I meant about letting you down. And why there haven't been many smiles in my rehearsals. I've been struggling and it shows."

"So we'll find a way to make the problematic numbers work," Rowan said.

He walked around the table and sat beside Alex. At first, Alex merely nodded at Rowan's suggestions, but as they paged through the score, Alex's coppery head bent closer to Rowan's dark one. Within minutes, they were so completely in sync that whenever one started to make a suggestion, the other finished the sentence.

Alex returned to rehearsal, brimming with renewed energy. Afterward, he hurried off to the green room to meet Rowan for a working lunch. I wandered back to the production office and discovered Bernie and Daddy hunched over the laptop.

I scolded myself for feeling jealous. I was grateful that Bernie had taken Daddy under his wing. Relieved that Rowan and Alex were adapting to their new relationship. But I still felt like the last girl picked at the junior high school dance.

❧

During the next two days, the "king and his courtiers" thing diminished, but at every break, I discovered Rowan deep in conversation with a different actor. I knew he would never coach the cast behind my back, but the situation gnawed at me and I finally decided to address it.

I found him in the Smokehouse with Gregory. As soon as I walked inside, they broke off their conversation and Gregory beat a hasty retreat.

"You're very popular," I noted.

"What do you mean?"

"All these little conclaves with the actors."

"I'd hardly call them conclaves."

"Well, what would you call them?"

"They're curious, Maggie. They want to know where I've been, what I've been doing . . ."

"What suggestions you have for improving their performances?"

"Some of them, yes."

He waited, watching me, until I was forced to ask, "And what do you tell them?"

"I don't tell them anything. I ask them what suggestions their director gave."

I was both relieved and ashamed. I felt even worse when Rowan asked, "Do you really think I would undermine your authority?"

"No! But as you pointed out, you're far more experienced than I am."

"I also pointed out that you had to stop comparing yourself to me."

"Well, it's damn hard to do that when half my cast is flocking to you for advice."

"That's not my fault."

"I didn't say it was!"

"Then stop blaming *me* for their behavior!"

Tension crackled through the Smokehouse, along with a decidedly chilly breeze.

"You're right. I'm sorry."

The temperature grew noticeably warmer. So did Rowan's expression. "And I'm sorry for shouting. Actors are needy creatures. You don't see the Mackenzies asking for my suggestions, do you?"

"They're too cowed by your reputation."

"It doesn't even occur to them. You're the one they need. It's ironic. The ones that came here for healing flock to you and the experienced actors seek me out."

"Because the Mackenzies trust me."

"They all trust you."

"Maybe." When Rowan blew out his breath in exasperation, I added, "Okay, so I'm hopelessly insecure. A few actors ask for a second opinion and I become a basket case."

Rowan took my hands. "That's not true, sweetheart. You've always been a basket case."

I pulled free, but he easily avoided my intended smack.

"I hate you!"

"Then why are you laughing?" he asked from a safe distance.

"Because I have a kind and generous nature."

His teasing smile vanished. "Yes. It's one of the things I love most about you."

"Hey, no fair."

"What?"

"Playing the love card. That trumps everything."

"I hope so."

CHAPTER 21
LET'S CALL THE WHOLE THING OFF

THE FOURTH OF JULY BROUGHT BLISTERING heat, but I was too excited to care. I was going out on the town. And I would have my lover and my father all to myself.

I put on my apricot sundress and hurried up the stairs to Rowan's apartment. When the door swung open, I flung my arms around his neck and kissed him soundly.

"Ready?"

"Jack's still dressing."

Deflated by his lack of enthusiasm, I asked, "You don't mind that we're going to the Chatterbox instead of picnicking at the high school? It's just so hot. And I didn't want you stuck in the kitchen, cooking all afternoon."

"It's fine, Maggie."

As he walked into the living area, I noticed something dangling from his back pocket. Before I could ask about it, he paused by the sideboard to pick up a rolled-up napkin.

"Would you put this in your purse?"

"Rowan, the Chatterbox may not be fancy, but they *do* have napkins. Not linen, but—"

"It's the silverware I'm concerned about."

Only then did I realize he'd wrapped his utensils in the napkin.

"Oh, God. I didn't even think . . ."

"I'll be fine if I use my own silverware. And I'm bringing my gloves. Just in case."

Gloves. Those were what I'd seen in his pocket.

I called up a mental picture of the Chatterbox. The booths were wooden, the tabletops, Formica, but the milkshakes came in those giant metal containers. You had to pour your shake into a smaller glass to drink it. Well, I could always pour his shake for him if he didn't want to don the gloves.

"Were you planning on driving into town?"

That one I *was* prepared for. I still remembered him retching as he staggered away from my car the night of Helen's heart attack.

"We'll walk. It's only half a mile."

He looked anything but reassured. "Are we likely to encounter any dogs?"

"You don't like dogs?"

"They don't like me. Well, Jamie's didn't. The first time Jamie brought him to the cottage, Blue charged out of the underbrush, baying like the Hound of the Baskervilles. I had to hide in the cottage until Jamie dragged him off."

Jamie Mackenzie — Rowan's first friend in this world. I knew he had arranged for Rowan to get a fake birth certificate and left him five acres of land in his will, but Rowan had not included the incident with Blue in *By Iron, Bound*.

"Why didn't you just use your magic to stop him?"

"I had far less control over my power then. I was afraid I'd kill the damn beast. Maybe Blue was just excited. I didn't stick around to find out. I just ran like hell."

Again, I called up a mental image, this time of Main Street. I went house by house, trying to remember who owned dogs, and came up with one golden retriever, a German shepherd, a dachshund, two pugs, and a couple of those yappy little "mops with feet" dogs.

"At least most of them are small," Rowan said.

"It's weird. I assumed animals loved the Fae."

"Many do. Especially the wild ones. I became quite good at charming birds, rabbits, squirrels. It made them much easier to kill."

"Jesus . . ."

"And Helen's cats adored me."

"I hope you didn't kill them, too."

He scowled. "Of course not. Although at times . . ."

"Rowan!"

"Well, they were always hanging about. It was a source of endless amusement to the staff, particularly when they were in heat. The cats, not the staff. They were so shameless Helen had to keep them locked in the house."

"Maybe Blue was doing the 'alpha male protecting his territory' thing, while Helen's cats—"

"Wanted to mate with me?"

Finally, a smile.

I'd always known travel would be difficult for Rowan. But if dinner in town required this much preparation, how were we ever going to have a normal life?

Think about it tomorrow, Scarlett.

For now, I just prayed that our celebratory evening wouldn't begin and/or end with all the dogs in Dale chasing us down Main Street.

Daddy remained blithely ignorant of Rowan's concerns. He was as excited as a kid about our outing. He might have forgotten his alcohol and drug use, but he seemed to recall every burger joint he'd ever eaten in. Maybe he had simply blocked out the bad memories.

Is that why he never talks about his family? Are we just another bad memory?

I became as silent as Rowan. It was too hot to chat, anyway. Even in my skimpy sundress, I was sweating like a stallion. Rowan looked as grim-faced and sweaty as the day of our first picnic when I'd been terrified he was having a heart attack.

"It'll be better when we reach the road," I assured him.

At least, there might be a breeze from a passing car. And I would have solid asphalt beneath my espadrilles instead of shifting gravel.

My anxiety increased as we trudged along the lane. Daddy's running monologue faltered. His surreptitious glances worried me more—as if he feared something was lurking in the tall grass. He flinched when a jay scolded us and let out a startled yelp when some insect buzzed past.

Maybe we should have driven, even if Rowan had to stick his head out of the car like a dog. Or maybe, as the old song advised, we should just call the whole thing off.

At the top of the lane, Daddy slumped against the low stone wall that ran along the road. Rowan just stood there, staring at the waves of heat rising from the asphalt. Sweat streamed down his face and plastered his shirt to his body. He closed his eyes and gulped at the hot air like a drowning man.

That decided me. "I'm going back for the car."

Daddy screamed.

I jumped about a mile and came down on the side of my espadrille. Pain stabbed my ankle, and I cried out. Rowan caught me as I staggered, then shouted, "Jack! It was just a chipmunk."

Daddy went ballistic and I broke my ankle over a fucking chipmunk?

Rowan had warned me. Just because Daddy enjoyed surfing the Internet didn't mean he was ready to face the world.

"Let's go back," Daddy begged. "Please?"

"We'll have to," Rowan replied. "Put your arms around my neck, Maggie."

A moment later, he was racing down the lane at the speed of Fae. The world blurred into a dizzying smear of green and blue and gold. Although Rowan was doing a five hundred yard dash carrying 139 pounds of hot, cursing female, he wasn't even breathing hard. But I could

feel the tremors coursing through his body as he rushed
me up the stairs to the apartment.

By the time Daddy arrived, I was ensconced on the
sofa, my ankle swaddled in ice packs, and Rowan had
started dinner preparations. Daddy collapsed into an
easy chair, winded and sweating and very apologetic.

"We'll go to the Chatterbox another day," I promised.
"And we can still watch the fireworks from Rowan's balcony."

Daddy waxed rhapsodic over Rowan's dinner of
steak, new potatoes, and salad—his closest approxima-
tion of the meal we might have had at the Chatterbox.
Not the celebration I had planned, but better than the
debacle we had faced an hour earlier.

As darkness fell, Rowan dragged a chair onto the balcony for me and the three of us watched the fireworks
explode beneath the fat, full moon. Daddy whooped and
I squealed. It was like time had rolled backward and we
were once again father and daughter, laughing together
and applauding each time another flower of colored
light blossomed in the sky.

Minutes after the big finale, Daddy's head began to
nod. As he toddled off to the sofa, Rowan leaned on the
railing and stared into the darkness.

"I've always experienced this world from a distance. I
watched the fireworks from this balcony every July. I saw
the first school bus roar past the lane every September.
I glimpsed the houses on the outskirts of Dale through
the bare-limbed trees of winter. I followed the changes
in the town in *The Hillandale Bee*. Heard about Hallee's
and the Golden Bough and the Mandarin Chalet from
the staff."

His shoulders rose and fell as he sighed.

"Tonight, I hoped I would finally see the world first-
hand."

"I'm so sorry," I whispered.

He bent to kiss the top of my head. "It's not your
fault."

"Yes, it is. Maggie Graham, Clumsy Professional."

"No. It was . . . it just wasn't meant to be. There will be other nights."

"Not with fireworks."

His lips moved lower, and I breathed in the faint aroma of wine. "Says who?"

CHAPTER 22
ROLE OF A LIFETIME

UNSATISFIED DESIRE DID MORE TO RENDER me sleepless that night than my sore ankle. My desire remained unsatisfied during the ensuing days. Whenever Rowan had a free hour at lunch, I had a meeting. When I was free, he had an extra music rehearsal. We couldn't even sit together during *Annie* for fear Fifi would go berserk. Instead, he and Daddy were exiled to the last row in the balcony.

My worries about Daddy were as hard to subdue as my hormones. He spent his days sequestered in the office and his evenings sequestered with Rowan. Daddy grew moody. Rowan grew irritable. I played peacemaker and wondered if Daddy was picking up Rowan's energy or if the enforced companionship was grating on both of them.

My father had always been the life of the party, the man everyone was drawn to. Had that merely been an act to disguise his insecurities? Or had the Borderlands destroyed his ability to interact with people?

"What did you expect?" Janet demanded. "That he would emerge from Rowan's apartment like a butterfly from its chrysalis?"

"No!" I lied. "But if he won't even mingle with the staff, what's the point of asking him to join us for the Follies?"

"Rowan never mingled."

"But he had contact with people. He was part of things."

Janet heaved a long-suffering sigh. "Fine. I'll host a barbecue after the Sunday matinee. If all goes well, we can invite Jack to perform in the Follies then."

I flung my arms around her. She cuffed me on the back of the head.

My excitement slowly leached away. The barbecue would give him a chance to get to know the staff, but ultimately, it was just one night of fun like the fireworks and the Follies. If he was going to become a part of this world, he needed something more.

That's when I realized the answer had been staring me in the face all along.

I called a staff meeting in the Smokehouse before the matinee. I'd already warned everyone not to breathe a word about the Follies to Rowan; I wanted to surprise him as well as Daddy at the barbecue. But I was reluctant to spring my other surprise without the staff's advice.

Once everyone was seated, I took a deep breath, flashed a winning smile, and said, "I'd like to offer Daddy Bill's role in *Into the Woods*."

For a moment, they just stared at me. Then Mei-Yin exclaimed, "Are you NUTS?" and everyone began talking at once.

"Wait! Listen!" I had to shout to make myself heard. "This is supposed to be a place where people can heal."

"It's supposed to be a professional theatre," Janet remarked.

"And Daddy's a professional actor."

"Was."

"He needs a purpose. And the only thing he knows is acting."

"Wasn't he a teacher?" Alex asked.

"He taught. There's a difference. Look, I know it's a risk. But he needs . . . something!"

"What role?" Rowan asked.

"Roles," Reinhard corrected. "The Narrator and the Mysterious Man."

Rowan shook his head. "The Narrator, perhaps. But not the Mysterious Man."

"It's the perfect role for him," I said.

"That's why you can't ask him to play it."

"You always talk about casting people in the roles they need. Well, Daddy needs—"

"Is this about Jack's needs or yours?"

I hesitated. "Both." As Rowan shook his head again, I added, "So leave me out of the equation. Don't *you* think he needs this role?"

"A character who abandons his wife and child? Who runs mad in the woods? Jack may be damaged, but he's not stupid. He won't even discuss his past with me, Maggie. You're asking him to act it out in front of the world."

"You asked Nick to do that in *Carousel*," Bernie noted.

"And look how that turned out," Rowan replied. "Jack's just not ready."

"Why not let *him* decide?" I asked.

"Because just offering him the role will bring up all the issues he wants to avoid. Trust me. It will be victory enough if he can play the Narrator."

It was not what I'd hoped for, but it was better than nothing. And maybe the show would help us connect as father and daughter as well as actor and director.

"It's been a long time since he's performed," Alex said. "Suppose he's not up to it? Or something happens to set him off?"

"I could understudy the part," Bernie said.

"Oh, Bernie, would you?"

"If Bernie understudies the role, he goes on for the matinees," Reinhard declared.

"What are you?" Bernie demanded. "My manager?"

"If you are going to add that to your long list of responsibilities, you deserve the chance to perform."

"You're right," I said. "We can split the role."

"What about the box office?" Javier asked.

"I could work the matinees," Catherine said. "If Bernie handles advance sales."

"You're working way too hard as it is," I replied.

"I can do it," she insisted.

"I'll run the damn box office," Janet said.

I swallowed hard. Everyone was working long hours
to make this season a success. And now I was asking
them to do more.

"I'm being completely selfish. You all have more than
enough to do. The Follies is plenty for Daddy to deal
with."

"And when the Follies is over?" Lee asked.

"Lee's right," Catherine said. "Jack needs more. And if
we have to work a little harder to give it to him, we can."

It took longer to dislodge the new lump that formed
in my throat. For the gazillionth time, I thanked God for
giving me this staff.

"Then we are all agreed?" Reinhard asked.

One by one, every head nodded.

"That still leaves us without a Mysterious Man," Hal
said. "Bernie can't play both roles. Not with all those
quick costume changes."

"I must have made a dozen calls after Bill left," I replied. "The professionals all turned me down. And the
locals were already committed to another show or a family vacation or—"

"I'll learn it," Rowan said. "If you find another actor
before rehearsals start—"

"Why bother looking?" Hal exclaimed.

"Because it might make Maggie uncomfortable to direct me."

I hesitated, knowing Rowan had directed the show
before. But if we could deal with the "king and his courtiers" issue, we could deal with this, too.

"Thank you. It'll be great having you in the show."

"You just want to order me around the stage."

"Well. That, too."

We shared a smile. Then Janet asked, "And what about Alison?"

"She has to find out about Daddy eventually."

"We're not talking eventually. Opening night is a month away. If Jack is too traumatized to consider the role of the Mysterious Man, do you think he'll be ready to see his ex-wife?"

"Who knows what he'll be ready for in a month?"

"I could always go on while she's here," Bernie said.

"But she'll still see Jack's name in the program," Janet noted.

"So I'll pay to have extra programs printed. And just list Bernie's name."

Mei-Yin groaned. "This is a recipe for DISASTER."

I shot a pleading look around the circle.

Reinhard sighed. "We will work it out. Somehow. I would suggest, however, that we avoid the term understudy when we broach this to Jack."

"Tell him I asked for someone to share the role," Bernie suggested. "Because I'm too old and feeble to handle all the performances. Then he'll feel like a hero."

"Feeble, my ass," I said. "*You're* the hero."

CHAPTER 23
A REAL NICE CLAMBAKE

I LEFT THE MATINEE AT INTERMISSION and raced up to the Bates mansion to help with final preparations for the barbecue. There wasn't much to do. Alex and Janet had supplied enough meat to satisfy the most raging carnivore. Bernie, enough beer to float a battleship. Catherine was bringing her Mexican bean salad, Mei-Yin, her German potato salad, and Hal, the fruited Jell-O with mini marshmallows that was a hideous—if hallowed—tradition at our gatherings. All that was left for me to do was throw some leafy green stuff together and set out the silverware and plates. At least Rowan wouldn't have to bring his own utensils; Janet always used real silver, too.

Mei-Yin fired up the grill with such maniacal enthusiasm that we all feared she would go up in flames. Self-immolation narrowly averted, we settled ourselves on the patio with pitchers of lemonade and daiquiris.

The rest of the staff began trickling in shortly after the matinee let out. But still no sign of Rowan or Daddy.

"The invitation was for 6:00," Janet reminded me.

I couldn't help hovering anxiously on the front porch. At 5:58, I saw them marching up the hill.

The screen door creaked, and I turned to find Janet observing me with a sardonic smile.

"What's wrong with being punctual?" I demanded.

"Not a thing."

The two men hesitated at the foot of the steps, then held up their containers.

"We brought dessert," Rowan said.

"Blueberry pie, apple pie, and peach cobbler," Daddy declared. "We baked them ourselves."

I suspected Rowan had done the baking, but I just smiled, happy to see his enthusiasm.

"The faery Betty Crocker," Janet noted.

"No more Fae comments," I whispered. "Bernie's here."

Daddy nodded solemnly, then marched up the steps and peered through the screen door. Rowan just looked up at Janet. She stared back at him for a long moment, then gargled something, which I took to be Gaelic. Rowan gargled something in reply. Her sardonic smile returned, but she merely ushered us inside.

"What was that all about?" I whispered.

"A Scottish tradition," he replied just as softly. "Janet offered me one hundred thousand welcomes. I wished her good health and every good blessing to those under her roof."

"You do this every time you go visiting?"

"Janet's never invited me to her home before."

"What are you talking about? She invited you here today. And to all the cast parties. Which you refused to go to until I dragged you."

"The cast parties don't count. She knew I wouldn't attend. And *you* invited me here today, not Janet."

"But you've been inside the house. After Helen's heart attack. And—"

"This is the first time Janet has ever personally invited me into her home. Asked me to sit at her table and break bread together."

"So it's a really big deal."

"It is to me."

I touched his arm lightly, and he smiled. Then we hurried after Janet and Daddy.

Rowan gazed longingly at the library, but when he entered the enormous country kitchen, his eyes widened.

"Kitchen envy?" Janet inquired.

"Kitchen lust," he admitted, placing his containers on the counter. His fingertips skimmed lightly over the marble while his gaze roamed from the stainless steel appliances to the gleaming white cabinetry to the terracotta floor.

"Pretty ritzy, huh?" Daddy remarked. "Janet must be loaded!"

Rowan grimaced. Janet just laughed. "That's me. The wealthy widow."

"A widow?"

I was appalled to detect a speculative gleam in my father's eyes.

"And determined to remain one," Janet said firmly.

As she led us into the sunroom, Daddy's head came up like an animal scenting the air. "Charcoal!" he exclaimed. Then rushed outside and trotted down the steps to the lower patio.

"The lure of the grill," Janet remarked. "Men can't resist it."

Apparently, Rowan could. He just continued to survey the sunroom: the hanging plants above the white shutters, the flowered upholstery on the love seat, the crockery vase filled with fresh-cut flowers.

"This room reminds me of Helen."

"It was her favorite place," Janet said.

"I can almost feel her here."

"I think I *have* felt her," I said.

I told them what had happened in Rowan's apartment and in my bedroom, the countless times I'd seemed to sense Helen's presence in the Bough. Always, I suddenly realized, when I felt sad or troubled or needed reassurance.

"That's when I feel her, too," Janet said quietly.

"Is it possible?"

"I don't know. I'd like to believe that she's watching

over us. Offering us reassurance when we need it. Just as she did in life." Janet blew out her breath impatiently. "First faeries. Now ghosts. Next, we'll have werewolves roaming the woods."

"Helen wouldn't allow that," I said.

"No. She never liked hairy men." Janet's gaze slid over Rowan. Then she strode onto the patio.

I started to follow her, then noticed Rowan's troubled expression. He rarely spoke of Helen, but I knew how much he must miss her. She had been his friend and confidante and—briefly—his lover. The one person on the staff with whom he could let down his guard.

"It must be a comfort," he said. "Living in this beautiful house. Feeling her presence."

I nodded.

"Even if—when—I get a real identity, I'll never be able to give you a home like this."

Dumbstruck, I just stared at him. "Who's asking you to?"

"I know you're not asking, but—"

"I lived in a shoebox in Brooklyn."

"You lived there. It wasn't your home."

"Yes. But the home I grew up in wasn't much bigger than your apartment." I shook my head, still reeling. "Jesus, Rowan. If all I wanted from life was a big house and a fancy car and expensive vacations, I would have set my cap for Long!"

"I just don't want you to be ... disappointed."

"I *am* disappointed! You say you know me and you still think that I need that kind of stuff to be happy!"

His frustration stabbed me. "Of course, you don't need it. But I need to feel I can take care of you."

I resisted the urge to shout, "I can take care of myself!" This was about his pride, his sense of self. I'd been so consumed with helping Daddy find his place in the world that I'd overlooked Rowan's struggles. And clearly, he *was* struggling, although he had hidden it from me.

"You helped me rediscover my past. You helped me

find my path. You gave me my father and $50,000 to start a new life. Most of all, you loved me enough to come back and share that life. From where I stand, you've given me an awful lot."

Some of the tension drained away, but he still looked troubled.

"You've done everything you can to support me when it must kill you to see all the changes at the theatre you built and ran. I can't promise it's going to get easier any time soon. But I swear you won't have to keep hiding in the shadows and watching from the sidelines. You'll direct again. And we'll work together and live together—and take care of each other."

His arms came around me. "You make it sound so easy."

"Hell, no! It'll be hard work. Even you might have a few gray hairs before this is over."

"Well, Bernie would find that reassuring."

I molded my body to his and whispered, "I don't want the house or the car or the vacations. I just want you."

And he obviously wanted me. He might be able to control his power, but the hard ridge in his pants was difficult to disguise.

"Get a ROOM!" Mei-Yin called from the patio.

We jumped apart. Rowan glared at Mei-Yin. As he started toward the patio, I caught his hand.

"I have a room, you know. Maybe we could . . . ?"

He hesitated, desire warring with discretion. Then he shook his head. "We'll find a time and a place to make love. For now, we'll just have to enjoy each other from a respectable distance."

❦

I had to enjoy Daddy from a distance, too. In true urmale tradition, he parked himself by the grill with the other men. Judging from the occasional laughter, they were all having a good time and that was the important thing.

Rowan made awkward conversation with the female contingent. At first, I thought he was still troubled by our conversation, but I gradually realized that in all the years he had worked at the Crossroads, he'd never actually socialized with his staff.

I plied him with daiquiris, and by the time we settled in around the picnic tables on the lower patio, he seemed more relaxed. But although he answered pleasantly whenever anyone addressed him, he took little part in the noisy free-for-all conversation.

By contrast, Daddy chatted easily with everyone as we chowed down on burgers, hot dogs, and bratwurst. Rowan and Catherine washed their meals down with milk, drawing a grimace from Daddy who drained the last of his Long Trail Double Bag Ale in a few deep gulps.

"How many has he had?" I whispered to Reinhard.

"Only one. I was the keeper of the cooler. Now, he has a new reason to dislike me."

"Great BURGERS," Mei-Yin called.

"Thank Jack," Lee said. "The man knows his way around a grill."

Daddy beamed. "It's all in the patties. Most people make them too thin. Three-quarters of an inch—that's my rule. And never flatten them with a spatula. Squeezes out all the juices."

Eager to involve Rowan in the conversation, I asked, "Are you getting all this?"

"Jack just won himself the role of head chef. For our non-fancy-schmancy meals."

When the laughter subsided, Janet said, "We were wondering if you'd like another role, Jack. In the Follies."

Daddy's eyes widened. Rowan slowly lowered his fork and stared at his plate. When he finally raised his head, the blank mask was firmly in place.

Why did Janet have to spoil this by fucking with Rowan? He obviously believed we were excluding him from the invitation.

She ignored my furious look and said, "Usually, it's just the staff that performs. But we're doing *Snow White and the Seven Dwarfs* and the doubling is a nightmare. Which is why we could use your help." Her eyes locked with Rowan's. "And yours. If you're so inclined."

Rowan took a sip of milk, slowly lowered his glass, and patted his lips with his napkin.

"Say something!" I demanded.

"Hush, Maggie," Janet said. "You're spoiling the moment. Rowan's drawing out the tension the way I just did. A fine theatrical tradition."

"And here I thought you were just screwing with me," Rowan remarked. "A fine Janet Mackenzie tradition."

They regarded each other as intently as they had outside the house. Then Rowan smiled and raised his glass of milk as if toasting Janet.

"It's nice to know some things haven't changed."

As I let out my breath, Rowan nudged Daddy. "So what do you think? Would you like to be in the Follies?"

"Of course! I still remember the show from my year. *Hansel and Gretel.* You were the wicked witch."

"Rowan was the wicked witch our year, too!" Bernie exclaimed.

"I'm always the wicked witch," Rowan remarked dryly. "And Catherine always plays the ingénue."

"Not this year," Catherine replied. "My big role is Sleepy. Not much of a stretch."

"I'm GRUMPY," Mei-Yin said. "Not much of a stretch for ME, either."

"I am Happy," Reinhard said, staring glumly into his ale.

"And I," Janet announced, "am the Evil Queen."

"So many comments spring to mind," Rowan murmured.

"Try to restrain yourself."

"So who *is* playing Snow White?"

I groaned and raised my hand. "I told them I didn't have the time or the energy or the ditzy soprano voice, but—"

"Weren't you complaining about casting when we met?" Rowan teased and laughed when I stuck out my tongue. "Do Jack and I have to guess our roles or are you going to tell us?"

"I was supposed to play the Prince and Sneezy," Lee said.

Daddy frowned. "But then you wouldn't have the right number of dwarfs at the end."

"Exactly. But now that you're onboard . . ."

"You want me to play the Prince!"

There was a horrifying moment of silence.

"Uh . . . no," Lee said. "We'd like you to play Sneezy."

I watched in agony as the emotions flitted across Daddy's face: disappointment, annoyance, truculence.

Rowan nudged him again. "Come on, Jack. An inveterate scene stealer like you should be able to add five minutes to the show with those sneezes."

A slow smile blossomed on Daddy's face. "Damn straight!"

I clapped my hands like the delighted child I was. "Then it's all settled!"

"No, it's not!" Rowan retorted. "Who am I playing? Let me guess, Janet. Dopey?"

"Tempting. Alas, we need you to play the old crone."

"But . . . that's the Evil Queen."

"The transformation is a bit daunting. We need some of that special Rowan Mackenzie magic to pull it off."

Rowan's face lit up, then creased in a frown of concentration. "I'll need a flash pot," he said, turning to Lee. "And a strobe."

"No problem."

"And I have to die spectacularly."

"Knock yourself out," Janet said.

"No, don't!" I protested.

"The old crone has to plummet to her death from a rocky crag," Rowan said.

"No plummeting. No crags."

Rowan smiled sweetly. His power teased through my

body, a coaxing caress that urged me to give in. I glared at him, and it subsided, but his pleading look remained.

"Fine. But if you break your neck . . ."

"Don't be silly. I'm a professional."

And a faery. He could probably plummet from a rocky crag and stick the landing like Mary Lou Retton.

We discussed the Follies over dessert and coffee. Rowan's baking won a lot of compliments, which seemed to surprise and please him. As the shadows deepened, Janet lit the votives on the picnic tables and Mei-Yin turned her pyromaniacal talents to the tiki torches.

The atmosphere encouraged Bernie to serenade me with "Some Enchanted Evening." The staff soon joined in. When they got to the ending with its reminder to "never let her go," everyone seemed to be looking at Rowan.

Maybe that's why he cleared his throat and said, "Well. It's getting late."

I nodded. "But before we go, Jack, there's one more role we wanted to discuss with you."

He grinned, showing blueberry-stained teeth. "I'd make a cute bunny."

"This is a role in *Into the Woods*."

He stared at me blankly.

"You know the show, right?"

You had the cast album. You listened to it a million times. You can probably sing every song in the score.

Daddy's fork clattered onto his plate. "You want me to be in a real show?"

"If *you* want to. One of our actors dropped out. Bernie volunteered to fill in, but . . ."

"It's just too much for me." Bernie took a trembling breath and morphed into the sad-eyed Puss in Boots. "I'm only good for two matinees a week. So I was hoping you'd play the Narrator at the evening performances."

Daddy frowned. "The Narrator?"

"The one who opens the show," I said. "And . . . narrates the action. Until they throw him to the giant."

I glanced at Rowan who was frowning, too. Uncertain what was happening, I laughed uneasily and added, "I'm afraid you won't get to die spectacularly. It all happens off—"

"That's a dual role," Daddy said.

"On Broadway, it was. But we're going to—"

"You want me to play the crazy man."

"No! Just the—"

"I get it! Let's cast Jack. It's the perfect role for him. He won't even have to act!"

I babbled out a denial, too horrified by his reaction to put a coherent sentence together.

"I won't do it! You can't make me!"

"Jack!"

Daddy turned on Rowan, his lips curled in a snarl. In that instant, he *did* look crazy.

"No one's asking you to play the Mysterious Man," Rowan said. "Maggie is offering you the role of the Narrator. That's it."

The fury in Daddy's face leached away and his uncertain gaze shifted to me.

"I didn't want to spring it on you as soon as you arrived. But I kept thinking: why should I scrounge up some inexperienced actor when I've got the man who played Billy Bigelow?"

For once, those words failed to work their magic. Daddy just shook his head. "That was a long time ago."

"But you're still an actor."

"I'm not sure what I am any more."

Suddenly, he looked far older than his sixty-three years. Old and small and unbearably fragile.

"Maybe this role will help you figure it out," Bernie said. "That happens a lot at the Crossroads."

CHAPTER 24

WHAT DID I EVER SEE IN HIM?

ON MONDAY MORNING, DADDY ACCEPTED the role of the Narrator.

On Monday evening, he had a panic attack and shut himself in Rowan's apartment.

On Tuesday morning, he laughed off the incident and announced that he was fine.

On Wednesday morning, he declared that he was never going to act again.

On Wednesday afternoon, he began giving helpful little suggestions to the actors. Then stormed back to the apartment when I told him he was overstepping his bounds.

On Thursday morning, he was all smiles and penitence, but the cast was eyeing him with misgiving, the staff was shooting me murderous glances, and Reinhard's hair was standing on end. Only the fact that mine was longer prevented it from rising heavenward, too.

Although Rowan appeared as preternaturally calm as ever, he was clearly struggling to control his temper—and his power. His frustration infected everyone. The actors sniped at each other; the younger staff grew moody or snappish. Even Reinhard and Alex couldn't always shield themselves and became increasingly short-tempered. Janet remained immune because she refused to set foot in the theatre.

Something had to change or none of us would live to see opening night. So on Friday, I suggested to Rowan that we have a little chat with Daddy over lunch.

Rowan scowled. "I am sick of chatting with Jack. I spend every waking hour with Jack. The prospect of eating lunch with Jack is about as appealing as eating cast-iron filings out of a cast-iron skillet with cast-iron utensils."

"I'll take that as a no."

"Maggie Graham. Perceptive Professional."

He stomped up the stairs to his apartment in a very unfaery-like manner. I muttered a few unflattering names under my breath, then whisked Daddy into town for lunch.

He marveled at how little Dale had changed, just as Mom had when she visited me for the first time. But where she had been suspicious of the town's timeless quality, Daddy was delighted by it.

"It's exactly the same," he exclaimed as we walked into the Chatterbox.

From the waitresses in their powder blue uniforms to the soda fountain stools at the counter to the jukeboxes in the cramped booths, the Chatterbox evoked a candy-coated past where kids were never more than naughty and parents never less than loving.

We slid into a booth, the wooden seats worn smooth by generations of Dale butts. My father studied the menu. I studied him.

He had talked about me that first night. Recalled the tent we had built, the games we had played. Since then, he had never brought up his family. Did he have to be on the brink of a mental breakdown before he could think about us? Was he avoiding the pain or didn't he feel any?

Look at me. I have the same auburn hair you had as a young man, the same smattering of freckles across my nose. You gave me your pointed chin and your blue-green eyes and your love of theatre. Can't you see any of that?

Obviously not. He just wolfed down his burger and

fries, moaned ecstatically over his chocolate milkshake, and flirted outrageously with Dot, our waitress. I picked at my tuna salad and kept the conversation light, unwilling to risk a public meltdown by broaching the subject of his recent mood swings.

Afterward, he insisted on stopping by the Bough. I warned him that it had changed, but I was still shocked when he took one look at the lobby and demanded, "Why can't people leave things alone? The Bough was great. It had character! Now it looks ordinary."

My mother had deemed it perfect. I'd thought so, too. But now I recalled the quirky old furnishings and the moth-eaten draperies and the Victorian gloom and wondered if I'd stolen everything that had made the Bough unique.

"Do *you* like the changes?" Daddy demanded.

"I should. I made them. I own the Bough, remember? I told you and Rowan that your first morning back."

Daddy mumbled, "Oh, shit." Then he shrugged and flashed that charming gap-toothed smile. "Oops."

I turned around and walked out.

His dismissive words had stung. That little "oops" totally pissed me off. Why was I surprised? He'd thrown the theatre into chaos this week and hadn't apologized for that, either.

"Charming, yes. But completely self-absorbed."

"Maggie!"

"And arrogant and superior."

"Wait!"

"Always standing apart, judging."

I flung open the car door.

"Please!"

I turned to find him standing on the curb, quivering with anxiety.

"It looks nice. Really. It's just . . . I loved the Bough the way it was."

"Always making excuses . . ."

I slumped against the car, suddenly exhausted. "I

loved it, too. But I worked really hard on redoing the lobby and it hurt my feelings when you called it ordinary."

"I'm sorry," he whispered.

"If you'd said that earlier, I wouldn't have gotten mad. An apology goes a lot farther than a shrug and a smile."

He stared at me as if I were chanting Hindi.

"Do you understand?"

"Yes. I was just . . . yes."

"Come on. I need to get to rehearsal."

Neither of us spoke on the short drive back, although Daddy kept stealing glances at me. After I parked the car at the theatre, I asked, "Do you want to tell me why you've been so up and down this week?"

His hands tightened on his thighs. I found myself studying them: the loose flesh, the network of ropy blue veins, the tiny spots of dried blood where he'd gnawed his cuticles.

"Are you worried about performing in *Into the Woods*?"

"What if I'm awful?"

"You won't be."

"But what if I am?"

"In all the years you acted, were you ever awful?"

His forehead creased in a thoughtful frown. "Well, I wasn't great in *Natalie Needs A Nightie*. But the material was so bad that—"

"You were actually in a play called *Natalie Needs a Nightie*?"

"In Scranton. Or Wilkes-Barre. Some place like that. I did a lot of dinner theatre. *There's a Girl in My Soup. Right Bed, Wrong Husband. Run for Your Wife*."

"I was in one called *Don't Start Without Me*," I confessed.

He smiled. Then his gaze slid away. "The thing is . . . my memory isn't so hot anymore."

I resisted the urge to pat his hand. I was his director now, not his daughter.

"The lines will come. It just might take awhile to get back in the groove." When my words elicited only a dispirited nod, I added, "I'll do whatever I can to help. Coaching. Running lines with you. But I can't have any more disruptions during rehearsals."

"It's Rowan's fault. He's making everyone nervous."

"Giving notes to my actors? That was Rowan's fault?"

"I was just talking with them."

"You were giving notes, Jack. And I won't have it."

"You're just mad because of what I said about the Bough."

"That's not true."

"And now you're taking it out on me!"

"That is not true!"

He scowled and looked away. I scowled and stared out the windshield.

Had he always been like this? Was I inventing a shared past as candy-coated as the world conjured by the Chatterbox?

"I want you to play this role, Jack. But if we can't work together . . ."

"We can."

"No more disruptions."

"Okay."

"And no more notes."

"Okay! Jeez . . ."

He slid out of the car. I slumped back in my seat and closed my eyes.

I was tired of pretending I wasn't his daughter, worn down by his apparent lack of interest in his family, and increasingly fearful that Rowan's assessment of his character was accurate. My mother's had been more charitable, but equally gloomy:

That lost boy quality . . . it drew a lot of people to him. Including me. I thought I could make him happy, give him what he needed, make everything right. Of course, I couldn't. No one could.

But I had to try.

CHAPTER 25

FASTEN YOUR SEAT BELTS

WITH DADDY ON A MORE-OR-LESS EVEN KEEL, I expected Rowan to even out as well. But when I walked into the theatre the next morning, the chill raised goose bumps on my arms.

It grew colder as I made my way through the stage left wings. The green room was empty. So was the hallway outside my office. The air felt noticeably warmer there.

I felt like a kid playing Blind Man's Buff . . . warmer, colder, really cold . . .

Which is how it felt in the Dungeon. Tension crackled like static electricity, raising the hairs atop the goose bumps.

When I heard muffled voices coming from the end of corridor, I started to run. Fae-powered anger sent a storm of adrenaline pumping through my body. I paused outside the closed door of the men's dressing room long enough to hear Rowan claim that Alex had begged for his help and then resented him when it was offered, and Alex retort that he had never begged Rowan for anything in his life and wasn't about to start now.

At which point I flung open the door and shouted, "Have you completely lost your minds? Stop it! Both of you!"

It wasn't exactly helping professional behavior, but I was too infected by their anger to care. The roiling tension subsided. The temperature rose a good ten degrees. Alex slumped onto a chair. Rowan stalked past the costume rack and leaned his hands upon a table. I studied his reflection in the mirror, but his long hair shielded his face.

Still shaking from the cold and the shock, I demanded, "What started this?"

Alex frowned. Rowan shrugged.

"I swear to God, if one of you doesn't start talking . . ."

"It was my power." Rowan straightened abruptly and turned to face me. "My control has been a bit . . . shaky lately."

"No kidding." When he glared at me, I said, "Sorry. Aftereffects."

Rowan's hand rose to knead the scar at his throat. He'd told me once that when he hurt someone, it throbbed. Judging from both men's expressions, it must be throbbing like hell.

"I apologize, Alex. I said a lot of stupid things I didn't mean."

"That makes two of us. It's so weird—understanding exactly what's happening but feeling helpless to stop it. I've always been bad at shielding myself. When I succeed, I feel like I'm going through life swaddled in cotton. When I don't, I act like a lunatic."

"So are we okay here?" I asked.

After a cautious exchange of glances, Alex nodded. Rowan hesitated, then said, "Alex, you and I have known each other for decades. I've worked with you more closely than anyone on the staff. Our relationship has always been . . . cordial."

Cordial? Jesus. My relationship with the maids at the Golden Bough was cordial.

Rowan's head swung toward me. "I never had the kind of relationship with the staff that you have. I didn't attend birthday parties or holiday dinners—or barbecues. A necessary precaution, I believed. To avoid . . . emotional entanglements. Even with Helen, I never really let down the walls."

"You did for Maggie," Alex said.

"More accurately, Maggie bulldozed the walls and I stood there in the rubble, blinking in shock." Rowan's tentative smile faded. "The point I'm trying to make is that I've never had a truly close friendship with anyone. I'm not even sure that I can. But I've watched all of you these last few weeks—laughing and talking and arguing with each other. Somehow, you manage to maintain that precarious balance between your personal lives and your professional ones. And I . . . envy that."

I wondered if Alex was as shaken as I was by that unexpected confession.

"Friendship's like any other relationship," I said. "It takes two to tango. If you never get out on the dance floor . . ." I grimaced. "Okay, stupid metaphor."

"Actually, it's a very good one," Alex said.

Rowan scrutinized him. "Did you resent my aloofness?"

"When I was younger, I sometimes wished I had the key to unlock the door, but I appreciated the dangers. Even without Momma's warnings—and Helen's example."

"And my power?"

"It always seemed as much a burden as a gift. But there were still times I was damn envious."

Rowan nodded, the blank mask on his face and the firm grip on his power hiding every hint of emotion.

"I always wondered what I might have done with that kind of power. If I could have been a world-class musician or composer instead of a high school teacher."

"You *are* a world-class musician and composer," Rowan said quietly.

Alex bowed his head. "Thank you for that."

I was surprised to hear the tremor in his voice. And more surprised that I was party to this conversation. Maybe I was the safety net Rowan needed to crack open the door.

"But I doubt you'll be recognized as world-class in

Dale," Rowan continued. "If you want that . . . if you need that . . ."

"I think about it sometimes, but . . . no. I'm happy in my little corner of the world. And I love teaching. Maybe that's something I inherited from you."

"From me?" Rowan echoed.

"By blood or by example. You're a teacher, too. You just have a different classroom."

Rowan nodded. Then he awkwardly stuck out his hand. Just as awkwardly, Alex rose and shook it.

"For what it's worth, Alex, I envied you, too. What you had with Annie."

Alex smiled, but the ache of his sadness throbbed through me.

"Maybe someday, you'll find— "

"Another Annie?" Alex shook his head.

"Another person to love."

Alex looked startled. Then he ducked his head and mumbled, "Sounds like one of Helen's impossible possibilities."

"I found Maggie. What's more impossible than that?"

Both men gazed at me, Alex with fondness and Rowan with a smoldering intensity that stole my breath. Then he abruptly strode out of the room.

Alex sank onto a dressing table. "In all the years I've known him, he's opened up to me just twice. Once, when Annie died. And again, in the letter he left when he returned to Faerie."

"It won't be easy for him," I warned. "The whole friendship thing."

"You're telling me? Still, he's making great progress."

Helen had said that during the early days of my rocky relationship with Rowan.

"But right now," Alex continued, "we've got to address this . . . situation."

"I thought he'd improve. Once Daddy settled down."

"Jack may get under Rowan's skin, but that's not why

he's strung as tight as piano wire. You two haven't had a moment alone since he returned."

That wasn't entirely true. We'd had about forty-five minutes altogether, which had included a few passionate kisses and one interrupted feel.

I could focus during rehearsal. It was afterward—during a break or a hurried lunch—that I found myself watching him like an obsessed schoolgirl. The way his tongue flicked out to retrieve a blot of mayonnaise from his lip. The way his jeans hugged his ass when he walked back to the Smokehouse. Those long fingers cradling a glass of milk.

I came out of my reverie to discover Alex grinning. "And here I thought you were handling it better than he was."

"Yeah. Right. In the middle of my meeting with Catherine about the set for *Into the Woods*, she started giggling. I couldn't figure out why until I saw her staring at the rolled-up script I was holding and realized I was giving it a hand job."

Alex burst out laughing. "I can't believe Catherine didn't tell me."

"She was being kind. And you better be, too. Otherwise, I'll never hear the end of it."

"I promise. But you and Rowan have to carve out some time alone or you'll drive everybody crazy."

"How? Even if we could find a free hour, Daddy's always around."

"Then tell Daddy to take a nice, long walk around the pond."

"He'll know exactly what we're doing."

"So will your staff. If we're in the theatre."

I grimaced, recalling Mei-Yin's "Get a room!" comment.

Alex's expression became stern. "You're going to have to accept that, Maggie. When Rowan's power breaks free, everyone in the vicinity will feel it. I doubt even he can control it at the . . . um . . . height of passion."

"I can't believe I'm having this conversation."

"Then take steps. If Rowan's happy ..."

"Yeah. I know."

I'd had *that* conversation with Janet two years ago.

"Tomorrow night's the cast party for *Annie*. I'll have Momma drag Jack up to the house as soon as the show's over. I suggest that you and Rowan arrive fashionably late."

CHAPTER 26
LET'S MISBEHAVE

A FAERY IN THE THROES OF SEXUAL anticipation is no less distracting than one in the throes of sexual frustration. It's just a lot more enjoyable for all involved. And that Saturday afternoon, everyone was involved.

As soon as I walked into the theatre, Rowan's desire raced through me like a brushfire. Reinhard must have anticipated my reaction because he was waiting by the stage door. He seized my arm to steady me, and the power immediately receded. But I was light-headed with longing and even Reinhard had to dab his forehead with a handkerchief.

"This is not good," he said.

"This is not good," I agreed.

"I will speak to . . . *Gott im Himmel!*"

A Category Five hurricane of lust blasted through me. Moments later, Mei-Yin strode through the wings bellowing, "LOVE is in the AIR!" She shoved Reinhard up against the wall and began devouring his mouth like a rapacious tiger.

When she finally came up for air, perspiration was dripping down Reinhard's face and he was wearing a decidedly goofy smile. Then he caught sight of me, frowned, and extricated himself from his wife. The earth resumed its normal rotation and Hurricane Mei-Yin was down-graded to a tropical storm.

"I will definitely speak to—"

As Reinhard broke off, I darted nervous glances around the theatre, seeking the direction of the next assault. A grim-faced Rowan marched down the stairs from his apartment. Daddy followed, looking as dazed as I felt.

"We're going for a walk," Rowan announced.

He strode out of the theatre, knapsack on his back, leaving Daddy to trail after him.

"I don't get it," I said. "It was never like this before."

"His power is stronger now," Reinhard said.

"And he's not GETTING any!" Mei-Yin leered at Reinhard and waltzed across the stage, singing "Some Day My Prince Will Come."

Reinhard mopped his forehead. "I will speak to the entire staff."

"Why? Rowan's gone."

"But the energy lingers, yes? And if the rest of the staff is like Mei-Yin . . ."

I groaned.

"Exactly. Come. We will round them up."

As we hurried across the stage, Reinhard stopped short and peered up at the balcony. That's when I noticed someone creeping up the stairs to the lighting booth.

"Hal!" Reinhard called.

Hal froze, then slowly turned toward us.

"What are you doing?"

"I just wanted to talk with Lee for a sec."

"You can talk later."

As Hal slunk back down the stairs, Reinhard's head jerked toward the stage right wings. "Where do you think *you* are going?"

Silence. Then: "I . . . forgot something," Javier said. "At the Mill."

Reinhard sighed. "You have twenty minutes."

"We'll only need ten!" Javier called. A moment later, I heard the pounding of footsteps and the slam of the stage door.

"How come they get to have fun and we don't?" Hal shouted from the balcony.

"Because they will be having fun off-site," Reinhard retorted. "If you and Lee cannot exercise a modicum of restraint, I suggest you do the same."

The door to the lighting booth banged open. Lee bolted down the stairs and grabbed Hal's hand, putting an end to any speculation regarding their capacity for restraint.

"If you are not back by the half-hour call, I will dock you both a month's salary!"

As they sped toward the lobby stairs, I said, "It's an epidemic."

Reinhard handed me his handkerchief. "It will pass."

Ten minutes later, Javier returned to the theatre, whistling a happy tune. Lee and Hal showed up soon afterward, leaving me to suspect they'd gone no farther than the Smokehouse. When I went down to the Dungeon to check on the cast, I heard suspicious moaning coming from the men's bathroom. I cracked open the door and hissed, "There are children here!" After which I fled to the picnic area to allow my raging hormones to subside.

Thankfully, most of the energy had dissipated by curtain time. The overture still sounded like a 33-rpm record played at 78 speed and the girls were a bit manic in the opening scene, but Amanda got us back on track with 'Maybe' and after that, the show proceeded normally.

I got a little misty at curtain calls, knowing this was the last time Amanda and her orphans would perform. I also realized Rowan and I needed to get to the cast party on time or I'd miss celebrating with the little ones whose parents would whisk them off after a half hour.

I briefly contemplated squeezing in a quickie during strike. Then I shuddered: Rowan's power plus a dis-

tracted cast and crew plus hammers, nails, and large set
pieces . . . talk about your recipe for disaster.

Sighing, I shooed the company out to the picnic area
for the usual post-matinee meal, courtesy of the Mandarin Chalet. Reinhard led the charge. When I spied him
getting into Mei-Yin's car, I realized he wasn't hungry for
Chinese food. Before the passenger door was even
closed, they were speeding off, trailing dust and the faint
sound of Mei-Yin's cackle.

I was still leaning against the stage door, smiling,
when Rowan suddenly materialized beside me. Before I
could do more than gasp, he grabbed my hand and pulled
me up the stairs.

"Rowan! Wait!"

"Can't."

"But the cast is right outside. If they feel—"

"They won't."

"If they hear—"

"They won't!"

"But Daddy—"

"Dinner. Janet's."

"I don't have any condoms!"

"I do."

"Where did you get—?"

"Lee."

"Lee bought you a box of condoms?"

Rowan paused on the threshold of his apartment.
"No. Lee bought me six boxes of condoms. Including
Magnum Ecstasy, Magnum Fire and Ice, and one with
climax control."

I started to giggle.

Rowan glared. "It was bad enough having to ask Janet
to invite your father to dinner. I'll never hear the end of
The Climax Control Crisis. Now do you want to do this
or not?"

"Well, I was kind of looking forward to my shrimp
and snow peas . . ."

He pulled me inside and kicked the door shut.

If Mei-Yin's uncontrolled power had been a Category Five hurricane, Rowan's was just shy of a nuclear meltdown. The aroma of honeysuckle and animal musk made me dizzy. Creamy warmth curdled between my legs. Molten heat flooded my body, and my knees buckled. Only his body pressing mine against the door kept me on my feet.

His tongue slipped between my lips, the sandpaper-rough cat's tongue I had fantasized about for weeks. I sucked on it, and a low growl rumbled in his throat.

My breasts ached, swollen and heavy in my bra. My kicky sundress rubbed unpleasantly against my shoulders, my ribs, my waist. The very air hurt my oversensitive flesh.

The shock of his fingers on my bare thighs made me gasp. Warm hands slid inside my panties, but as Rowan pushed them down, they got caught somewhere north of my knees.

I shimmied wildly. Rowan cursed.

I heard the sound of ripping fabric, and the pressure around my knees gave way to the shivery sensation of nylon skimming down my legs and settling atop my feet.

I clawed at his shirt. Rowan batted my hands away and began fumbling with the buttons on his jeans. I moaned, nearly weeping with frustration. He seized the waistband of his pants and gave a mighty tug. Buttons clattered onto the hardwood floor like hailstones.

He dug a packet out of his pocket. Holding one end in his teeth, he ripped it open, then spat the sliver onto the floor.

He seized my hand and turned toward the bedroom. "No. Here. Hurry!"

His mouth claimed mine again as I fell back against the door. His knuckles brushed my bare belly, sending shock waves of desire through me. I stared into those glittering green eyes, mesmerized by the golden sparks flashing in their depths. Then his hands cupped my bottom and he lifted me as effortlessly as he had torn open his jeans.

I wrapped my legs around his hips. Visions of *The Godfather* danced in my head: Sonny Corleone giving it to the bridesmaid, and—for some unknown reason—fat Clemenza drawling, "Leave the gun. Take the cannoli." Then Rowan's cresting desire swept away all thoughts of Corleone and cannoli and I just hung on for dear life.

It was over in seconds, shattering my previous Olympic orgasm record. My legs oozed off his hips to dangle in the air like a rag doll's. His heart thudded against mine, as rhythmic as the blood pulsing in my ears. Then I made out another sound—just as soft, just as rhythmic—that seemed to be coming from outside the apartment.

Rowan cursed. A moment later, I identified the sound as footsteps pattering up the stairs.

The Olympic judges would have deducted points for my dismount, but I managed to stick the landing. After that, it was all I could do to stagger into the bedroom and collapse on the bed.

The latch rattled once. Twice.

"The door won't open," my father complained.

"No," Rowan said. "It won't."

"I left my script in your knapsack."

"Get it later."

"But Janet's going to run lines with me after dinner."

"I have company, Jack."

There was a long silence. Then a soft chuckle. "Well, why didn't you say so? Hi, Maggie!"

I pulled a pillow over my face. Then threw it aside and called, "Hi, Jack!"

"I thought I felt something weird. Now I know what it was. Hot monkey love!"

Rowan cleared his throat. "I'll get your things."

"Jeez, if you wanted some private time, you should have just asked. Next time, tell me to take a walk around the pond. That'll be the code."

I almost wished Alex was here to share this moment.

Rowan's boots thudded on the floorboards. The front door creaked open.

"Here's your script. And your notebook. And a pen. Enjoy dinner."

"I will. We're having fried chicken and potato salad and—"

The door slammed.

I made a brief effort to sit and gave it up; my limbs felt like they were weighted down with rocks. In spite of the ceiling fan, the bedroom was stifling. That's when I noticed that the door to the balcony was closed. As were the skylights. With any luck, Rowan's precautions had prevented the cast from hearing my final shriek of ecstasy.

The soft sound of footsteps alerted me to his approach. He hesitated in the doorway, then strode through the bedroom and wrenched open the sliding door.

For a moment, he stood there with his back to me. It was unpleasantly reminiscent of his behavior the night of my first Olympic orgasm. But when he turned toward me, he looked so miserable that I struggled into a sitting position.

"If you ever doubted the selfishness of the Fae, you saw ample evidence of it just now. I acted like a stag in rut."

"Well, I acted like a cat in heat, so I guess it all evens out."

"And you're not upset."

A statement, not a question; he could feel that I wasn't.

"A little unnerved, maybe. It was kind of like ... that first time."

"At least that night, I tried to control my power and failed. Today, I didn't even try. I wanted you and I just ..."

"Got what you wanted?"

He winced.

"That was supposed to be a joke."

"And you're supposed to be angry!"

"And *you're* angry because I'm not?"

"I just ... I don't understand! I drag you up the stairs.

I pull you into the apartment. I mount you like an animal . . ."

"I could have said no when you were dragging me up the stairs. Or when you asked if I wanted to do this. Your power wasn't influencing me then." I patted the bed, and he sank down beside me. "What happened wasn't exactly what I expected. But I wanted you, Rowan. You must have felt that."

"Yes, but—"

"That's why I'm not mad."

The tension in his body drained away, but his frown remained. "It was supposed to be perfect. Our first time together. I wanted it to be slow and beautiful and romantic. Yet when push came to shove—"

"So to speak."

That won a small smile from him.

I mustered my energy and leaned forward to plant a kiss on the tip of his nose. "So this time we ended up with wham, bam, thank you, ma'am. And Daddy pounding on the door. Next time, we'll do slow and beautiful and romantic. Okay?"

He just stared at me. "I can sense your feelings, your moods. Sometimes, I can even guess what you're thinking. But I'll never be able to understand you, will I? Not completely. Or predict how you'll react."

"Well, how dull would that be?"

"Predictable isn't dull. It's reassuring. And safe. And—"

"Dull. People aren't predictable, Rowan. Life isn't predictable."

"It was. For me. Once. Then I met you."

"You're supposed to smile now and say it was the best thing that ever happened to you."

"It *was* the best thing that ever happened to me. But it was also . . . frightening. It still is. I've never behaved like I did today. Even when I was young and stupid and susceptible to every shift in emotion. Ever since I came back, I feel like I'm walking on quicksand. I'm not even sure who I am any more."

Did he even realize he was echoing my father's words? I considered assuring him that he, too, would find the answers he needed. Instead, I cupped his face between my hands.

"You're a faery in a human world. A man without an identity. A director who's not directing. And a lover who's spent almost no time with his beloved. If you weren't unsure, you'd be nuts! But it'll get easier."

"Promise?"

I crossed my heart. "And when we're old and gray . . . well, when I'm old and gray and you're still raven-haired and handsome and we have to pretend you're my son or you have to do the whole glamour thing in order *not* to look like my son because we'd totally creep people out if they saw us together and we were making out . . . I forget my point . . ."

"We'll laugh about this?"

"Absolutely."

Rowan nodded. But his smile was disturbingly bleak.

BLEAK PRETTY MUCH DESCRIBED HELL WEEK, too. Even with a cue-to-cue Sunday afternoon and a walk-through of the scene changes Sunday evening, Monday's tech rehearsal lasted a brutal five hours.

The set was simple enough—a stepped unit with two playing areas for the children's bedrooms upstage left and right and a larger central area for the other interior scenes. The maze and greenhouse would be created downstage. Hal had also built a painted "frame" around the proscenium arch that looked like elaborately turned wrought iron until the lights came up for the finale to reveal it as a flower-bedecked arbor.

Lee's lighting set the mood: a fiery Indian sky and a cloud-filled one in Yorkshire; the ghostly blues of the storm sequences and the amber pools of light that illuminated the dreary mansion; the silvery moonlight that poured through the door to the secret garden in the final moments of Act One and the brilliant sunlight that flooded the garden at the end of the show. But all those effects required a zillion cues and twice that many stops and starts to ensure that they were coordinated with the music and scene changes.

A few of Hal's design elements had to be raised and lowered from the flies: two crystal chandeliers for the ballroom, large portraits of Lily in the gallery, damask draperies in Archibald's library. Unfortunately, one bank of draperies kept getting stuck in mid-flight, adding a Salvador Dali-esque touch to the Yorkshire sky. The portraits were more obedient, but the empty frame in which Michaela was supposed to stand swayed back and forth as if she were on the deck of the Titanic.

The other set pieces were placed and cleared by the actors. Most were easy—a garden bench here, a settee there. What they couldn't carry on was supposed to roll smoothly. Given the Crossroads tradition of reluctant rolling, Catherine had been zealous about her casters—a bit overzealous judging from the way Colin's bed whizzed onto the platform, accompanied by the startled shrieks of its occupant.

However, the giant topiaries in the shapes of stylized birds and flowers took top honors in the "Neither Smooth nor Seamless" competition, turning "It's a Maze" into a rousing Edwardian bumper car sequence. Every time an actress brushed against them, her dress clung to the damn things like Velcro. The ghosts spent more time tugging at their skirts than wafting.

And then there was the mist. Our fog machine had been recalcitrant during *Brigadoon* and surly during *The Fantasticks*. Now, it was gleefully bent on world domination. By the end of tech, the atmosphere was more *Jekyll and Hyde* than *The Secret Garden*.

Rowan gave me a magical neck rub. Janet gave me whisky. Between the two, I managed to sleep.

Our first dress rehearsal was rocky. Our second was marginally better. Whatever substance Hal applied to the topiaries mitigated their desire to snatch at the women's clothing. Whatever magic Alex applied to the pit band helped them discover volumes other than fortissimo. The set changes more or less worked. The actors more or less found their pools of light. The Dreamers wafted, menaced, and comforted at most of the right moments. Michaela looked and sounded beautiful, Gregory looked and sounded tormented, and Roger avoided filial fondling. Hal's costumes were flat-out gorgeous. Gregory's worked so well that I serenaded Hal with a non-Lerner-and-Loewe approved version of "I've Grown Accustomed to His Hump."

Daddy skipped both dress rehearsals. He said he wanted to be wowed opening night. I just hoped he—and the rest of the audience—would be.

I approached the opening without my usual blend of hope, terror, and excitement. Even with the staff, the possibility of disaster had always existed. When a faery's got your back, the "anything can happen in live theatre" vibe dissipates—especially since we had discussed the moments that required a little magical boost.

I yearned for my days as an actress when Rowan's magic had been mysterious and thrilling and occasionally unnerving. The whole idea of planned magic felt wrong.

Nancy's "break a leg" phone call lifted my spirits. Having lived through Hell Week of *Brigadoon*, she knew how to transform this one from a hair-whitening disaster into a series of comical misadventures.

By the time my mother called, I was able to greet her with a cheery hello.

"What's wrong?" she demanded.

"Nothing's wrong."

"You sound too cheery."

"I was trying to disguise how exhausted I am."

"Well, you failed. Was Hell Week awful?"

"No more than usual. But the show will be fine. You'll see for yourself on Saturday."

There was a brief silence, then a sigh. "Sue's mother has taken a turn for the worse. The hospice people think it's only a matter of days. Flaky Leila and her husband are doing some shamanic circle thing this weekend. Laura said she'd try to fly in next week. By then, her grandmother will be in the ground."

As her tirade escalated, a shameful feeling of relief washed over me: at least now we wouldn't have to worry about hiding Daddy. I didn't want Sue's poor mother to die or Sue to be grief-stricken or Mom to be worried about her best friend, but I had to admit the timing was terrific—and that I was an awful person for thinking that.

"There's a special circle in Hell for unfeeling daughters," my mother declared.

"I feel bad!"

"I'm talking about Laura and Leila. Anyway, I hate to leave you in the lurch, but . . ."

"Of course, you have to be there for Sue."

"I'll pay for the room. And the tickets."

"We'll fill the room. And sell the tickets. Just let me know when you're coming up and—"

"It'll have to be closing weekend. We have a birthday party for Chris' granddaughter next Saturday."

"I'll put aside two tickets. And if there's no room at the inn—"

"You'll put us up in a stable?"

"Only if you arrive on a donkey. And pregnant."

"Round up some wise men to offer me gold and frankincense and I'll consider it."

"No myrrh?"

"Ancient embalming fluid is not my idea of a hostess gift."

"I'll talk to Janet. I'm sure she'd be happy to put you up."

"*I'll* talk to Janet. You have enough on your plate." There was a brief pause. Then she said, "How are . . . things?"

"If you mean Rowan, they're okay."

"Just okay?"

"I've hardly seen him since . . ."

He ravished me against the front door.

". . . Hell Week started. We'll have more time together during *Into the Woods*."

"Yes. I suppose you will."

Her voice was heavy with disapproval. She'd been

openly skeptical about the wisdom of casting Rowan and our ability to work together.

"So the two of you are . . . ?"

"We're fine, Mom."

"Don't get defensive."

"I wasn't . . . okay, I *was* defensive. But I hate that you want this to fail."

"That's not true! I want it to last a lifetime." In the silence that followed, I could practically hear her choosing her words. "I'm just afraid it won't."

I sighed. She sighed. We avoided talking about Rowan. By the time I hung up, my cheery mood had vanished.

"Snap out of it!" Janet ordered. "You've got more important things to worry about than your mother's opinion of Rowan." When I stared at her blankly, she exclaimed, "*The Secret Garden*? Opening night? Ring any bells?"

"I don't have to worry about the show. Rowan will work his magic. Everyone will be awed . . ."

"Is that what you've been in such a funk about?"

"I don't know. Maybe. It just feels so . . . predictable."

"Theatre? Predictable? You've got to be kidding. And since when has Rowan pulled all the strings? There were plenty of flubs in *Brigadoon* and *The Sea-Wife* and *Carousel*. Rowan's magic is the icing on the cake. And he'll use it as sparingly as he always has."

"But when you know the garden will look real at the end of the show, it kind of kills the anticipation."

"You're on the inside now, Maggie. Knowing how the magic works is never as much fun as watching the magician pull a rabbit out of his hat. It's our job to make the hard work look effortless and the magic seem like a cool special effect or an especially wonderful performance. But we can still marvel at those moments. Because *we* know they're really magical."

CHAPTER 28

IT'S BAD LUCK TO SAY GOOD LUCK ON OP'NING NIGHT

WHETHER JANET'S WORDS GOT ME OUT OF my funk or I realized I was being a total drama queen, I was back in my groove by that evening: the heart racing, cotton-mouthed, armpit-soaked, stomach-lurching, everything's-coming-up-roses-unless-we-bomb excitement of opening night.

I stopped in Rowan's apartment when I arrived at the theatre. Daddy preened when I complimented him on the seersucker shirt and chinos I'd bought for him. Then Rowan walked in from the bedroom.

"Catherine and I did a little online shopping."

The black leather pants were the same ones he'd worn to *The Sea-Wife*'s opening, but the silk shirt was new. The deep green made his eyes sparkle like emeralds.

He shrugged, as if his beautiful shirt had suddenly shrunk two sizes. "I just wanted to do you proud on your opening night."

"You always do me proud. And you look gorgeous."

"So do you."

His gaze traveled over the green sarong that Hal had insisted I wear. I'd resisted at first; I'd worn it my final night with Rowan and it carried too many sad memories. But Hal claimed the bamboo pattern was perfect for opening night of *The Secret Garden*. And the warmth of Rowan's gaze made me happy I had acquiesced.

"I carried the memory of you in that dress every day we were apart."

I let out a shaky sigh and reluctantly said, "We better get down to the green room."

"Not yet. Jack and I have an opening night gift for you."

Mystified, I followed them into the bedroom. On the bed I discovered a jug of detergent, a bottle of fabric softener—and two stacks of neatly folded clothes.

Most women wouldn't get weepy about grown men doing their own laundry, but for my men, it was a milestone.

"Rowan didn't like touching the machines," Daddy said. "Even with gloves. So I did most of the work."

"You also said that bleach brightens everything," Rowan said. "Fortunately, I insisted on a test run."

He opened the armoire and pulled out the jeans he'd ripped open during our quickie.

"The tie-dyed look'll come back," Daddy declared.

"And I'll be in the fashion vanguard when it does," Rowan replied.

"It's the best present you could have given me."

"Don't worry," Daddy said. "He got you flowers, too. But it's bad luck to give them to you before the show."

I nodded. "And tonight, we don't want anything but good luck."

⚓︎

When we gathered in the green room for our toast, I discovered why Hal had been so insistent about my sarong—and why Rowan had taken the unusual step of wearing a green shirt: the entire staff had gone not-so-secret garden. Alex sported a red rose on the lapel of his tuxedo. Reinhard had tucked a green pocket square into the breast pocket of his black suit. Hal had chosen a mauve shirt for the occasion, Lee, a gold one. Janet wore a pale green silk sheath, Catherine, a breezy little flowered number, and Mei-Yin, a scarlet dress with white plum blossoms. As captain of the stage crew, Javier was doomed to wear black, but he sported a goofy circlet of flowers on his head—our ninja Queen of the May.

I got predictably sniffly, Janet predictably rolled her eyes, and even Catherine took a tiny sip of champagne during our toast.

Although Janet and Reinhard flanked me as I led warm-ups, it was the faery lounging against the back wall of the green room who made the magic. As many times as Rowan's power had touched me, I had never deliberately called it forth. As I instructed the cast to close their eyes, I felt like an ancient priestess summoning the elemental forces of the universe.

My toes tingled as his power touched them. My feet grew heavy, as if rooted to the very bedrock of Vermont. A steady vibration rose up through my legs, like sap rising in the spring.

Heat flushed my body as the power flowed up through my belly and chest. My voice fell into a rhythmic chant. My fingers uncurled like new leaves. My body swayed like a sapling, moved by an otherworldly force as ageless as wind and sun and time.

I was caught in the spell yet standing apart, observing its effects. Driven by the growing urgency of the power yet directing it from my little island of calm.

Rowan sensed every shift in my emotions and responded as I framed the words for the cast. We were dancers, our spirits moving together instead of our bodies. We were music, he the song and I the singer. We were separate yet linked by the power flowing between us and through us, between and through the clasped hands of those in our circle.

Twin powers—Fae and human—feeding us and feeding on us, charging us with anticipation and excitement, racing around the circle, pulsing through every body, every mind, every spirit as the song built to a relentless climax.

"Let it go!"

The energy burst free on a wave of cries and groans and sighs. Even the cast members who had performed in *Annie* looked dazed. But they had never experienced a warm-up powered by Rowan Mackenzie.

"Just breathe."

His power retreated on a wave of love that told me more clearly than any words that our brief communion had touched him as deeply as it had me.

Maybe that's why I jettisoned my usual speech and simply said, "Hold on to that power. Bring it to the stage. And we'll make magic here tonight."

❧

The house lights began to dim as Rowan and I slid into our seats. Daddy swiveled around and flashed a grin. "Janet's my date."

Janet gazed heavenward before whispering, "Turn around and behave."

Daddy winked at me and obediently faced the stage. The house lights faded to black. Rowan gave my icy hand a reassuring squeeze. A spot picked up Alex in the orchestra pit. He acknowledged the applause with a quick nod and took his place at the piano.

The rustle of a program. The creak of a nearby seat. The palpable anticipation as if the theatre itself were holding its breath. Then the brass section launched into the "Prelude."

After three short measures of "A Bit of Earth," the strings introduced "Come to My Garden." My heartbeat ignored their serene strains to gallop along with the racing counterpoint of the woodwinds.

The full orchestra took up the melody. The majestic tempo grew slower. My heartbeat sped up. The brass and woodwinds dropped out, leaving only the throb of strings. I took a series of calming breaths as harp and bells shimmered up the scale in the mysterious motif of the "Opening."

A pool of amber light picked up Natasha sitting

downstage right, studying a gilt-framed photograph. The motif sounded again and behind the scrim, a cool lavender light picked up the ghostly figure of Lily on the upstage left platform. Michaela's voice made me shiver with pleasure as she sang the gentle lullaby about the flowers she would keep safe in her garden.

As the lights slowly faded on her, the sky behind the scrim glowed orange, revealing the Indian Fakir on the upstage center platform. Thankfully, Paul no longer resembled Bert Healy with a turban. He even managed to avoid teetering when he lifted a foot in the slow, stylized movement Mei-Yin had taught him.

Before I could wonder if she was giving him some magical help, Larry entered and bent to kiss Natasha's hair. My fingers involuntarily tightened on Rowan's, knowing that our first technical hurdle was looming.

Instead of the bed called for in the script, Hal had come up with the idea of using a stylized canopy that would rise from the floor as the Fakir chanted, like a cobra emerging from a snake charmer's basket. After the fly operator raised it to the right height, four actors would install poles and stretch the gauzy fabric out to create an open-sided canopy. While the idea was cool, the effect was usually spoiled by actors juggling poles and fabric.

As Larry lifted Natasha, the scrim rose. A quartet of actors dressed as Indian servants emerged from the wings. As the groups moved slowly toward center, the tent shimmied upward. The servants seized the four corners of the long swath of fabric, slipped their poles into them, and backed away just as Larry gently laid Natasha in her "canopy bed."

There were appreciative murmurs from the audience. I squeezed Rowan's hand in thanks and felt his love warming my fingers.

He used his magic as sparingly as Janet had predicted: to control the mist that snaked obediently around the actors' ankles, to make the topiaries glide smoothly around the stage, to calm Ethan when he dried up in his first scene, and to give Neil the extra nudge he needed to transform "Winter's on the Wing" into a joyous rite of spring.

The "Final Storm" erupted with lightning and thunder, drawing gasps from the audience. The frenzied singing of the Dreamers gave way to the ominous "Mistress Mary, Quite Contrary" round. Natasha appealed to the Dreamers, but they glided past her like living topiaries, brandishing their red handkerchiefs.

Rowan suddenly tensed. I glanced at him, then back at the stage, wondering what had disturbed him. Natasha conveyed Mary's growing terror perfectly as she wove in and out of the maze of Dreamers, desperately searching for her father. Maybe Rowan was concentrating on controlling the mix of voices so that each individual line came through clearly against the choral singing of "It's a Maze."

As the Dreamers slowly circled Natasha, Daddy began shifting in his seat. Was he simply restless or did he have to pee? Well, Act One would be over in a few minutes. He could certainly wait that long.

I forced my attention back to the stage, but I couldn't concentrate because of Daddy's infernal squirming.

Janet's head snapped toward him. She whispered something, but he just rocked back and forth in his seat.

My impatience vanished at his obvious distress. I leaned forward to reassure him, but when I touched his shoulder, he cried out and batted frantically at the air.

Heads turned in our direction, audience members distracted from the action unfolding onstage by the personal drama playing out in the house.

Rowan's forearm thrust me back in my seat. He slid forward to rest his hand on Daddy's right shoulder. Daddy moaned, and I pressed my fist to my mouth to keep from doing the same.

I'd worried that the vivid special effects might frighten some of the children, but my father knew too much about stage magic to be this upset. Had the ghostly

Dreamers triggered some awful memory of the Border-
lands? Did Mary's futile attempt to escape the maze of
Dreamers remind him of his terrified flight from the
Crow-Men?

The number built in intensity, the Dreamers' "Mistress Mary" chant underscored by the dissonant blare of
horns and the wild twittering of the piccolo and the relentless beat of the timpani. In a few moments, the terrifying music would segue into the soothing melody of
"Come to My Garden" and the nightmare would be
over. If Daddy could just hold on, if Rowan and Janet
could keep him calm for ten more seconds . . .

Daddy quivered like a dog straining at its leash. Natasha darted through a pool of light, red hair washed to a
pale strawberry blonde by the white light.

Only then did I understand my father's distress. I was
too shaken to move. All I could do was sit there as the
music reached its frenzied peak.

A single oboe played "Come to My Garden." Natasha
flung herself into Larry's arms, father and child reunited
at last.

The Dreamers began drifting offstage. I leaned forward to touch my father, to let him know without words
that I shared his anguish.

Rowan shoved me back and clambered over me just
as Daddy leaped to his feet and shouted, "No!"

There were startled exclamations from the audience.
Still frozen in their embrace, Natasha and Larry broke
character to stare into the house. The oboe faltered, then
picked up the melody once again.

Daddy tottered down the aisle. Tears welled in my
eyes as he raised his arms to embrace his lost child.

To embrace me.

My fingers dug into the worn nap of his abandoned
seat, still warm from my father's body. Only by gripping
the seat hard could I keep from jumping up and running
down the aisle and crying, "I'm here, Daddy. I've always
been here."

Rowan seized Daddy's left arm. Janet seized his right.

The music swelled, mercifully covering the rising tide of whispers. Soothing magic rippled through the sostenuto of the strings as Alex tried to calm musicians and audience alike. I felt the steadying throb of Reinhard's power and the determined beat of Mei-Yin's, urging everyone to focus on the stage.

As Michaela stepped aside to reveal the door to the secret garden, even those seated around me settled back in their seats. Their soft "Ahh" told me that the door had swung open, silhouetting Natasha in a flood of moonlight.

I didn't see it. I was still watching the shadowy figures escort my struggling father out of the theatre.

CHAPTER 29

HOLD ON

I HAD NO TIME TO DEAL WITH MY EMOTIONS. When the house lights came up a moment later, I had to concentrate on damage control. I delegated my available staff to handle the audience and asked Bernie and Frannie to deal with the board. As Long made a beeline toward me, I beat a hasty retreat to the Dungeon to check on the cast and found Reinhard outside the women's dressing room.

"They are fine," he whispered. "I told them it was Jack and . . ." He shrugged uncomfortably.

They had all witnessed Daddy's outbursts. This was just another crazy Jack moment.

Natasha, God love her, was more concerned about Daddy than the fact that he had spoiled her big moment. Most of the other women were mollified when I told them he had been overcome by their performances, but a few grumbled that he had ruined their opening night.

"Be glad the guy got into it," Debra snapped, "and focus on Act Two."

I shot her a grateful look and continued down the hall to the men's dressing room. Larry still seemed a little nonplussed, but Otis' reassuring presence was calming everyone. I squeezed his arm, got a firm nod in return, and moved on to the musicians' green room.

Trapped in the pit—and assuaged by Alex's magic—

they were just puzzled because the underscoring had fallen apart. Alex had his arm around the shoulders of the poor oboe player, clearly bolstering his sagging confidence with Fae magic.

I arrived at the breezeway to find staff and board doing their best to downplay the incident. The audience members who had been sitting near Daddy still seemed shaken, but Mei-Yin and Lee were working them hard. Lee's power pulsed with strength and calm, while Mei-Yin's crackled with humor. The odd combination worked. My racing heartbeat slowed and I felt the urge to laugh the whole thing off—just some poor old guy who'd gotten carried away by the magic of theatre. Things could be worse, I thought, as I raced up to Rowan's apartment.

Then I heard the shouting.

I flung open the door and hurried inside to find Long stalking around the living area and Janet clinging to his arm.

"Jack's asleep in the bedroom," Janet informed me. "Rowan gave him a tranquilizer."

I nodded my understanding of her faeryspeak. Before I could assure Long that everything was under control, he said, "What the hell just happened? What's *wrong* with that man?"

"Nothing's wrong with him," I replied, trying hard to keep my voice level.

"First, those disturbances in rehearsals . . . oh, I heard all about them. Is he mentally unbalanced or—?"

"No! And keep your voice down or you'll wake him up."

"Let's all keep our voices down," Janet advised. "And let's not overreact because Jack got caught up in the show."

"He's an actor, for God's sake! How could he get *that* caught up in the show?"

"He's been through a lot!" I exclaimed. "So cut him a fucking break, Long."

Long's eyes widened, but I was too sick with worry to care.

"Why don't we all sit down?"

I hadn't even noticed Rowan standing in the doorway, his voice and power radiating calm. The tension in the room dissipated. I sank into an easy chair, limp and weak-kneed. Janet and Rowan guided Long to the sofa. They sat on either side of him, Janet clasping his hand, Rowan gripping his forearm.

"The show brought back some painful memories for Jack," Rowan said.

"He just wasn't ready to deal with them," Janet murmured.

"But he'll be fine."

"And so will the show."

"Actors are resilient. They're used to dealing with little bumps during a performance."

"And that's all this was."

"There's nothing to worry about."

"Nothing at all."

Long nodded, soothed by their soft voices and their seductive Fae power. Then he blinked and asked, "Should I make some sort of announcement before Act Two? To reassure the audience?"

Rowan patted Long's arm. "That might draw more attention to the incident. Better to go on as if nothing had happened, don't you think?"

"Yes ... better to go on ..."

Janet squeezed Long's hand. "If anyone asks, we'll say that Jack was taken ill."

"Yes ... that's good ..."

Brainwashing my board president was *not* good. And observing the way Long's head bobbed obediently made me a little queasy.

Get used to it, Graham. This is what it will be like living with a faery. There will always be suspicions to quell, truths to avoid, lies to invent.

Rowan ushered Long toward the front door, one

hand resting lightly on his shoulder. Long hesitated, then eased free.

"I know he's your friend, Rowan. But as president of the board, my first responsibility is to this theatre. No matter how much I may sympathize with Jack's problems, the fact remains that he's a disruptive influence."

"I'll look after Jack. And I give you my word, there will be no more disruptions."

"That's not your job."

"But it *is* my responsibility."

Long shook his head. "The Crossroads Theatre isn't a . . . a halfway house. If this man is as deeply troubled as I suspect, he needs professional care."

"He needs the Crossroads," I said. "He was an actor once. He could be again."

"And when he's ready, I'll be the first to welcome him back."

"Back?" I echoed.

"I'm sorry. Jack has to leave. Tomorrow."

"No!"

Rowan's power lanced through me, an urgent plea for silence. Janet advanced on Long, her cold eyes belying the warmth of her smile.

I couldn't let Long send Daddy away, but neither did I want to watch them break him. And they *would* break him. Long might be less susceptible to their brainwashing, but he would not be able to resist it forever. It would eat away at his resolution, transform his objections into complacency, convince him to do what they wanted—what we wanted. Could I let them do that when his concerns were perfectly valid?

"Stop!" I exclaimed.

Rowan and Janet shot me identical looks of disbelief; it was the first time I had ever noted any resemblance between them. Long merely seemed puzzled.

"You can't send Jack away. I've cast him in *Into the Woods*." As Long's expression shifted into outrage, I quickly added, "He needs to act again. He needs to find a purpose in life."

"Why is it our responsibility to give him that?" Long demanded. "And why are you so worked up about him? You've only known the man a few weeks."

"He's my father."

Long gaped. Janet sighed. Rowan just watched me.

"My mother divorced him more than twenty years ago. She took her maiden name again and changed mine, too. I got an occasional postcard from him and then ... nothing. Until Rowan brought him back to me. He didn't recognize me. He doesn't even know I'm his daughter."

My voice broke. Rowan hurried to my side, his arm and his power steadying me.

Long glanced toward the bedroom. "He doesn't know?" he whispered.

Rowan shook his head. "We thought the shock might be too much for him."

"That's why he got so upset tonight. He was seeing *me* on that stage, not Natasha."

Rowan's anxiety flashed through me, then vanished as he tamped down his power. All the time he'd been dealing with Daddy, he must have been worried sick about me.

"He's had a hard life," I told Long. "But he's coping. And he's excited about performing again. The Narrator is only a small part. I've asked Rowan to play the Mysterious Man."

"Rowan!" Long exclaimed.

"You saw him as Billy Bigelow," Janet reminded him. "He can certainly handle the Mysterious Man."

"That's not the point! I should have been informed. About all of this."

"You're right," I agreed. "I'm sorry. But—"

"What happens if Jack can't go on?" Long demanded in a furious whisper. "Or—God forbid—he breaks down onstage?"

"Bernie is understudying the role. And he'll be playing the matinees."

"Bernie's in on this, too? Good God, what else have you been keeping from me?"

"I'll be with Jack during rehearsals and the show," Rowan said. "I can keep him calm and focused."

"You didn't do a very good job tonight," Long noted.

"No. He caught me . . . off guard. That won't happen again."

"I know it's a risk," I said. "But I'm asking you to trust our instincts. To trust *me*." Careful to keep my voice soft, I added, "He may be my father, but I love this theatre. If I thought he couldn't handle the stress—or turn in a good performance—I would never suggest this."

Long frowned. "Letting him stay is one thing, Maggie. But putting him in the show . . ."

"Come to the Follies," Rowan urged. "See how he does in that."

"He's in the Follies, too?"

"A kind of dress rehearsal," Rowan said.

"That's hardly the same as performing on the main stage."

"It'll be fun," Janet assured him. "I'll even wager Jack will exceed your expectations. If I win, I'll make you dinner. If I lose . . ." She flashed a teasing smile. ". . . I'll make you breakfast."

To my astonishment, Long blushed. Then he nodded brusquely. "But if I decide he's not ready to perform in *Into the Woods*, that's the end of it. Agreed?"

I nodded meekly. I even worked up a grateful smile; I only hoped it was half as convincing as Janet's kittenish one.

No matter what happened at the Follies, I would never permit Long to send my father away. Daddy had finally opened the door to his past, and I was going to help him walk through it.

CHAPTER 30

HEY, OLD FRIEND

THANKS TO THE SHITLOAD OF FAE POWER circulating through the theatre, Act Two went off without a hitch. When the lights came up on the final scene, even I gasped when I beheld the brilliant red and gold of the roses, the deep green of the foliage, and the otherworldly blue of the sky. When Archibald embraced Colin and Mary, I sniffled along with the audience, my vision blurred by tears and the shimmering light that suffused the stage.

I wished Daddy could have seen it: the transformation of the garden, the transformation of all those touched by its magic. I wished he could have seen Archibald and Colin reunited. And I wished that life imitated art. I didn't expect that Mom and Daddy and I would ever stand in Helen's sun-drenched garden, all wrongs forgiven, all happiness restored, but for the first time I had real hope that some of those old wounds could be healed.

For the next two days, he remained closeted in Rowan's apartment, emerging only to apologize to the cast for "getting carried away" and to come to Janet's house to run through *Snow White* with the rest of the staff. He seemed so relieved to throw himself into our rehearsal that I gave up any thought of telling him I was his daughter. It was far more important for him to shine during the Follies.

Nancy's arrival offered a welcome respite. Even if I could only escape for a few hours, dinner at the Bough would give me a chance to decompress.

When I invited Frannie to join us for a drink, she shook her head. "I'm waiting for the couple who've booked the Honeymoon Suite to check in."

"So sit where you can see the lobby."

After a brief hesitation, she agreed, and for the next fifteen minutes, I enjoyed the rare treat of talking about ordinary things like the weather, the economy, and the recent coyote incursions in Dale. Then Frannie jumped up and exclaimed, "I think Mr. and Mrs. Louis just came in."

"Maybe I should go out and—"

"No. You gals enjoy your dinner." She winked at Nancy and whispered, "If you get any juicy gossip about Maggie and Rowan, be sure and pass it along."

As soon as Frannie disappeared into the lobby, Nancy pounced.

"Something's happened."

"You and my mother should start a detective agency."

I waited until Beth presented our salads and retreated to the kitchen. Then I plunged into the saga of opening night. Nancy expressed cautious optimism about Daddy's breakthrough, but her expression clouded when I described the aftermath with Long.

"You used the F-word?"

"I was upset. I apologized later. And was very sweet. Well, sweet for me."

"Don't shrug this off!" she exclaimed with rare heat. "Rowan allowed you to talk like that because he loved you. But you can't do it with Long."

The arrival of our dinners saved me from answering. When Beth departed, I said, "I know I should follow Janet's example and smile and coax and cajole. It's just . . ."

"Cajoling isn't your strong suit. But at least treat Long with respect. And when he drives you crazy, count to five before you say anything."

"Not to ten?"

"You'd never make it that far." Nancy picked up her fork and set it down again. "I know you love your father. And you want him to be happy. But you can't sacrifice your future for him."

"It won't come to that. Long will—"

"It's not only Long. There's Rowan to consider. And Alison. And your staff. I don't want to see you jeopardizing those relationships because you're putting all your time and energy into developing one with your father."

I poked my grilled trout, appetite gone. I was all too aware of how little time I had spent with Rowan, how much extra work I had thrust onto my staff. And every day that I allowed to pass without telling my mother about Daddy seemed a betrayal of the closeness we had forged. I doubted my father would ever give me the kind of love and support I received from them.

And from the woman sitting across the table from me.

"You're absolutely right," I said. "And now, enough about Daddy. Let's talk about you."

She described her added workload at the library in the wake of the budget cuts and her poor mother's case of shingles. In the middle of a story about her cat's ear infection, she broke off abruptly.

"This is about as much fun as discussing your fight with Long."

"Who cares? Sometimes, life is crappy bosses and shingles and ear infections. So what did the vet say about Dante?"

Only when coffee arrived did she casually mention that she'd gone out on two dates with a college professor named Ed.

"Two dates? And I'm only hearing about it now?"

"Well, we just had the second date last night and—"

"Wait. Start at the beginning."

Through a combination of wheedling and relentless interrogation, I got most of the details. Nancy assured me it was "too soon to tell" if anything would develop, but her faint blush and soft expression indicated things were developing pretty fast.

When she said she had a surprise for me at tomorrow's matinee, I was sure she was going to produce Ed. I waited outside the theatre in a fever of anticipation. But Nancy arrived alone.

"No Ed?"

She surveyed the horde of people streaming toward the lobby and suddenly grinned. "I brought someone else. Two someones, actually."

A bass voice bellowed, "Yo, Brooklyn!" And the burly figure of Lou Mancini waded through the crowd like a T-shirted and tattooed Moses parting the Red Sea.

I managed to squeak, "Yo, Joizey" before Lou engulfed me in a bear hug. Then squeaked again as his girlfriend Bobbie shouldered him aside and treated me to an equally rib-bruising embrace.

"Why didn't you tell me you were coming?"

"We wanted to surprise you," Bobbie said.

"And we sure as shit did," Lou added.

Bobbie punched his shoulder. "It's a kids' show," she informed Lou in an undertone. "So watch your language, asshole."

"How long are you up for? Can you stay for the Follies?"

"Hell . . . heck, yes!" Lou said. "That's why we came up this weekend. Got into the Bough last night and—"

"Wait. You're not . . . are *you* Mr. and Mrs. Louis?"

"That was Frannie's idea. In case you started poking around."

"We nearly had a heart attack when she told us you and Nancy were in the dining room," Bobbie said. "We ran all the way upstairs. And—oh, my God, Maggie—our suite's gorgeous!"

"Yeah. But I kinda miss my crappy old room." Lou nudged Bobbie. "We had some good times up there."

"We know," Nancy said. "Our room was under yours."

Lou's bellow of laughter made several nearby patrons wince and earned him another punch from Bobbie.

"I just can't believe you're here. Rowan will be so happy to see you. Maybe we can all go out for a quick dinner after the show."

Too late, I recalled all the reasons why that would be a really bad idea: mad dogs, special silverware, projectile vomiting.

"Or grab some Mandarin Chalet grub and eat in Rowan's apartment."

Lou and Bobbie exchanged awed glances. "*The* apartment?" Bobbie said.

"Maybe you should check with Rowan first," Nancy suggested.

"We can check with him now," I said as Rowan edged through the crowded lobby.

He kissed Nancy's cheek, squeezed Bobbie's hand, and staggered only a little as Lou enthusiastically pounded his back. But when I mentioned dinner, his smile slipped.

"We don't have to go out," I assured him. "Just take some Chinese food up to your apartment."

"I wish we could, but Alex and I are meeting to discuss music rehearsals for *Into the Woods*."

"What about lunch tomorrow?" I suggested.

"I'm helping with setup for the Follies."

"There's plenty of time for that after the matinee."

"Lee and I are still working out some of the special effects."

"But—"

"It's not a problem," Nancy said, shooting me a quelling glance.

Lou nodded. "A man's gotta do what a man's gotta do."

"We can talk after the Follies," Bobbie said.

But their smiles failed to hide their disappointment.

Rowan's fingers rose to his throat, kneading the scar that was hidden beneath his tightly buttoned collar. "Maggie and I should get backstage. I'll see you after the show."

I smiled brightly and allowed him to take my arm, but as soon as we rounded the side of the barn, I shook off his hand.

"You haven't seen them in two years. Lou and Bobbie came all the way from Jersey! And you couldn't make time to have dinner?"

"In my apartment."

"Where else can we go? You refuse to go out. The cast will be eating in the picnic area."

"So you invited them to my apartment."

"I thought it would be fun!"

"But it's *my* apartment, Maggie. You might have asked whether I wanted guests."

"Okay. Yes. I'm sorry. But—"

"I've never even invited the staff to my apartment. Except Helen, of course."

I knew he'd never socialized with the staff until this summer, but I'd assumed that Alex had been there to work on the shows. Certainly, most of the staff had been inside—Lee and Hal when they stormed the barricades the night of my first Olympic orgasm, the rest to pack up Rowan's things. But none had been invited guests.

Rowan glanced at the milling crowd, then took my arm again and led me into the Smokehouse. He closed the door and regarded me gravely.

"I'm not like you, Maggie. You're at ease with people. You know what to say. How to . . . fit in."

"How are you going to learn to fit in if you lock yourself away?"

"I won't always . . . I was thinking of hosting a party for the staff after the season is over."

"Why wait? Throw a cocktail party before the Follies."

He stared at me, aghast. "I can't invite guests over on such short notice."

Sometimes, I forgot that he had learned human manners in the nineteenth century.

"Newsflash. You don't need to send engraved invitations. Especially to old friends who are all going to be at the theatre that afternoon."

"But—"

"Ask Nancy and Bobbie and Lou to stop by for the last half hour. That way, the staff will be flattered that they got first dibs, and the others will be flattered that they were included."

"All those people . . ."

"Nobody will mind. They'll be having too much fun."

"Maybe *they* will."

I put my arms around his neck. "Say yes."

"That's coercion."

I kissed him. "Say yes."

"Unfair coercion."

I deepened the next kiss and felt his groan rumble against my mouth. "Say yes?"

"I believe the correct term is 'uncle.' "

I slipped free and clapped my hands. "A new Crossroads tradition."

"Dear gods. From a cattle call of a cocktail party to a new Crossroads tradition in ten seconds."

"It's better this way. Get it over with fast. Like pulling off a Band-Aid."

"The perfect analogy."

"Oh, stop being a grumpy old faery. You'll have a great time. Just give me a shopping list and I'll pick up everything you need tomorrow morning. I'll even help with prep."

"You in the kitchen? That almost makes this worthwhile."

"I can cook! Some things. And I can certainly chop and peel and do the grunt work."

"Maggie Graham, Sous Chef." He studied me a moment, then said, "You never give up, do you?"

"Maggie Graham, Pit Bull." My smile faded as I took in his serious expression. "This is the easy stuff, Rowan. If we can't do this—"

"We can. I can."

CHAPTER 31

IT TAKES TWO

I SHOULD HAVE KNOWN ROWAN WOULDN'T be content with cheese and crackers. It was only by dint of considerable persuasion that I got him to include veggies and dip—or what he called crudités with tarragon aioli.

Daddy fled after the first fifteen minutes. I soldiered on in Hors D'oeuvres Hell.

"The point is having people in," I said as I eviscerated a cucumber. "Not to win an award from *Gourmet* magazine."

"If we're going to do this," he replied, stirring his lemony fennel slaw, "we're going to do it right. The cucumber cups need to be smaller. They're an—"

"If you say amuse bouche one more time, I'm serving up bacon-wrapped faery testicles."

"I'd prefer Graham on the half shell."

Our chuckles died at the same moment. I slowly lowered my knife. He slowly lowered his spoon.

"We're alone," Rowan said. "We have an hour until the actors arrive for the matinee. And we're making hors d'oeuvres. Does that strike you as incongruous?"

"No. It strikes me as crazy."

He took my hand and led me toward the bedroom. En route, he paused by his desk, ripped a page out of his new journal, and scrawled, "Jack. Take a long walk around the pond."

I taped the note to the front door and closed it firmly. "What's the lady's pleasure?"

My face grew warm.

Rowan grinned. "Graham on the half shell, it is."

The first time we had made love, we'd been a little awkward and more than a little desperate for the fulfillment we had postponed for so long. Later, the knowledge of our parting cast a bittersweet shadow over our lovemaking. As for our wham bam quickie, that didn't count as lovemaking at all.

Now, I could simply enjoy him. The otherworldly paleness of his body. The smoothness of his skin. The soft folds of flesh between his thighs, the most alien part of his anatomy and the one he had hidden from me the longest. The pink rosebud of a penis peeking out shyly, then rapidly losing its shyness as it shot skyward.

His hands gliding over my skin. His cheek rubbing against my thigh. That cat's tongue teasing between my legs.

I think I screamed shortly after that. And made some unearthly noises. Rowan didn't seem to mind. After he'd reduced me to a quivering Jell-O woman, he rested his chin on my belly and summed up with a succinct "Yum."

When he reached for the box of condoms, I stayed his hand. "I have a better idea."

I've never been Frieda Fellatio. The preliminaries are fine. It's the inevitable ending that always gives me trouble. Which is why I'd never ventured into this territory with Rowan. But the way his eyes widened when he realized what I intended and his little moan of pleasure when I seized his hips and pulled him toward me encouraged me to take the plunge.

Unfortunately, I didn't factor in the effect of faery power. It's hard to give a guy a hummer when you're gasping and moaning yourself.

I finally raised my head and said, "Rowan. Can you tamp down the power a bit?"

I felt like Santa in the animated *Rudolph the Red-Nosed Reindeer* special asking Rudolph to turn down his nose. But this little experiment was never going to reach a satisfactory conclusion while I was experiencing secondhand arousal.

Rowan stared into space, his eyes glazed with pleasure. When I tapped his thigh, his gaze finally focused. "I'm not sure . . . it's very difficult . . ."

"Maybe we should give this up and—"

"No! I'll try. Very hard."

There were a couple of dicey moments when his desire flooded my body and I was sure he'd have to finish without my assistance. But Rowan clamped down on his power and I clamped down on Rowan and, apart from the moment when his fingers tightened involuntarily in my hair, the inevitable ending proved oddly satisfying. Oddly for me, that is. He tasted the way he smelled, sweet and musky and warm. I licked up every delicious drop and smiled smugly as he collapsed onto the bed.

"That was amazing," he breathed, giving my not-so-inner Aphrodite an added boost.

"You mean no one's ever—?"

"You know perfectly well you're the only person who's ever seen me naked."

"Well, you don't necessarily have to see the flagpole to polish the chrome."

He gave a startled yelp of laughter. "In my day, it was discreetly called the French way."

"In your day, they didn't have chrome to polish."

"Gods. I wasn't sure I was going to make it."

"A credit to your control."

"A credit to my imagination. I pictured myself going off like an unattended fire hose and—"

It was my turn to yelp.

He propped himself up on his elbow and grinned. "I don't suppose you'd care to polish the chrome again?"

"I'll get lockjaw. Besides, the actors will be arriving soon and you can't possibly . . ."

My eyes widened.

Rowan lay back and folded his hands behind his head. "Faeries have extraordinary recuperative powers."

"Smug bastard."

"Chrome polisher."

I pinned him to the mattress and straddled him, a pretty easy task since he wasn't putting up a fight. Then I kissed him, and he shivered.

"Is that what I taste like?"

"Mmm-hmm."

"Did you . . . was it . . . ?"

"Yum."

<hr>

I was more aware of the pleasant ache between my legs than the performances at the matinee. Afterward, I raced back up to the apartment and found Daddy perched on the sofa, scowling at the plate of crudités.

"I told him that was all he could have," Rowan called from the kitchen, "until everyone arrives."

Fortunately for Daddy, there was a knock on the door a few minutes later. I hung back to let Rowan greet his guests. The men solemnly shook hands. Mei-Yin clapped him on the shoulder. Catherine gave him a quick peck on the cheek.

Janet brought up the rear. She hesitated on the threshold, just as Rowan had the day of the barbecue. They went through the same Gaelic gargling. Then Janet stepped inside and I let out my breath in relief at surmounting another hurdle.

"No need to stand in the office," Rowan said a little too heartily. "Let's all go into the other room."

Hal let out a soft shriek as he entered the living area; obviously, he'd never seen it. Nor had Bernie who gave a low whistle and murmured, "Man, oh, Manischewitz, such a hayloft."

Because of the Follies, we were serving nonalcoholic beverages, but I couldn't resist buying two bottles of champagne to mark the occasion. Rowan opened one, splashed a swallow into Catherine's glass, and filled the rest.

"As you probably guessed, this was Maggie's idea. I have to admit I was . . ."

"Horrified?" Janet prompted.

"Taken aback," Rowan conceded. "But she assured me it would be fun. So a long overdue welcome. To colleagues. To family. To old friends."

We clinked glasses, all of us savoring this extraordinary moment. Then Daddy said, "Can we eat now?" and we exchanged solemnity for laughter.

Daddy circled the room like a shark as he sampled hors d'oeuvres. The rest of us milled around and exclaimed over Rowan's food.

"You MADE this?" Mei-Yin demanded, examining a basil leaf topped with a tiny ball of pine nut-coated goat cheese.

"Maggie helped."

"Mostly, I gouged out cucumber cups for the salmon mousse."

Hal popped a mango shrimp in his mouth and mumbled, "Yum."

I studiously avoided looking at Rowan.

"I'll never fit into my Follies costume," Hal declared. Then he immediately plucked a puff pastry from Lee's plate. "Ooh! What are these?"

"Lemon parsley gougeres," I informed him.

"Goo-who?" Lee asked.

"Who cares?" Catherine replied. "They're terrific."

Her happy laugh gave me almost as much satisfaction as her heaping plate. Morning sickness seemed to have given way to a rapacious appetite. And although she would probably fall into bed after the Follies, her face—if not exactly glowing—was less drawn.

"I had no idea you were such a good cook," Javier said.

Daddy paused long enough in his circling to note, "There aren't any mini-hot dogs."

"Try a bacon-wrapped date," I advised.

"Try . . . what *are* these, anyway?" Bernie asked.

"I hope you're not kosher," Rowan said.

"Only at Passover."

"Prosciutto crostini with lemony fennel slaw."

Alex laughed. "I never imagined I'd hear those words coming out of your mouth."

"You're as bad as Maggie. I informed her that the miniature quiche is properly called a mushroom pomponnette and—"

This time, everyone laughed. Hal picked up two tiny quiches and exclaimed, "Two—four—six—eight. Who do we appreciate? Rowan. Rowan. Rowan!"

Rowan looked pleased but confused until I explained the "cheerleader with pom-poms" allusion.

For the next hour, he was a consummate host, unerringly finding something to appeal to each of his guests: explaining the origin of the battered trunk to Javier; lingering with Alex by the antique melodeon; showing Janet the silver-framed photograph of Jamie and his family.

When he saw Reinhard gazing raptly at one of the bookcases, he nudged me and whispered, "Library lust." As we wandered over, Reinhard carefully removed one volume and cradled it in his hands. "I still cannot believe you own a first edition of this."

I craned my neck, and he turned the book so I could read the faded lettering on the bright blue cloth cover: *Adventures of Huckleberry Finn, Tom Sawyer's Comrade*.

"Holy crap," I whispered.

Rowan smiled. "The first book I ever owned—and the first novel I ever read. I preferred travelogues and newspapers that offered me glimpses of the world. But I enjoyed *Roughing It* so much that Jamie's son Andrew bought me that."

"Do you know how much this is worth?" Reinhard asked.

Rowan shook his head.

"At a guess ... twenty to thirty thousand dollars."

"Holy crap," I whispered again.

Even Rowan looked shocked. "Well, at least now I know I can support myself."

"You're not selling it," I told him flatly.

"No. It has too much personal history. But most of the other first editions are just ... old books."

"You should have them appraised," Reinhard said. "I am no expert, but I have a friend who is an antiquarian bookseller. She will give you an honest estimate."

"Thank you, Reinhard." Rowan cocked his head. "I believe the other guests are arriving."

A few moments later, he ushered Lou, Bobbie, and Nancy into the living area. After the hugs, kisses, and backslapping concluded, I steered them over to Daddy. Nancy eyed him intently as she shook his hand.

"It's nice to meet you, Jack. Maggie's told me so much about you."

Lou settled for a more casual "Howya doin'?"

"Better," Daddy replied, drawing uncertain glances from Lou and Bobbie.

I brandished the plate of cucumber cups. "Hors d'oeuvres, anyone?"

"I won't lie to you."

"Rowan made the salmon mousse himself."

"I went through some bad times."

I tramped on Daddy's foot. "But right now, he's enjoying the party."

"Oh, sure. But don't get your hopes up. There aren't any mini-hot dogs."

It was only a matter of time before someone asked Lou and Bobbie about their status. Naturally, that someone was Mei-Yin who demanded, "When are we gonna hear WEDDING bells?"

Bobbie blushed. "Well, now that you mention it . . . next spring."

Rowan's voice rose above our excited babble. "This calls for more champagne!"

As we raised our glasses, I wondered if our friends would ever toast our engagement or witness our wedding vows. Then I silently intoned my "one day at a time" mantra and reminded myself to enjoy this moment, this day, and the company of good friends.

Half an hour later, I shooed Nancy, Bobbie, and Lou out to the picnic area to grab some pizza with the rest of the audience. Rowan shooed the staff off to the Smokehouse to get into makeup and costumes.

Our first party. And everything about it—except the hors d'oeuvres—had been wonderfully ordinary.

"Post-party depression?" I teased as Rowan collapsed on the sofa.

"Post-party exhaustion. Do you think they enjoyed themselves?"

"They had a wonderful time. How about you?"

"It wasn't as bad as I thought it would be."

"Didn't you have any fun at all?"

"Yes," he replied, a faint note of surprise in his voice. "Once I stopped trying so hard and just let things . . . happen."

"There's hope for you yet, Mackenzie."

He heaved himself off the sofa. "Stop patting yourself on the back and get to work, Graham."

I banished my uncertainties about the future, content to revel in the wonderfully ordinary task of cleaning up after our guests.

CHAPTER 32

QUIET PLEASE, THERE'S A LADY ONSTAGE

IF THE STAFF WAS NERVOUS ABOUT DADDY'S DEBUT, they hid it well. As we changed into our costumes behind the screens Hal had set up, there was a lot of good-natured teasing about *my* debut. Last year, I'd been too overwhelmed to take a role in the Follies. This year, my stomach was aflutter with nerves and mushroom pomponnettes.

When I emerged in my costume, the staff applauded. I laughed when I beheld my adorable forest creatures.

Over their tights, the staff wore shapeless knee-length serapes in various shades of brown and gray. Mei-Yin — our resident squirrel — had a bushy gray tail attached to her serape. Catherine had a bunny's powder puff. Alex's head was crowned with a stag's antlers. In his black eye mask, Javier looked more like a dashing cat burglar than a raccoon. But a morose-looking Reinhard won top honors with his enormous moose antlers.

"The cast will lose all respect for me."

"They'll be too busy admiring your rack," Hal replied.

"Honey, my drapes are stuck again."

As Lee fiddled with the draping that hung over Hal's full-length mirror frame, the door to the Smokehouse opened. We all froze, but it was only Bea.

"My God," she said when she saw Mei-Yin and Reinhard. "It's *The Adventures of Rocky and Bullwinkle*."

Reinhard scowled. "If you have come to call places, please do so."

"Places!" she sang out, still grinning. "Break a hoof, Dad."

I adjusted Daddy's floppy dwarf cap. "You'll be great." *Please, please, please let him be great.*

Rowan kissed my cheek. "Just have fun. Both of you."

I slipped out the Smokehouse door and eased aside so that Janet and Hal could squeeze in behind the backdrop that hung from the branches of the maples. The recorded overture blared from the speakers, prompting cheers and whistles from the assembled actors. When the lights came up to reveal Janet in her evil queen glory, they responded with a low "Oooh." But Hal got the first laugh of the evening when he pulled open his draperies. He'd kept the weird mask from the Disney cartoon, but the rest of his costume was pure Carmen Miranda, complete with a towering headpiece of apples.

There were some giggles when I launched into "I'm Wishing." And even more at Catherine's echo, which veered between Minnie Mouse and Marlene Dietrich. Lee got some laughs with Prince Charming's constipated voice. But Bernie's Huntsman brought down the house as he gamely attempting to stab me while inching forward in his walker.

The friendly forest creatures were a hit. So was the entrance of the dwarfs, who marched over from the breezeway carrying lanterns. I watched Daddy anxiously, but he "heigh-hoed" as fervently as the rest and shamelessly hammed up his sneezes: stuttering, staggering, regaining control, only to lose it again; clinging to a very un-Happy Reinhard; goggling at a very Dopey Javier; and finally unleashing such a storm that the rest of us careened around the acting area.

"You're doing great," I whispered to him. And was rewarded with a smile and a snuffle.

I danced with the dwarfs, spinning from one pair of hands to the next. It was almost like my dream, but I was so much happier now. Daddy had joined our dance and although Rowan could only watch from the shadows, his pleasure bubbled through me like the champagne we had sipped at our cocktail party.

When it came time for the Queen's transformation, I was the one watching from the shadows. As Janet drank her magic potion, the strobe light kicked in, making her contortions positively eerie. Her gown billowed as she whirled in a circle. The flash pot went off, emitting a small cloud of sickly yellow smoke. It cleared to reveal a hook-nosed, hunchbacked Rowan shrouded in a long, black cape.

The collective gasp from the audience was followed by wild applause. Awe changed to laughter when Rowan dipped his apple into the cauldron and pulled up a succession of different objects: a softball, a cantaloupe, and a scarlet brassiere with cups large enough for watermelons. I didn't know whether he used faery glamour to pull off the trick or merely some ordinary sleight of hand, but I laughed as delightedly as the audience.

When he arrived at the dwarfs' cottage, it struck me that this was the first time we would play a scene together in front of an audience. The few words we'd exchanged in *Carousel* didn't really count. Another first—for both of us.

"Make a wish," he croaked, proffering the shiny red apple.

For a moment, I forgot where I was. I just saw those familiar green eyes looking out from that almost unrecognizable face.

I wish I could help you find your place in this world. I wish that you could direct again. I wish you could let the staff into your life and discover how those friendships can nurture and sustain you. I wish you could trust me to share your worries. I wish I could give you a child with my red hair and your green eyes. I wish I could always be with you. I wish I could spare you the pain of watching me grow old and die.

Rowan's eyes widened. Then he lifted my chin and whispered, "One wish."

I snapped out of my daze and dutifully wished for my prince to come and carry me away to his castle where we would live happily ever after.

He pressed the apple into my hands. I raised it to my mouth and bit into it.

Colors exploded before me—probably some weird lighting effect that made the sparks in Rowan's eyes flash gold and silver and apple red like the fireworks we had watched from his balcony. The apple slipped from my fingers. I seemed to float to the ground, but that must have been Rowan's magic easing me earthward.

In the blackout that followed, he pulled me to my feet a good deal more brusquely and quick-stepped me behind the backdrop.

"I'm fine," I whispered, although I was still a little dazed. "Go die spectacularly."

His kiss bruised my mouth and shocked me back to reality. His spectacular death scared the shit out of me.

One minute, he was racing through the audience, pursued by a horde of screaming dwarfs and the next, he was scrambling up one of the trees by the Smokehouse. He edged his way onto a branch and looked down where I was huddled in the shadows, gnawing on my fist.

"It'll be great!" he whispered. Then he leaped for the Smokehouse roof.

There were a few screams from the audience. I nearly bit off my index finger.

A spotlight picked him out as he clawed his way up the roof. Although I knew he was just making it look difficult, I gasped each time he slipped. He struggled to his feet, hampered by his long skirt, then tiptoed along the roofline like a tightrope walker.

He paused to shake a fist at the dwarfs and suddenly lurched sideways. His arms pinwheeled as he fought for balance. I told myself he was acting, that his magic would protect him if the four mattresses behind the Smokehouse didn't, that we would laugh about this later unless I murdered him first.

He flung out a hand in a final, desperate effort to save himself. With a despairing screech, he toppled backward off the roof.

More screams, including mine. Someone seized my arm, and I screamed again.

"Get on the table," Bea whispered.

"What?"

"Your bier."

"Shit."

I snagged my foot in the draping around the bottom of the table. Then I disentangled myself and crawled onto my makeshift bier. The hinges creaked as Bea lowered the plexiglass lid over me. I folded my hands across my heaving chest and tried to take shallow breaths.

To the accompaniment of the Prince's "One Song," the crew hauled up the backdrop. My faithful dwarfs rolled the table forward and—I prayed—locked the wheels. Hal marched on to narrate the tale of the Prince who had searched far and wide for his fair maiden. The lid creaked open and I suppressed a sigh of relief as cool air flooded in.

Lee's lips touched mine. Then touched them again. He lifted me up and plastered a big wet one on my mouth, but when I refused to awaken, he abruptly released me.

As I flopped back on my bier, he whined, "She's supposed to be revived by true love's first kiss."

"Maybe YOU'RE not her true love," Mei-Yin declared.

The dwarfs lined up for their try at reviving me. Javier slobbered all over me in an appropriately Dopey way, but the rest were very decorous. Then it was Grumpy's turn. Mei-Yin ground her mouth against mine for so long that I finally tapped her on the shoulder.

She grinned. I glared. Then I got back into character and exclaimed, "Oh, Grumpy! It was you all along."

After which I went home with my dwarfs, the Prince

danced off with his Carmen Miranda Mirror, and we all lived happily ever after.

❦

"If you ever scare me like that again," I warned Rowan after I'd changed into my street clothes, "I will kill you!"

"But wasn't it spectacular?" he asked, eager as a child.

"Spectacularly scary." I smacked him, then rounded on Mei-Yin. "And what was with that kiss?"

"You LOVED it!"

Our high spirits evaporated when we discovered Long waiting outside the Smokehouse. Daddy shrank back against Rowan. The rest of the staff clustered around him; whatever reservations they had, he was part of the pack — and Long was not.

Judging from Long's frown, he caught the "us against him" vibe. But he just smiled and said, "Congratulations, everyone. I can't remember when I've had so much fun. Although I nearly had a heart attack when you fell off the roof, Rowan."

"All carefully choreographed, I assure you."

Long's gaze rested on Daddy. "I can understand why Maggie was so eager to have you in *Into the Woods*. I'm sure you'll be a wonderful addition to the cast." He waved away Daddy's stammered thanks and shot Janet a rueful smile. "I guess this means I can only claim dinner."

She chucked him under the chin. "A very nice dinner."

As the staff hurried toward the breezeway for the reception, I lingered to thank Long. With Nancy's admonitions fresh in my mind, I was more than usually gracious.

His smile vanished. "I'm not giving him a free ride, Maggie. Just a chance to prove himself. And only because he's your father. If there are any outbursts or disturbances, I'll pull him from the show."

My chin came up. "I'm the director, Long. If he can't handle the role or causes any problems, *I'll* pull him."

CHAPTER 33
WE CAN MAKE IT

THE NEXT MORNING, I SHARED A BRIEF FARE-WELL BREAKFAST with Lou and Bobbie and Nancy, then plunged into rehearsals for *Into the Woods*. I'd always loved the show. Okay, maybe there was too much moralizing in Act Two and maybe the songs weren't as strong as those in Act One, but once I became executive director, I was determined to mount a production. It didn't matter that Rowan had done the show before. It captured the essence of the Crossroads: its history, its secrets, and its undercover mission of helping people find their paths through life.

Like all good fairy tales, it was about the wishes people make and the quests they take to fulfill them. A Baker and his Wife, cursed with childlessness by the vengeful witch from next door. A collection of fairy-tale characters—Cinderella, Little Red Ridinghood, Jack from "Jack and the Beanstalk"—that must break out of their predetermined stories and make difficult choices to survive. A lighthearted Act One that morphs into a dark and dangerous Act Two, in which consequences can be deadly and wishes can only come true through collective effort and sacrifice. And of course, the Mysterious Man, who abandons his wife and child, but returns to guide his son the Baker through the darkest hours of his life. Plus a great book by James Lapine and a Stephen

Sondheim score that made you laugh one moment and cry the next.

What's not to like?

Alex suggested we start things off by running the prologue, a thirteen-minute musical scene that introduced all the principal characters. Since the prologue consisted of nine—count 'em, nine—interwoven scenes, I was more than a little nervous about the possibility of starting things off with a train wreck. But Alex's instincts were sound. There were stumbles, of course, but when they sang that final "and home before dark," there were cheers and whistles from the rest of the cast and high fives among the performers.

I watched my father whooping it up with the others and felt a wave of pride. Yes, Rowan and I had run his lines with him dozens of times. But Daddy had performed like the pro he once had been—and might become again.

We split up after that, Rowan and Alex working musical numbers in the Dungeon and Smokehouse, while I blocked onstage. By the end of the afternoon, I was so jazzed by our progress that I seized Rowan's hands and exclaimed, "Let's go out to dinner!"

"Out?"

"Alex and Mei-Yin are working 'Ever After' tonight. We've got the whole evening free. Let's celebrate!"

"Good idea," Alex agreed. "You've been chained to this place ever since you returned, Rowan. About time you got out and saw the town. What there is of it."

"But what about Jack?" Rowan asked.

"I'll take him along to dinner at Momma's."

"It's all settled," I declared. "I'll meet you in the lobby in half an hour."

I skipped up the hill and into the Bates mansion. Janet leaned over the upstairs railing and remarked, "Either you've decided to play Little Red Ridinghood or it was a good rehearsal."

"Into the town without delay to celebrate this perfect day ..."

"A good rehearsal. I'm delighted. You can stop singing now."

"Into the Chatterbox, we may decide to share a milkshake."

"You and Rowan?"

I nodded and hurried up the stairs.

"He's actually leaving the grounds?"

I paused on the top step. "Sure. Why?"

"Nothing. Have a good time."

"You, too! Alex is bringing Daddy up to dinner."

"Oh, goodie."

"Stop. Daddy likes you."

"Yes. I know."

"What does that mean?"

"Nothing."

"You're full of meaningful 'nothings' this evening. Do you know something I don't know?"

"I know a great many things you don't know. I am—"

"Wise beyond your considerable years. Someday I hope to hear all about your date with Calvin Coolidge. But right now ..."

"Go. Have fun. You can tell me all about it when you come back."

I laughed. "I only tell you about my awful dates."

But she'd already walked into her bedroom and closed the door.

❦

By the time I selected a flowered skirt and scoop-necked blouse, my bedroom looked like a tornado had blown through. I left my cast-off clothes where they'd fallen, pulled on my sneakers, and threw a pair of sandals into my tote bag; no way was I ruining another outing by turning my ankle. I flew through the house, packing up additional supplies, and hurried back down the hill.

Rowan was waiting outside the barn.

"You look so pretty and summery."

I pivoted in a circle, my skirt swirling around my thighs. "And I feel as corny as Kansas in August."

His smile was oddly wistful. "Still in love with a wonderful guy?"

"Yeah. But you're nice, too." I grinned and pointed toward the road. "And . . . they're off!"

Like the nineteenth-century gentleman he was, he took my tote bag, but frowned as he inspected its contents. "Do you really think we need bottled water?"

"In case you get warm."

"Couldn't you just spray us with this thing?" he asked, pulling out the plant spritzer.

"Sure. But that's mostly to scare off the dogs."

Thunder rumbled faintly in the distance.

"Looks like it might rain," Rowan noted.

"I put umbrellas in the bag."

"Ah."

"We could take the car if you—"

"No."

As we walked up the lane, I yapped about our dinner options. With both the Bough and the Chalet closed on Monday nights, it came down to the Chatterbox or Duck Inn.

"Duck Inn is basically pub grub. But they have a liquor license."

"Ah."

"If you want a strawberry milkshake, though, we should go the Chatterbox."

"Yes."

"What are you in the mood for?"

His anxiety prickled through me.

"No biggie," I assured him. "Decide when we get to town. I'll eat anywhere. I'm just happy to be going out to dinner with you."

His power surged, laden with such apprehension that I drew up short.

"What is it? What's wrong?"

Sweat popped out on his forehead, as if conjured by my words.

"Rowan? Talk to me."

Instead, he sank onto the low stone wall.

"This isn't going to work."

"What isn't going to work?"

"I've tried, Maggie! You have no idea how hard I've tried. But I can't do this."

He's leaving me.

He swore he wouldn't.

Mom was right.

You misunderstood. He wouldn't walk out of your life again.

Oh, no? Watch him!

You know this man.

He's not a man. He's a faery.

He loves you.

Not enough.

Stop. Think. Don't blurt out something you'll regret.

I raised my eyes to heaven, hoping for some celestial guidance. All I found were thunderclouds piling up like dirty cotton balls.

I took a deep breath and asked, "What are you talking about?"

"This! Dinner!"

My breath leaked out in a shaky sigh. I sat beside him, mostly to keep my knees from buckling.

"If you didn't want to go out . . ."

"I *can't* go out!"

I shook my head, completely baffled.

"I can't go out to dinner. I can't even step into the road!"

"If you're talking about the curse . . ."

"The curse was lifted. But I am still bound."

Finally, I understood what must have happened on our abortive Fourth of July outing, why he was always inventing excuses to avoid going to town, why he was drenched with sweat.

I laid my hand over his clenched fist. "You know what this is, right? A classic panic attack. You were a prisoner so long that your body is going nuts at the prospect of leaving the property."

He jerked his hand free and stalked away. "I am well aware of the nature of my . . . dysfunction. That has not helped to effect a cure."

"Don't be so hard on yourself. This is only the second time—"

"No, Maggie. It's not the second time or even the twenty-second time. I tried to step into the road the first week I returned. Every night after Jack fell asleep, I walked up this lane. And every morning before dawn, I tried again—and failed again."

That long, lonely walk, shrouded in darkness but buoyed with the determination that this time, he would break free. And then the longer, lonelier walk back to his apartment, bowed down by yet another failure. Repeating that ritual night after night. Locking away his fear and humiliation in the daytime to present a confident facade to the world.

"He's actually leaving the grounds?"

Clearly, Janet had suspected the truth—just as Alex had picked up on Rowan's sexual frustration. They had their Fae power to guide them. I had only my human senses. And they had failed me. Why hadn't I looked deeper?

"Why didn't you tell me?"

He whirled around. "Because I was ashamed!"

The hot flush of his humiliation roiled through me. His angry eyes met mine. Then his gaze slid away and he slumped atop the wall.

Okay, Graham. You're the helping professional. Start helping.

He'd spent several lifetimes learning to lock away his emotions, consigning his fears and hopes and doubts to the unresponsive pages of his many journals. I had read some of those journals. Shared his bed. Heard his bitter

confessions about the willful misuse of his power. I had
felt his grief and anger, longing and despair resonating
inside of me. I had even experienced the agony of being
bound by iron. And still, I felt pitifully unprepared for
this moment and all too aware that the words I chose —
or failed to choose — might change our relationship forever.

Touch had always unlocked his emotions. And humor.
This sure as hell didn't feel like a situation that humor
could remedy, so I'd have to rely on touch.

I wriggled between his knees and rested my hands on
his shoulders. A shudder rippled through his body, but
his emotions remained carefully shielded.

"First off, I love you. And these panic attacks don't
make me love you or respect you less. We'll deal with
them. Together. But I can't help if I don't know what's
troubling you."

"I didn't want to worry you," he mumbled.

"Worry me. Please. I don't have your power. I don't
know what's going on inside your head. I either miss the
clues or feel like I'm putting together a puzzle with half
the pieces missing. We have to be able to talk. To be honest. And to trust each other."

His gaze finally rose to meet mine. "You thought I was
leaving you."

Fucking faery powers.

"Yes. And then I stepped back and decided — "

"Not to kill me?"

His small smile left me wobbly with relief. But I knew
my lack of trust had wounded him, even if he was carefully shielding me from his pain.

"I'm sorry I doubted you. I wish I could say it'll never
happen again. But . . ."

"It will. Whenever we're put to the test."

"We're going to face a lot of tests, Rowan. And if you
always know what I'm feeling and I'm always in the dark,
it'll only make them harder. Just let me in. Tell me what
you're thinking. If you blame me for doubting you — "

"No. I've had doubts, too. When I'm with you—or when I'm working—I forget about the obstacles. But at night ... the Fae only require a few hours of sleep. That leaves a lot of time to think. And the night breeds ... dark thoughts."

"But the sun is shining now." I scowled at the lowering sky and added, "Well, it's shining behind the clouds. And we have the whole evening ahead of us. We'll make dinner. We'll make love. We'll chase away the darkness."

His arms went around me. I cradled his head against my breast.

"Let's go home," I whispered.

"No."

Gently, he freed himself from my embrace. Then he rose and turned toward the road.

"You don't have to prove anything to me."

"I know. I have to prove it to myself."

He took a single step forward and stopped, the toes of his boots a mere inch from the black macadam—like the night of the *Brigadoon* cast party, when he had hovered just beyond the patio of the house he had vowed never to enter.

But he had reconsidered that vow, made in the first flush of anger and hatred for the Mackenzies who had imprisoned him. If he could enter Janet's house to comfort Helen after her heart attack, then surely, he could conquer his fear now.

He took a deep breath. Then another. A drop of sweat oozed over his eyebrow. He blinked it away.

A muscle jumped in his cheek as he gritted his teeth. A shudder racked his body. He wiped his palms on his jeans. Clenched and unclenched his hands.

And then his head drooped.

I stepped into the road and thrust out my hands.

"You can do this."

Rowan backed away.

"Take my hands. We can do this."

He shook his head and continued retreating.

"Rowan! Please!"

He bared his teeth. Then he threw back his head and bellowed his anger and frustration and defiance to the sky.

His unleashed power blasted through me. I staggered backward, gasping. Saliva filled my mouth, as hot and delicious as the rage scalding my body.

Like a berserker out of some ancient tale, he charged, hair streaming behind him, eyes wild and unseeing, mouth open in a roar of fury that tore an answering scream from my throat. The thunder of his footsteps shuddered through the earth, shuddered through my body.

And suddenly, I was laughing, fury banished by exultation, blood-pounding rage transformed into a light-headed giddiness that made me reel.

Hands grasped my arms, steadying me. Green eyes— still a little wild, still flashing with the echoes of his power—stared into mine.

The soft huff of his breath against my face.

The nasal blast of a horn.

We clutched each other and stared at the vehicle bearing down on us. Then Rowan whisked me into his arms and out of the road and we fell back against the stone wall, laughing and breathless.

The pickup truck eased onto the grassy berm. The driver leaned over to peer out the passenger window. I spied a familiar John Deere cap and beneath it, the frowning face of my board treasurer.

"Hi, Mr. Hamilton!"

"What the hell are you two doing? Playing chicken?"

"Something like that."

"Well, cut it out. You're too old for such foolishness."

Rowan whooped. I seized his shirtfront before he toppled backward off the wall.

"He been drinking?"

"No. We're just . . . we had a really good day."

Mr. Hamilton shook his head at the unfathomable

weirdness of theatre people. "Next time you have a really good day, stay out of the road."

"Yes, sir."

His head withdrew into the truck, an anxious tortoise retreating into its shell. I stifled a giggle with one hand and waved good-bye with the other. Then Rowan and I exchanged grins.

"I couldn't walk into town now to save my life," I admitted.

"I'm not even sure I can make it to the barn."

I shoved a hank of wet hair off his forehead. "You did it."

"*We* did it. I'm sorry I lost control like that."

"It worked. That's what matters."

He raised my hand and pressed his lips to my palm. "Have I mentioned that I love you?"

"Not for ages. An hour, at least."

"I love you, Maggie Graham."

"I love you, Rowan Mackenzie."

❧❧

We took a cool shower and made love. Fixed dinner and made love again. I knew I should dress and go back to the house before Daddy returned from rehearsal. Instead, I fell asleep in Rowan's arms—and awoke in them the next morning.

It was the first time that had ever happened. Every other time I had slept in his bed, he woke long before me and only returned to the bedroom when he sensed I was waking. Maybe he had stayed with me to avoid disturbing Daddy.

Before I could ask, there was a soft knock.

So much for a clean getaway.

Rowan slipped out of bed and padded to the door. "What is it, Jack?"

"Janet left something for Maggie."

"Leave it outside the door, will you?"

"Okay."

"Was there anything else?"

"I made coffee. And put out some crumb cake."

"Thank you."

"Rehearsal starts in an hour."

"We'll be there."

"I thought . . . until then . . . maybe I'd take a walk around the pond."

"Thank you, Jack. That's very thoughtful."

"See you at rehearsal. You, too, Maggie!"

"Okay!" I sang out.

Janet's mysterious offering turned out to be a shopping bag filled with a change of clothes, my makeup bag, a toothbrush, and a note that read, "Dear Heloise. Congratulations on breaking out of the cloister. Try not to appear too saddle sore at today's rehearsal. Janet. P.S.— please extend my congratulations to Abelard on *his* escape. It's about time."

I merely folded the note without reading it aloud. But Rowan said, "She sensed what I was going through, didn't she?"

"I think so." I gently traced the centuries-old scar at his wrist where once he had tried to kill himself to escape the degradation and agony of the iron.

"It doesn't matter. It's over now."

He stretched out beside me and I let my fingers drift across his chest, marveling yet again at its smoothness.

"Did you stay with me all night?"

"Yes."

"Just lying here? Awake?"

"I slept for a few hours. The rest of the time, I just listened to you."

It was impossibly sweet: Rowan holding me in his arms, listening to the soft sound of my breathing.

"You snore."

I bolted upright. "I do not!"

"You snore and snuffle and mutter and thrash. You're a very lively sleeper."

"I'm surprised you didn't sell tickets."

"It was endearing!"

"Snoring. Endearing."

"Yes. It was so . . . unexpected. Like you."

He pressed me back onto the mattress and kissed me. Expecting the usual developments, I was surprised when he rolled over onto his back.

"I've never fallen asleep with anyone. The Fae always sleep alone. Each in his own secret place. That way no one can find you when you're vulnerable."

"Well, it's always hard sharing a bed when you're used to—"

"It's more than that. I can't shield myself when I'm asleep. I've always worried that I might sense my partner's dreams. Or that hers could bleed into mine. I think that might have happened last night."

I fought down my panic. Although I knew Rowan would never deliberately invade my dreams, it still felt like my last bastion of privacy had tumbled.

"Say something. Please."

The upwelling of love caught me off guard. He could have used his power to sense what I was feeling. But he was deliberately shielding himself to restore the privacy I might have lost during the night.

"Well, I'll tell you one thing: we're not sleeping in separate beds."

His embrace was bruising, but his lips were very gentle as they roamed over my face. "Tell me what you dreamed."

"The same dream I've been having for months. I was alone in a forest glade . . ."

"Dancing with fireflies."

Another shiver of panic, but smaller this time and easier to subdue.

"I've had the same dream," he whispered. "All summer."

"All . . . ? But how is that possible?"

"I don't know."

"Did you see the staff? Were they there?"

"No. You were alone."

So it was not my dream, but his—or some strange blending of the two.

"You sensed my presence. I thought at first you would run away, but you waved your hand, beckoning me. And when I hung back, you ran across the glade and pulled me out of the shadows and ordered me to dance."

"God. Even in dreams, I'm a bossy cow."

"You started twirling around and told me to twirl, too. I was oddly . . . clumsy. But you took my hands and spun around and around with me. And the fireflies surrounded us in light—beautiful golden light. And we were laughing and happy. And then . . ."

"And then?"

"The fireflies vanished. And so did you. And I was alone in the dark."

The desolation in his voice shocked me. I rested my left palm against his chest and raised my right to cup his cheek.

"You're not alone. I'm right here. And I'm not going anywhere."

Neither of us wanted to state the obvious: that one day, death would take me away from him. Maybe that's why I kissed him so fiercely—to drive away that specter.

When he didn't respond, I kissed him again, more gently. I let my hands and my mouth offer the reassurance we both needed: that we would have thousands of nights together, thousands of days to work and play. We would celebrate the end of summer by walking in our woods. We would lie together, warm beneath our blankets, while snow silently drifted onto the skylights. We would see the first crocuses bravely pushing through the snow in the spring and stand on our plateau, admiring the fiery glory of autumn.

Trust me, my hands whispered as they skimmed over his back. Cherish what we have, my body urged as I guided him inside of me. Give me your doubts and your fears; I am strong enough to bear them. Fill me with your magic; I am brave enough to accept it.

His heart pounded against mine. His power ebbed and flowed, eternal as the tide. Golden sunlight poured through the skylights, caressing our bodies, seeping through flesh and bone and blood to dance inside us like a cloud of fireflies, the light pulsing to the rhythm of his power, the rhythm of our bodies.

A single note, bittersweet and beautiful, vibrating with possibility, blossoming into fullness. An answering chord, resonating with my love, my longing, my hope. Melody and harmony, faery and human. Bodies and hearts and spirits entwined in a single song that swept us over the edge of the precipice and carried us safely back to earth again.

Share my dreams and I will share yours. Offer me your heart and I will give you mine. Trust me, my love. And, together, we will defy all the powers of this world and Faerie to come between us.

ENTR'ACTE
THE JOURNAL OF ROWAN MACKENZIE

She astounds me. Her strength, her determination, her bull-headed stubbornness that sees every impossible obstacle as an annoying hurdle.

And her love. Not fascination, which I have encountered from many humans. Or awe, which the elders assured us was our due from such an inferior race.

Love.

As a child, I sniggered at the stories about humans who stumbled upon our kind and wandered mazed through the world for the rest of their days. I smiled indulgently at their depictions of our realm and dismissed as sheer invention those stories in which a human outwitted the Fae.

We knew all their tales. Throughout the ages, the Fae have slipped through the veil to lurk outside their homes or stand just beyond the light of their fires, watching and listening.

Only when I returned to Faerie and was inundated by the questions of my clan did I appreciate the symbiotic relationship that has evolved between human and Fae. If they are fascinated with us, we are just as intrigued by them: their minds, so easily controlled; their senses, so easily beguiled; the gamy smell of their flesh; the hairiness of their bodies. Try as we might to hide our wonder behind a facade of disparagement and detachment, we have always marveled at the fire they carry inside, the passion with which they devour life, the fierce emotions that roil through them: fury and joy; grief and longing; hatred and love.

283

Even after living among humans for centuries, I could not adequately describe those emotions to my clan. When I tried, they regarded me with confusion and thinly veiled contempt.

What is more pathetic than a Fae in thrall to a human?

Yet Maggie has never made me feel pathetic. Furious, incredulous, uncertain, joyful, but never pathetic. Even when I revealed the shameful truth about my panic attacks and the recurring dream in which she always, always leaves me.

How can she love my weaknesses? Do they make me seem more human?

I must never suggest that; Maggie would fly into a temper if I equated weakness with humanity. Besides, so many of the human qualities the Fae ridicule as weaknesses are—paradoxically—their strengths: their blind loyalty to those they love; their willingness to accept the flaws of others; their ability to forgive.

I maintained a distant professionalism with Reinhard, yet he stores my belongings without ever knowing if I would return for them. I brushed off Alex's overtures of friendship for decades, yet he risks the possibility of being hurt again to try and forge a genuine relationship with me. Janet can put aside a lifetime of resentment to invite me into her home. And Maggie can forgive me for leaving and open her heart and her life to me again.

Will I ever understand them? Will I ever understand her?

Yet I trust her with my heart and my life. I have shared my secret name. I will even risk sharing my dreams. But how can I share the truth of what really happened on opening night of *The Secret Garden*?

It might be kinder if I did. It would help her understand Jack's determination to go on seeking the elusive portal to Faerie. And prepare her for the inevitable moment when he tells her he is leaving—again.

But she is so confident that this show will change him. And perhaps she is right. I have to give her—and him—the chance to find out.

So I will lock away the truth. I will let Maggie believe that Jack saw his daughter on the stage, that he rushed to aid his child in her moment of peril. I will let her overlook the obvious: that the peril had already passed when Jack leaped up, that child and father had already found each other, that it was only when the Dreamers drifted away that Jack cried out in despair.

Just as he cried out when my clan slipped into the forest on that long ago Midsummer.

Nearly thirty years since that night. And Jack is still running after the faeries who beguiled and abandoned him, his longing only whetted by the passage of years.

Oh, Maggie, your love is your greatest strength and your greatest weakness. It blinds you to the truth about your father—and the truth about me.

No matter how many times you pull me into the light, I will always have to retreat into the shadows. One day, you will grow tired of coaxing me out.

And when that day comes, I will lose you.

ACT THREE

EVER AFTER

CHAPTER 34

DON'T RAIN ON MY PARADE

I FLOATED THROUGH THE NEXT WEEK on Cloud Nine. Performances for *The Secret Garden* were great. Rehearsals for *Into the Woods* were great. Life was great.

So what if Jessica was struggling with the role of the Baker's Wife? She'd get it eventually. So what if Kanesha was tentative? So was Cinderella in Act One. I'd make it work. I could make anything work.

The students playing Little Red Ridinghood and Jack blended smoothly with the adults. Our Baker was rock solid. Our Rapunzel was a terrific singer. Our two princes—one a Mackenzie, the other a professional—got along so well you would have thought they'd been friends for years. And they looked so much alike—tall, dark, and handsome—that Mei-Yin dubbed them TweedleTim and TweedleTom.

Directing Rowan was a breeze. He brought a hint of danger to the mysterious man that nicely offset the comic moments.

Best of all, Daddy was happy and confident. The reservations of his cast mates faded when there were no further outbursts or bragging about his past performances. As the week progressed, he even began joining them for meals.

I was thrilled that he was making friends, delighted that he was getting out into the world—and a little hurt

289

that he could dump me so easily. I knew it was stupid. I was the one who had pushed him to mingle. Now, I was acting like an abandoned child.

Been there, done that, not doing it again.

I made up my mind to let Daddy fend for himself and enjoy my time alone with Rowan.

After which I promptly began lurking: inventing some vital item I needed at the grocery store so I could drive past the Ptomaine Stand at lunchtime, popping into restaurants for takeout while he was eating dinner. Hal chided me for reverting to Maggie Graham, Stalker. Janet advised me never to consider a career as a private investigator.

Rowan just said, "Let him go, Maggie."

"I am letting him go. I'm just following at a discreet distance."

"If you're so discreet, then why did Jack ask me if you were checking up on him?"

"Oh, God. What did you say?"

"I lied and said you were running errands."

"Did he believe you?"

Rowan gave me his "What do you think? I'm a faery!" look.

Debra's rendition of "Stay with Me" inadvertently put an end to my lurking. She captured the Witch's fury at discovering Rapunzel has admitted the prince to her tower; her bitterness at learning she is not "company enough;" her fear about the dangers lurking in the world; and her tender plea for Rapunzel to remain a child, safe with the mother who loves her. As I watched that rehearsal, I realized I'd run through all those emotions in my relationship with Daddy. If I hadn't begged him to remain a child, I'd certainly shadowed him like an overprotective mother.

Been there, done that part deux.

I backed off and prayed that the greatest danger he would encounter in the world was the fat content of the Ptomaine Stand's burgers.

Our first run-through went so smoothly that I was shocked when the staff began speculating about when the other shoe would drop.

"We've got a terrific show," I protested.

"A terrific Act One," Alex corrected.

"So let's enjoy the moment."

"You know who you sound like?" Mei-Yin asked. "The BAKER'S Wife. Right before the giant SQUASHES her."

"A tree squashes her."

"The point is she gets SQUASHED."

I waved away Mei-Yin's observation. Of course, Act Two would be more demanding; the show got a lot darker, characters died left and right, and those that remained faced difficult choices. But the cast was strong and united, and I was confident we could pull it off.

Some of the credit went to Otis and Debra. With only the tiny part of Cinderella's father to master, Otis spent most of his time calming nervous Mackenzies and running lines with Daddy and the kids. Even the professionals seemed to rely on his easy laugh and quiet strength to ease them through the occasional rough patch. If Otis was the cast's unofficial den mother, Debra had become its head cheerleader, her acid humor balancing his warmth, her "let's get this done" practicality offsetting his easygoing attitude.

"She reminds me of you," Rowan commented as we shared a hurried dinner.

"Funny, talented, helpful . . ."

"Skeptical, bossy, opinionated . . ."

I tossed my half-eaten breadstick at him and exclaimed, "Finally!"

"Finally?" he repeated, neatly snagging the breadstick in mid-flight.

"A joke. You've seemed so . . . preoccupied this week."

I waited for an explanation, but he merely returned the breadstick to my plate.

"Look, if you're uncomfortable being directed by me—"

"No." He poked an asparagus spear and said, "Your mother's coming up next weekend to see *The Secret Garden*."

"I'll tell her to leave the spoon at home."

"I'm more concerned about her meeting Jack."

I sighed. "She can't. Not then, anyway. The last thing Daddy needs before Hell Week is that kind of drama. She's coming up the next weekend for *Into the Woods*. Maybe by then . . ."

"Why not wait, Maggie? Until the season's over. You have enough to deal with without telling Jack you're his daughter and engineering this meeting."

"But—"

"All we have to do is keep him out of her way for two weekends. Have Bernie go on as the Narrator the night she's here. Print up programs that list his name instead of Jack's. Let's save the drama for the stage."

While I hated the continued subterfuge, I knew it would save Daddy a lot of stress during *Into the Woods*. And it would give us more time to get to know each other, which would make the revelation that I was his daughter easier for both of us. Maybe by the time *Into the Woods* closed, he'd have worked out what he wanted to do next. Knowing he had his life in order would impress Mom far more than seeing him in yet another musical.

"It's a deal."

Rowan's relief surprised me; obviously, he'd been a lot more worried than he'd let on.

"So she's arriving Friday?"

"Saturday. There's some retirement party at Chris' law firm Friday evening."

"Then Jack and I will go to the cottage before the matinee—"

"We'll have to ask Janet to keep him under wraps. Chris wants the four of us to have dinner Saturday. Don't worry, I told Mom you'd make dinner here because we wouldn't have enough time to go out between shows.

And don't yell at me for not telling you sooner. I didn't want you to start obsessing."

"I do not yell," Rowan replied. "Or obsess."

He spent the next fifteen minutes interrogating me about my mother's favorite foods. When I pointed out that this qualified as obsessing, he flashed a rueful smile. "It's just . . . it's our first meal together. I want everything to be perfect."

"All you have to do is wave your magic wand and we'd eat sawdust and think it was great."

"That would be cheating. I want her to see me, not my magic."

"Beguile her with mushroom pomponnettes instead of faery glamour?"

"I want her to accept me as a man. As a human."

Touched by his serious expression, I reached across the table and squeezed his hand.

"She will."

On Sunday, the other shoe dropped with God-like vengeance.

A storm knocked out the power around lunchtime. Bernie dealt with the hassle of canceling the matinee. Alex soldiered on with music rehearsals in Janet's candlelit parlor. Lee hooked up the generator to light the Smokehouse. After turning my script with staging notes over to Reinhard, I raced to the hotel.

Fortunately, most of our paying guests had checked out that morning. Frannie handed out flashlights to those who remained. Our backup generator churned out enough juice to power the emergency lights in the common areas and the coolers in the kitchen. We served up sandwiches and beer that evening, and cast members and tourists alike joked about our adventure.

After two days of staging scenes in the soggy meadow, the adventure had palled and the cast had begun sniping at each other. I soothed and cajoled. The staff churned out Fae power to ease the tension, focus tired minds, and boost confidence.

Much to my surprise, my father used his charm for the same purpose. He flashed that gap-toothed grin. He made silly jokes. He complimented cast members on their comic timing, their singing, their death scenes. And he seemed utterly sincere. Even when he shifted the charm to someone new, the person he'd just abandoned regarded him with an affectionate smile.

For the first time I understood why he had been so successful onstage and off. He made each person feel like the center of his world. He'd done it to me after the Ms. Pac-Man debacle just by asking me about my day and encouraging me to talk about rehearsals. I wondered if his behavior stemmed from genuine concern or a need for approval or simply a desire to avoid unpleasantness.

Frankly, I was too grateful about the results to care. Cloud Nine might be a little gray, but at least it was no longer scudding over the horizon.

❧❧

The power came back on Wednesday morning. With that hurdle behind us, I set my sights on the next one: helping Jess find the strength and humor in the Baker's Wife.

"If she's so strong, why does she sleep with the Prince? Just because she quarreled with the Baker . . ."

"Her defenses are down. She lets herself be swept off her feet. She realizes it's a mistake, but it helps her understand who she is and what she wants—and to appreciate the life she has."

"And then she gets crushed by a tree."

"Well . . . yes."

"Is that supposed to be God's punishment?"

"I prefer to think of it as dramatic irony, but if God's punishment works for you . . ."

"No. It just seems so unfair. She makes one mistake . . ."

"'People make mistakes,'" I quoted from "No One is

Alone." "Because she lingers with the Prince, she's under that tree when it falls. Because the Baker's father steals the magic beans, the Witch is cursed by her mother. And in revenge, the Witch lays a curse on the Baker's family. Act One is all about spells and magic and making choices. Act Two is about the consequences of those choices. Untangling the spells. Relying on ourselves instead of magic."

I might have been describing the history of the Crossroads Theatre—and my family. Rowan's fascination with humans led him to break his clan's rules about approaching them. Because he seduced an innocent Mackenzie girl, he was cursed by her mother and abandoned by his clan. In a vain effort to lift that spell, he worked another to call the Mackenzie descendants to the Crossroads. My father answered that call. And one fateful night, he stumbled on Rowan's clan and fell under the spell of their glamour.

Maybe this was the summer we untangled the spells and our lives.

Observing Jess' frown, I tried to get back on track.

"Her mistake makes her human—and vulnerable. And her loss forces the Baker to step up to the plate. Same thing happens with Jack and Little Red and Cinderella. They lose their lodestones and have to grow up. Like we all do. We learn to make our own choices, find our own paths. And if we're lucky, we find people along the way who can help us."

Mom. Rowan. Nancy. Helen. Everybody on the staff. They all guided me, no matter how many twists and turns the path took.

"The stronger you are, the harder your loss will hit the Baker—and the audience."

"I don't feel very strong. Especially around Brian."

"He's overcompensating."

"Because he doesn't trust me."

I hesitated. "Because he's scared. So he's trying to control the situation."

"Like the Baker."

Like me that first season.

Jess studied her script. She was one of those people whose appearance suggested that her primary goal was to slip through life unnoticed. Medium height, average weight, ordinary features, indefinite age somewhere between twenty-five and thirty-five.

And then she raised her head and I was struck anew by her thoughtful expression and the intelligence of those brown eyes. She was a quiet pool that seems unremarkable at first glance, but whose depths you discover on closer inspection.

Like Nancy.

"I know someone like Brian," Jess said. "Scared underneath and trying really hard to hide it."

Hard to say whether that "someone" was a parent or a lover or a friend—or what effect this summer would have on their relationship. But I finally understood why Jess had come here. And even if the choices that lay ahead were tough, I knew she had the strength to make them.

"Brian's a good guy," I finally said. "And a good actor. Talk to him. Work your scenes. If you need me to step in, I will. But I think you can handle this without me."

❦

Our Act Two run-through got off to a rocky start, but the solid performances of Debra and Rowan helped steady the others. The cast was close to mastering the rapid-fire lyrics of "Your Fault" and the intricate dance steps in the finale. And both Jess and Kanesha were beginning to bring out their characters' inner strengths.

I skipped Friday's performance of *The Secret Garden* to spend the evening with Rowan. He had to scurry down the back stairs from the kitchen now and then to smooth over the usual rough spots with his magic, but it was still nice to have some quiet time together.

When he returned from ensuring that Act Two was off to a good start, he refilled our wineglasses, lifted my feet off the sofa, and settled them across his lap. By the time he finished the foot massage, I had devolved into a state of boneless bliss.

But I couldn't help asking, "The show will be okay, right?"

"The show will be fine."

"Debra's great. Much better than I was when I played the role at Southford. I was good at the big moments, but I went for the cheap laughs."

"Well, that was before you came to the Crossroads."

"And you took me under your beneficent wing?" I raised my hands and salaamed as best I could from my reclining position. "I am not worthy, O great one."

"I'm not great," he assured me solemnly. "Just very, very good."

I stuck out my tongue. "Do you suppose she's a Mackenzie? Debra, I mean."

"I don't know."

"You don't?"

"It's not like they have a particular scent, Maggie. Or a plaid aura."

"I thought you always knew."

"Of course I knew. They were only ones who came here. But I don't have a blood tie to the Mackenzies. Except to the staff, of course. If you're really curious about Debra . . ."

"The important thing is that she found something here she needed."

"Yes. A job."

"More than a job. She's mellowed since the beginning of the season."

"Maybe."

I pushed myself into a sitting position. "Are the Mackenzies supposed to have a monopoly on the Crossroads? Professionals and community theatre actors might need help, too, you know."

"The Mackenzies don't want a career in theatre."

"Neither do most of the others. Debra's the only one

who's actually making a living at acting. The other 'professionals' are doing what I did: bouncing from one non-Equity job to the next and holding down a crappy job between gigs to pay the bills. Sure, some are hoping for their big break. But most just love the theatre too much to give it up."

"If they can't make a living at it, aren't we doing them a disservice by encouraging them to believe that they can?"

"I don't think we're doing that. I think—I hope— we're giving them skills that will help them succeed on and off the stage. Same as the Mackenzies. There must be thousands of people who need this place, who could learn something about themselves by working here. I want to give them that chance. It's not a betrayal of what you set out to do. It's just . . . expanding the mission."

Rowan frowned. "And magic? Where does that fit in?"

"The same way it always has. When you left, we all thought we had to become a normal theatre in order to survive. But it's the magic that makes this place special. I want that. I want this to be a place that changes lives, just like it changed mine. And I know that sounds like Maggie Graham, Helping Professional, but—"

"That's who you are."

"Are you so different?"

"I don't have your illusions about people. And I don't want you to be . . . disappointed."

"Are we talking about the theatre? Or Daddy?"

"Both."

BY THE TIME THE MATINEE LET OUT Saturday, Daddy was in lockdown at the Bates mansion, dinner preparations were complete, and the air in Rowan's apartment was redolent with the earthy aroma of mushroom pomponnettes.

"You look beautiful," I told Rowan who had donned his green silk shirt and black leather pants for the occasion.

"So do you," he replied, surveying my kicky sundress.

"Are you as calm as you look?"

"Absolutely. When Alison walks in, I'm going to call her Mom and give her a big kiss."

"You better be wearing a brass jock strap."

He laughed and shooed me downstairs to keep watch.

When Chris' Accord eased down the lane, I hurried out of the lobby and ran after it like an excited puppy. Mom crawled out of the car, submitted to a brief hug, and noted, "You look appallingly blissful."

"I am. How are *you*?"

"Tired."

She made a brief detour to greet some of the cast members who were enjoying the usual post-matinee supper in the picnic area. As soon as she turned toward the barn, her pleasant smile vanished. She marched toward the stage door like a prisoner about to enter Stalag 17.

"This is going to be a disaster."

"No, it won't," Chris assured me. But his expression was almost as grim as my mother's.

"Is it dinner with Rowan? Or something else?"

"It was just a really long drive."

We followed Mom up the stairs to the apartment. Rowan took one look at them and said, "You both look like you could use a drink."

As he ushered them into the living area, Chris gave a low whistle. Mom, of course, had seen it during her less-than-cordial meeting with Rowan two summers ago. Praying our dinner would go better, I darted around like a hummingbird on crack as I set out the hors d'oeuvres.

I heard another whistle and turned to find Chris examining the bottle of wine on the sideboard.

"You really pulled out all the stops, Rowan."

"Wait'll you taste the mushroom pomponnettes," I promised.

My mother's lips pursed; clearly, she thought Rowan was trying too hard. She thawed a little after her first glass of wine, but her chilly politeness was almost worse than outright rudeness. Rowan pretended not to notice, but when he went into the kitchen to put the lamb chops on the grill, I plunked myself on the sofa next to her.

"He's worked really hard on this dinner," I said in a furious whisper. "Could you at least try to meet him half-way?"

Mom had the grace to look abashed. She took a deep breath, put on a happy face, and said, "I thought Maggie was exaggerating when she praised your cooking. Now I know better. If you get tired of the theatre, you can open a restaurant in town."

Rowan glanced at me, then shook his head. "I'm already keeping a wary eye out for your spoon. I don't want to be looking over my shoulder for Mei-Yin's cleaver."

"Look on the bright side," my mother said. "A cleaver would be quick."

"Thank you, Alison. That *is* a comfort."

I began humming "Always Look on the Bright Side of Life." Chris obligingly chimed in with the whistles. Rowan laughed. Even Mom smiled.

Apart from her brief interrogation about how Rowan had spent his time away—and whether he had reconciled with his mythical father—dinner went more smoothly. But both Mom and Chris seemed . . . off. Maybe it *was* just the long drive. I hated to think of them enduring the return trip tomorrow.

When I mentioned that, Chris said, "We're not. We're going to stick around and play tourist next week."

I managed to avoid shrieking, but my face must have conveyed my panic because Mom said, "Don't worry. We won't be underfoot. We'll do some sightseeing and come back Thursday after *Into the Woods* opens."

"And since you'll be done with rehearsals," Chris added, "we'll have all day Friday to visit. Maybe go on a day trip, the four of us."

I banished the mental picture of Rowan vomiting out the back window of Chris' car and plastered a smile on my face. "That's great! I'm not sure if the Rose Garden Room's available next Thursday, but—"

"It's all taken care of," Chris said. "Frannie booked us into a room down the hall for Thursday night."

"Wonderful," Rowan said. "You'll have much more fun playing tourist than driving back and forth two weekends in a row. Where are you going? Or are you just going to wander?"

I gave a derisive snort; Mom was as likely to wander through Vermont as she was to hitchhike.

After favoring me with a quelling glance, she began describing their itinerary. Rowan astonished me by commenting on all the sites she mentioned and offering suggestions for others to consider. If I didn't know better, I'd have believed he had actually visited them.

"It's worth a side trip to see the Quechee Gorge," he urged. "The Grand Canyon of Vermont, they call it. If you don't want to walk to the bottom, you can still get a marvelous view from the bridge. Better still, take a hot air balloon ride. I've always wanted to do that." His expression grew dreamy. "Imagine floating through the sunset with the world drifting by beneath you. Like Phileas Fogg in *Around the World in Eighty Days*."

"It probably costs an arm and a leg," my practical mother noted.

"But for the experience of a lifetime ..." Rowan sighed. Then he brightened. "You should come up for fall foliage season. The town will be crawling with leaf peepers, but there's a place nearby with incredible views. I took Maggie there for a picnic."

"It was our first date. Rowan packed up his entire kitchen—silver, crystal, bone china. And the food ... poached salmon, grilled quail ..."

"That's some first date," Chris said.

"It wasn't as romantic as it sounds. More like the opening round of a boxing match. Both of us probing, trying to find out what made the other one tick."

"But it was a beginning," Rowan said. "The first time we really opened up to each other."

As we shared a smile, an enormous sense of peace filled me. We'd come a long way since that afternoon.

My smile faded when I caught Mom studying me. Chris was studying Mom, his expression grave.

Was that why they seemed off? Were they having problems?

Stop borrowing trouble. The evening's finally going okay. Slice up the blueberry pie, dish out the ice cream, and thank God for small favors.

To my relief, they seemed to enjoy *The Secret Garden*. We waited in the green room to greet the cast and Mom found a special moment in each of the principal actors' performances to praise. But as Rowan and I walked them through the lobby, she said, "It's not an easy show, is it? The story, I mean. There's so much bitterness and anger and lost dreams."

"But there's a happy ending."

"Musicals are nice that way. Life is rarely so accommodating."

I shot a glance at Rowan who obligingly dragged Chris over to examine a poster. I led Mom toward the parking lot and asked, "Is everything okay?"

"Yes. No. Sue's mother died."

Without thinking, I blurted out, "It took long enough." Then clapped my hands over my mouth, aghast at my insensitivity.

After staring at me in shocked disbelief, Mom threw back her head and gave a great bellow of laughter. Then she pressed her fingertips to her lips. We stood there like two "Speak No Evil" monkeys until she lowered her hand and whispered, "I said the very same thing."

"We're going straight to hell," I whispered back.

"Nonsense. She was a dreadful old harridan. And she made Sue's life a misery."

"How is Sue?"

The last traces of amusement fled. "Sad. Angry. Bitter. Guilty. The whole experience made me feel . . . old."

"You're not old!" Unwillingly, I noticed that the unforgiving fluorescent lights in the parking lot cast shadows under her eyes and deepened the faint grooves around her mouth. "Sixty-two is practically middle-aged these days."

"Only if you live to be a hundred and twenty," she remarked dryly. "When the morning paper comes, you know the first section I read? The obituaries. A sure sign I'm getting old."

"Or that you're ghoulish."

"Well, there *is* that."

"I wish you'd told me all this when we talked on Sunday."

"You sounded so happy. I didn't want to spoil that." She grimaced. "Instead, I spoiled dinner."

"No, you didn't."

"Promise you won't say awful things about me when I'm dead."

"I don't say awful things about you now! I don't think you're a harridan."

"And . . . ?" she prompted.

"And you very rarely make my life a misery."

To my relief, that wrested a smile from her.

"Hey!" Chris called. "Are you two finished whispering?"

Mom motioned the guys over and said, "I was being maudlin. Another sign of impending decrepitude."

"You're the least decrepit woman I know," Rowan said.

"Your opinion doesn't count. You're just trying to win me over."

"Am I succeeding?"

"I'm still deciding."

"Told you she was tough," Chris said. "You had *me* at the mushroom pomponnettes."

Mom hugged me. "It was a wonderful show, Maggie. And a wonderful dinner, Rowan."

The first time she'd ever called him that. Hard to tell whether he felt the earth teetering on its axis, too. He merely shook her hand and thanked her.

"Breakfast at the Chatterbox?" I asked.

"No. Sleep in and get some rest. You have a busy week ahead. I'll call you Thursday when we get into town."

"Call me sooner if you want. To talk about the trip. Or . . . whatever."

"I'll call you Thursday," she said firmly.

As the car eased up the lane, Rowan said, "All in all, I thought it went pretty well." When I merely nodded, he asked, "Didn't *you* think so?"

"Yes," I assured him.

"She called me Rowan. That was a big step."

I hugged his arm. "Yes. It was."

"But . . . ?"

I told him about my conversation with Mom, adding, "I was afraid she and Chris were having problems."

When Rowan remained silent, I asked, "They're not, are they?"

"I don't know," he replied. "I sensed something during dinner. A certain . . . sadness. Maybe it was the specter of mortality."

"But you don't think so."

"I don't know," he repeated. "But I'm glad they'll be able to spend some time together. They deserve a chance to relax and enjoy each other. And so do we. So let's have fun tonight and celebrate another successful show."

I nodded. But I wished I could skip the cast party. All I really wanted to do was hurry after my mother and find some way to dispel the sadness that shadowed her.

CHAPTER 36
SEE WHAT IT GETS YOU

WAS RELIEVED TO DISCOVER THAT DADDY'S EVENING had been less stressful than Mom's. He had grilled burgers with Bernie and Mei-Yin, helped Hal string paper lanterns around the patio, and beaten everyone at Monopoly. Apart from asking why we hadn't brought our guests to the cast party, he seemed disinterested in our "out of town friends." I provided a hushed summary of my evening to the staff while we were setting out beer and wine and platters of food.

A rousing chorus of "The House Upon the Hill" heralded the arrival of the cast. Those who were making their first pilgrimage to the Bates mansion surveyed their surroundings with awe. The veterans made a beeline to the dining room.

The partying began in earnest after the kids departed with their parents. Most of the staff and crew left shortly afterward; they had to be back at the theatre at nine o'clock to begin loading in the set of *Into the Woods* and knew better than to incur the wrath of Reinhard and Lee by showing up late.

I wandered through the house, laughing at some of the war stories of our rehearsals and making a special effort to spend time with the cast members who would be leaving tomorrow. But the strain of dinner was telling on me and by one o'clock, I was yawning.

"Time for bed, Cinderella?" Rowan asked.

"Past it. Mind if I bunk with you tonight? The party will go on for at least another hour."

He offered a convincing imitation of Long's leer. "I was hoping you'd suggest that."

"Just to sleep."

"No hanky-panky?"

"No."

"No makin' whoopee?"

"Uh-uh."

"Not even a little Graham on the half shell?" he whispered. And laughed as I frantically shushed him.

"Have you seen Daddy?"

"Not lately. Why?"

"I don't want him up to all hours drinking."

Rowan cocked his head and gazed thoughtfully at the chandelier in Janet's foyer. After about ten seconds, I said, "Hello? Earth to Rowan?"

"He's out back," he announced with a smug smile.

"If only you were that good with lost keys. I'll grab my stuff and roust him out."

"Meet you on the front porch."

I threw a change of clothes and some cosmetics into my carryall, snatched up my purse, and headed back downstairs. I breathed a sigh of relief when I stepped outside. After the stuffiness of the house, the cool air felt delicious.

Cigarette smoke drifted skyward, shrouding the patio in a haze. Cast members chatted together, some faces illuminated by the lamplight shining through the windows, others dyed pink and gold and bilious green by the paper lanterns hanging from the branches of the maple tree. Spying no sign of Daddy's signature white hair, I slowly descended the steps, guided by the soft glow of the luminarias in their paper bags.

A couple was strolling in the garden, their shadowy figures barely visible as they moved in and out of the small pools of light shed by the solar lanterns. I felt a pang of regret that Rowan and I had never wandered through the moonlit garden. But there would be many nights for that after the season ended.

The couple turned to each other. I expected them to kiss, but after a moment, they moved apart and started toward the house. At which point I mentally scolded myself for spying and directed my gaze to the lower patio.

The guttering flames of the tiki torches revealed Daddy sitting atop a picnic table, feet planted on the bench, elbows resting on his knees. As I drew nearer, his head turned and he lifted his paper cup in salute. That's when I noticed the champagne bottle lying on its side next to his thigh.

"How come you're sitting out here all alone?"

"Got too noisy for me."

His words were clear; maybe he hadn't had as much to drink as I'd feared.

"Plus, I was enjoying the view." He gestured toward the garden with his cup. "Did you see them?"

"It's bad manners to spy," I said primly.

"But you see some pretty interesting things. Want to know who it is?"

"I do not. They deserve their privacy."

"Then how come you're peering at them, trying to make out their faces?"

"I am not peering. I'm just . . . enjoying the view."

As the couple passed one of the post lanterns on the drive, I caught my breath. There was no mistaking the coppery gleam of the man's hair or the identity of the woman whose face was turned toward him.

Alex and Debra?

I froze as they mounted the steps to the patio, but they were too intent on each other to notice Daddy or me. When they were safely out of earshot, I whispered, "Oh. My. God."

Daddy giggled like a naughty boy. "Who'da thunk it, huh?"

"Rowan must have. I'm going to kill him for not telling me."

Was that why Debra needed to come to the Crossroads? To find Alex?

I reviewed every interaction I'd witnessed. They clearly liked each other and enjoyed working together. Debra joked with him. Alex teased her. But they did the same with me.

"Maybe they just wanted to take a walk," I said.

Daddy snorted in disbelief.

"Let's go back to the apartment. We'll pump Rowan for info."

"Sure you two wouldn't rather be alone?"

"I'm too tired to do anything but sleep. And I won't get much around here."

As if to prove my point, a dreadful rap version of "Come to My Garden" floated down from the house.

Daddy sighed. "Time was I could perform in the evening, party till dawn, and rehearse all day. Not anymore. Must be getting old."

It was a painful echo of my mother's words, but Daddy seemed rueful rather than sad.

"One for the road?" he asked, reaching for the champagne bottle.

I tossed my carryall onto the table. "Okay."

He righted the champagne bottle, poured a slug into his cup and handed it to me. Then he raised the bottle and said, "Here's to my first Hell Week in a couple of decades."

"The first of many."

I tapped my cup against the bottle and took a small sip. Daddy lowered the bottle without drinking.

"What? No toast?"

"Can't very well drink to that one."

"Why not?"

"I think we both know my acting days are numbered."

"We haven't even opened yet and you're throwing in the towel?"

"Oh, it's been fun. And I appreciate you taking a chance on me."

"There will be other shows, Jack. And better roles."

"It's not that."

"You want to get back into teaching?"

"Teaching? Hell, no. I got bigger plans." He glanced around the patio, then whispered, "Come on. You know."

I shook my head.

"I'm going to Faerie, of course."

The world became utterly silent, as if his words had swallowed the muted buzz of conversation from the upper patio and the ratchety chorus of night insects. From a great distance, I heard my croak of laughter. The hoarse caw of the crow in the maple tree. The jeers of the shapeshifters in the Borderlands, mocking me for imagining I could hold him here.

Daddy mistook my reaction for delight and laughed with me. If he had looked at my face, he would have realized his mistake, but his rapt gaze was fixed on the forest, a dark, formless mass barely visible in the light of the waning moon.

"Rowan said I shouldn't tell anybody, but I knew you'd understand."

Something wet on my hand. Champagne from the paper cup crushed between my fingers.

"Everybody thought I was crazy. My wife. The doctors. But I found a way in. Took me years, but I found it."

He rocked back and forth, hands gripping his knees, as if to restrain himself from racing into the forest.

"If only I'd come to Rowan in the beginning. It kills me to think of the time I wasted. Not that I regret reaching the Borderlands. I saw things you can only imagine. But I knew I'd only touched the tip of Faerie. Sometimes, I glimpsed it through the mist. And heard that music."

High-pitched and silvery, like the rippling glissando of a harp.

I must have made some sound because my father peered at me. "Don't worry. Rowan already told me he wouldn't leave. But he doesn't have to, see? That's the beauty part. He just has to open a portal and bam! I march out of this world and into the other one. Piece of cake. In a way, I owe it all to you."

All I could do was stare at him.

"Well, Lee helped. His lighting, anyway."

When I just continued staring, Daddy exclaimed, "*The Secret Garden*! The storm at the end of Act One. It was like Lee had been there that night."

His gaze returned to the forest. "For years, it was just bits and pieces. Like a dream you half recall the next morning. The leaves rustling in the breeze. The thunder rumbling off in the distance like timpani. The sky shuddering with heat lightning. The whole forest seemed to shimmer. But that wasn't the lightning."

He drew in a deep, trembling breath and let it out on a sigh.

"Oh, Maggie, if you could have seen them. You can't judge by Rowan. He's trying to pass as human. It was like they carried the light of the sun and the moon and the stars inside. And when they came gliding through the trees—like a cloud of fireflies . . ."

Just like that other Midsummer. The fireflies dancing in the meadow. The glowing ball of light vanishing into the woods. The night Caren and I had come so close to discovering the secret of the Crossroads and glimpsing what my father had seen decades earlier.

"I'd forgotten most of it until opening night. But with the lights and the music and the Dreamers drifting onstage, circling around that little girl . . . that's when all the bits and pieces finally fit together. And when the Dreamers left . . ." His voice caught. "It was like I was losing *them* all over again."

My father leaping out of his seat. His desperate shout. That frail figure tottering down the aisle, arms outstretched.

It was not me he'd seen on that stage. It was not me he wanted.

He was reaching for them.

He had spent half his life pursuing them. Why had I been stupid enough to imagine he would stop?

"I begged Rowan to open a portal that night. But he wouldn't. He said I'd promised to do the Follies and *Into the Woods* and told me I had to honor my commitments. And he was right. It would have been wrong to walk out. But after the season's over . . ."

I sank onto the bench. Daddy slid down beside me.

"He'll open a portal if *you* ask him. I know he will."

I forced myself to look into his eager face. "So you're just going to turn your back on this world?"

The steadiness of my voice astonished me. Even more astonishing was my calm—as if I'd always known I would face this moment and had been preparing for it since the night he had crept out of the theatre.

Daddy drew back, frowning. "Look, I'm grateful for everything you and Rowan have done. But there's nothing for me here."

"There's your wife."

"My ex-wife."

"And your daughter."

He shifted uncomfortably on the bench and stared off into the darkness. "She's better off without me."

"How do you know?"

"Because I know Allie. My ex."

My calm shattered. He was only one who had ever called her by that nickname. Mom had always hated it.

"She'd have taken good care of her. Brought her up right."

"You don't even want to see her? To find out?"

"I'd just screw her up. Again. Besides, she's a grown woman now."

"Thirty-four."

"Something like that."

"Not 'something like that.' Exactly that."

"So she's thirty-four. And I'm a crappy father for not remembering, okay?"

"No, Jack, it's not okay."

I slowly rose and stared down at him. I was shaking with anger and had to take a moment to regain control of my voice.

"Maybe your life got turned upside down because of what happened here. Maybe any man would have fallen apart. And maybe your wife had no choice but to divorce you. But you had a child. And you abandoned her."

"I did what I thought was best," my father mumbled.

"For you! You always did what was best for Jack Sinclair. A couple of visits after your wife kicked you out. A couple of postcards saying 'Daddy will always love you.' How many birthdays passed before she stopped hoping for a card? How many times did she cry herself to sleep, wondering why you had forgotten her?"

My father leaped to his feet. "I didn't forget! I never forgot!"

His breath was coming as hard and fast as mine, his eyes glaring with the same anger, his chin stuck out with the same belligerence. And he was blind to the resemblance.

"Even now, you can't see it, can you?"

His anger shifted into something else—wariness, perhaps. Or fear.

"What the hell are you talking about?"

From the direction of the house, I heard someone shout my name. Dully, I realized it was Rowan. Well, he'd started this tangled chain of events by calling my father to the Crossroads. It seemed only fitting for him to be here for the big climax.

"Let me help you put the bits and pieces together, Jack. Just like opening night of *The Secret Garden*. Alison reverted to her maiden name after the divorce. And she changed little Maggie's name, too."

His eyes flew wide. He shook his head and stepped back, only to bump into the picnic bench and collapse gracelessly onto it. And all the while, his eyes remained fixed on my face, scanning my features the way I had cataloged his that first night.

"Oh, Christ . . ." he whispered.

The footsteps pounding toward us abruptly halted. Then they resumed, much more slowly. They stopped again, so close behind me that I could feel the heat of Rowan's body.

I wasn't aware of edging away until I discovered that I was standing much farther from the picnic table. Nor was I sure if I had unconsciously tried to distance myself from them or if I was trying to preserve the strange bubble of calm that surrounded me again.

Not calm, really. Emptiness.

"Why didn't you tell me? Why didn't either of you tell me the truth?"

He seemed strangely insubstantial—as if part of him had already left this world.

Rowan's gaze remained fixed on me as he quietly explained: Jack's fragile mental state, the shock, waiting for the right time. The same words he had offered when Jack discovered how much time had passed. Always, it seemed, we kept circling back, revisiting the links in the endless chain of spells and curses, explanations and excuses. Yet nothing ever really changed.

"I should have realized. There were so many clues."

I had been just as blind. Longing for the transformational ending of *The Secret Garden*, I had created the same kind of fantasy that Mary imagines in "The Girl I Mean to Be:" the characters in a picture-perfect setting, all wounds healed, all wrongs forgiven.

If I had been less caught up in that fantasy, I might have recognized the clues Rowan had given me: his fear that I would be disillusioned, his plea to postpone Mom's meeting with Jack, his quiet warning that I needed to let him go.

So many clues—and I had ignored them all.

Like father, like daughter.

"I'm sorry, Maggie. If I had known . . ."

"Would it really have made a difference?"

Although I'd spoken gently, he winced.

"Would you honestly give up Faerie for me? For anyone?"

His hesitation answered me more clearly than any words.

I nodded and began walking toward the steps.

"Magpie . . ."

My breath whooshed out like I'd been punched in the stomach. Rowan's anxiety stabbed me. I flung up my hands, warding off Jack's words and Rowan's power. Then I slowly turned.

"I will always be your daughter, Jack. But I am not your Magpie. I'm Maggie Graham. The executive director of the Crossroads Theatre. Call tomorrow is at one o'clock."

I started up the steps, only to discover Alex hurrying down them and Janet watching from the upper patio. As Rowan started toward me, I shook my head.

"No."

Although my voice was little more than a whisper, both men stopped short.

Such a tiny word to hold such power.

Rowan spoke my name, his voice low and urgent, his power pleading with me to stay.

"No," I repeated.

I took the only escape route available and hurried down the steps to the drive.

CHAPTER 37
LEAVIN'S NOT THE ONLY WAY TO GO

TOO LATE, I REMEMBERED THAT I HAD PARKED MY CAR at the theatre after my morning trip to the grocery store. Not that I could have reached the garage anyway. I barely made it to the drive before I heard Rowan's footsteps behind me.

I veered up the hill toward the side of the house.

"Maggie!"

The ground was terraced, each level connected by a short series of steps. But it was a steep climb and I was panting before I reached the halfway point.

"Wait!"

The light streaming from the windows flung bands of illumination across the level ground at the top, but here, I had only my memory and the unpredictable moonlight to guide me. Twice, I stumbled, but managed to regain my balance and keep moving.

"Talk to me, damn it!"

I had no breath to talk and no desire to stop, although my body was drenched with sweat and my legs had begun to ache. As I mounted the final set of steps, a blur of movement to my right startled me. The next thing I knew Rowan was blocking my path.

It seemed childish to dodge around him. Worse, it was useless. He'd just pull his "faster than a speeding bullet" act to thwart me again.

He had the good sense not to touch me with either his hands or his power. I didn't want to be touched by anything Fae at that moment. Janet, Alex, Rowan ... all of them sensing every emotion, battering at my defenses. That was why I had left. With all their fucking magical power, you'd think they would understand that and leave me alone.

"Talk to me. Please."

"I can't do this, Rowan. Not right now."

I started walking. Rowan kept pace beside me.

"The evening of my panic attack. You said we had to be able to talk. To deal with things together."

"I also said we had to be honest."

He checked suddenly, but caught up with me a few paces later.

"I wanted to tell you the truth. But you were so happy during rehearsals for *Into the Woods.* I just couldn't bring myself to hurt you."

"I know."

Again he checked and hurried to catch up with me.

"But ... I don't understand ..."

"Glass houses, Rowan."

"What?"

"I've been lying to my mother all summer. Trying to protect her. Why should I be angry at you for doing the same thing?"

"But—"

"I'm angry at myself. For being stupid enough to believe he could change."

"Now that he knows you're his daughter—"

"He might stay out of some sense of obligation, but he'll always want Faerie more than me."

My voice cracked and I pressed my lips together. I felt more than saw Rowan's hand come up, but I just quickened my pace.

The parking lot was an oasis of fluorescent light. Rowan must have thought I was going to the apartment because he had to veer sharply to follow me to the car.

As I fumbled for my keys, he slapped his palm against the window.

"Where are you going?"

"I don't know."

The hotel was booked. I didn't want to wake Hal. Besides, then I'd have to contend with Lee's Faedar.

"You shouldn't be driving when you're upset."

"I'm fine."

"Please. Let's go up to the apartment and—"

"I don't want to go to the apartment!"

"You can't just drive around all night."

"Maybe I'll crash in the lobby of the Bough. It doesn't matter! I just need to be alone."

"I'll take Jack to the cottage. You'll have the apartment to yourself."

"I need to get away, Rowan. From everything and everyone that reminds me of Faerie."

His hand slipped from the glass. His shocked expression shattered what was left of my self-control.

I blurted out an apology, flung open the car door, and slid inside.

"Are you coming back?"

His voice sounded hollow, as if every emotion had been drained.

"I'll be here for load-in."

It took three tries before I managed to shove the key into the ignition. I slammed the door and backed out so quickly that the car skidded on the gravel.

As I neared the top of the lane, I glanced into the rearview mirror. Rowan was still standing in the parking lot.

His small, lonely figure blurred. I gripped the steering wheel hard and hit the accelerator.

❧❧

I made it about half a mile before I pulled over and indulged in the release of tears. Then I blew my nose and kept going.

I drove aimlessly, grateful for the dark, winding roads that forced me to concentrate on my driving. But I kept seeing Rowan's forlorn figure. I was angry with myself for hurting him, angrier still that his persistence had driven me to it—and terrified to realize that I couldn't bear to be near him.

Had Mom felt like that when she kicked Jack out? Or had love leached away long before that?

Thank God, I had never told her that Jack had returned. Just imagining what I might have put her through brought on another fit of the shakes. Better to envision her sleeping peacefully beside Chris, untroubled by the ghosts of our past. Ghosts had no place in this world. And Jack Sinclair had no place in our lives.

The lyrics of "No More" kept running through my head, an ironic counterpoint to my turbulent thoughts. No more giants, the Baker pleaded. No more witches or curses or lies. But even he realized that he couldn't ignore them, any more than he could forget the false hopes, the reverses, the good-byes . . .

Damn Stephen Sondheim. Why did he have to write my fucking life into a musical?

I turned on the radio, hoping to drown out the lyrics, but the brief bursts of music vanished as soon as the car descended a hill.

At some point, I realized I was hopelessly lost. If my car had a GPS, I might have been able to punch in the name of one of the rare streets I passed. Lacking that, I just kept driving until I stumbled onto Route 9. Unsure of my bearings, I turned west. Within a few miles, I realized I was heading toward Bennington rather than Dale.

I wished I could keep driving. I wished I could crawl back into my protective bubble.

No more feelings. No more questions. Just running away. Escaping the ties that bind.

That was the Mysterious Man's solution. And Jack's. *Like father, like daughter.*

But the Mysterious Man warned the Baker about the dangers of wandering blind. Which was exactly what I'd been doing for the last hour.

I could never outdistance my thoughts or escape the ties that bound me to the Crossroads. With every mile that separated me from the theatre, I became more conscious of them: the concern of my staff, the bewilderment of my father, and most of all, the anguish of the man who loved me.

The man I still loved. But my blithe confidence that we could surmount every obstacle had been shaken.

No matter how human he acted, Rowan was innately different. He had powers I would never understand, weaknesses he could never conquer. If I couldn't accept that, I should break it off now.

But would I be able to do that? Even if I wanted to? Maybe I was ensnared by Fae glamour as surely as my father. Or maybe that was simply the nature of love. Another sort of trap—and just as dangerous.

"Give him a chance, Mom."

"To do what? Break your heart a second time?"

"That won't happen."

"You know who you sound like? Me. Thirty years ago."

Was I repeating her mistake—trying to make Rowan over into something he wasn't, something he could never be?

Always more questions. Just different kinds.

But one thing I did know. Like it or not, I *was* Magpie, the child pounding her fists on the window as her father walked out of her life. And Maggie Sinclair, the girl who watched her identity disappear just as her father had. Without those girls, Maggie Graham would never have made that fateful journey to the Crossroads.

So many spells. So many ties. Blood and friendship. Duty and obligation. Commitment and love. How do you break free without dooming yourself to loneliness? Even then, the ghosts are always there, lurking in the shadows of memory. Sooner or later, you have to face them.

Rowan had taught me that.

I waited for a truck to roar past, then made a quick U-turn. Running again, but this time, back to the family I had been given and the family I had chosen.

Although I was driving faster, the odometer seemed to spin more slowly. By the time I coasted into Dale, my eyes felt like they were lubricated with sand. Main Street was deserted at this hour, but the streetlamps were so bright after the dark road that they made me squint.

I slowed as I approached the Golden Bough. It was tempting to hide out there, to snatch a few hours of sleep on one of the sofas in the lobby. But there were too many people back at the theatre who were waiting and worrying about me.

I was already gliding past the hotel when I saw the figure sitting on the porch steps. I tramped on the brake, and the Civic shuddered to a halt.

It seemed to take an hour to cross the street, yet my breath came so fast, I felt like I was running. All the while, Rowan sat there like a statue. Only when I reached the porch did I notice the unceasing tremor rippling through his shirt.

I imagined him hesitating in the parking lot. Running up the lane. Hesitating again as he reached the road before racing through the darkness to town—the town he only knew secondhand from the stories of others. Had he paused for a moment to take in his first view of Dale? Or simply hurried down Main Street, searching for the Golden Bough?

And then the long, lonely vigil, watching and waiting and hoping.

His breath caught as I raised my hand, then leaked out in a strangled sigh when my fingertips touched his cheek.

I drew his head to my breast. As he flung his arms around my waist, his power burst free, flooding my senses with tremulous relief, the ache of sorrow, and a stab of fear so sharp that I winced.

We had embraced like this the evening I had confronted him at the theatre, daring him to love me. Now, we clung to each other like survivors of a shipwreck, both aware of how close we had come to foundering.

I pressed my lips to his hair and breathed in his scent. Not the musky-sweet aroma of desire, but the bitter tang of fear and despair.

"Are you coming back?" he had asked. Stupidly, I had told him I would return for load-in. But he had known I would never walk out on the show. He had been asking if I was walking out on him.

Maybe it would always be like this for us—this pulling away and coming together. Maybe that was inevitable between human and faery. But I had to believe that we could bridge our differences, that love and trust and time would bind us together more strongly.

His silk shirt was damp with perspiration. I stroked his back, his shoulders, the knotted muscles in his neck, my hands silently assuring him of my love, my commitment. But silence had proven to be our enemy and caused too many misunderstandings. I needed to speak the words—as much for me as for him.

"I'm here, Rowan. I can't promise I'll never bolt again, but I will always come back."

The fear receded, but his sorrow whispered through me. And something else that made no sense to me.

Wonder.

When he raised his head, I saw only his eyes. So impossibly green. So clearly Fae. Only when his fingertips touched his cheek did I notice the damp track running down it, glistening in the light of the porch lantern.

"You made me weep," he whispered.

"Oh, Rowan. I'm so sorry."

"No. You don't understand. The Fae can't weep."

His gaze searched my face as if I were a stranger.

I brushed my fingertips against his cheek and drew back, startled. His tears felt . . . thick. Like the glycerin used in films to simulate real tears.

He seized my hand and brought it to his mouth. His lips closed around my middle finger, and he sucked it gently. Then he raised his index finger to my mouth.

Salty, yes. But also something sweet. Like honey.

"Am I becoming . . . human?"

I shook my head helplessly. "Maybe the Fae don't weep because nothing ever touches them deeply enough. But now that you've learned to love . . ."

"I've learned the fear of losing it."

The fear that had haunted his dreams this summer. And made him weep tonight.

"I just wish I hadn't been the one to teach you that."

"Who else could?"

I nodded, shouldering the burden of my guilt and the risks of loving him. Never again would I believe we could sail over every hurdle as easily as we'd conquered his panic attacks. The knowledge left me forlorn, as if we had lost something nearly as precious as what we had found tonight.

I took his hand and led him to the car, only to draw up short when I realized he couldn't possibly ride in it.

"I'll park behind the hotel. And we'll walk home."

His fingers tightened on mine. "We'll drive."

Tears rose in my eyes. I blinked them away and shook my head.

"We'll drive," he repeated.

I rolled down all the windows and turned the vents on high. Then I leaned over and opened his door. As soon as he slid inside and closed the door, I tramped on the accelerator and sped back to the theatre.

When I reached the lane, I slowed just enough to avoid ripping out the undercarriage of the Civic. Even before I stopped the car, he flung open the door and stumbled outside. I hurried around the car to find him gulping great lungfuls of air. But he didn't get sick. He just nodded gravely, as if he'd proved something to himself—and to me.

As I glanced up at the apartment, he said, "Jack's at the house. We didn't think he should be alone."

I thought longingly of Rowan's bed, then resolutely turned toward the house.

"You don't have to see him tonight."

"I'm not going there to see him. Janet will be waiting up. And Alex."

"How did you know Alex was—?"

"His car's still in the lot."

We walked up the hill hand in hand. The lights were still on in the house, but it was quiet now. As we neared the porch, the screen door swung open, and Janet and Alex walked outside. He was still in his tuxedo, although he'd removed his tie and jacket. Janet had donned her old terry cloth robe and she held my carryall in her hand.

"I'm sorry I worried you."

They nodded, their eyes on Rowan, their faces betraying the same wonder I had seen on his when he had wept. Although the traces of his tears were gone, Janet's power was strong enough to have sensed what had happened at the Bough.

If Rowan felt that his privacy had been invaded, I saw no sign of it. He even managed a weary smile when Alex gripped his shoulder.

"The important thing is that you're home," Janet said.

She nodded to Rowan and returned my hug with surprising fierceness. Then she thrust out my carryall and declared, "If you pull a stunt like that again, I'll evict you."

Rowan and I walked to the apartment in silence and undressed by moonlight. We were too exhausted to make love. It was enough to hold each other.

The last thing I remembered was the steady throb of his heartbeat under my hand.

CHAPTER 38
PROMISES, PROMISES

I HAD THREE JOBS DURING LOAD-IN: to set out the coffee urn and the Chatterbox pastries in the lobby; to clean up after the feeding frenzy; and to stay out of everyone's way in between. Usually, I enjoyed the camaraderie with the crew, but the events of the previous night weighed on me.

I had dreamed again of that glade in the forest. But instead of dancing with the fireflies, I chased after them, while Rowan chased after me, both of us helpless to capture what we sought. And when the fireflies abandoned the glade, we were left to stumble through the darkness, each blind to the other.

My dream or Rowan's or some tangled mix? I only knew that I awoke to that same forlorn feeling I had experienced on the steps of the Bough—and the fear that neither Rowan nor I was strong enough to follow the path we had chosen.

As the early birds on the crew swarmed the lobby, I saw Lee eyeing me with concern. I beat a hasty retreat into the house. The back doors of the barn were open. It reminded me of the ending of *White Christmas*, only instead of a Currier and Ives snow scene I saw Catherine and Javier wheeling a giant storybook through the breezeway—and Rowan walking out of the stage right wings as if he carried the weight of the world on his shoulders.

"Jack's upstairs. He was hoping to speak with you."

The other burden we both had to carry. This one, I would have gladly thrust aside. But I had to face him sometime. Better to clear the air now than have all those feelings simmering during Hell Week.

"Would you rather talk to him alone?" Rowan asked as I mounted the steps to the stage.

"You're as much a part of what happens to him as I am. Just . . ."

"Keep out of it?"

"Keep your magic out of it. Unless he goes off the deep end. Let us feel what we feel without smoothing out the rough edges." As we walked through the wings, I asked, "Do you think he *might* go off the deep end?"

"He's nervous about seeing you, but all in all, he's surprisingly calm."

Maybe subconsciously, he had suspected the truth and been bracing for it, just as I had been braced for his revelation about going to Faerie.

Jack was hovering in the middle of the living area. Against my will, I was touched that he had dressed with such care, choosing khaki slacks and a short-sleeved shirt instead of his usual shorts and T-shirt.

His smile was hesitant, like a kid who wasn't sure if he was going to be scolded or praised. Maybe that was the real Jack Sinclair. The boy who never grew up. My personal Peter Pan.

He waited for me to sit on the sofa, then glanced at Rowan for direction. Rowan merely sat in one of the easy chairs and after a moment, Jack perched on the other one.

He studied me uncertainly, the actor awaiting his cue. I refused to give him one. If I was kind, he'd respond with warmth and charm. If I seemed angry, he would try remorse. This time, he would have to improvise. I just hoped that whatever he said was genuine, not playacting.

He glanced around as if seeking inspiration, then blurted out, "Do you hate me?"

Startled, I replied, "No. I don't hate you."

"That's what I kept worrying about. The only child I'll ever have. What if she hates me?"

I found myself recalling the words in Rowan's journal: *"His insecurity throbs like a heartbeat. He is so eager for me to like and respect him."*

"I didn't want to leave. Or drop out of your life. But it was hard. Thinking about you. The longer I stayed focused on finding a portal, the easier it was to let everything—everyone—go. And I know that makes me a shitty father and a shitty husband, but . . ."

He paused, waiting for me to speak—probably hoping that I would deny it. When I remained silent, he added, "It was only after I got to the Borderlands that I could really let myself think about you."

Again, that hesitant smile.

"It's so hard to believe that you're all grown up. My Maggie—the one in my head—she's still a little girl, even though I knew that she—that *you* had gone to college, gotten a job. The Borderlands, it was always changing. But you stayed just the same."

It had been like that for me, too. Both of us frozen in time for the other.

"I just wanted to say . . . I'm sorry. I know that doesn't make up for anything, but . . ." He took a deep breath and slowly let it out. "If you want me to stay, I will."

I was surprised to feel my throat tightening. Last night, I had written him off, convinced that he had no place in my life. Now, my heart thudded against my breastbone.

"Why don't we just focus on the show for now? And on getting to know each other. If you still feel that way after *Into the Woods* closes, we'll talk about it then."

His relief was so obvious that it hurt.

You can't do this again. The endless cycle of hope and disillusionment.

"There *is* something we should talk about, though. Mom's coming into town Thursday. I haven't told her about you. And for now, I don't think we should."

"You want me to stay out of the way while she's here? Sure. Why upset her?"

I suspected he was more eager to avoid any potential unpleasantness than spare Mom's feelings, but I just said, "That means no going out with the cast. And Bernie plays all the performances while they're here."

"They?"

"Mom and Chris—the man she's been seeing for the last couple of years."

"She never remarried?"

I shook my head.

"Huh. I figured she'd settle down with some nice, steady corporate type."

His clear disdain for the nice, steady corporate type—like Chris—made me snap off a curt, "No."

"What? You blame me for that, too? I can't help it if she never got over me."

"The man has ballocks the size of basketballs and an ego to match."

"Sorry to burst your bubble. She got over you a long time ago. But you'd hurt her so badly that it took years before she could trust a man again."

"It wasn't like everything that happened was my fault! She wasn't the easiest person to live with, either. Everything in its place. Everything just so. I can count on one hand the number of times she did anything spontaneous."

If anyone else had said that, I would have admitted the assessment was pretty accurate, but I was damned if I'd let him belittle her.

"Can you blame her? Living with you? Always running off. Gone for weeks at a time. If she wanted everything just so, it was to bring a little stability into her life. And mine!"

"She's been like that as long as I've known her. Always scared of life. Of taking a chance."

"She took a chance on you. Look where that got her."

"It was different in the beginning. I was the bad boy

who jolted her out of her groove. And she loved it! But she couldn't just enjoy the ride. She had to start in on me to quit acting. Settle for a boring job like the one she had at the bank. Well, I wanted more!"

"And it was always about what *you* wanted, wasn't it?"

"I tried! I gave up theatre for teaching. And I stuck it out, even though there were days I wanted to put a bullet in my head. You know how mind-numbing the nine-to-five grind is. You tried it yourself before chucking it for the theatre."

"Then I chucked theatre for the nine-to-five grind again. I might still be doing it if I hadn't come here."

He stared at me in bewilderment. "I thought you were like me, but you're not, are you? You're like Allie." He jerked his thumb at Rowan. "And there's *your* bad boy."

"No."

"Right now, it's all romance and magic and hot monkey love. But a couple of years down the road, you'll be after him to change. To be ordinary."

"No."

"Or you'll start wishing you'd settled for a banker or a lawyer or a dentist. And then Rowan'll be out in the cold. Just like I was!"

"No!"

It was too close to the bone, too close to the fears that Rowan and I had shared in the night.

"You don't know anything about me. Or Rowan. I can't predict what the future holds for us, but we're going in with our eyes open. I don't know what the future holds for you and me, either. We've got a month to find out. Just don't sign on to become part of my life if you're going to bolt at the first sign of trouble."

"Maggie . . ."

"I'll see you at the run-through."

I stalked out of the living area and flung open the front door. The hammering onstage only added to the painful throb of my headache. I walked outside and sought the relative privacy of the Smokehouse.

As I sank onto a chair, the door opened again. Rowan circled behind me and rested his hands on my shoulders, but he used only the gentle pressure of his fingers to knead away the tension. Maybe he was still obeying my request to keep his magic out of this.

"What do you want from him, Maggie?" As I tensed, he added, "I'm not suggesting that you should excuse anything he's done in the past. I'm asking what you want from him *now*."

"I want him to be honest."

"But he was honest. Yes, he was trying to justify his behavior. But he was also very perceptive. About Alison. And us."

Which was why I'd gotten so angry.

"Was he right?" Rowan asked in that same quiet voice. "Do you want a nice, normal, ordinary life?"

I jumped up from the chair and shoved it out of the way. "Who doesn't? But I gave that up when I signed on to be executive director of this place. And I gave up looking for a nice, normal, ordinary guy when I fell in love with you. I don't want a banker or a lawyer. And unless Bernie will marry me, I don't want a dentist, either."

It killed me that his smile was so sad. The same smile I had seen at the end of our last summer when we knew we were going to lose each other.

I punched him on the chest with both fists and kept raining blows on him, driving him back against the wall.

"Goddamn it, Rowan. Don't you give up on us!"

I never saw his hands move. I just discovered my upraised fists trapped by his imprisoning fingers.

"Then don't you give up on us, either!"

His mouth claimed mine, bruising my lips. Then it softened, anger shifting into hunger, into the same desperate need I felt.

And then I heard Hal calling my name.

Rowan's hands fell. I stepped back.

"You should go see what he wants."

"Yes."

But we just stood there, staring at each other.

"I'm not giving up," Rowan said.

"Neither am I."

We sealed the pact with our usual handshake. Instead of releasing my hand, Rowan gripped it harder.

"Remember all those things I said about how the journey's never over and learning valuable lessons along the way?"

I nodded.

"I like your way better. Let's cut right to the happy ever after."

His smile was confident. But he was skilled at disguising his fears.

CHAPTER 39
I WANT TO MAKE MAGIC

JACK TIPTOED AROUND ME FOR THE REST OF THE DAY. Finally, I took him aside and assured him I wasn't angry. He assured me that he just wanted Rowan and me to avoid the mistakes he and Mom had made. I assured him that I understood. We assured each other to death and although it really didn't change anything, it did cut some of the tension.

The staff went into "circle the wagons" mode just like the night Rowan returned. Only this time the interloper was my father. I had to plead with Lee to refrain from ripping Jack's head off and beg Alex to stop looking at me with sad, puppy dog eyes. Hal bit his lip every time he saw me, Catherine patted me every time she passed, and Mei-Yin spoke in such dulcet tones that I wanted to scream, "I'm okay! Really!"

I knew they all meant well, that they loved me and were trying to help me deal with this situation. But I didn't know how to deal with it, either. What I wanted most was to thrust aside my personal problems and focus on the show.

As usual, Reinhard—ever stalwart, ever silent— understood that. He must have spoken to others because the hovering abruptly ceased and we all got back into show mode.

Everyone got a much-needed lift when we saw the set for *Into the Woods*. The cast actually applauded.

Like the characters in Act One, it was mostly two-dimensional. Painted cutouts of two enormous trees framed the stage, their branches curving over the proscenium arch. Banks of twisted trees flanked a tiered rock formation at center. Our local Cub Scout troop had collected the leaves that Hal had laboriously added to the netting of the forest's "canopy."

Rapunzel's tower and the tree that hosted the spirit of Cinderella's mother were also trompe l'oeil miracles. Like the three giant storybooks in place at the start of the show, these were hinged and could be opened and closed by the actors or crew.

I let the cast explore a bit, then sent them off to change for the costume parade. It was the first time they'd seen each other in fairy-tale drag and there was a lot of "oohing" and "aahing" over the transformations. Jack's gray suit looked natty if bizarrely out of place among the peasant garb, uniforms, and ball gowns. Rowan looked more like an adorable ragamuffin than a Mysterious Man; I'd have to wait until he donned his gray wig and beard at dress rehearsal to get the full effect.

Not so TweedleTom. Even without the hair pieces and ears, he looked wonderfully wolfish in his furry leggings and tail, clawed gloves, and black sequined jacket. His bare chest came in for almost as much comment as his costume, especially after his cast mates realized that the "fur" was all Tom.

"Watch out," Debra warned. "One of the locals might skin you and set you out before a fireplace."

Everyone was on such a high afterward that I wished we could plunge right into the run-through, but I knew we needed to work the stickier bits of business first. So we spent the next hour opening and closing the storybooks, the tower and the tree; practicing the Wife's "fall" from the rock formation; and raising and lowering the "tree limb" on which the Baker and Jack kept watch for the giant.

We'd flown in set pieces plenty of times, but never a pair of actors. Lee had tested it for half an hour before the costume parade, and although he assured Brian and Connor that it was safe, they looked petrified the first time they descended from the flies. By the fourth time, though, Connor was having so much fun that he began rocking their narrow platform like a Ferris wheel seat.

Brian shrieked. So did I. Lee shouted, "Quit messing around! Or I'll cut the bit and you'll do the scene on top of two stepladders."

We actually needed rolling stepladders so the actresses playing Rapunzel and Cinderella's dead mother could ascend to their bowers. Mira—the aforesaid dead mother—chose that moment to announce that she was afraid of heights.

"Did she even look at my sketches?" Hal demanded in a furious whisper. "Am I supposed to put the ghost of Cinderella's mother in a stump?"

"Let's just deal with it."

Even with two stagehands helping her on and off the ladder, she was still a wreck. In the end, Javier had to mount the ladder behind her and put his arms around her waist while Mira clutched the ladder's railing in a death grip and shakily sang her solo.

Through it all, Rowan sat in the front row, silently gauging how much magical help cast and crew might need on opening night.

We held the run-through after our dinner break. There was so little seat squeaking from Long that I actually swiveled around to make sure he was still there. He gasped so loudly at the Witch's transformation that I was glad Hal had permitted Debra to do the scene in costume.

When the run-through concluded, he shouted, "Bravo!" And as soon as I finished giving notes, he hurried onstage to praise the actors.

"The transformation worked beautifully," he told

Debra as the rest of the cast trooped down to the dressing rooms. "I don't know how you managed it. No, don't tell me. You'll spoil the magic."

The transformation was anything but magical. Shrouded in a voluminous hooded cloak, no one could tell that Debra was already wearing her younger self's white satin gown and sequined slippers. After she drank the magic potion, she reeled upstage. While the audience was agog at the Mysterious Man's dying revelations, Debra was ripping off her flesh-colored clawed gloves, prosthetic nose, and bushy eyebrows. She stuffed those into a hidden pocket in her cloak, slid off her gray wig, and even had time to apply the red lipstick that had been secreted in the goblet.

A flare from the flash pot. A puff of smoke. Debra dropped her cloak and voila! The crone had transformed into a glamour puss. In the few seconds before the blackout, everyone was too busy gawking at the gown and the blonde wig to notice that the glamour puss still had age lines on her face.

The most magical moment in the show and we accomplished it without any faery magic at all.

It would have been cool if Rowan could have cast a glamour across Debra's features to make her look youthful, but it was simply too risky. Even when he had directed the production, he'd done it the old-fashioned way, unwilling to arouse suspicion.

After Long left, Debra asked, "Is that how you worked it when you played the Witch?"

"Hey! I never told you I played the role. Who spilled the beans?"

She glanced at the pit, and Alex sheepishly raised his hand.

"Sorry," Debra said. "Didn't mean to out you."

"It's okay," I said. "And no. We used a double at Southford. I ducked offstage; she staggered on in an identical cloak. Poof. Reveal. Blackout. Applause."

"That would be easier, you know."

"Yes, but it was so damn obvious. At least, the audience knows you're working hard."

"Especially with my hooked nose hanging off my face."

"That was only the first time. It looked great tonight."

And would look even better during the show. If Rowan refrained from using his magic to effect the transformation, he would certainly jump in to help Debra do so.

"Did the makeup read okay?" Debra asked.

"You looked beautiful," Alex replied.

He smiled up at her. She smiled down at him. Then Alex made a big deal about collecting his score and Debra hurried off to change.

As soon as was humanly possible, I dragged Rowan up to the apartment and demanded, "Is something going on between Debra and Alex?"

"They certainly light up around each other."

"They do?"

"Well, you wouldn't notice."

"No. Of course not. I'm a mere human."

"I only meant that there's nothing about their behavior to give them away."

When I filled him in on their moonlit stroll in the garden, his eyebrows rose.

"I thought you'd be happy."

"I've always hoped Alex would find someone to share his life. I just never imagined it would be someone like Debra." His expression grew thoughtful. "Then again, Annie was pretty domineering."

"You're kidding. I always pictured her as ... well ... like Helen. Sweet. Kind. Loving."

"She was. But she was also strong-minded. A match for Janet any day. Which was probably a good thing for Alex. Sometimes, he needs a push."

"Maybe we should—"

"No."

"You don't even know what I was going to say."

"You were going to suggest we give Alex a push."

"Damn faery . . ."

"Let them be, Maggie."

"You cast Lou and Bobbie opposite each other."

"And after that, I let them be."

"Sometimes people need a little push."

"And sometimes they need to figure things out for themselves. As you have reminded me on more than one occasion."

CHAPTER 40

ALL I WANTED WAS THE DREAM

THE EXTRA TIME WE SPENT WORKING THE PROBLEM AREAS paid off. We were out of tech in three hours instead of our usual five; even Reinhard was in danger of ascending to Cloud Nine. When I settled into my seat for dress rehearsal, I was filled with confidence.

The stage lights came up to reveal the open storybooks with their fairy-tale characters in a frozen tableau: Cinderella by the hearth with her broom; the Baker and his Wife preparing bread; and Jack and his Mother flanking Milky-White, the wooden cow that resembled a giant pull toy on casters. The right page of each book showed the interiors of the three cottages. On the left, Hal had painted the opening lines of the story in elegant calligraphy, each beginning with the traditional "Once upon a time."

All that remained was for Jack to enter and utter those same words to open the show.

Although I had seen him make that entrance a dozen times, my heart still sped up when he strode out of the wings. He nodded approvingly at the tableau and crossed to his position by the stage right proscenium arch.

The spot came on.

He turned toward the darkened house.

And stood there.

For about two seconds, I thought he was milking the moment. Then I noticed his glazed expression.

He'd had his lines down the first week of rehearsal. Had performed perfectly during the final run-through. But now Jack Sinclair—the man who had boasted about his performance as Billy Bigelow, who had given acting tips to the cast of *The Secret Garden*, who had been a professional actor for more than ten years—Jack Sinclair had dried up.

His mouth snapped shut. His Adam's apple rose and fell as he swallowed. Alex's head jerked stage right, his hands upraised to cue the pit band. Long's seat gave an ominous squeak. And still Jack remained frozen, blinking like the proverbial deer in the headlights.

Rowan would never leave him hanging out to dry. Maybe Jack was simply too terrified to respond to the gentle nudge of Rowan's power.

Seconds after the thought crossed my mind, Jack started visibly at what had to be a much stronger jolt of Fae power. He swallowed again. Opened his mouth.

"Once upon a time . . ."

The words came out in a strangled whisper. My heart went "da-DUM" along with the opening chords from the pit band. Instead of continuing the narration, Jack lapsed into silence. The actors forged ahead. I gripped the seat in front of me and prayed he would recover.

He did. But instead of introducing Cinderella's Stepmother and Stepsisters, he muttered the lines he had just missed.

The number went downhill from there. At some point, he simply stopped talking and stood there with his head bowed. Although critical information was lost—like the fact that Rapunzel was the Baker's sister—Sondheim's lyrics held the story together.

The director in me noted that with dispassionate interest. The daughter wanted to rush onstage and lead that dejected figure out of the spotlight's glare.

I was halfway out of my seat when he slunk offstage.

As I sank down again, two hands patted my shoulders: Bernie and Catherine, silently lending their support.

The curtains parted to reveal the forest. I tried to concentrate on the wonderful maze of light streaming through the trees and the characters' journey into the woods, but I was too conscious of the minutes ticking away until the Narrator's return at the top of Scene 2.

I swiveled around and whispered to Bernie, "If he doesn't come back, I'll need you to go on."

Bernie nodded toward the stage. I whipped around and found Jack in place. He spoke his line clearly enough, but he seemed to be in a trance. I wasn't sure if he was grasping for words or if he was merely repeating the ones that Rowan was magically feeding him.

Three musical numbers passed before he returned to introduce Rapunzel. The glazed look had left his eyes, but only in the final moments of Act One did he seem to be in character.

I stayed away from the Dungeon at intermission, fearful that my presence would only distract him further. Instead, I hurried up the stairs to Rowan's apartment.

Although I had just seen him in full costume and makeup, it was still bizarre to be greeted by a Mysterious Man in long gray wig, false beard, and rag picker's motley.

When he asked, "How bad did it look?" I knew he was referring to Jack's performance rather than his appearance.

"After the meltdown? A little . . . robotic. But okay at the end. How much of it was you?"

"Most of it."

It was hard to tell if he was tired with all the age makeup. The weariness in his voice might only have been the same disillusionment I felt.

I followed him through the living area. His dining table now held an eight-bulb makeup mirror, a wig stand, and a partitioned makeup case filled with brushes and pencils, foundation and sponges, powder and rouge, vials of spirit gum and remover.

As he resumed his seat before the mirror, I asked, "Are you okay?"

"The top of Scene 2 was the worst. I had to calm Mira and feed Jack his lines. Very . . . schizophrenic." He plucked a makeup pencil from his case and began re-touching the age lines on his forehead. "In the past, I've always directed my power at a group or an individual. Same power. One focus. This is the first time I've had to help two people with two distinct problems at the same time." In the mirror, his gaze met mine. "So I guess that's what I've learned from doing the show."

"And we haven't even opened yet." I rested my cheek lightly against his, careful to avoid smudging his makeup.

"Sorry I didn't have any power to spare for you."

"I'm fine. I just hope Jack makes it through Act Two."

"The Narrator's death occurs well before my resurrection. So I should be able to concentrate on him. If he needs me."

I straightened with a sigh. "Of all the problems I knew I'd face with him, I never expected this one."

"Neither did I. He seemed fine during warm-ups. No more excited or nervous than any of the others. It was only after he walked onstage that I felt his panic."

"Will he be able to perform tomorrow?"

Again, his gaze met mine in the mirror. "I don't know, Maggie. Maybe he'll work out his jitters tonight."

Jack seemed more confident in Act Two, but that might have been the effect of Rowan's power. Much as I wanted him to have the opportunity to perform, Rowan had others in the cast who might need him. I couldn't allow him to become Jack's personal Energizer Bunny. If Jack needed that level of support, I would have to pull him.

As soon as Lee brought up the house lights, Long hurried down the aisle toward me. Before he could speak, I said, "I don't know what happened with Jack." I kept my voice low, conscious of the cast waiting onstage for notes. "But I'll deal with it, okay?"

"I know you will. And I know you'll do whatever's best for the show. I just wanted to tell you I was sorry. For your sake and his. I know how much it meant to you to have him in the show. And I think it meant just as much to him."

His response was almost as unexpected as my father's meltdown. Funny thing was, I'd dealt with that calmly. Long's support brought me to the verge of tears.

He sighed. "I really should know better by now. When things go wrong, a lecture stiffens your resolve and kindness upsets you. Maybe one day, I'll figure out the rules."

"Maybe one day, I'll be able to take either the lecture or the kindness without losing it."

Long cleared his throat. "Yes. Well. The cast is waiting. I'll say something brief and inspirational and get out of your way."

All summer, I had dreamed of a new relationship with my father. Instead, I seemed to have stumbled into one with my board president. As we walked toward the stage, I recalled Long's habit of popping in at unexpected moments, of attending run-throughs and dress rehearsals as well as most of the performances. I'd always suspected he was checking up on me. Maybe he was simply lonely.

Long uttered his few inspirational words. My speech was equally brief and consisted mainly of telling the cast how proud I was—and that I wanted to run the Act One opening early tomorrow afternoon. After I staged the curtain calls, I let Jack leave with the rest of the cast, unwilling to ask him to stay behind and shame him in front of everyone. He hurried off to the Dungeon, visibly relieved at his easy getaway. It was Otis who lingered.

"He'll settle down," he assured me.

"I hope so."

He regarded me silently, then said, "It's tougher when it's family."

Without thinking, I replied, "Tell me about it." Then I stared up at him in shock. I hadn't told the cast that Jack was my father. And I knew none of the staff would reveal that, either.

"How did you know?"

"Didn't at first. Then I started noticing little things. Like the way you both stick your chin out when you're angry. And how you took such care with him. You're good to all of us, but it was different with Jack."

I nodded, still a little stunned.

"He hasn't figured it out yet, has he? That you're his daughter."

"He didn't know in the beginning, but he does now."

But only because I had told him. It revealed so much about both men that Otis—a relative stranger—had seen what my father had missed.

"Families can be one tangled up mess sometimes," Otis said. "Or the greatest blessing in the world. Usually both."

"At the same time."

"If there's one thing I've learned this summer it's to keep trying to untangle that mess. You taught me that, Maggie. Don't you go forgetting it."

The staff gathered in the green room and waited for the cast to leave before we began the debriefing. Jack was the last to emerge from the Dungeon. He flashed a nervous smile when he saw us and started when I took his arm and led him down the hall toward the production office.

"Can you believe I went up on my lines? I've never done that in my life. But I'll be fine for the opening."

"Why don't you sleep on it? You can let me know tomorrow if—"

"I don't need to sleep on it. I'm ready!"

I noted the truculent thrust of his chin with brittle amusement.

"Okay. I'll see you at one o'clock to run the opening. If that goes well, great. But if I think your nerves are getting the better of you, Bernie goes on."

Without a word, he stalked down the hallway and disappeared around the corner. I slowly walked back to the green room. I knew the staff would support whatever decision I made. I just hoped it was the right one.

"He says he can go on. I'm not so sure. I'll decide after tomorrow's rehearsal. Either way, Bernie, I need you to be ready. I can't risk a meltdown like we had tonight. If Jack's out, you can dress with the rest of the cast. Otherwise . . ." I glanced at Rowan who nodded. "Use Rowan's apartment. It'll only undermine Jack's confidence if he sees you in the dressing room."

"Whatever you say."

"Javier, please make sure Bernie's armchair is stage right so we can move it out in a hurry if Jack folds."

"Do we really need the chair?" Bernie asked. "I feel like such an old fart sitting there."

"But you look like the guy who used to introduce *Masterpiece Theatre*."

"Only small, balding, and Jewish."

"It works, Bernie. Yes, it saves you from all those entrances and exits. But it's like you're actually telling the story to the audience."

"Maybe we should try that with Jack," Hal ventured. "I could put together a storybook. A smaller version of the ones onstage. And paste his scenes into it."

Once again, I found myself torn between my roles as daughter and director. This time, the director won.

"We've all bent over backward to help Jack. Either he performs the part as rehearsed or he doesn't perform at all."

CHAPTER 41
NO MORE

JANET AND I WERE YAWNING OVER OUR COFFEE the next morning when she suddenly shoved back her chair and jumped to her feet.

"What's wrong?"

"Rowan. Something's upset him."

"What?"

But she had already run out of the kitchen. By the time I recovered from my shock and stumbled to the front door, she was racing down the hill, bathrobe billowing behind her like giant blue wings.

I tore after her, terrified that Rowan had been hurt. She must have sensed my fear because she stopped at the bottom of the hill and waited for me to catch up with her.

"He's fine."

"Then . . ."

"I don't know, Maggie!"

As we approached the theatre, I noticed the stage door hanging open. Then I saw Rowan standing in the picnic area.

His wet hair hung in unruly tangles over his bare shoulders. Tiny rivulets of water oozed down his back. As we hurried toward him, his shoulders rose and fell. Then he turned.

"What is it? What happened?"

"It's Jack. He bolted."

"Bolted?"

"He said he wanted to take a walk. I could feel his restlessness, so I agreed. I'd just gotten in the shower when I felt this stab of panic . . ."

I searched the treetops for the crow that must have frightened him. Only when I registered the sympathy—the pity—on Rowan's face did I finally understand.

Last night's bravado had crumbled. And instead of talking to me or asking Rowan for help, Jack had run off.

Why was I surprised? It was what he did best.

Rowan was still talking, but his voice failed to penetrate the roaring in my ears and the pounding of my blood and the pressure inside my head.

"Son of a bitch!"

I slammed my fist into the trunk of a tree.

The pain felt good, a refreshing shock to my system. Then, of course, my hand just hurt like hell.

Rowan's fingertips glided over the abrasions, trailing cool relief, just as they had that afternoon two years ago when I'd fallen in the woods. Circling back to the past yet again. This whole summer seemed like one endless circle with stumbles in all the same places.

"I'm sorry, Maggie."

"You're not his keeper."

"He's probably gone to the cottage. I saw him running . . ."

"Into the woods?" I gave a short, bitter laugh. "I thought he might bolt when he found out I was his daughter. Or when he learned Mom would be here."

But naturally, he was more concerned about his performance.

"I think he was too embarrassed to face you. To admit that he couldn't do it."

"And he thinks it'll be easier to face me after this?"

"He doesn't think, Maggie. He just reacts in the moment."

Which works great onstage. In real life, not so much.

"I'll get dressed and go after him."

"No."

No more stumbling around the circle.

No more chasing the false hopes and impossible dreams.

Just . . . no more.

***

The show was a huge hit. I was happy for the cast—especially Bernie. The audience warmed to him the moment he walked onstage. He unhurriedly made his way to the armchair, hung his cane over one of its wings, unbuttoned his suit coat, and eased himself onto the leather seat with a little grunt. Then he surveyed the darkened house with a smile that said, "Okay, folks. I'm settled in. You do the same."

That was the only moment I felt really connected to the show. The rest of the time I was far away, noting the laughter and the applause and—near the end—the occasional sniffle. It was the same at the reception afterward: I heard myself saying all the right things to the cast and the audience and the press, but it was like I was playing a role without fully inhabiting the character.

When Jack was still AWOL the following morning, Rowan again volunteered to go to the cottage. I told him to suit himself; I had no intention of accompanying him.

He was gone most of the afternoon and arrived at the house alone. By then, I was dressed to meet Mom and Chris for dinner.

"Was he at the cottage?" Janet asked.

Rowan nodded.

Stupid to feel relieved. As stupid as spending the day worrying that he was lying in the woods with a broken leg or a broken neck. Especially since I would have cheerfully broken his legs *and* his neck after what he'd done.

"He's sorry he ran out," Rowan said.

"He's always sorry when he runs out."

"I took him some food. And clothes."

"You're kidding."

"I didn't think you'd want him to go hungry."

"I don't care if he starves!"

"You don't mean that."

"Don't tell me what I mean."

"You're just angry."

"And don't tell me what I feel! I'm just glad he's out of our hair while Mom's here."

"And after that?" Janet asked.

"He'll get hungry."

"So it's back to the 'starve him into submission' plan?"

"I'm not . . . look, he chose to run off. Why should we reward that behavior by ferrying food to him?"

"All right," Rowan said. "If that's what you want."

"Am I supposed to feel sorry for him? To plead with him to come back? I've spent too much of my summer — and my life — doing that. If you want to play Meals-on-Wheels, knock yourself out. Just don't expect me to play helping professional. Not this time. Jack can spend the rest of the goddamn summer at the cottage for all I care. The only way I'm talking to him again is if *he* comes to *me*."

CHAPTER 42

IF MOMMA WAS MARRIED

I TOOK A LOT OF DEEP BREATHS ON THE DRIVE to the Bough, knowing Mom would pick up on my emotions in a heartbeat. I just hoped I could put her off the scent by telling her it had been particularly hellish Hell Week. At least that wouldn't be a lie.

Although I was only a few minutes late, I found Chris pacing the lobby.

"Sorry. Last minute hair crisis."

"Not a problem," he replied, treating me to his usual affectionate hug. "Your mom's still getting dressed. Want to grab a drink in the lounge?"

"God, yes!" When my reply drew a startled look, I said, "Sorry. Aftereffects of Hell Week."

Might as well start planting the seeds now.

The lounge was only half-full, mostly locals enjoying a quick brew before heading home. We snagged two pints and hunkered down at a table near the back of the room. We both took fortifying swigs of ale. Then Chris thumped his glass on the table and said, "I wanted to talk with you. Alone."

For half a second, I thought he was going to tell me that Mom had finally accepted his proposal. But his gloomy expression hardly suggested a prospective bridegroom bubbling over with excitement.

"I asked your mother to marry me—again. And she turned me down again."

"But . . . why?"

"She says she's happy with the way things are."

"But you're not."

"I'm sixty-four, Maggie. I want more than sleepovers on the weekend and dinner on Wednesday. I want to go to sleep with her at night and wake up beside her in the morning. I want to vow before God and my family and friends to spend the rest of my life with her. Maybe that's hopelessly old-fashioned, but—"

"No. It's lovely."

I wanted the same thing.

Groping for something to reassure him, I said, "People stay in committed relationships for years without getting married. Look at Lee and Hal."

"At least they live together. She won't even consider that. Look, I know her marriage to your father was a disaster. And that it's taken her a long time to get over it. Hell, it took six months before she'd even go out with me. But she's been divorced for more than twenty years and we've been together for two. If she thinks I'll run out on her the way he did—if she doesn't know me any better than that by now . . ."

"You're nothing like my father. And she knows that."

Chris stared into his ale. "I'm sorry to unload on you like this. I just . . . I don't know what to do."

"We'll think of something," I promised.

❦

Chris picked at his food, while Mom nattered on about the glories of Vermont. When our coffees arrived, he pushed back his chair and announced that he needed to take a walk.

Mom waited until the sound of his footsteps faded, then said, "He's even more transparent than you are. Obviously, he's told you everything."

I nodded.

"I don't know why he felt compelled to involve you."

"Because he didn't know where else to turn."

"Maggie, Chris and I have been over and over this. He wants to get married. I don't."

"Do you love him?"

"Don't be silly."

"Yes or no."

"Of course I love him," she snapped. "But I like my independence, too."

"Being married doesn't necessarily mean you lose your independence. Reinhard and Mei-Yin are hardly joined at the hip."

"That's different."

"How?"

"Because it is! Now let's drop this."

"Are you willing to risk losing him?"

"It won't come to that." Her fingernail tapped a nervous tattoo against her coffee cup. Then she must have realized what she was doing, because she folded her hands in her lap and asked, "Shouldn't you be getting to the theatre?"

"No."

We glared at each other and retreated to our coffees.

Another frontal assault would be ineffective; when Mom was upset, she tended to fight rather than withdraw or admit her feelings.

Gee, who does that sound like?

I attempted a conciliatory smile. "You could move in together. If you didn't want to take the plunge. That would—"

"Only encourage him to believe that, sooner or later, I'll agree to marry him."

I gave up on conciliatory and went for the bombshell. "Is this about Daddy?"

Her coffee cup rattled violently against the saucer. "If you think I'm still carrying a torch for Jack Sinclair—"

"No. I think he hurt you so badly that you're afraid take a chance with Chris. You're scared he'll leave you like Daddy did. So you're pushing him away before he can."

"Thank you, Dr. Phil." She flung her napkin on the table and signaled the waitress. "But I'm afraid our time is up."

❧❧

I spent most of the show going over those conversations. I could understand if Mom didn't want to discuss her personal life with me—or take advice from her daughter. But if she refused to open up to the man she loved, the relationship seemed doomed. Her chance for lasting happiness was slipping through her fingers, and Chris and I seemed powerless to prevent it.

I could think of only one person who might.

I followed Rowan to his apartment after curtain calls. Without bothering to remove his makeup or costume, he poured us each a healthy slug of whisky, waited for me to take a sip, then sat beside me on the sofa. He nodded sympathetically as I described the problems Mom and Chris were facing, but when I broached my plan to deal with them, he drew back, frowning.

"You want your mother to talk with Jack?"

"I don't *want* them to talk. But I can't think of anything else that might jolt her out of the past and save her relationship with Chris."

"It's their relationship, Maggie. It's up to them to save it or not. I don't think we should be interfering in their lives."

"This from the faery who's been calling Mackenzies here for more than a hundred years."

"I called them, yes. But I never forced them to confront their problems."

"You pushed me hard enough."

"But I never said, 'It's all about your father.' I let you discover that for yourself. Over the course of three months. Do you really think your mother will take one look at Jack and decide she wants to marry Chris?"

"Maybe not, but—"

"And what if it makes matters worse? This isn't like giving Alex a little push toward Debra."

"Don't you think I know that? But I can't just stand aside and watch things fall apart. She's stuck, Rowan. And unless something happens to ... unstick her ... she's not only going to lose Chris, she'll never be able to move on with her life."

"Then let me use my power to—"

"No."

"I'm not talking about brainwashing her. Just reminding her that she loves Chris and doesn't want to lose him."

"She already *knows* she loves Chris and doesn't want to lose him. And when your power wears off, she'll be right back where she is now."

"At least, talk to Chris first. See if this is what *he* wants."

"I can't. If he's part of this, it will only convince her that he can't be trusted."

Rowan shook his head. "She'll be furious, Maggie."

"I know."

"She might never forgive you."

"I know!"

"Do you really want to risk everything? Not just Chris' relationship with your mother, but yours, too?"

"No! But I don't think I have a choice."

The next morning, though, I called Nancy before she left for work. I'd brought her up to date on The Life and Times of Maggie Graham when she made her opening night "break a leg" call. It took less than a minute to fill her in on the latest installment.

She was silent for so long that I expected her to offer the same objections as Rowan. Instead, she said, "I think they *should* meet. Not because it will save her relationship with Chris; that's something they have to work out for themselves. But she has a right to know about Jack."

"Even if he's ... moving on at the end of the season?"

"I think so. But you know how I've hated this cat-and-mouse game you've been playing. Think how relieved you'll be to get everything out in the open."

Except the fact that my father was "moving on" to Faerie. And my lover was opening a portal so he could get there.

That afternoon, Rowan accompanied me to the cottage. I spent most of the walk steeling myself to face Jack again—and mentally vowing to keep our conversation short, sweet, and drama-free. This was a straightforward business proposition, after all, not a reconciliation.

Jack answered Rowan's knock. His smile faded when he saw me.

As he began stammering an apology, I said, "I need you to do something for me, Jack. And if you're willing, I promise that after the season is over, Rowan will open the portal to Faerie for you."

I watched the shifting play of emotions across his features: confusion, wariness, disbelief, shock—and finally, a joy so profound that tears filled his eyes.

Once, perhaps, he had regarded me with such joy. Now, only the Fae could evoke it.

After all that had happened, the upwelling of grief surprised me. Resolutely, I swallowed it down. I was accustomed to losing my father. The important thing now was to keep my mother from losing Chris.

CHAPTER 43
I PROMISE YOU A HAPPY ENDING

OVER THE NEXT TWENTY-FOUR HOURS, my confidence eroded. After watching me pace the living area, waiting for Mom and Chris to arrive, Rowan said, "We can still call this off. Just leave Jack in the Smokehouse and send Alison and Chris off to do some sightseeing after lunch."

"Let's play it by ear. Maybe they've patched things up and we won't have to do anything."

One look at their faces convinced me that the "patching up" scenario was wishful thinking. When lunch concluded, I offered a silent prayer that I was not about to make the biggest mistake in my life and sat Mom and Chris down on the sofa. I sank into an easy chair. Rowan perched on the arm and took my hand between his.

"Mom. There's something I have to tell you."

"Oh, my God, you're pregnant."

"No! No. I am definitely *not* pregnant."

Mom heaved a sigh of relief. Then she frowned. "Well, you're not getting any younger," she noted in one of her maddening about-faces. "And if you two intend to stay together, I hope you've at least discussed—"

"Let's save kids for another day, okay?"

She studied me suspiciously, then leaned back on the sofa with a groan. "Oh, Lord. This is like those TV shows where the family stages an intervention to save their drug-addicted loved one. Only you're intervening in our relationship. Thank you, no."

"Mom . . ."

"Chris and I are grown-ups, Maggie, and we'd appreciate it if you would—"

"Daddy's here."

As Mom went rigid, I hurriedly launched into the same story I had fed Nancy weeks ago, a truer depiction of Jack's life than the version he and Rowan had concocted for public consumption: the letter that was eventually forwarded to Rowan; his cross-country trek; the chance meeting with a group of hikers that led him to a dilapidated cabin in the mountains; and his eventual return to the Crossroads with Jack in tow.

"I wanted to tell you all of this when you came up for *Annie*, but Daddy was . . . well, he was a mess, and I decided to wait until he was more like his old self, and I'm sorry to spring it on you like this, but I thought . . . I thought . . ."

My voice ran down. Mom stared at her clasped hands, her lips compressed into a tight pink line. Then her head came up and she fixed Rowan with a cold stare.

"Why did you have to interfere?"

"He's Maggie's father. And I knew she loved him. Should I have left him there? Living like an animal? Knowing he'd never survive another winter?"

"No. You should have taken him to a hospital."

"I tried. He ran away."

My mother's laugh was bitter. "That's his answer to everything. You could have notified the authorities. They would have removed him forcibly and seen to it that he got the care he needed."

"We were miles from anywhere, Alison. No cell phone reception. No roads."

"Then you should have lied! Taken him to town and turned him over to people who could help him."

"I couldn't do that. He'd put his trust in me."

"So you brought him here."

"Yes."

"Knowing it would only turn Maggie's life upside down."

"Yes."

"Knowing she was probably better off without him."

"Yes."

"And now what?" She turned that burning gaze on me. "You're going to become his caretaker? Waste years of your life like I did?"

"It won't come to that."

"My God, Maggie! Don't you think I said that? I spent most of my marriage trying to change Jack Sinclair. And when I couldn't, I spent the rest of it trying to keep him from going off the deep end."

"He's better now."

"Running a telephone hotline doesn't qualify you to diagnose or treat mental illness. And unless he's given up this ridiculous search for ... other worlds ... then he *is* mentally ill and he needs professional treatment, whether or not he wants it."

"When you see him—"

"I have no intention of seeing him."

"What?"

"I've gone through hell for Jack Sinclair. I am not starting down that path again. And I pray to God you'll abandon it. Because there is no happy ending here. If he's sick, he'll have another breakdown—and another and another until you have no choice but to commit him. And if he *is* better, he'll leech off of you just long enough to get his life together and then walk out—again. Either way, he'll ruin your life and break your heart in the process."

"He can't break my heart. He doesn't have that power over me any longer."

Maybe the weariness in my voice convinced her that I was stating a fact rather than protesting.

"As for ruining my life, he won't be around long enough to do that. He's moving on after the season ends."

"Moving on? Where? To do what?"

"I don't know. Neither does he."

"Typical. And what happens a month from now—a year from now—when you get another desperate cry for help?"

I shrugged. "I'll help him."

"Then he'll hold you hostage for the rest of your life."

"He's my father. I can't just turn my back on him. But I won't allow him to hold me hostage. And you shouldn't either."

Her puzzled frown cleared. "Now I get it. Honestly, Maggie, did you really think I'd take one look at Jack and change my mind about marrying Chris?"

I avoided looking at Rowan who had said exactly the same thing.

"Okay, it was a stupid idea!"

"No, it wasn't," Chris said quietly.

Mom's head snapped toward him. "Were you in on this?"

"No. But if Maggie had come to me with the idea, I would have said, 'Let's try it.' At this point, I'm willing to try anything."

"Then try accepting how I feel! All of you."

She grabbed her purse and started for the door.

"There's one more thing you should know."

With obvious reluctance, she turned to face me.

"Whether or not you want to see Jack now, you might see him tomorrow night. He's playing the Narrator in *Into the Woods*."

"I thought Bernie—"

"Bernie's his understudy. And he's playing the matinees. If Jack can't go on—"

"Don't pull him for my sake."

"It's not that. He froze during dress rehearsal. And . . . couldn't go on opening night."

"Froze? Jack?" Mom shook her head in disbelief. "Of all the things you've told me today, that's the most unbelievable. Was it because of me? Did he know I would be here?"

"He learned that days ago. Just after I told him I was his daughter."

"He didn't figure that out himself? All he had to do was look at you. But that's Jack. Too wrapped up in himself to notice anyone else." Mom studied me for a moment, then nodded. "That's what you meant when you said he didn't have the power to hurt you any longer."

"Partly. But I've had a chance to get to know him this summer. And he's everything you always claimed. Charming. Clever. Childish. Self-absorbed. You warned me. So did Rowan. But I thought I could . . . fix him. Talk about 'The Impossible Dream.' If something's really impossible, why waste time trying?"

"If you believed that," Rowan said, "you would never have risked loving me." He took my chin between his thumb and forefinger and tilted it up. "People do change, Maggie."

"You *wanted* to change."

"I wanted *you*. As far as changing . . ." His thumb caressed my chin. "As I recall, you pretty much had to drag me kicking and screaming the whole way."

"As I recall, I did a whole lot of kicking and screaming myself."

We stared into each other's eyes. Then we both became aware of the silence in the room. I ducked my head. Rowan cleared his throat and rose.

"Yes. Well. As Alison said, enough dissection for one day."

"Where is he?" my mother asked.

"Jack?"

"No, the Easter Bunny. Of course, Jack!"

"In the Smokehouse. Look, you don't have to—"

"I know I don't have to. Let's just get this over with."

"I'll bring him up here," Rowan said.

But Mom was already marching to the front door, leaving the three of us to scamper after her like school-children following an impatient teacher.

Short of knocking her down, there was no way to

reach the Smokehouse first to warn Jack. As it was, when she flung open the door and stopped dead, we barely managed to avoid piling up behind her like The Three Stooges. I edged past and found her staring at Jack in shock.

He acknowledged her reaction with a hesitant smile. "You should have seen me when I first got here. I looked like something the cat dragged in."

Maybe it was the use of one of her favorite phrases that made her shudder. Her hands tightened on the handle of her purse. Did she realize she was holding it in front of her like a shield?

The same way Daddy held his guitar when he met me.

"You look great," Jack said. "Pretty as ever."

My mother gave a disparaging snort. "Your eyesight is failing."

"Same old Allie."

"Not quite. Time changes everyone." She glanced at me. "Isn't that a song from some musical?"

"Maybe you're thinking of 'Time Heals Everything.' "

"The lyricist was clearly an optimist."

"The title is ironic," Rowan said quietly.

"In that case, I'll have to listen to it sometime."

A long silence ensued as they continued to study each other. Finally, Jack said, "Maybe we should walk down to the pond." He shot a pointed look at Chris. "So we can talk in private."

"Talk about what? Where you've been? What I've been doing for the last two decades?" Mom shook her head.

"Well, Maggie thought we should talk."

"Maggie thought the mere sight of you would send me running to the altar. This is Chris Thompson, by the way. The man I've been seeing for the last two years."

Jack and Chris exchanged stiff nods. Neither extended his hand.

"Maggie ought to know better," Jack said. "Once you make your mind up, there's no budging you."

"How do you know?"

"I just meant—"

"I know what you meant. You always thought I was hopelessly stuck in my ways."

"And you always thought I was a screwup."

"You *are* a screwup, Jack." Her voice was surprisingly gentle. "But our marriage was probably doomed from the beginning. The only good thing to come out of it was Maggie. She's the reason I'm here. Not to demand apologies or point fingers or stumble down memory lane. Now what is this nonsense about you freezing onstage?"

The abrupt shift in conversation left us all adrift. Jack shot me a reproachful glance and muttered, "It's been a long time since I performed."

"Are you saying you can't act any longer?"

"Of course I can act!"

"Then stop making excuses and do it! Rowan put his life on hold to find you. Maggie's turned this theatre upside down to make a place for you. It's time to step up to the plate, Jack. I'll expect to see you onstage tomorrow night. And by God, you better give the performance of a lifetime."

"It's only a small role."

"What's that old theatre proverb? 'There are no small roles, only small actors?' "

"I hate that saying!" Jack and I exclaimed in unison.

Our reaction drew a reluctant chuckle from Mom. "God, Jack. I can't believe you didn't realize she was your daughter."

"She's your daughter, too. First time she yelled at me, she said, 'An apology goes a lot farther than a shrug and a smile.' How many times did you remind me of that?"

"About a million."

I recalled the strange look he'd given me when I said that. But he still hadn't put the pieces together. Maybe he'd been afraid to try.

"So," Mom said, "if we're done here, I'll see you after the show, Jack."

"Allie? You don't . . . hate me, do you?"

"No. I don't hate you."

She sounded infinitely weary. How many times had he asked that over the course of their marriage? And how many times had she given him the same tired reassurance?

"All the hurt and pain and mistakes we made . . . it was a long time ago. I can even forgive you for vanishing from your daughter's life, because I think that was the best thing you could have done for her."

Jack nodded eagerly, but I was stunned that she could wave aside his abandonment.

"But while I might be willing to forgive the past, I am holding you accountable for the present. And the future. If you hurt Maggie again, I *will* hate you. You've been given a second chance to play a part in your daughter's life, Jack. Don't screw it up this time."

She strode out of the Smokehouse. Chris and Jack seemed shell-shocked by her vehemence. On Rowan's face, there was open admiration.

I ran after her. When she heard me calling, her steps slowed, then stopped.

"I'm sorry. I shouldn't have put you through that."

"No. You were right. I did need to see him."

"Are you okay?"

"Just . . . tired."

I hooked my arm through hers, and we walked toward the parking lot. Mom finally broke the silence to ask, "When you told him you were his daughter, did he ask if you hated him?"

I nodded.

"Still so desperate to be loved."

Rowan had written something similar in his journal. I wondered if Jack hungered for love or merely for expiation.

"Maybe that's why he became an actor," Mom mused. "All that love pouring over the footlights."

"That's not love. It's applause. Adulation."

"It's the only kind of love Jack could handle. The love of strangers. Real love requires that you give something in return."

"And that doesn't make you bitter?"

"I'm bitter about the wasted years. But I meant it when I said I don't hate him. Frankly, I don't feel much of anything. I never expected that. You love someone. You live together. You bring a child into the world. And in the end, there's nothing left. I find that very sad."

"It is."

"Maybe Rowan was right to bring him back, but I wish for your sake that you could have held on to your happy memories of him." She sighed. "How awful has it been for you?"

I watched Chris and Rowan walking toward us. Then I turned back to Mom and asked, "Do you want to go somewhere? Just the two of us?"

"Yes," Mom said. "I'd like that."

❧❧

We ended up at Woodford State Park. Although there were a couple of cars parked by the trail entrance, the lakeshore was deserted. It was an unprepossessing spot for a chat, the overcast sky as gray as the waters of the lake. The rack of canoes provided the only cheery note, the bright colors—yellow, red, orange—a startling contrast to the pine trees lining the shore like grim, green soldiers.

"It's not exactly Rehoboth," I said.

"More like the lake in that Montgomery Clift-Elizabeth Taylor movie. The one where he takes Shelley Winters out canoeing so he can kill her."

"That's a real pick-me-up."

"This from the woman who refers to Janet's lovely home as the Bates mansion."

We sat on a weathered wooden bench near the strip of sand that constituted the beach and I told her as much about my summer as I could. She punctuated my monologue with the occasional sigh, but her head jerked toward me when I described the night I ran away.

"I know. Another like father, like daughter moment."

"Maybe. But you came back. And the two of you seem okay now."

"I think so."

I could hear the uncertainty in my voice and feel my mother's intent gaze.

"The honeymoon isn't exactly over, but we've had our share of ups and downs."

"Good. That means you're going into this with your eyes open."

I'd told Jack we were. But were anyone's eyes really open when they were in love?

"When I met Rowan, I thought you were falling for a man just like your father. The boyish charm. The eagerness to please. And that strange watchfulness. Like he was gauging my reactions and choosing the most appropriate response."

That description of their first encounter was so accurate it was scary. And it was a scary-accurate description of my father, too.

"But I'll grant a lot of leeway to a man who'd spend months searching for his girlfriend's father. And who looks at you the way he does . . . like you were the only person in the room."

"The same way Chris looks at you."

Her cheeks grew faintly pink.

"Did Daddy ever look at you that way?"

"In the beginning. When he was trying to win me. But after he had . . ." She shrugged.

"So you're okay with Rowan?"

Mom sighed. "Yes. But he still scares me, Maggie. There are scars on that man's soul."

"Everybody has scars."

"But some can't be healed."

I wondered if she was talking about herself as well as

Rowan, but I just said, "He's helped heal some of mine. I'm trying to do the same for him."

"That won't be easy. Rowan's a bit . . . murky at times, isn't he?"

"Yeah." It was my turn to sigh. "Is Chris ever like that?"

She stared out at the lake. "Chris is like the water in the Caribbean. So beautifully clear you can see right down to the bottom."

❧❧

We returned to the theatre to find Chris and Rowan sitting on a bench by the pond.

"Seems everyone is gazing at water this afternoon," Mom noted.

"Actually, we just got back from a hike," Chris said. "Rowan showed me the plateau where you two had your first picnic. Talk about a romantic spot. Well. Not so much for Rowan and me. But if you two had been with us . . ."

I saw exactly what Mom meant about clear waters. His love for her shone through his eyes, his smile, the very way his body leaned toward her.

For a moment, she allowed her love to shine just as clearly. Then she frowned and said, "We should let Maggie and Rowan get ready for the show."

As their car pulled out of the parking lot, Rowan said, "I'm beginning to understand why you wanted to intervene. He's a good man. And they're good for each other."

"But I'm not sure they're going to make it. Or if I helped them."

"You opened the door, Maggie. Like I do when I call the Mackenzies. You can't push them through it, any more than you can push your father."

"That's not what you wrote in your journal the summer he was here: 'If anyone can save Jack Sinclair from himself, his daughter can.'"

"You can't save someone who doesn't want to be saved."

"I suppose that's the lesson I had to learn this summer."

Rowan put his arm around my waist. "The summer's not over yet."

CHAPTER 44

YOU'LL NEVER BE ALONE

JACK APPARENTLY WANDERED UP TO THE HOUSE after the rest of us left the theatre. He was gone by the time I returned, but Janet said that they had spent the afternoon sitting in the sunroom.

"Just . . . sitting?"

"He talked about the early days of his marriage. And when you were a little girl."

"Did it ever occur to him to share those memories with me?"

"Maybe he needed a dress rehearsal."

"Don't remind me of dress rehearsals."

"One thing I do know: he didn't want to be alone. Every time I got up to do something, he trailed after me like a lost puppy."

"You must have loved that."

"Actually, it was rather sweet." At my disbelieving look, she added, "Don't worry. I'm immune to Jack Sinclair's charm. But he's adrift right now. And a little lonely."

If so, he was back on track by the Saturday matinee when he swore up and down he was ready to go on that night. I just nodded and made sure Bernie was on stand by. As soon as Jack headed down to the dressing room, I slipped upstairs to Rowan's apartment.

"How is he?" I asked.

"He seems fine."

"He seemed fine before he bolted."

"He won't bolt this time. He has something to prove —
to himself, to Alison, and to you."

"That's what it took? Mom daring him to screw up?"

Rowan shrugged. "Stranger things have happened.
Especially in this theatre."

When Jack reported to the green room for warm-ups,
he seemed as calm as Rowan had claimed. And when
Reinhard called places, he gave me a brisk nod.

I did the same as I slid into my seat next to Mom. She
shrugged, but her hands relaxed their death grip on her
purse.

The house lights began to dim. The murmur of conversation hushed. A program rustled. A seat squeaked.
Someone coughed. I took a deep breath.

The lights came up on the stage, and there was a smattering of applause at the storybook tableau. Then Jack
walked onstage.

I heard Mom catch her breath. Maybe it was the gray
suit. Or the haircut he'd gotten in town that morning. He
looked exactly like the nice, steady corporate type he had
disdained — or the well-dressed English teacher he might
have remained if luck or fate or faeries hadn't changed
his life.

He strolled to his position. His gaze swept the darkened house. Then it returned to the center section where
we were sitting. Maybe I only imagined that it lingered
on Mom, but his smile was strangely wistful.

"Once upon a time . . ."

The orchestra launched into the opening number, the
jaunty staccato beat of strings and piano driving the vocals of the cast and Jack's narration. As the characters
made their wishes, two of mine came true: my father was
performing again and my mother was witnessing it.

She chuckled at Cinderella's diffident description of
the ball, laughed at the self-centered "agony" of the
princes, but when the Witch implored Rapunzel to give
up her wish to see the world, she became very still.

I knew "Stay with Me" would remind her of the years we had been estranged from each other, the eagerness with which I abandoned my childhood home for college. Each new job, each new role had been an adventure. I never thought about my mother returning to that empty house at the end of the day. When I thought of her at all, it was with a mingled sense of guilt and duty. She'd kept her fears and her doubts to herself and let me go my own way. I wasn't sure I could be as strong if I ever had a child.

Jack's performance surprised me. He brought a sly humor to the role I had never seen in rehearsal, as if he and the audience were sharing an inside joke. It was utterly different from Bernie's folksiness and made the Narrator's death even scarier.

When Bernie played the role, I always felt disbelief when that moment arrived. How could anyone throw this nice old man to the giant? It was like murdering Mister Rogers. Or Santa Claus.

This time, I shared all the Narrator's emotions: nervousness escalating to desperation; the momentary relief when his tormentors backed off; and then the terror of being dragged across the stage and shoved into the wings where the giant awaited her sacrifice. I felt oddly betrayed because Jack had promised the happy ending we got in Act One. If the joke could turn so viciously on him, no one was safe.

I shifted uneasily in my seat and heard others doing the same. It was as if the entire audience feared that something might emerge from the darkness to snatch us from our uncomfortable seats and our comfortable lives and drag us into the unknown.

Was that Rowan's magic or Jack's performance or some strange amalgam of the two?

The few light moments in Act Two shone brighter for that, but there was a nervous undercurrent to the laughter, as if the audience was still searching the shadows for danger. I floated in and out of the show, adrift in the shadows of memory:

My mother's pain throbbing through me as the Witch lamented Rapunzel's death, the muted sadness of watching me drift away all those years ago made sharper by the fear that she might lose me again to the siren call of my father's charm.

The sour taste of bile filling my mouth as the characters hurled accusations at each other, their bitter voices replaced by Rowan's and mine the night he revealed the truth about himself and about my father.

Shock turning my body rigid when the Mysterious Man appeared, no longer Rowan in his tattered costume but that terrified Rip Van Winkle who had tottered out of the theatre and back into my life.

No more visions.

Rowan's face, the unfeeling mask of Faerie. His voice, filled with familiar gentleness. As if the Mysterious Man's resurrection had rendered him both more otherworldly and more human.

Faery-green eyes weeping honey-sweet tears.

Rowan's face becoming my father's, filled with the excitement of exchanging the ties that bind for the thrill of the unknown. Brian's filled with my mother's weariness as she confessed that all the pain and anger and love had been reduced to ashes.

Once upon a time . . .

My father spinning tales about fantastic worlds. My mother cautiously explaining why Daddy had to leave. While I listened and watched, looking to them to learn what to be, what to feel, where to turn.

Careful what you say.

My eight-year-old self, staring at the newspaper clippings of Daddy's shows, wishing he would come back. My thirty-four-year-old self, staring at Jack's name in the program, wishing he would stay.

Careful what you wish for.

And hidden in the shadowy wings, the one who had cast the spell that brought father and daughter to the Crossroads; cast another to erase a man's memories of the magic that had touched him one Midsummer night; watched the unexpected consequences wrought by time and fate and human nature; and returned to restore order, only to discover that some spells are beyond Fae magic to repair.

Oh, careful what spells you cast, my love. For even you with all your power cannot always tell where they will lead. And then it is left to us to untangle them. Stumbling along the path, guided only by the magic we humans possess: determination, instinct, love.

Into the woods and out of the woods. And maybe—if we're very lucky—we earn our happy ever after.

The finale brought me back to the show. The audience clapped along with the music, as relieved and happy as if they had survived a dangerous journey. But after the red velvet curtains closed, my mother remained in her seat, staring at the stage.

I touched her arm lightly, and she started as if awakening from a dream.

"It was like the night I saw *Carousel*. When it seemed like you were singing to me. Only this time, I saw my whole life flash before me. The handsome prince who is charming, but insincere. The witch whose daughter keeps pulling away. The crazy man darting in and out, in and out ..."

Clearly, whatever magic Rowan had worked had affected her, too.

Impulsively, I blurted out, "You know you won't lose me. No matter what happens with Jack."

Her eyes widened. "How did you ... ? All right, now you're scaring me."

"I'm sorry. I just ... that's what came to me. When I was watching tonight."

"Yes. Well. Let's just say I was grateful when Cinderella began singing 'No One is Alone.'"

"You're not alone," Chris said.

"I know," she replied, her voice as quiet as his. "And I know I'll never lose you, Maggie. I'm far too adept at hunting you down wherever you might go." Her nod was as brisk as Jack's before the show. "We'd better move along. Jack will expect to see us at the stage door."

Chris frowned, but followed us into the lobby. It took awhile to make our way through the crowd; people kept stopping to congratulate me. Their faces held a mixture of pleasure and uncertainty, as if they, too, were still feeling the effects of the show.

Friends and family members of the actors gathered in small clusters near the stage door. Jack hovered in the doorway, scanning their faces. Then he spied us and began edging forward, his head turning this way and that to acknowledge the congratulations.

His steps faltered as he approached us, his smile a little nervous.

"So. What did you think?"

"It's funny," Mom said. "I thought it would be a straightforward role. But you really held the whole show together, didn't you? And the moment they threw you to the giant . . . that was terrifying."

Jack's expression clouded. "Yeah. It was."

I wondered again how much Rowan had done to create the power of that moment. But Jack was watching me, clearly awaiting my reaction.

"It was a great performance. You took the role—and the show—to a whole new level."

"Thank you. That really . . . it means a lot." He shot a quick glance at Mom. "I guess you'll be leaving in the morning."

"Yes. So I'll say good-bye now."

She thrust out her hand. He clasped it gingerly. It was the first time they had touched and it lasted only a few seconds before both backed away. But they continued staring at each other, as if they recognized that this would be the last time they would ever meet.

"Maggie says you plan to leave after the season's over."

"Well . . . probably."

Mom blew out her breath impatiently. "What are you going to do with yourself, Jack? You're not a kid anymore. You can't just wander."

"I know, Allie. Maybe this time, I'll figure out where I belong."

"Still searching for enlightenment?" Her voice held resignation rather than the bitterness I remembered from my youth.

"Still searching, anyway."

"Well, someday I hope you find what you're looking for."

"You, too." He stepped closer. "Is he good to you?" he asked, ignoring the fact that Chris was standing a few feet away, glowering at him.

"He's very good to me. And very good *for* me."

Resentment tightened my father's features. Then it was gone, replaced by that same wistful half-smile I'd seen at the top of the show.

"I'm glad," he said, almost to himself. "You did a good job with our girl. I knew you would. But . . . well . . ."

"She's temperamental," my mother noted. "Like you."

"But she's got her feet on the ground. That she gets from you."

Did they see only the strangers they had become as they gazed at each other? Or the parade of their younger selves? The college students caught up in the first throes of romance. The young couple trying to keep that romance alive as he flitted from gig to gig. The happy parents, united in the love of their child. The older ones, torn apart by bitter quarreling and an obsession neither could understand.

For a moment, I thought they might embrace. Then Mom nodded and turned away. Chris tucked her hand into the crook of his elbow. My father watched them until they were lost in the crowd. Then he gave me a shaky smile and walked slowly back to the theatre.

People ebbed and flowed around me, their noisy chatter punctuated by occasional bursts of laughter. I felt removed from all the excitement and suddenly, very alone.

And then I felt them all around me. Reinhard's power, as steady as the throb of a heartbeat. Janet's as bracing as cold water on a hot day. Alex's warmth. Lee's protectiveness. Mei-Yin's determination. The quiet strength that was Catherine. The brighter flash of concern that was Javier. And for the first time—very faint—a bubbly upwelling of sympathy and love that could only be Hal.

And the center of all those separate powers and the source of most of them—Rowan.

I felt him slipping past the clusters of people behind me, making his slow, steady way toward me. His hands came down on my shoulders. His love rippled through me.

I leaned against him and closed my eyes.

No one is alone.

CHAPTER 45

TIME HEALS EVERYTHING

MOM'S DEPARTURE WITH CHRIS seemed to cue a mass exodus from Dale. The professionals bolted after the matinee to audition for their next gigs. The Bough emptied as the Mackenzies embarked on day trips. The local actors and staff resumed their everyday lives.

It was the natural order of a summer stock season, but my sense of loss was greater this year, knowing that my father would soon leave my life—and my world—forever. I'd hoped we could spend some of that time getting to know each other, but he left the apartment early every morning to walk in the woods and only returned as the light was waning.

"He'll come around," Rowan assured me. "In his own time."

But there was little time left.

Instead of using mine to research grants, I moped around the theatre. Alex, too, was moping, and I was certain it was because Debra had left for New York. When I found him drifting aimlessly around the garden Tuesday morning, I dragged him to the apartment for lunch.

"Look at us," I said. "We spend half the summer complaining about how overworked we are and we can't even enjoy our freedom."

"You need to start thinking ahead," Rowan said.

"We are," Alex replied gloomily.

"Thinking about the theatre, I mean."

I inscribed another figure eight in my gazpacho. "Debra had this idea for a murder mystery series at the Bates mansion."

Alex poked at his salad. "She mentioned that to me, too."

"It's not exactly part of our mission, but it might be fun. And it would bring in money. Do you think Janet would go for it?"

Alex shrugged. "She's always complaining that she's bored during the off-season."

He sighed. I sighed.

Rowan said, "What about that reading series you were telling me about? The one to showcase new works by Vermont playwrights."

"That's not until the spring. The scripts have just started coming in. But there's always the Christmas show."

"You're doing a Christmas show?"

"Do you even look at the program?" I complained. "There's been a notice in every one! We're doing *A Christmas Carol*. Long loves the story. Ghosts. Redemption. New beginnings."

The perfect summation of this season at the Crossroads.

"He loves all the children's roles even more: Cratchits and carolers and street urchins. He's sure we'll make a fortune. But so far, Alex and I haven't found a version we like."

Alex's fork clattered onto his plate. "My God. I'm so stupid. There's our version!"

"You guys wrote a musical adaptation of *A Christmas Carol*?"

Rowan nodded. "The first show we ever wrote together."

"Mostly as a lark," Alex said. "We started talking and the next thing you know, Rowan presented me with a draft."

"Why didn't you suggest it from the start?" I demanded.

"It felt wrong to do it without Rowan," Alex replied. "And once the season got underway, I was too busy to even think about Christmas."

"We'd probably want to make some changes," Rowan said. "We've both learned a lot about putting a musical together since then."

"The plot's not going to change," Alex replied. "And most of the songs are done. The orchestrations will take a couple of weeks, but—"

"Whoa, whoa, whoa!" I exclaimed. "You're starting school soon. When will you have time to—?"

"I'll make time! Besides, Rowan and I work fast."

"We wrote *The Sea-Wife* in six months," Rowan added, catching Alex's enthusiasm. "This is just polishing."

"If we put our minds to it, we could have the whole thing ready by mid-October."

"And begin rehearsals in early November," Rowan said.

They turned to me, a freckled face and a pale one, both alight with excitement.

"I'll need the completed script before the September board meeting," I warned them.

"But we're a known commodity!" Alex protested.

"A winning commodity," Rowan added.

"I still need to let them read it. If they want to."

Rowan shoved back his chair. "I must have a copy somewhere."

"I still have mine," Alex said, following Rowan into the office. "If you can't find yours, I'll dig it out this afternoon and—"

"Here it is!" Rowan crowed. "On the shelf with our other shows."

I found them sitting thigh-to-thigh on the floor, their heads bent over a green binder. I considered volunteering to make another copy, but they had already begun dissecting the opening number, exclaiming over some bits and groaning over others.

Reluctant to become an unnecessary third wheel, I wandered down to the production office and pulled out my lesson plans for the new after-school program for elementary school kids. I jotted some notes, went through my inbox, then slumped back in my chair.

Alex had something to look forward to when Debra left. Rowan had a project to fill the next two months. But the project I wanted to focus on—getting to know my father—was going nowhere.

So focus on something else, Graham.

I picked up the phone and called Long.

When I told him about the Mackenzie-Ross adaptation of *A Christmas Carol,* he exclaimed, "That's wonderful! I'll call the board today and let them know."

"Umm . . . shouldn't they vote on this?"

"A new musical by Rowan Mackenzie and Alex Ross? What's to approve?" Then he added, "They're not doing some radical reinterpretation, are they? The Ghost of Christmas Past wandering around in the nude."

"I sincerely doubt it. Apart from the sensation it would cause, it would be way too chilly for the poor actor."

"I suppose we do need an official vote. Boards can be so tiresome sometimes."

"Tell me about it," I replied without—as usual— thinking.

Long just chuckled. "I'll e-mail everybody today and ask them to weigh in. I'm sure they'll be thrilled. And once it's approved, I'll announce it before the remaining performances of *Into the Woods.* If you think that would be appropriate."

"It would be perfect."

There was a brief silence on the other end. Then Long said, "I didn't get a chance to speak with your mother after the show, but I saw her talking with Jack."

"It went okay. Better than I thought it would. But it was . . . stressful. For both of them."

"And for you. A lot to deal with in one week. And that show Saturday night! It was excellent," he hastily added. "But . . . strange. Harder to watch somehow."

When I told him my theory about Jack's performance and the joke that unexpectedly turned around to bite him—and the audience—in the ass, he said, "Yes, you might be right. But everyone I talked with afterward seemed delighted. Maybe it was just us. Because we were expecting one thing and got something different."

Much like Long himself. From the moment I'd met him, I had pegged him as one sort of man, but this season, he had turned out to be something else.

"Well, you must have a million things to do," he said. "And I need to get out those e-mails. I'll let you know as soon as I've heard back from the board."

I resisted the urge to keep him on the line, to soak up some of his excitement. Everyone seemed to be caught up in the Christmas spirit except me.

Rowan must have sensed that. He appeared in the doorway a few minutes later and said, "Alex has gone home to search for the music. We're going to meet tomorrow afternoon to play through the score. Want to join us?"

"Love to. When do I get to read the script?"

"How about tomorrow morning?"

"What's wrong with right now?"

"I thought we might walk into town. See the sights. Have dinner at the Golden Bough."

I jumped up and hurried around the desk. Then I hesitated. "Are you sure you're ready for this?"

"Absolutely."

I flung my arms around his neck and buried my face against his shoulder.

"He'll come around," Rowan whispered.

OUR WALK TO TOWN WAS UNIMPEDED BY SLAVERING DOGS. It was the cats that slowed us down.

A succession of furry wraiths darted through the grass and twined around Rowan's ankles, purring in adoration. When he attempted to remove the first one, it went limp, as if his touch had induced a fainting spell. The next treated his fingers to a lascivious tongue bath. When I tried to extricate the third, it shot me a disdainful glance, dug its claws into Rowan's pants, and hung on with grim determination.

We shambled and stumbled and shooed our way past the large houses outside of town, only to glance back and discover a line of cats trailing after us. Rowan broke into helpless laughter, then a tremulous rendition of "There's a Parade in Town," made even more discordant by the yowls of his admirers. When I pointed out that his Pied Piper act might blow his cover, he called on his magic to gently discourage his feline courtiers.

The human inhabitants of Dale were as curious as their cats. If they didn't exactly faint, they popped out of shops and restaurants to greet me and exclaim over Rowan.

"Do you know everyone in town?" he asked after our shouted conversation with Mrs. Grainger who was a dear, but deaf as a post.

"It's a really small town."

But there was no denying that Rowan was a bigger draw than the Fourth of July parade.

As yet another wave of admirers approached, he seized my hand and pulled me into the General Store.

"Well, if it isn't Rowan Mackenzie," Mr. Hamilton exclaimed.

Every head swiveled in our direction. Fortunately, most were tourists, who went back to their browsing.

Rowan greeted Mr. Hamilton pleasantly, but his wide-eyed gaze swept the scuffed floorboards, the exposed wooden beams, the woven rugs that hung over the railing on the second floor, and the moth-eaten heads of various dead animals that eyed us glassily from the shadows near the rafters.

"This is what a General Store *should* look like," he declared. Then he spied the widowed Kent sisters making a beeline toward him and darted off.

Mr. Hamilton watched Rowan prowl through the narrow aisles filled with Vermont-made products plus a hodgepodge of stuff ranging from dishware to clothing to camping equipment.

"Doesn't get out much, does he? First time I remember him coming to town in all the years he's lived here."

"He was claustrophobic. Or agoraphobic. Something phobic."

"That's what I heard, too. Doesn't seem to bother him now, though."

"I think he got treatment. While he was away."

As Rowan clambered up the steps to the second floor—pursued by the indomitable widows—Mr. Hamilton frowned. "Not afraid of heights, is he?"

"Heights he's okay with."

For half an hour, Mr. Hamilton and I discussed the weather, the Blueberry Festival, and *A Christmas Carol.* Then Rowan zoomed up to the counter and paused to study the rack of postcards.

"That's what we need. A postcard of the theatre."

As he took off again, I exchanged a long look with Mr. Hamilton. "Why didn't we think of that?"

"Beats me. Every shop in town would carry them. Out-of-town ones, too, I bet."

"If we get them printed up soon, we could have them in stores by fall foliage season."

Mr. Hamilton tugged his right earlobe, a sure sign that he was calculating expenses.

"Why don't I work up some figures?" I suggested. "We can go over them before the September board meeting."

As he beamed approvingly, Rowan strode toward us again and laid two beeswax candles and a wallet on the counter.

"Who's the wallet for?"

"Me."

I refrained from pointing out that he had nothing to put in it. He hadn't made a dime all summer and had repeatedly refused to accept any of the money he had given to me.

After studying the glass jars of penny candy for five minutes, he selected a striped stick of sarsaparilla.

"Would you like one?"

"No, thanks. But let's get a licorice one for Jack."

I unzipped my purse and froze when Rowan pulled a wad of bills out of his pocket. With a proud smile, he paid for his purchases and carefully slid the remaining money into his new wallet.

As soon as I dragged him outside, I demanded, "Where did you get all that money?"

"Never mind."

"Did you sell one of your books?"

"Not an old one."

"*Which* one?" I persisted.

"*To Kill a Mockingbird*."

"You own a first edition of *To Kill a Mockingbird*?"

"Not anymore."

"But how could you let it go? It's such a wonderful story."

"And I can still enjoy it whenever I like. Reinhard bought me a paperback copy after he arranged the sale."

"I should have known Reinhard was in on this." I lowered my voice to ask, "How much did you get for it?"

"Guess."

"Five thousand dollars?"

He glanced around before whispering, "Fifteen thousand."

"Holy crap!" I exclaimed, drawing giggles from two passing kids.

"Reinhard's holding most of it. I just have what's in my lovely new wallet." He glanced up and down Main Street. "Now where?"

"Hallee's. But we have to hurry if we want to get there before it closes."

Although Hallee's was just across the street, it took us fifteen minutes to escape the new tide of well-wishers that surrounded us. I groaned in disappointment when I discovered the door was locked. Rowan stared at the window display, transfixed.

"It's Hal's annual tribute to blueberries," I explained.

The display featured the usual assortment of scantily clad mannequins, all sporting blue lingerie: blue panties and bras, blue teddies and negligees. A mannequin in a blue corset cradled white bowls of blueberries beneath her breasts. Two male mannequins in tight blue briefs posed with pies like discus throwers. Off to one side, a mannequin in a blue negligee leaned languidly against a white picket fence. Her left hand toyed with her sparkly "sapphire" necklace. Her right proffered a single blueberry to the male mannequin—in obligatory blue thong—that reclined at her feet amid a veritable ocean of berries. High above, a blue moon smiled benignly.

"Merciful gods," Rowan breathed.

"Wait until apple season. He's planning a Garden of Eden theme."

Rowan was still mesmerized by the display when the door to the shop banged open and Hal flew out.

"Oh, my God! I can't believe it. You're here. In Dale!"

As he burst into "Miracles of Miracles," the door opened again and Lee walked out, grinning. "When Hal and I saw you through the window, we just about—"

"Do you like it?" Hal interrupted. "The display?"

"I love it. It's sexy and funny and inventive. Just like the man who created it."

Tears welled up in Hal's eyes. With a tremulous cry, he ran back into the shop.

Lee caught the door before it swung shut. "He's just verklempt," he told Rowan.

"Ver—?"

"Ask Bernie," Lee and I chorused.

As we entered the shop, the pink velveteen curtains at the back parted and Hal emerged, dabbing his eyes with a tissue.

"I'm fine," he insisted. "Lee, Maggie—talk among yourselves. I have to give Rowan the tour. Oh, where to begin? Accessories? Gowns? Nightwear!"

While Hal played tour guide, I idly sifted through a rack of camisoles and corsets.

"Who buys something like this?" I asked Lee, holding up a plaid prep school uniform with cutouts around the breasts.

"You'd be surprised. I just wish his high-end stuff sold as well as the kitsch. He makes out pretty well on the costumes he designs for the drag queens, but when he opened the shop, he planned to sell all custom-made clothing. People just aren't willing to shell out the bucks for it."

I glanced at Rowan and Hal who were in hushed consultation in nightwear. "Mr. Hamilton and I were talking about making up a series of postcards of the barn. What if we expanded the idea to include note cards featuring Hal's artwork?"

Lee's face lit up. He seized my arm and dragged me over to Rowan and Hal. "I'm taking over the tour, Hal. Maggie needs to talk with you."

Hal was even more excited than Lee. "We could do

different versions. Reproductions of the pen-and-ink sketch on the program. Original watercolor renditions of the barn. I could do a whole Dale Collection! The barn. The General Store. The town hall."

"Hallee's."

Hal shook his head. "The tourists will want Ye Olde New England Towne." He gasped and clutched my arm. "A gift shop. We need a gift shop with theatre tchotchkes. T-shirts, hats, note cards, books, posters. My posters!"

For a moment, we were both transported into the wonderful world of merchandising. Then I descended to earth.

"One step at a time. First, work me up some prices I can show the board. Then we'll tackle the gift shop."

We hurried over to share our latest brainstorm and found Rowan and Lee examining a pair of black leather boots with stiletto heels.

"Just what I need. I fall over my feet when I'm wearing sneakers."

"But think how well they would go with this leather bustier," Rowan said.

"I'd sweat like a horse. Come on, I'm hungry."

We made it about fifty feet down Main Street when a barrel-like figure stormed out of the Mandarin Chalet.

"So you FINALLY made it into town!" Mei-Yin exclaimed. "This calls for a CELEBRATION. A special DINNER!"

"That's what we were planning," I said.

Her eyes narrowed to slits. "Where?"

"Why, the Chalet, of course," Rowan lied smoothly.

"GOOD answer!" She flung out her arms. "WELCOME to the Mandarin Chalet. Where EAST meets WEST. And the ELITE meet to EAT!"

When dragons flank the doorway of a giant gingerbread house, you expect the interior to be a hellish amalgam of *Flower Drum Song* and *The Sound of Music*. I'd been shocked the first time I walked into the Chalet and found nary a dragon or cuckoo clock in sight.

The snow-covered mountains in the mural would
have felt equally at home in Sichuan Province or Swit-
zerland, as would the intricately carved wooden screen
that separated the restaurant from the bar. Soft pools of
light illuminated the tables, while the rose and gold accents conjured a glorious sunrise. Throw in the faint music that combined sounds from the natural world with
harp and flute, and the Chalet felt like a mountaintop
retreat or a relaxing day spa.

"So what do you THINK?"

Although Mei-Yin was beaming, a discordant twang
of anxiety shivered through me.

"It's so restful," Rowan said. "Exactly what I need after all the excitement today."

Her relief surprised me; clearly, Rowan's approval
meant as much to her as it had to Hal. But she just whispered, "Makes people STAY longer. And SPEND more."

She snatched up a sheaf of menus and marched off.
Although it was only 6:30, the restaurant was already
half full, mostly with the AARP crowd, all of whom regarded us avidly, all of whom expected us to stop and
chat. When we finally reached the corner table where
Mei-Yin waited impatiently, we both sank gratefully
onto our chairs.

"Order whatever you want," Mei-Yin said. "Chinese,
Swiss, Mexican . . ." She punctuated each cuisine by slap-
ping a different menu on the table. "I'll have Max cook
you up something SPECIAL." She slapped the wine list
down, too, then snapped her fingers at a hovering busboy. "YOU! Clear off these utensils and bring out the
REAL silverware."

"You keep the family silver here?" I asked.

"Just a couple of place settings. When Reinhard and I
try out one of Max's new recipes, we like to do it up in
STYLE."

More likely, she had brought the silverware in after
Rowan's return in anticipation of the day he would dine
at her establishment.

Rowan just thanked her quietly and watched her march back to the kitchen.

The restful atmosphere was somewhat undermined by the staff's obvious terror of offending their boss' special guests. Ice rattled like chattering teeth as the busboy tiptoed over with the water pitcher. Our server's voice shook as he announced the specials. Both relaxed so quickly that I knew Rowan must have called on his power to calm them.

Mei-Yin emerged from the kitchen with her stepson in tow. Max was a younger version of Reinhard from the premature gray of his brush cut to his stocky build. He even gave a little bow when Rowan rose to shake his hand.

"It's an honor to have you here."

"And a long overdue pleasure for me. But with all these choices . . ." Rowan waved his hand at the pile of menus. ". . . Maggie and I are at a loss. What would you recommend?"

As the two men launched into a protracted discussion of menu options, I brought Mei-Yin up to speed on recent developments. She demanded good dance music for Fezziwig's party and the opportunity to play the killer in our yet-to-be-approved Halloween murder mystery. But she also suggested that until we scraped together funds for a gift shop, we set up tables on the breezeway at intermission to· hawk merchandise. And volunteered to teach some movement classes for the after-school programs if I got swamped. Which seemed likely given all the new initiatives.

Max announced our dinner selections. Rowan's main course sounded like a phlegmy sneeze, mine like the worst salad ever imagined. They turned out to be veal strips in a cream sauce and a cold sausage salad that was unexpectedly delicious. Mei-Yin and Max lingered long enough to share a toast, then left us to savor our meal.

Dinner in town—another first. And Rowan's sweet smile made it even more perfect.

When we passed on dessert, our server brought us coffee and a small bowl filled with chocolate-dipped strawberries. What he didn't bring was the check.

"It's on the HOUSE!" Mei-Yin declared when Rowan called her over.

"I can't let you do that."

Once more, her eyes narrowed into dark, dangerous slits. "You gonna tell me what you'll 'LET' me do? In MY restaurant?"

"No, of course not. I just—"

"GOOD! It's SETTLED."

We thanked Max and Mei-Yin profusely. And after she had escorted us to the door, Rowan pressed a kiss to her cheek.

"You are a very gracious lady. And you made this an evening I will never forget."

Her happiness zinged through me, but all she said was, "Don't get run OVER walking home."

Rowan caught my arm as I turned toward the theatre. "What about the Bough? Don't I get to see all the changes you've made?"

"We could do that another time."

"Nonsense," he said, steering me down the sidewalk. "Besides, Frannie's feelings will be hurt if I don't stop in."

From the rapidity with which Frannie descended, I suspected she'd been watching our progress from the front windows. But Iolanthe still reached us first. I caught a blur of movement near the front desk. A moment later, she was draped over Rowan's boot.

"Cats like Rowan," I told Frannie.

"My goodness. I can't remember the last time I saw her move that fast."

"I can't remember the last time I saw her move."

Naturally, Frannie insisted on showing him around. And naturally, Iolanthe insisted on accompanying us. But her burst of energy had faded and she yowled so plaintively that Rowan finally picked her up. She spent the rest of the tour cradled against his chest. Now and then, her paw came up to touch his cheek, as if she—like Frannie—had difficulty believing that Rowan Mackenzie was actually here. The cast members in the lounge took his presence in stride, but of course, they had no way of knowing they were witnessing a minor miracle.

Rowan declined a drink, but when we returned to the lobby, he said, "The hotel looks beautiful. It reminds me of Helen's sunroom."

Frannie and I exchanged startled glances.

"You're right," Frannie said. "Maybe it was Helen's spirit guiding us all along."

Rowan smiled. "Maybe so. She'd be so happy to know that you're watching over the cast."

"And even happier to see you two together again." As the grandfather clock struck ten, Frannie added, "It's late. You better run along. I'll give you the rest of the tour next time you're in town, Rowan. I'll even show you the room Maggie stayed in during her season. Where she laid awake nights dreaming of you."

"Frannie!" I protested.

"Well, you did, didn't you?"

"Yes! But you're not supposed to tell him that. It'll give him a big head."

"Rowan's head's just fine. Now scoot, you two."

Rowan carefully deposited Iolanthe in the inbox and we started for home. The streets were already deserted, everyone in Dale tucked in for the night. We said little, content to mosey along in silence. My heart was filled with happiness at sharing Rowan's adventure in town and my mind was buzzing with ideas for the theatre. Astonishing that Rowan's casual mention of a postcard could lead to so many new possibilities.

As we walked up the hill to the house, I said, "This has been a perfect day."

"Has it? I'm glad."

I stopped, struck by the eagerness in his voice.

"What?"

I was so stupid. I knew he'd suggested this outing because he'd seen how depressed I was. But even if he'd
enjoyed seeing Hal and Frannie and Mei-Yin, he'd also
had to rub shoulders with strangers, endure an endless
succession of little chats, an endless exchange of stupid
pleasantries. If the cocktail party with the staff had been
a challenge, this afternoon must have been agony.

"What?" he repeated.

Before I could reply, the screen door creaked open
and Janet walked onto the porch with Jack trailing behind her.

Hands on hips, she surveyed us with a frown. "Well, I
hope *you've* had fun. *I've* been on the phone all goddamn evening. Half the population of Dale has called to
inform me of Rowan Mackenzie's historic visit. There
will probably be an article in the next edition of *The Bee*:
" 'Local Recluse Tours Town. Citizens Agog.' "

Rowan proffered the two beeswax candles. "By way
of apology." Then he produced the penny candy for Jack.
"Maggie thought you might like this."

Jack held the stick up to the porch lantern, then slowly
lowered it and stared at me. "Licorice. My favorite."

"I know."

An awkward silence descended. Janet poked her elbow into Jack's ribs. He cleared his throat and said, "I
was thinking. Maybe tomorrow, we could all go on a picnic. If you'd like."

I stared at Janet who enjoyed picnics about as much
as Rowan liked long car rides, and promptly burst into
tears.

Jack looked horrified. Rowan put his arm around me.
Janet said, "Oh, for God's sake, stop bawling like a constipated calf."

I snuffled like a congested calf and said, "That would
be lovely." Then I remembered. "But Alex—"

"Alex called," Janet said. "He forgot he had a dentist
appointment tomorrow. So he'd like to postpone playing
through the score until Thursday."

I knew damn well there was no dentist appointment. I fought the return of the constipated calf and whispered, "Okay."

"Good," Janet said. "I am now going to reheat my dinner for the third time."

As the screen door slammed behind her, Jack said, "I guess I'll head down to the apartment. Unless you want me to take a walk around the pond."

"I think we're both a little worn out," Rowan said. "I'll see you down there."

"And I'll see you tomorrow," I said.

Rowan led me over to the old wooden porch swing. I listened to the mournful creak as we rocked gently back and forth, then asked, "Was it awful for you today?"

"No. Well. A little daunting. All those people . . ."

"I'm so sorry. I should have realized—"

"No," he repeated. "I loved seeing Hal's shop and Mei-Yin's restaurant and your hotel. All the places I've been hearing about for so many years. I just never expected such a welcome. Such . . . kindness. Humans really are quite magical, aren't they?"

"Kindness isn't magical."

"It is to me. Kindness, compassion, love. Those qualities are alien to the Fae. And innate to humans."

"But they're not magical."

"Yes, Maggie. They are. *You* are. Look at what you've accomplished this season. You helped your mother come to terms with her past. You forged a disparate group of actors into a company. You made the staff partners in this theatre in a way they never were when I was director. You laid the groundwork to make the Crossroads financially viable. You pushed and pulled and dragged me into this world that I had only glimpsed secondhand. You've done far more with your magic than I ever did with mine."

"How can you say that? I know what your power can do."

"But don't you see? No matter how beautiful or ter-

rifying or extraordinary the magic of Faerie is, its ultimate purpose is to disguise. Human magic . . . reveals. I
never understood that until this summer. It's like when I
call the Mackenzies. My magic sets the stage, but human
magic—your capacity to love, to change—that's what
makes the drama unfold."

His smile was a little sad, as if the revelation had diminished him somehow.

I squeezed his hand. "I loved the nice, normal, ordinary day you gave me. But I love your magic, too. You
can calm me with a touch or carry me to the brink of
ecstasy. You can make paper flowers bloom and help an
actress overcome her fear of heights—and help heal a
lost soul like my father. Your magic is the most wondrous thing I've ever known in my life. Never forget that.
Or think that I want you to be like other men."

His love flowed into me and through me, as strong as
the earth, as boundless as the sky.

My father had said that the Fae carry the light of the
sun and the moon and the stars. And maybe they did.
But Rowan's love shone with the soft glow of the fireflies
that danced in our dreams.

CHAPTER 47
STAY WITH ME

WE WERE BLESSED WITH A BEAUTIFUL DAY for our picnic, but the cool breeze reminded me that autumn was quickly approaching. The four of us tramped along the trail, content to savor the peacefulness. Occasionally, our pace slowed as we skirted a boggy area. In springtime, those places had been a riot of wildflowers: carpets of white-petaled bloodroots giving way to shy violets, yellow trout lilies, red trillium, and the green sprawl of jack-in-the-pulpit. Only after I'd walked the woods in spring did I fully understand what Alex had wanted us to capture during "June is Bustin' Out All Over:" that giddy relief at feeling the world awaken.

When I mentioned that, Janet snorted. "And to think, she once thought spring peepers were birds."

"Well, who knew frogs could sing?"

"When she came back to the house one fine spring day and told me about the beautiful buttercups she had found, I decided to take her in hand."

"Marsh marigolds?" Rowan guessed.

"Yellow violets," Janet replied.

"Yellow violets?" Jack echoed. "Well, no wonder you got it wrong. Talk about your oxymoron."

"Thank you," I said. "And as for you two, cut me a break. I lived in cities all my life."

"You had Prospect Park," Rowan said.

393

"Which I hardly ever got a chance to visit."

"And the one in Wilmington. What was it called?"

Jack inscribed a slow crescent through the leaves with his boot.

"Brandywine Park," I finally said. "And it was hardly the hundred acre wood."

"Just some open space along the river," Jack added. "With picnic tables and barbecue grills."

A tiny step for mankind, but a giant leap for father and daughter.

The conversation drifted to other topics, but when we stopped at the ancient beech, I told my father, "The first time I saw it, I thought of that tree on the Brandywine. The one with the roots that could hide pirate gold or a family of gnomes."

Jack stared at me in astonishment. "I can't believe you remember that."

Rowan seized Janet's hand to help her ascend the hill to the plateau. After a moment's hesitation, Jack took mine. When we reached the top, we exchanged shy smiles like kids on their first date.

But that's what this was. And Janet and Rowan were the chaperones easing us through it with food and conversation and sensitivity.

We talked mostly about the theatre, but somehow our discussion of *A Christmas Carol* led to a comparison of Christmas celebrations in Dale and Wilmington, just as Rowan's story of building his first snowman with Jamie's children encouraged Jack to talk about the first time he went sledding and broke his nose.

During those two hours, I learned more about my father than I had ever known, including the shocking discovery that he'd had an older brother who had died when Jack was thirteen. Less shocking was the revelation that Jack had been considered "the bad Sinclair boy" who had grown even wilder after Jimmy's death.

Although he quickly changed the subject, it was obvious that acting had saved him from getting into serious trouble, that the theatre was more of a home than his parents' house. What better place to forget his troubles—as a teenager and as an adult? And what better way to do it than by becoming—for a few hours, at least—someone else?

I'd done it myself.

The stage was playground and therapist's couch. The one place we could safely explore our fears, our hopes, our deepest selves. A place where the laughter was approving, where we could bask in the applause and the admiration—and yes, the love—of our audience.

Little wonder he was drawn to Faerie. It was another sort of playground—more fantastical, more dangerous, and infinitely more alluring. And unlike a theatre where the magic vanished as soon as the curtain came down, its glamour never faded.

That was the first of many conversations with my father—and many walks in the woods. Somehow, it was easier to talk under the open sky, maybe because it allowed us to walk the trails in silence if we preferred.

Cautious at first, we skirted the difficult parts of our shared past to concentrate on the happy memories. But as the season neared its conclusion, we began sharing stories from the years after he had left. His were often confused and disjointed, the description of a glorious sunset over the red rocks of Sedona suddenly shifting into a vision of Stonehenge at sunrise—as if his memories were as mutable as the landscape of the Borderlands. At such moments, I glimpsed the fragile, confused old man I had met in June. It saddened me to realize how much of his life was lost—and frightened me to think that the glamour of Faerie would blot out his remaining memories.

Including his memories of me.

By piecing together his stray comments I managed to fill in some of the blanks of his final years in this world. Dark years, mostly, when his money was gone and he lived hand-to-mouth, picking up work where he could find it, staying in one place only long enough to make enough cash for the next leg of his journey. The homeless shelters he resorted to when there was no work and no money. The struggle to find the clarity of mind to continue his quest.

He was far more at ease listening to me talk about my life, offering only an occasional quiet comment. I had rarely seen his introspective side. And while I was grateful to discover this other Jack Sinclair, it made the prospect of losing him more painful.

Perhaps he felt the same for during the final week of *Into the Woods*, his silences grew longer, his expression more troubled. When we returned to the theatre Thursday afternoon, he suddenly blurted out, "I can stay. If you want me to."

Once before, he had made that offer and been relieved when I didn't accept it.

I nodded to one of the picnic tables and sat down opposite him. Choosing my words carefully, I said, "Of course, I want you to stay. But most of all, I want you to be happy. Do you really want to give up Faerie for this world?"

"I wouldn't have to give it up. Just . . . postpone going for awhile."

"And what would you do here?"

"I suppose I could teach."

"Do you *want* to teach?"

His shoulders sagged. "Not really."

"It's okay to want Faerie. You've been looking for it most of your life."

"It was all I had. But now . . . I just keep thinking about what Allie said. About getting a second chance and not screwing it up."

"We're bound to have regrets. No matter what you choose. If you go, I'll miss you and you'll feel guilty. If you stay, *I'll* feel guilty for keeping you from Faerie. And you might be bored out of your skull."

My weak attempt at humor failed to evoke a smile.

"It's not like the clock runs out when the curtain comes down Saturday night. Let's both think about what we want. And talk about it again on Sunday."

His performance that night was more solemn, as if the decision he had to make weighed on him. I listened to "Stay with Me" and longed to speak those same words to him. I wanted to protect him from the unknown dangers of Faerie, to assure him that the theatre was his home, that I was his home.

Rowan had told me that the night he returned. But Rowan loved me more than my father ever could.

When Kanesha hobbled onstage, wearing her one golden slipper, and began to sing "On the Steps of the Palace," the song seemed an ironic commentary on my situation. Cinderella was trying to make a decision, too. And like me, she was stalling. Should she allow the Prince to find her or just keep running? Was she better off at home where she was safe but unhappy? Or with her prince in a palace where she would always be out of place?

It was a jolt to realize that her words reflected Jack's dilemma far more than mine. To stay or to run. To remain in the safety of this world or exchange it for the dangers of one where he would always remain an outsider.

Cinderella's decision was not to decide, but to leave a clue—a shoe—and let the Prince make the next move. A clever choice that neatly absolved her of responsibility.

Like Cinderella, my father was afraid of making a choice for fear it might be the wrong one. And like her, he had left his own clues: his assertion that he would stay—if I wanted him to; his fear of screwing up; his compromise of postponing his departure—and his decision— a little longer.

He had always allowed Mom to make the tough choices. He was waiting for me to do the same.

If I forced him to choose, he would stay. For a few weeks, a few months. That was easier than hurting me.

And if, like Cinderella, I chose not to decide?

We would drift along. I would offer him a role in the Halloween murder mystery. The role of Scrooge in *A Christmas Carol*. I would use the glamour of theatre to combat the glamour of Faerie. And for a few weeks, a few months, it might work.

But then the show would close and the New Year's celebrations would end. The long, dark days of winter would creep by. And faced with the piercing cold and the gray-white silence of this world, his eyes would turn to Faerie, the longing greater, the need to see it more urgent.

I would watch him grow increasingly restive and resent him. He would sense my reaction and feel guilty. The tentative relationship we had built this summer would slowly erode and we would end up angry and alienated.

Cinderella's song ended in a dizzying confection of clever rhymes and clever compromise. But although we had both learned something new, our choices were very different.

❧

After the show, I found Rowan waiting for me at the top of the stairs. Whether he knew my decision, he certainly sensed my turbulent emotions. He poured two glasses of whisky and together, we waited.

Jack's steps slowed when he saw us sitting on the sofa. At Rowan's gesture, he sat beside me. Knowing a long preamble would only make him more anxious, I said, "I've been thinking about our conversation this afternoon. It means the world to me that you offered to stay. But you lost your heart to Faerie years ago. And that's why I think you should go there."

His head drooped, and he began to tremble. For a moment, I thought I'd made a terrible mistake. When he looked up, there were tears in his eyes.

"You're so much like your mother. So strong."

I took his hand between mine, feeling the rough calluses on his fingertips, the loose, dry skin on the back of his hand. He had been in the prime of his life when he found the portal to the Borderlands, but he was older now. Was desire enough to sustain him in that other world?

"It's okay, Daddy. Everything'll be okay."

A single tear oozed down his cheek. "It's the first time you've called me that."

"I lost you for awhile. And Magpie, too. But we found them again during these last few weeks. And they'll always be with us. No matter where we go."

CHAPTER 48

HARD TO SAY GOODBYE

WHEN DADDY WALKED ONSTAGE FOR THAT FINAL PERFORMANCE, his gaze fastened on me as it had on Mom. His face held the same wistfulness. And his voice was hushed as he spoke the magical words he had so often used to begin one of his tales: "Once upon a time ..."

That night, he offered me the tale of our lives: the charming, weak-willed prince; the marriage that began with passion and ended in separation; the baby who represented the hope for the future; the young girl eager to see the world; the stranger who emerged from the past to weave his way into his child's life once again. The choices made. The lessons learned. The regrets. The losses.

Nancy sat beside me, her hand clasped in mine. She had arrived without Ed, claiming he had a dreadful summer cold. For once, her instincts were wrong. It would have cheered me to share their joy, to see the blossoming of their relationship, to know that on this night of endings, something wonderful was beginning.

But as the cast took their final curtain call, I decided she'd been right, after all. It would be better to meet Ed in September when he was more than an antidote for grief, when the four of us could simply enjoy spending time together and share the happiness of being in love.

I moved through the cast party with Nancy and Rowan beside me and the staff hovering nearby, their faces radiating concern and love. It was eerily reminiscent of the *Carousel* cast party on the eve of Rowan's departure. But I was stronger now. And although I would grieve for my father, I was grateful for the gift of time we had been given—and determined to use what time we had left to help him prepare for the journey that lay ahead.

But first, I had to deal with other departures. I spent Sunday morning at the hotel, helping Frannie with checkout and bidding a final farewell to my Mackenzies.

"Don't fret about your daddy," Otis said. "He's a tough old bird for all he looks like a good wind'll knock him over. And just 'cause he's leaving doesn't mean he'll never be back."

I managed a smile. My father had returned to me once, his resurrection as miraculous as the Mysterious Man's. But there would be no miracle this time. The choice I had made brought with it the knowledge that I would never see him again, never know if he was safe or happy—or even if he was alive.

"Well, *you* better come back," I said. "Bring Viola up for a vacation."

"You can count on it."

Debra was one of the last to leave. As she looked around the lobby, she said, "I'm actually going to miss this old place."

"Then you should consider a return engagement. I'm preparing the budget for a Halloween murder mystery night. If the board goes for it, I'll need someone to help run it. And then there's *A Christmas Carol*. You'd bring a new level of feistiness to Mrs. Cratchit."

"Great. Another mother with a dead child. Can't I just be a ghost and scare the crap out of kids?"

"The Ghosts of Christmas Past and Present are up for grabs. Rowan's got his eye on the Ghost of Christmas Yet To Come."

"Well, he's appropriately wraithlike."

"Name the role and you've got it. I can offer you the same fabulous salary you got this summer. And a room at your favorite Vermont hotel."

"At least, I won't roast like I did this summer."

"You won't sleep much, either. Every time the heat comes on it sounds like 'The Anvil Chorus.'"

"You really have to work on your sales pitch."

"Think about it," I urged her.

Caught by my serious tone, she nodded. "Okay. I will." She turned to go, then hesitated. "You survived without him most of your life. You can do it again."

Before I could reply, she strode out of the hotel, leaving me to wonder if she and I had traveled parallel paths through life.

I hoped I would find out, but only time would tell if I could lure her back to the Crossroads. No matter what Rowan said, people sometimes needed a little push. And my sales pitch wasn't really pushing. It was just my version of calling the Mackenzies. If Debra answered the call, I would sit back and let the drama unfold. And maybe tweak it a bit like any good director.

I was heading back to the front desk when the bell over the front door jangled again. I turned to discover Bernie and Reinhard walking into the lobby.

The last bird was flying home.

"You know, Reinhard doesn't have to drive me back today," Bernie said.

Much as I would have liked him to remain, I shook my head. How could I explain all the gear we were purchasing—or why Rowan and I were escorting my father into the woods instead of driving him to an airport or train station?

"You're the best," I whispered as I hugged him.

"I'll be back for the September board meeting. You need me before, you call."

Gregarious Bernie and gruff Reinhard. One had been my first friend in the cast. The other had begun as hectoring stage manager and become my rock. Always in the background unless a crisis arose. Always lending me his quiet strength. Advising me, scolding me, but never saying, "You must do this." He allowed me to take risks and hovered nearby in case I crashed and burned, hiding his worries lest they add to mine.

He was more of a father to me than my own.

Impulsively, I threw my arms around him. When I finally released him, his smile was strangely tender and I knew he had sensed what I'd felt. Then his frown returned and he said, "So. The hugging is finished. Now, we go."

I called Mom that afternoon. When I told her that Daddy was moving on, there was a long silence. Then she asked, "Are you okay?"

"I told him he should go."

"I figured that. Are you okay?"

"Yes. Mostly. It's the right decision."

"That doesn't make it easier."

"No. But it's not like when Rowan left. I have a life now. Things to look forward to."

"Do you want me to come up?"

"Not for my sake. But if you want to see him again . . ."

"No." Her voice was as firm as mine. "Good-byes aren't your father's strong suit. And we already said ours."

"How are things with you and Chris?"

Another silence, even longer than the first. "Things are . . . okay."

"Meaning . . . ?"

"Meaning we're working on it and stop prying."

"You pry into my life all the time."

"I'm your mother. That's my job."

"You sound like the Witch in *Into the Woods*."

"I didn't lock you in a tower for fourteen years. Or blind your Prince Charming."

"No, you just threatened to castrate him."

"Not lately. How is Rowan?"

"He's good. *We're* good."

I wished I could tell her that he had ventured into town three times since that first dinner. That he had endured the short car ride to Hill with just a trace of queasiness. That he had made similar trips to have dinner with Hal and Lee, to visit Reinhard's office and Javier's antique store. Instead, I talked about the final performances of *Into the Woods* and my mixed feelings at facing the end of another season.

As we were about to hang up, I asked, "Is there any message you want me to give Daddy?"

"No." Then she added, "Tell him to take care of himself. And try not to go nuts again."

❦❦

Daddy and I both went a little nuts during the days that followed. We had agreed to give ourselves a week after the show closed to gather the supplies he needed. I sat him down Monday morning to create a list. We rush-ordered some things via the Internet and scoured the shops of Dale and Bennington for everything else. Between the freeze-dried foods and the all-weather gear, I felt like a mother preparing her little boy for his first camping trip—on Mount Everest. But at least, the frenzy of preparations distracted us from his imminent departure.

By Saturday, all that remained was the farewell barbecue at the Bates mansion. Neither Daddy nor I ate very much; the "Last Supper" overtones were all too obvious. But we did our best to keep up a good front until Rowan's blueberry cobbler had been demolished and Reinhard rose from his place at the picnic table.

"So. Tomorrow Jack will leave us. And like all farewells, this one brings a mix of emotions. We are sad to see him go. Even I, who was not so sure that he should stay in the first place. But. He is about to embark on a great adventure. One he has longed to take for many years. And for that, we should be happy."

His gaze lingered on me for a moment before drifting around the table.

"Those of us who remain are very lucky. We know the joy of finding our heart's desire."

He smiled at Mei-Yin. Lee pressed a quick kiss to Hal's cheek. Javier rested his palm on Catherine's stomach. Alex stared at his plate, thinking of the wife he had lost and perhaps, the woman who might fill that void in his heart. Janet watched him. Then her gaze rose to my bedroom window. To Helen's bedroom window.

I twined my fingers through Rowan's. I'd always hated that line near the end of *The Wizard of Oz* when Dorothy announces that if she ever goes looking for her heart's desire, she will search no farther than her own backyard. If it isn't there, she tells Glinda, she never really lost it to begin with.

But sometimes, you don't know what you've lost. And even when you do, you might have to go farther afield to find it. It had taken me years to reach the Crossroads. My father had traveled much farther and spent far longer on his quest. And although he had yet to find his heart's desire, we *had* found each other.

"As Jack resumes his journey, I offer this blessing. One that my mother taught me a very long time ago."

Reinhard raised his mug of beer. Benches scraped against brick as we rose, bottles and glasses uplifted.

"May the road rise up to meet you. May the wind be always at your back."

Around the table, voices softly chanted the words of the traditional Gaelic blessing.

"May the sun shine warm upon your face, the rains fall soft upon your fields."

Rowan's arm around my waist. Daddy's eyes shining with unshed tears.

"And until we meet again, may God hold you in the palm of His hand."

It was the perfect ending to our dinner and to my father's season at the Crossroads. But when we returned to the apartment, we discovered the farewells were not quite finished.

"Christmas came early this year," Rowan said.

A giant wicker basket sat on the sofa, filled with assorted boxes wrapped in Christmas paper and bedecked with ribbons and bows. I understood now why Rowan had sent us ahead to the barbecue. He had been setting the scene—again.

"A few things from the staff," he said. "They thought it might embarrass you to open them at the barbecue."

"It's too much," Daddy whispered. "How will I ever thank them?"

I exchanged a glance with Rowan and said, "Write each of them a note."

"But what will I say?"

"I'll help you."

There was a Swiss army knife from Javier and Catherine, antibiotics and detailed instructions on their use from Reinhard. Mei-Yin had contributed a wicked looking cleaver, Bernie a dozen toothbrushes and enough dental floss to strangle the entire population of Faerie. Hal's small watercolor painting of the barn made my throat tighten. Lee's gift of aftershave and condoms made us laugh.

Alex's gift touched me the most. The tiny digital recorder came with a plastic baggie filled with batteries and a note that explained that he had programmed a selection of show tunes as well as two Crossroads musicals: *Into the Woods* and *Carousel.* If my father never saw my face again, my voice would be with him, singing, "You'll Never Walk Alone."

Daddy abruptly excused himself and hurried to the bathroom. By the time he returned, we both had our emotions under control.

There was only one gift left, a small envelope that

bore Janet's handwriting. Daddy pulled out a rectangular piece of paper and gave a soft cry.

It was a photograph of me. Janet must have used an industrial strength telephoto lens to get the close-up of my profile. The sunlight streaming over my left shoulder turned my hair to fire. The right side of my face lay in shadow, but you could still see my pensive expression as I stared off into the distance, lost in thought.

"When was this taken?" Rowan asked.

"I don't . . ."

And then I remembered. It was the afternoon of Arthur's funeral. I'd gone out to the garden to seek a little peace before our final dress rehearsal.

"Midsummer's Eve," I whispered.

"You look so faraway," Daddy said.

I had seen that same look on his face, always at odd moments when he thought no one was watching. A little dreamy, a little sad. My father yearning for Faerie and I, for the lover I had lost to it.

"There's one more thing," Rowan said.

He held out a small manila envelope addressed to Janet. Daddy and I exchanged startled glances when we saw my mother's return address label.

"What would she be sending to Janet?" I asked.

"I think she wanted someone else to see it first. And decide whether to pass it along. There was no note. So we're not sure if she intended it for Jack or for you."

"You open it," Daddy said.

The top of the envelope had already been slit. Inside was a smaller envelope. From its size and shape, it might have held a greeting card. But it was another photo, its colors faded with age.

The bottom of the Christmas tree filled the background. Discarded wrapping paper and open boxes were scattered around it. I was probably four or five years old, dressed in my red-and-white candy cane pajamas with the feet. Crushed to my chest was Moondancer, the unicorn My Little Pony I had wanted so desperately. And sitting opposite me, his mouth open in the same round "O" of delight, was my father in his Rudolph the Red-Nosed Reindeer pajamas and goofy antlers.

Both of us so impossibly young, so impossibly happy.

"This is for you," I said as I passed the photograph to him.

My voice was as steady as my hand. But of course, I had seen that picture countless times. Its twin was in one of my old scrapbooks—pasted there by my mother.

Daddy's breath caught. He studied the photograph for a long moment. Then he walked over to his battered old backpack, unzipped a compartment, and withdrew something from it.

It was another photograph, the colors even more faded, the corners ragged. But it was the same Christmas. I was asleep under the tree, clearly worn out by the festivities. Moondancer was still clutched to my chest, but my head rested in my mother's lap. Her hand was frozen in the act of brushing my hair off my face. Hers was almost masked by the dark waterfall of her hair, but you could just make out the tender curve of her mouth as she gazed at me.

I wept then, as silently as my father. For the happiness we had known and lost. For the man who had safeguarded this photograph for decades. And for the woman who could forgo blame and resentment and anger to offer him another keepsake of that time—once upon a time—when we had been a family.

CHAPTER 49
THINGS BEYOND THIS EARTH

I SPENT A CHEERLESS MORNING HELPING DADDY write his farewell notes and listening to the incessant pounding of rain on the roof. I was on the verge of demanding that we postpone his departure when the rain abruptly ceased. Like a scene from a Biblical movie epic, the dark clouds parted and sunlight streamed into the apartment.

Daddy's mood brightened just as quickly. "Good-byes aren't your father's strong suit," Mom had told me. But his relief still hurt and as usual, I did a poor job of hiding my feelings.

"It's not that I want to leave," he explained. "I just hate dragging it out."

"Maybe it would be best to say your good-byes here," Rowan said. As I started to protest, he added, "I don't want you there when I open the portal. You know what happened to Jack after his encounter with my clan. It's even more dangerous for a human to look upon Faerie. All the legends tell us that."

"You told me most of the legends were crap."

"Most of them are. But the allure of Faerie is very real. Do you want to spend the rest of your life always seeking it, always wanting it? Will you risk everything we have here, just for a few more moments with Jack?"

I gnawed my lip, bitterly acknowledging the truth of
his words. But I wasn't ready to say good-bye. Not yet.

Rowan sighed. "All right. Come with us as far as the
cottage. You can wait there while Jack and I go on alone.
Agreed?"

"Agreed," I whispered.

I put on my boots. Rowan shouldered Daddy's bulging backpack. Daddy grabbed his guitar and Rowan's
knapsack and left the apartment without a backward
glance. I wondered if he would leave me the same way.

The birds mocked me with their cheerful warbling, as
did the chinks of brilliant blue sky that peeked through
the forest canopy. The earth had a better handle on my
mood, releasing my foot with reluctance each time I
sank into a soggy mass of leaves and pine needles and
mud.

The rain had transformed the low-lying places into
swampland. We picked our way around the worst spots
and tottered across others on fallen logs. The rain-slick
leaves made climbing the smallest rise a monumental
effort, even with Rowan steadying us as we clambered
up one side and skidded down the other.

It was almost a relief to see the stone walls of the cottage through the trees. The glade lay deep in shadow,
although sunlight still gilded the treetops.

Rowan gazed skyward. "We have a little time left.
Let's rest here for a few minutes."

We scraped our boots against a rock by the doorway
before traipsing inside. The first time I'd entered the cottage, I'd shuddered to imagine Rowan living in this
gloomy little room. After slogging through the woods, I
was just grateful to slump onto one of the benches flanking the wooden table.

Rowan unearthed supplies from his knapsack: a plastic
bottle of lemonade, a crusty loaf of bread, a bunch of
grapes, a hunk of cheese. He retrieved crockery plates and
cups from the hutch near the open fireplace and laid them

on the table as well. Then he took a bone-handled knife from a drawer and sliced off cheese and bread for us.

Daddy stoically shoveled food into his mouth. I picked at the grapes. Rowan studied me. Desperate to break the silence, I asked, "Is the portal nearby?"

"Not far," Rowan said evasively.

"Has it always been here? In these woods?"

"It's not a physical place, Maggie. The Fae can open a portal anywhere."

"Then why did we come all the way out here?"

"Opening a portal leaves traces of energy behind, no matter how carefully I seal it. Although they fade quickly, it would be unwise to draw attention to the theatre or Janet's house. And since my power is weaker than most of my kind, I have to choose a place where all four elements are present—earth, air, fire, and water."

We lapsed into silence again. When Daddy finished eating, Rowan carefully wrapped the remaining food in linen napkins. As he reached for the backpack, Daddy said, "I'll do that."

"All right. And then we'd better be going."

Rowan slung Daddy's guitar across his back and walked outside. Panic quickened my pulse as I hurried after him.

"Can't I go just a little farther with you?"

"No. And I want you to promise not to follow us." When I hesitated, he added, "I don't want to use my power to keep you here. I'll need all of it to open the portal. But if you won't give me your word—"

"I'll stay."

His arms came around me. "I know you want to be with him. But it's safer this way."

I swallowed hard and nodded. Daddy emerged from the cottage with his pack on his shoulders, and I swallowed again.

As many times as I had imagined this moment, I'd never come up with the right words of farewell. How do you say good-bye to a father you barely know but whose presence has been with you every day of your life?

As I groped for something to say, Rowan reached into the pocket of his jeans.

"I meant to give this to Maggie one day. But I think you need it more."

He thrust his fist toward Daddy and opened his fingers. I gasped when I saw the gold ring in his palm. Daddy backed away, shaking his head.

"Take it," Rowan said brusquely. "There are markings on it my clan will recognize. It might ensure your welcome."

"Or they might think I stole it."

"My chief warded it against theft. They'll know it came to you as a gift."

I gazed at the ring of faery gold—the ring Rowan had surely meant to give me on our wedding day. With shaking fingers, I plucked it from his palm. The ring was warm from his body and seemed oddly heavy for such a small circlet of gold, but if there were markings on it, they were too small—or too magical—for me to see.

Rowan's sweet smile brought on a fresh upwelling of tears. I blinked them back and held the ring out to my father. He slid it onto his pinkie, grunting a bit as he wiggled it over the swollen knuckle. Then we just stared at each other.

"I'm lousy at good-byes," he said. "But you know that."

"I wanted to buy you a gift. Like the staff did. Something to remember me by."

"Do you think I could ever forget you?"

They might make him forget. They might banish every memory he had of this world, including our years in Wilmington and these last two months.

"I just wish I had something to give you."

"Oh, Maggie. You've already given me so much."

Our embrace was clumsy, the stupid backpack making it hard for me to hold him. Finally, I wriggled my hands beneath it so I could hug him. Even after two months, he was still so thin I could feel every rib.

"Be happy, Magpie."

He wrenched free, staggering a little from the weight of the backpack. Rowan took his arm to steady him. Then he led my father away.

The leaves squelched obscenely as they walked across the glade. I swiped my fists across my eyes and followed the bobbing red backpack as it moved deeper into the woods.

I should have told him to be happy. I should have begged him to be safe.

I should have assured him that these last two months have been a gift. I should have promised him that he would always have a home at the Crossroads.

I should have asked if he had a message for Mom. I should have asked him to stay.

The backpack was just a red spot among the trees, as small as Rudolph's nose on those silly pajamas.

I should have told him that I loved him.

The red spot grew brighter as Daddy walked into a patch of sunlight. As I opened my mouth to call to him, it vanished.

Oh, God . . .

Something gleamed in the sunlight. A tiny spark no bigger than a firefly.

The ring. He must have turned back to look at me one last time. He must be waving good-bye.

I ran to the edge of the glade, waving frantically as I shouted, "I love you, Daddy!"

The spark disappeared. For just an instant, I glimpsed that spot of red. Then it, too, was gone.

Had he heard me? If not, Rowan would tell him what I had said. I tried to take comfort in that as I trudged back to the cottage.

I wiped off the cups and the plates and returned them to the hutch. Screwed the cap back on the bottle of lemonade and returned it to Rowan's knapsack. Found a broom in one corner and tried to sweep the drying mud from the floor. I looked around for another task—anything to keep busy—and spied something on the bed that interrupted the patchwork pattern of the quilt.

Even in the gloom, I made out the moose-headed cows. The T-shirt had been carefully folded and obviously left for Rowan. Daddy must have placed it there while we were outside.

I frowned when I saw a dark smudge on one corner of the shirt. As I attempted to brush it away, I touched something hard. Wood, I realized, as my fingers curled around it. I carried it to the doorway, seeking more light, but the glade was as shadowy as the cottage.

I fumbled around the hutch, feeling along shelves and opening drawers until I found a box of matches. I lit two candles and carried them over to the table. Then I sat down to examine the mysterious object.

It was a model of a bird—a crow judging by the black substance that covered most of its body. Too dull and rough to be paint. Charcoal, perhaps. Was it some sort of protective talisman he had carved in the Borderlands to ward off the Crow-Men?

The body had been worn smooth. Only the grooves of the tail feathers were faintly discernible under my fingertips. The charcoal had chipped away on the wings and belly, leaving patches of bare wood. I stroked the belly gently, then frowned at the smudges I left behind and the white residue on my fingertips. Chalk?

Even then, it took another moment for me to grasp the truth.

Not a crow. A black-and-white bird, carefully carved, carefully painted with whatever materials he could find, and carefully preserved for decades to remind him of the child he had left behind.

His Magpie.

I don't know how long I sat there, sobbing. Minutes, probably, although it seemed like hours. Finally, I rose and wiped my face with the same towel I had used to clean the dishes. Then I carried the magpie back to the bed and set it atop the T-shirt.

As I turned away, I noticed something pale peeking out from under the bed. I crouched down and picked it up.

The photograph must have slipped out of his back-pack when he set out his gifts. I had to hold it close to the candles to determine that it was the faded picture of Mom and me, the photo he had carried for more than twenty years, preserved just as carefully as the magpie.

I ran out of the cottage and plunged into the woods, shouting Rowan's name. He would open the portal at sunset. There was still time to reach them. There had to be.

I skidded into a tree trunk and clung to it for a moment, gasping. The shadows under the trees were too thick to risk running. One misstep might bring the disaster of a twisted ankle, a wrenched knee. But my mind screamed at me to hurry.

I shoved the photo in the back pocket of my shorts. If I dropped it, if I lost it . . .

Don't think about that. Just keep moving.

I clawed my way up a slope, slipping and sliding on wet pine needles. At the top, I paused, trying to get my bearings. The sky was a deeper blue now, but up ahead, the trees thinned, and the light was brighter. All I could do was follow the dying sun.

I sidestepped down the slope, reeling from one tree trunk to another to keep from falling. When the ground leveled out, I quickened my pace. I forced myself to ignore the sharp stitch in my side, to concentrate on the next step and the next and the next after that. If I thought about my father vanishing from this world before I could reach him, the panic would rise like bile.

I searched the shadows for tree roots that might trap a foot, vines that could ensnare an ankle. But still, I tripped over something hidden under the leaves.

Pain lanced through my wrists as I tried to break my fall. My cry was cut off as I bellyflopped onto the ground. Precious seconds ticked away while I lay there, panting. Only when the cold dampness penetrated my T-shirt did I drag my forearms through the muck and use them to leverage myself onto my knees.

The light through the trees was now a rich orange-gold. The twittering of the birds grew louder as they saluted the sunset. But even their chorus failed to drown out the sound of splashing water.

I gave a hoarse croak of laughter when I realized how close I had come to sliding headfirst into the stream. I'd made so much noise crashing through the woods that I had failed to hear it. For once, my clumsiness had served me. Rowan needed water to open his portal and this stream meandered through the thin screen of saplings. Between them, I could make out the undulating line of the distant hills, dark against the bright stripes of the rose-colored clouds.

I staggered to my feet and clambered along the muddy bank, ignoring my sodden clothes and the cold that made my teeth chatter and the sharp throb of pain in my left wrist. As I neared the saplings, I opened my mouth to shout Rowan's name.

A hill blurred, and I blinked to clear my vision. But it wasn't the hill or my vision. It was the air just beyond the trees, roiling and churning as if caught in a whirlpool.

The whirlpool shuddered. A sliver of light cracked open the sky like a lightning bolt. But the lightning was golden. As golden as a cloud of fireflies.

The rough bark of a tree beneath my fingers. The golden light blessing my eyes. The stream laughing as it tumbled over the hillside, past a small outcropping of rock below me, past a man with his arms upraised and another with a red pack and a guitar.

A rainbow shimmered in the air where the dying rays of the sun sliced across the thin cascade of water. A warm breeze caressed my face, carrying with it the dizzying aromas of roses and honeysuckle, ripe berries and sweet grass. And glorious birdsong that shamed the pitiful chirps from the treetops.

And music . . .

High-pitched and silvery, like the rippling glissando of a harp.

And singing . . .

The sweetest of harmonies, augmented by a deep vibration that pulsed through me like a second heartbeat. So might crystals sound if they could sing. So might the heart of the world sound if it could beat. Add one voice, change one thread of the song, and it would be diminished.

Then the chorus swelled, and as beautiful as it had seemed before, this was the sound of perfection. I yearned to be part of it, to blend forever in the pure, glorious, aching joy of that song.

Another rainbow, more beautiful than the first, growing out of the shelf of rock, arcing toward the portal of golden light where stars now danced like fireflies. A rainbow bridge, shimmering with otherworldly brilliance, pulsating with the steady tattoo of that heartbeat.

The man with the red pack places his foot on the bridge. His giddy laughter shivers through me and I laugh with him.

And suddenly, I am scrambling down the rocky hillside, slipping through the waterfall's spray, leaping onto the shelf of rock, running past the man with the upraised arms, running after the lucky one on the rainbow bridge.

"Maggie!"

My steps falter. I know that voice. It comes from behind me, so it must belong to the man with the upraised arms.

The man on the bridge hesitates and looks back. I know that face. But it is so much older than I remember.

The music urges me onward. The golden light fills my eyes. But another power rips through my chest, cleaving heart and spirit alike.

"Maggie! Please!"

The man and the bridge blur just as the hill did.

"Run, Jack!"

Something is wrong. Even the golden light seems to sense it for the stars are winking out one by one.

The man on the bridge starts running toward the light. I have to stop him. There is something I have to do, something I have to give him.

"Maggie!"

Three times, he has called my name. Three times for a charm. Where did I learn that?

Warmth enfolds me. A breeze kisses my cheeks. The scent of lavender fills my nostrils.

"Rowan will always carry you in his heart. We all will. Remember that, my dear. And know that you will always have a home at the Crossroads."

The breeze whips my hair across my eyes, obscuring the rainbow bridge and the flickering portal and the golden light of Faerie.

"Goddamn it, Maggie! Don't you give up on us!" that broken voice shouts.

The siren call of the music beckons me. The sweetest music I will ever hear in my life.

I cover my ears to block it out. And then I turn my back on Faerie and stumble into Rowan's arms.

FINALE AND CURTAIN CALLS

CHAPTER 50
YOU ARE MY HOME

I WAKE TO THE BLARE OF A CAR HORN. I cannot understand why the skylights have disappeared. Then I remember: I am in the guest room of Alison's home in Delaware.

I relax when I sense Maggie's presence somewhere in the house. I barely remember stumbling inside yesterday evening, nor when I have ever slept through an entire night. Hardly surprising after that hellish car ride.

Pale slivers of sunlight leak between the panels of fabric at the far end of the room. I realize now that they cover a sliding glass door. How strange that my bedroom in this house has one, too.

I slip on my dressing gown, pad over to the doors, and fumble in the gloom for a cord. The blinds ratchet open, treating me to a depressing vista: a grid of asphalt; a collection of narrow townhouses, and a fortresslike structure that must be the hospital. I spy a patch of green that might be grass, but no trees anywhere. Still, sunlight slants through the warren of buildings; we will have a nice day for the wedding.

I pull open the door and am greeted by the reek of car exhaust and gasoline and garbage. A blessing for humans that their senses are so muffled; how else could they stand to live here?

I shove the door closed and sink onto the bed. My

muscles ache from vomiting, my stomach—my whole body—a hollowed-out shell. That I survived at all is due largely to Maggie's new convertible.

When she suggested buying one, I pictured a long, sleek automobile with fins or one of those sporty little roadsters driven by international playboys and middle-aged men seeking to reclaim their youth. Our car is rather stumpy. But Maggie quoted a lot of initials that apparently proved it was a sound purchase in spite of its horrifying price.

I made it through Vermont, Massachusetts, Connecticut, and New York with only mild queasiness and windburn. Then we reached New Jersey.

The rain forced us to put up the roof. After that, we had to pull over every fifteen or twenty miles. I now have the dubious distinction of vomiting at every rest stop and exit on the southbound side of the New Jersey Turnpike. Doubtless, on our return trip, I will become acquainted with those on the northbound side, although Maggie has suggested another route that will allow me to see the "scenic" parts of the state.

I will have to take her word that they exist. After marveling at the incredible sprawl of New York City, I recall little of New Jersey other than that endless highway studded by giant signs advertising dating services, insurance companies, and an adult club. And an airport where the giant planes soared so low that I feared they would land atop us. The roar of their engines made me shudder as much as the car.

I force myself to my feet. After mistakenly stumbling into a closet, I discover the bathroom next door. I have to use a washcloth to turn on the nozzles in the shower, but the hot water revives me. As I reach for the shower curtain, I feel her entering the bathroom.

She perches on the toilet seat, still dressed in her long flannel nightgown and slippers. A steaming cup rests on the sink's faux marble countertop. I breathe in the scent of ginger that rises from the cup and from Maggie's body.

Her gaze sweeps over me, and a quiet smile blossoms on her face—the same smile with which she greeted me when she awoke in my bed. A night and a day after that mad dash through the woods with Maggie's body cradled in my arms and her blood bathing my hand. A night and a day after she looked onto Faerie and I thought I had lost her.

"How are you feeling?" she asks.

Like the discarded carapace of a cicada.

"Hungry."

"I'll make you some scrambled eggs and toast after you get dressed."

As she turns to leave, I climb out of the tub, carry her hand to my lips, and press a kiss to her palm.

"I love you," I tell her, as I have every morning since she returned to me.

"I love you, too," she replies as she always does. But this time, she frowns. "I'm okay, Rowan. Really."

But I can't help recalling that wild creature who laughed as she raced for the portal, heedless of the blood running down her leg where she cut herself on the rocks, heedless of the pain of her sprained wrist. Heedless of me.

She will always bear the scar on her knee. It is the other scars I fear more: the ones on her soul and her mind and her heart.

Her hands come up to caress my face. "I'm here, Rowan."

She said that the night we found each other at the Golden Bough. And promised then that she would always come back to me.

And she did. It still amazes me that she possessed the willpower to turn away from the portal. As often as I have claimed that human love is greater than the power of Faerie, it was only at that moment that I saw the proof of it.

I want to pull her into my arms. I want to bury myself in her softness and use my body to drive away the memories. But I cannot risk losing control of my power with Alison in the house.

Maggie flings a bath towel at me. "Get dressed. The wedding's in two hours."

"How's Alison?"

Her laughter refreshes me far more than the shower. "Solid as a rock. I'm more nervous than she is. Ever since she decided to take the plunge, it's been full speed ahead." Her kiss is brisk and businesslike. "Don't dawdle, Amaryllis."

I laugh at *The Music Man* reference and obey. But as I dress, my mind returns to that evening in the woods. Someday, perhaps, I will stop blaming myself for allowing her to come with us to the cottage. As for failing to sense her presence, I was almost as helpless as Maggie, all my power bent on opening the portal and holding it open until Jack made the crossing.

I almost lost him when I saw her. That outpouring of love, that desperate plea for her to stay . . . and the terrible knowledge that if I continued to use my power to try and stop her, the portal would collapse and Jack would be trapped between the worlds. Not in the Borderlands, but in that other land where legends claim lost spirits dwell.

Maybe Helen *was* there, just as Maggie insists. If I could not sense Maggie's presence, I could have overlooked hers as well. It comforts me to believe that her spirit was watching over us. Might still be watching over us.

But I am baffled by some of Maggie's other claims. The light and the music, yes. But I saw no stars inside the portal—just the green hills of Faerie barely visible through the misty sunlight. Did she imagine the stars and the rainbow bridge and that chorus of voices? Or does every human experience Faerie differently?

Reinhard and Janet were there to hear her halting recollections. When we exchanged glances, she asked, "Doesn't anybody believe me?"

"Of course, we believe you," I assured her.

She laughed a little when she realized we were parroting lines from *The Wizard of Oz*. Then she looked up at me and said, "But anyway, Toto, I'm home. Home."

That's when I knew she had truly returned, touched by Faerie but not lost to its power.

Janet urged me to banish her memories of the portal. But I recalled Maggie's insistence that humans sometimes needed to work things out for themselves. Her promise that, together, we could deal with my panic attacks. And most of all, that she had chosen me over Faerie. If she had the strength to do that, I must let her deal with the memories. And stay close so that I may help her.

But for now, I must push them aside. I will not allow them to spoil this day for Alison and Chris—or for Maggie and me.

❧❧

I imagined that this wedding would be like those I had seen in the movies of *The Sound of Music* and *Camelot*. A glorious affair with hundreds of people in attendance, music swelling, and the bride and groom garbed in their finest clothes.

But there are only twenty of us gathered on Alison's tiny patio, mostly Chris' family and friends: his sons and daughter, their spouses, a small tribe of children, and a man named Frank whom everyone calls Biff and his wife Barbara whom everyone calls Babs. Instead of a white gown, Alison wears a simple dress the same pale blue as the October sky. Maggie's is the deep russet of an oak leaf.

A high wooden fence shields us from the street, but not from the second-story windows of the neighboring houses or the occasional blare of a car radio. At least, we are gathered under the open sky instead of inside a clerk's office.

The minister stands before the sundial. The white stole atop her robe is embroidered with a motley assortment of religious symbols. Apparently, this means that she is qualified to unite people of many faiths. Her welcome is pleasant but brief. Then Alison and Chris step forward. Maggie and Biff take their appointed places as maid of honor and best man.

It seems so . . . unceremonious, so lacking in the ritual that should mark this occasion. But I forget about that as Alison and Chris speak their vows. Her expression is as soft as it was in the photograph that Jack preserved. His is earnest, and he recites his words breathlessly, as if he cannot believe this is really happening.

Their love fills my spirit with joy, as does Maggie's tearful smile. I wonder if she imagines the two of us standing before our friends, speaking the words that will bind us together in the eyes of the world.

Janet assures me it will happen. She has even offered to arrange everything with the "acquaintance" she retained the last time she changed her identity. I would merely have to sell one of my first editions to pay for the false papers this person would procure. I had hoped to avoid that, to pretend I was an illegal immigrant and eventually earn a green card and then full citizenship. But even illegal immigrants have birth certificates and driver's licenses and credit cards. Don't they?

I wish I could seek Chris' advice, but that would mean more lies. And how can I put him in the position of honoring such confidences as my lawyer and withholding damaging information from Alison?

My concern for Maggie has absorbed me for the last six weeks, but soon, I must take steps. The board is preparing next year's budget. Even if I wait until May to sign a contract and receive my first paycheck . . .

A burst of applause interrupts my daydreaming. The ceremony is already over and Maggie is hugging her mother. I wait with Alison's friend Sue at the fringes of the small crowd to allow family members to greet the new couple first. As I step forward, Chris pulls me into a hard embrace. Alison shocks me by doing the same.

We troop into the living room where the caterers have set out hors d'oeuvres. I am—as Maggie would say—underwhelmed. But the others are too happy to notice what they are eating. And after several glasses of champagne, even I can look charitably upon limp asparagus spears wrapped in prosciutto.

I gravitate helplessly toward the children. A feast for the eye and the spirit. I approach them with caution, but their parents seem delighted by my interest, so I calm fretful babies and play horsey with the toddlers and try to nod intelligently as the older ones demonstrate the wonders of their handheld computer games. I am more comfortable when a little girl shoves a crayon into my hand and demands that I help her color two gremlins with the improbable names of Bert and Ernie.

I look up to discover Maggie watching me with that same quiet smile. I wish again that I might give her a child, but it is too soon to discuss that. For now, I will anticipate the birth of the newest member of the Crossroads family. According to Catherine and Javier, he—or she—will arrive shortly before the equinox. What more perfect symbol of spring could there be?

As Alison and Chris go upstairs to change, I abandon my selfish indulgence of playing with children to guide Sue onto the patio. We chat about Alison and Chris, but her mother's death shadows her happiness. I use my power to drive some of the shadows away. Perhaps before Maggie and I return to Dale, I will be able to do more.

Maggie runs out of the house and exclaims, "Hurry! They'll be leaving any moment."

As we rush toward the front porch, she orders me to grab a fistful of rose petals from the dish by the door. Rice, apparently, is no longer de rigueur.

The vista from the front porch is far more pleasing than the one from my bedroom. Although the houses are still lined up like soldiers, the tree-lined street soothes my senses. There are only a few golden leaves among the green. Autumn has just begun to touch Wilmington, while back in Dale, the fall foliage is nearing its peak.

A shout goes up behind us. Alison and Chris scamper through the crowd. We throw our rose petals and shout good wishes and wave as the car pulls away. It seems impossible that they will share dinner tonight in the Bahamas.

I doubt I will ever see the beautiful blue Caribbean. I would have to be carried off the plane on a stretcher. But I never thought I'd survive this trip, so perhaps there is hope for me yet.

In the meantime, there is still the beautiful gray Atlantic. Maggie has hinted that we might leave early and stay for a night at the Jersey Shore. I pray it is nicer than the Turnpike.

The guests disperse. The caterers pack away the leftovers. Maggie kicks off her shoes and collapses onto Alison's rock-hard settee with a grunt.

"Never wear new shoes to a wedding," she says, crossing her ankle over her knee to massage her foot.

"Let me do that."

She takes the precaution of stacking pillows at the end of the sofa; the carved wooden arm of the settee looks as comfortable as a shillelagh. Then she leans back and swings her feet into my lap. The slippery feel of her stockings sends a shiver of desire through me. As I dig my thumbs into the ball of her foot, she purrs like Iolanthe.

"I'm a foot rub whore."

"That's all right. I'm a grocery store whore."

She laughs. "At least foot rubs are sensual. You're the only man in the world who finds grocery shopping an erotic experience."

I close my eyes, happy to surrender to these memories, to exchange the light and music of Faerie for the glare of fluorescent bulbs and the soft drone of pop songs. Perhaps grocery stores are as alluring to the Fae as Faerie is to humans.

Shelf upon shelf of brightly colored boxes and cans. Fancifully named breakfast cereals like Count Chocula and Lucky Charms, which Maggie refused to purchase. Towering cumulous clouds of paper towels and napkins and toilet paper. Slabs of meat glistening beneath plastic wrap. Mounds of shrimp peeping out of the ice like buried treasure. Geometric stacks of apples—green and red and gold. Leafy vegetables reclining under a misty spray. The mingled aromas of fresh-baked bread and ripe bananas, coffee and cocoa, floor wax and fish.

And that deli department ...

Earthy cheeses and salt-cured meats. Briny olives and phallic pepperoni. The lascivious pink of the hams. The plump curves of the roast beef. Whole chickens weeping thick tears of barbecue sauce as they revolve in basted bliss upon a spit.

It was all so beautiful, so bountiful, so ... arousing.

We barely survived the short car ride home. I was too excited to be queasy—or to control my power. We dropped the groceries by the doorway, wrestled off the necessary clothing, and went at it on the office floor. Maggie was still laughing when she climaxed.

She laughs again as her toes investigate the bulge in my pants. "Someone's thinking of naughty things," she chants in a singsong voice.

"Someone wants to do naughty things," I chant back.

"Later. I'm too contented right now." She sighs. "They looked happy, didn't they?"

"Yes, they did."

"I can't remember the last time she seemed so happy."

"Did she ever tell you why she changed her mind?"

"Nope. She just announced that they were getting married and told me if I acted smug and self-satisfied, I wasn't invited." Maggie's smile is entirely smug and self-satisfied. "Sometimes, a little push is exactly what people need. Look at Alex and Debra."

"They're not at the altar yet. Debra's not even in Dale."

"She'll be there next week to prep for *Murder at the Mackenzie Mansion*. A little murder. A little mystery. A little Cratchity Christmas cheer. Who knows where it might lead?"

I serenade her with a brief rendition of "Matchmaker." Her hand flails briefly, but I am safely out of range of her intended smack.

"Know what I think?" she asks.

"That Debra came to the Crossroads to find Alex."

"No, Mr. Smarty Pants Faery Man. I think Debra came to the Crossroads because she needed all of us. What we have there. Our family. Alex was just the cherry on the sundae."

Her expression softens. Is she recalling the morning she awoke to find Janet and Reinhard and I at her bedside? And the others crowding in behind us, their faces filled with such love, such relief?

This after the long vigil in the apartment. Lee prowling around like a caged animal. Mei-Yin snapping at everyone. Hal alternately weeping and declaring that it would be all right, that it had to be all right. Catherine and Javier making food that no one ate because they had to do something other than sit there and wait.

Janet's energy resonating with the same fear that had screamed through her the night of Helen's heart attack. Alex so bowed down with grief that he suddenly seemed an old man. And Reinhard who silently stitched her wound and bandaged her hands and wrapped her wrist. Only when he was certain that she was safe in mind as well as body did he leave the apartment—and return a few minutes later, his eyes reddened from weeping.

I shared their love, their anguish, their fear, their relief—and they shared mine. And in that night and that day, I became part of their family, as blood alone had never made me. The unexpected gift that came from that ordeal.

"Penny for your thoughts?" Maggie asks.

"Just thinking about family."

Maggie yawns hugely. "Better stop with the foot massage before I start snoring."

"We could always take a nap," I suggest casually.

"Yeah, yeah. I know exactly what kind of a 'nap' you have in mind."

"Well, you'd nap afterward."

"Mmm . . . let's wait until later. We can snarf down leftovers, watch a cheesy movie in the rec room, and make out."

My spirits brighten. We have often made love, but never made out. I understand it involves extensive foreplay.

"So what *would* you like to do?" I ask.

A look of determination crosses her face. "Let's go for a walk."

"On your sore feet?"

"Sucker. I just wanted a foot rub."

We change into comfortable clothes and walk toward the towering buildings of downtown Wilmington. Then Maggie turns back. I wonder if she has forgotten something at the house, but we continue past it.

I let my hand brush against the trunks of the trees we pass. Their roots wreak havoc with the sidewalk, but their energy feeds me more than any of the food I consumed.

The houses on our right give way to an open tract of land. A pretty little brick church with a gambrel roof sits upon it. According to the sign, it is older than I am. I find it oddly comforting to find another relic of the past here, thriving in the shadow of the skyscrapers.

Beyond it, I glimpse a hillside of trees. I am so engrossed in them that I fail to notice the sound of rushing water until we reach the end of the street. I knew the Brandywine was close to Maggie's childhood home, but I never imagined it was only two blocks away.

Her good spirits have evaporated, and I realize that this is a test for her.

We take our lives in our hands as we dart across the roadway, dodging cars that are traveling far too fast. We follow a narrow canal that parallels the river—the mill-race, Maggie informs me. The path is crowded with pedestrians, eager to enjoy the crisp afternoon. Dogs strain at their leashes as I pass, but a flick of my power deters them from further investigation.

Maggie has lapsed into an ominous silence, but when I take her hand, I receive a quick smile.

Although her mood worries me, my power swells in relief as we walk among the trees. Opening the portal drained me and my concerns about Maggie's recovery prevented me from spending September at the cottage as I usually do. Perhaps when we return home, I will go there. Maggie will be working. I can use the time to finalize the script for *A Christmas Carol* and still return to her every night.

We cross a small footbridge. I smile as my boots sink into the soft grass. So good to feel the earth beneath my feet again. Beyond the river, I spy a parking lot, some sort of statue, and an allée of cherry trees that must be glorious in the spring. When I notice the picnic tables, I realize this must be Brandywine Park.

"That's the zoo," Maggie says, pointing to some stone structures half-hidden among the trees. Her finger moves left. "You can't really see the monkey house from here. Not until the leaves fall."

But I *can* see a steep expanse of grass, which must be Monkey Hill, where she and Jack chased fireflies.

We have spoken of him only once. The morning she awoke, I reassured her that he was safe. She wept because he had left without the photograph; even the reminder that he still had the other two failed to console her.

I expect her to talk about him now, but we merely retrace our route. Instead of turning up the street to her mother's house, she leads me toward a terrace of white stone overlooking the river. I lean against the railing, my senses cheered by the water eddying around the rocks in the shallows.

Maggie's anguish rips through me.

My hand automatically reaches for her. She is standing as still as a statue, gazing across the river. I cannot imagine what has upset her. Then I notice a partially uprooted stump clinging precariously to the bank.

"Is that . . . ?"

She nods, and the tears in her eyes overflow.

I put my arm around her and gaze at the remains of the tree that sheltered pirate treasure and a family of gnomes and a little girl's dreams.

Maggie dashes away the tears with the back of her hand. "Talk about symbolism."

Her chin trembles, but she thrusts it out defiantly. She refused to succumb to Faerie. She will not collapse under the weight of this sight. She is as strong as the roots of the gnome tree that stubbornly resist the efforts of nature and man to dislodge them.

Her defiant expression fades and she takes a shaky breath. "I just wish I knew if he was safe. If he was happy."

I don't care if he's safe or happy. Twice, Jack Sinclair has nearly cost me the woman I love. Had he been anyone else, I would never have spent all those months searching for him.

But he is Maggie's father. And for her sake I say, "The ring will ensure at least one night of hospitality. And with his talent for song and storytelling, I believe my clan will let him stay. Happy? I think so. As much as he might regret leaving you, he's better off in that world than drifting aimlessly through this one."

"And what if they tire of him like they did before?"

Doubtless they will. Jack can be fitfully entertaining, but I cannot believe he will hold their interest forever. But again, I search for words that will reassure her.

"It's just as likely he'll tire of them. With so many

clans to visit, so much else in Faerie to see, I can't imagine Jack staying in one place very long."

"A wandering minstrel."

"Aye."

She smiles, and I silently bless Gilbert and Sullivan.

"Let's go back to the house," she says, "and open a bottle of wine."

When I hesitate, her brows come together in a puzzled frown.

I had always intended for this moment to take place on the plateau with the glorious autumn foliage for a backdrop. But even a faery director must occasionally improvise. And this place, this moment when past, present, and future converge feels right.

I take her hands and stare into the face I love more than any in this world or the other—and all the beautiful words I have memorized evaporate. Instead, I blurt out, "Marry me."

Brilliant, Rowan. Just brilliant. What woman could resist such a poetic outpouring?

Yet Maggie's eyes are shining and her face glows with an inner radiance more glorious than the afternoon sunlight.

"Yes," she whispers. "Oh, yes."

Her mouth is soft against mine, but her arms are strong and sure as they pull me closer.

I grope for the ring in the pocket of my jeans, then hesitate. She notices the gesture and the hesitation, and a small tremor ripples through her.

"I'm sorry. I should have given you the ring later instead of reminding you—"

Her fingertips press gently against my mouth. "Reinhard was right. Every parting holds joy and sadness. Maybe it's fitting that every new beginning does, too. I'll look at this ring and remember the other one. But I'll also remember that it might keep him safe. That you brought him back to me and gave us this summer and helped him find his heart's desire." Her thumb traces the outline of my lips. "I've already found mine."

My hand trembles shamefully as I slip the ring onto her finger. As she stares down at it, I resist the urge to probe her emotions. I chose the ring within moments of walking into the jewelry store in Dale. The bands of gold and silver to represent the intertwining of our lives. Emeralds for her birthstone and mine—at least according to the false birth certificate Jamie procured for me long ago. And the diamond because ... well ... an engagement ring is supposed to have a diamond.

Now, I only notice that the diamond is small, the emerald chips flanking it even smaller. I should have bought a more expensive ring. I should have let her choose one herself.

She holds her hand before her face. Then her eyes meet mine.

"It's perfect."

She flings her arms around my neck and I hold her tightly. A horn blares. We look up, startled, as a car whizzes past. Two young men stick their heads out of the windows, grinning and pumping their fists. I don't know whether they're cheering or jeering. And I don't care. Maggie's softness fills my arms, her scent fills my nostrils, and her happiness fills my spirit.

Abruptly, she pulls away. "I have to call Mom. And Nancy. And Janet and Hal and Reinhard and ... no. Tomorrow. I'll call them all tomorrow, Scarlett. Tonight is just for us."

For the first time since Jack's departure and her brush with Faerie, the shadows are gone. They will return, of course. You cannot have sunlight without shadow.

But the past cannot hold us hostage. And to my dazzled eyes, the future shines more brightly than the golden light of Faerie.

Barbara Ashford

Spellcast
978-0-7564-0729-2

Spellcrossed
978-0-7564-0729-2

"[A] novel about the transformative power of the theater...a woman with an unsettled past...and the intersecting coincidences that move her toward the future. Maggie is relatable and her journey compelling. Four stars."
— *RT Book Reviews*

"[A] charming fantasy novel. Maggie Graham is enchanted and bemused by the Crossroads Theatre...but it takes Maggie a while to really grasp just how magical it is. Readers will figure it out much sooner, but there's enough mystery (not to mention romance) to keep readers interested.... A slightly bittersweet but appropriate conclusion left me wanting more, in fine theatrical tradition."
— *Locus*

To Order Call: 1-800-788-6262
www.dawbooks.com

DAW 206

Gini Koch
The Alien *Novels*

"This delightful romp has many interesting twists and turns as it glances at racism, politics, and religion en route. Darned amusing." —*Booklist* (starred review)

"Amusing and interesting...a hilarious romp in the vein of 'Men in Black' or 'Ghostbusters'." —*Voya*

TOUCHED BY AN ALIEN
978-0-7564-0600-4

ALIEN TANGO
978-0-7564-0632-5

ALIEN IN THE FAMILY
978-0-7564-0668-4

ALIEN PROLIFERATION
978-0-7564-0697-4

ALIEN DIPLOMACY
978-0-7564-0716-2

ALIEN vs. ALIEN
978-0-7564-0770-4
(Available December 2012)

To Order Call: 1-800-788-6262
www.dawbooks.com

DAW 160

Laura Resnick

The Esther Diamond Novels

"Resnick introduces a colorful cast of gangsters and their associates as she spins a witty, fast-paced mystery around her convincingly self-absorbed chorus-girl heroine. Sexy interludes raise the tension...in a well-crafted, rollicking mystery." —*Publishers Weekly*

"Esther Diamond is the Stephanie Plum of urban fantasy! Unplug the phone and settle down for a fast and funny read!" —Mary Jo Putney

DISAPPEARING NIGHTLY
978-0-7564-0766-7

DOPPELGANGSTER
978-0-7564-0595-3

UNSYMPATHETIC MAGIC
978-0-7564-0635-6

VAMPARAZZI
978-0-7564-0687-5

To Order Call: 1-800-788-6262
www.dawbooks.com